HEY, MISTER MARSHALL

USA TODAY BESTSELLING AUTHO

SAFFRON A. KENT

Copyright

This is a work of fiction. Names, characters, places, and incidents are either the product of the author's imagination or are used fictitiously, and any resemblance to actual persons living or dead, business establishments, events, or locales, is entirely coincidental.

Cover Art by Najla Qamber Designs
Editing by Olivia Kalb & Leanne Rabesa
Proofreading by Virginia Tesi Carey

June 2022 Edition

Published in the United States of America

Other Books by Saffron A. Kent

Bad Boy Blues
(St. Mary's Rebels Book #0.5)

My Darling Arrow
(St. Mary's Rebels Book #1)

The Wild Mustang & the Dancing Fairy
(St. Mary's Rebels Book #1.5)

A Gorgeous Villain
(St. Mary's Rebels Book #2)

These Thorn Kisses
(St. Mary's Rebels Book #3)

Medicine Man
(Heartstone Series Book 1)

Dreams of 18
(Heartstone Series Book 2)

California Dreamin'
(Heartstone Series Book 3)

A War like Ours

Gods & Monsters

The Unrequited

Blurb

At eighteen, Poe Blyton's life is in shambles and the reason is Alaric Marshall.

After her mom's death, he appeared out of nowhere and became Poe's controlling guardian. When she protested his tyranny, he had the audacity to send her away to an all-girls reform school. A school full of iron-clad rules and regulations.

But at least she's graduating soon.

Until Alaric himself arrives at the school as the new principal and takes that away from her as well.

That devil.

He's really asking for it, isn't he?

And Poe is going to give it to him.

It doesn't matter that her sworn enemy has the prettiest dark eyes she's ever seen. Or that he looks really, really good in his boring tweed jackets. So much so that she wants to rip them off his body and see what's underneath.

Because scorching hot or not, her new principal or not, Poe is going to ruin Alaric's life.

Dedication

For every troublemaking, chaotic and wild soul out there. May you find peace in your complexity. And for my husband, who loves all parts of me, troubled and otherwise.

Troublemaker

(n; as defined in the dictionary)
One who causes mischief or difficulties
Synonyms: Rabble-rouser, mischief-maker and Poe Austen Blyton

Renaissance Man

(n; as defined by Poe and *not* the dictionary)
History expert; or, a scholar who studies the Renaissance era and wears tweed jackets with elbow patches
Synonyms: Alaric Rule Marshall

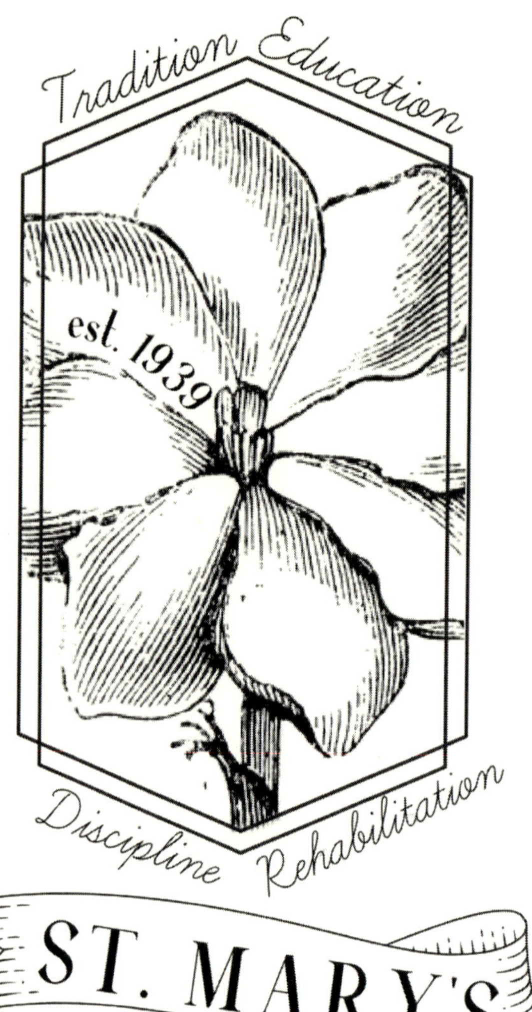

ST. MARY'S SCHOOL

FOR TROUBLED TEENS

Part I

The Devil + The Harpy

Chapter One

Middlemarch

Four years ago

If there is one thing I know how to do well it is to plot.

I know how to make a plan. How to work out the details

How to align all the stars and fit all the moving pieces together.

Which means it's going to be a very bad day for him.

My victim.

Well, victim sounds sort of ominous. Murderous even.

I promise I'm not going to kill him.

I'm only going to make him *wish* that he were dead. Or at least wish that he'd never heard my name or allowed me to set foot in his mansion.

In his very stupid and ancient-looking mansion that's been my home for the past week.

So here I stand, at the second story window, hiding behind the heavy cream-colored drapes as I keep watch over the looming wrought iron gates that mark the entrance of this massive property.

Waiting for him.

Black clouds are gathering up in the sky, and the very air seems hot and heavy, swollen, ready to burst open any second now. And just as lightning flashes across the sky, those hell gates open and I go on the alert.

A sleek black car enters and travels steadily, silently over the graveled pathway, right up to the marble steps where it comes to a stop. My heart thumps in my chest as I wait for my victim to emerge.

And when he does, I move too.

Because it's showtime.

I collect everything that I need from the foot of my bed and walk out of my room, slowly and silently.

To listen.

Just when I hear a door slamming shut below indicating that he's in place – in his study specifically; which is where he goes after he comes back from work – I take off.

I go down the stairs and turn left at the landing, rushing toward the kitchen.

Stopping at a storage room, I go inside. I find a stepladder and climb up to the vent. I pop the grill thingy out and hoist one of the things — a cage — that I brought with me and put it inside, before pulling up and getting inside myself. I crawl through the short space and when I reach another grill thingy, I stop and look through the slats.

Into the grand kitchen.

Usually it's bustling with activity but right now, at seven in the evening, everyone has gone home.

Except Mo.

The head housekeeper with a mop of silver hair and a warm smile.

Who lives here and is currently busy warming up dinner for him.

For a second as I watch Mo, scooping out spaghetti and meatballs and pouring that creamy red sauce over them, I hesitate. What I have planned for him also involves Mo, and I like Mo.

Even though I've only known her for a week, I think Mo is cool.

She's really gone out of her way to make me feel comfortable in this strange house and in this strange situation. The rest of the staff is nice too, if I'm being honest. But Mo has been the friendliest.

Unlike her master.

Who's yet to have a conversation with me.

It's okay though. I'm going to change that tonight.

Keeping my eyes on Mo, I fish out my phone from my jeans pocket and dial the home number; Mo had me program it into my cell for emergencies. The call connects and I hear the ring, both through my phone and in the hallway.

As expected, Mo puts the pasta away and goes out into the hallway to pick up the phone.

Because *he* never picks up the phone. Even when he's home.

I guess he's just too good to talk to people, isn't he?

Fucking asshole.

But this time, it works out in my favor.

Muting the speaker, I leave the line open through which I can hear Mo's voice. I pop open the grid thingy again, take the mouse out of the cage – the one I bought from one of my contacts in New York; yeah, I have sources – and dangle my arm out to simply let it go. Like a champ, it jumps out of my palm and lands on the counter. From there, it skitters away, choosing to stay stuck to the black and white vintage backsplash as it makes its way to the stove.

I quickly pop the grid back in and climb out of the duct. I peek my head out of the storage room to see that, annoyed, Mo has hung up the phone and is now walking back into the kitchen. Since the coast is clear, I get out of the storage room and run back the same way I came to take my position.

This time, I hide myself in the bathroom that's located right across from his study and wait, hoping that it works.

And it does.

A couple of minutes later, I hear a shriek.

It's Mo.

It makes me feel bad. Because as I said, Mo has been good to me and I'm using her weakness against her: mice. She's afraid of them; she told me so herself.

But it needs to be done.

At the heel of her scream, I hear the door to his study open with a snap. Followed by the sound of loud footsteps — his — jogging down the hallway.

Perfect.

I slip out of the bathroom and sprint across to his study, and step inside his lair.

Which is made of books.

That's my very first thought.

There are books on the wall-to-wall bookshelves. There are books on the floor. There are books on his giant wooden desk. There are books *under* the desk even. And don't even get me started on the coffee table in front of a leather couch in a nook, and the side tables and that long console table behind the couch. And then there are papers and documents strewn about on just as many surfaces as the books.

And in the midst of all those papers, there's smoke rising. From a cigar.

Which sits on an ashtray.

By a thick tumbler of whiskey, I notice. Or at least, I *think* it's whiskey, golden brown and shimmering.

So this is his lair then. I've never seen it before; he keeps this room locked when he's not home.

Books, cigar and whiskey.

Not to mention, leather.

There's so much leather in this room. Leather chairs, leather couches, his leather-bound books.

Apparently, he is a history professor. Specializing in something called the Renaissance era. He's actually the head of the department — the *youngest* head of the department — Mo said with pride.

"How old is he?" I asked when Mo told me.

"Thirty-one." Mo chuckled. "Well, to your fourteen-year-old brain, I'm sure he sounds ancient. But he's quite accomplished for his age. Two PhDs. Head of the department. Countless papers and grants. He recently got a grant to head an archeological dig over in Italy. It's quite prestigious. But that's not all, actually. He also sits on the city council. Is on the board of various museums and schools and things. I guess he just does everything, but history is his main interest."

The Renaissance man, I thought.

You know because he studies the Renaissance era.

Wow.

I mean, just imagine being so passionate about something — even though it's something as boring as history — that you spend years studying it, analyzing it, freaking absorbing it.

But anyway.

I don't have time for this.

I have a plan to execute and I only have a few minutes to do it before he gets back. So I look around, trying to find a perfect spot.

Ah, the wall right across from the couch.

I walk over and get to work. Pulling out the red spray paint that I pocketed back in my room, I write on the wall: 'Die Mr. Marshall, Die. PS: I'm not your fucking prisoner. Stop ignoring me.' I also draw a skull beside it to drive my point home.

It's not a threat, per se.

But it's shocking enough to get his attention.

Which is exactly what I'm looking for.

On that note, I go back to the coffee table and pick up his whiskey. I drain it down — hating the ever-loving shit out of it — before going for his cigar. I put it out on the ashtray, pocket it, and then I'm running out of there.

I'm going back up to my room, where I'll lie in wait.

Until he comes to find me.

My victim.

Mr. Marshall.

Chapter Two

He doesn't.

Come to find me, I mean.

It's been over twenty-four hours and there's no sign of him.

Last night after I ran back to my room, I waited.

I waited for hours and I thought I was doing pretty well until I opened my eyes — I don't remember closing them — and it was morning. Or rather late morning. Frantic, I tore out of my room and ran down the stairs. Mo was in the kitchen, and as soon as she saw me she smiled, served me breakfast.

I waited for her to mention the mouse or the spray-painted wall in his study but she never said a word. When I asked about him, she gave me the same answer in the same friendly tone that I've been getting for a week now: he's gone to campus and has lectures and then he has a city council meeting. No mention of what happened last night, or what I did, nothing.

And now it's night.

Actually it's the middle of the night and I can't sleep.

So I've been wandering around the mansion and my wanderings have brought me here.

To the roof.

There's a small balcony a few doors down from my room and it has a spiral staircase that leads up to the roof. I stand at the edge, my palms on the concrete railing, and look at the sprawling grounds before me.

Not that I can see much of anything.

For a variety of reasons.

The very first one is that I *can't* see. Not without my glasses, and I am only now realizing that I left them in my room.

And secondly because I'm crying.

I'm crying because I'm angry. And I'm frustrated and because I'm trapped here.

In this strange mansion. And in this strange town.

With a strange man who doesn't even talk to me.

And that's because my mother is dead.

She died in a car crash three weeks ago while on her way to an impromptu vacation in Florida. A vacation I had no clue about.

It wasn't unusual, you see.

Her jetting off to vacations and exotic locations.

Because my mother is – *was* – Charlie Blyton.

Yeah, *the* Charlie Blyton.

The famous daytime soap opera actress.

And so her schedule has always been busy.

Too busy. At least for me, her daughter.

She'd leave for places, and I'd find out about it days later. And this time I found out about it when they called the house with the news of her accident.

And now I'm stuck here in this town that I know nothing about when New York has always been home for me and I want to go back.

God, I want to go back so badly.

So so badly that standing here, crying and blind — also getting drenched because it's been raining pretty hard since yesterday; the third reason I can't see much — a new plan forms in my head.

About running away.

Yes.

Maybe I should simply run away.

Run back to New York and figure all the details out later.

I mean, I wanted to do this the right way, okay?

That was the whole point of my prank yesterday. That was why I wanted to get his attention.

So we could talk.

So I could make him understand that this is not the place for me. I don't belong here. I belong back in New York. The amazing city that I grew up in.

So he needs to let me go.

Sniffling, I squint through the rain, trying to see the clearing that surrounds this place. It's a blur right now, through tears, rain and poor eyesight. But I know that the clearing is a vast carpet of green. And then there are thick woods that border this whole property. I'm not sure how dense these woods are but I'm pretty sure I could find my way through them if I wanted to.

I could do anything I wanted to.

"You're a badass, Poe," I say to myself, wiping my tears off; not that it matters in the rain, but still. "You're a fucking badass. You can do this. You can go back to New York. How hard can it be to navigate a bunch of trees really?"

"That's the wrong way."

At the sudden words coming from behind me, I jump and whirl around, my hand on my chest, my back pressed against the concrete railing.

And there, standing at a distance from me, is the man I've been constantly thinking about.

Every second of every day, for the past two and a half weeks.

Ever since I heard his name.

Alaric Marshall.

Actually, Alaric *Rule* Marshall.

"What kind of a name is that?" I remember asking Marty, my mom's lawyer. "Rule."

"Well," he said, shifting in his seat, inching up his glasses, "it's his name."

"It's a bullshit name," I said, sitting across from him in my mom's office back home. "Who the fuck is he?"

His white bushy eyebrows went up at my curse but he did reply, "Well, uh, he lives in Middlemarch, the town Charlie grew up in. And from what your mother has mentioned, the Marshalls were close to the Blytons, your grandparents. They were family friends. Now, your grandparents are dead, and your father's whereabouts have always been unknown. So in her will, Charlie has indicated that if something should happen to her, the Marshalls are to have custody of you. Specifically a Mr. Theodore Marshall. This was a very far-fetched thing, you understand. No one was expecting this to happen, Poe. Least of all your mother, and well, she had to name *someone* and no one else —"

"If I'm to be in the custody of this Theodore Marshall," I spoke over him, "then I'm going to ask you again: who the fuck is this Alaric Rule Marshall? What, his older, more boring brother? Father?" Then, after a second or two, "*Grand*father?"

He could be a grandfather.

Because the name sure sounded like it belonged to a ninety-year-old man with a mop of white hair and gold-framed glasses like Marty.

Marty inched up those glasses again. "Well, Mr. Theodore Marshall is not capable of handling your care anymore. He's been indisposed for a couple of years. Health reasons. And all his affairs and responsibilities have been taken over by his *son*. Alaric Marshall is the son." When I went to interrupt him again, Marty went on, "But rest assured, I have checked and double-checked all the details. I remember Charlie mentioning that she went to school with Mr. Marshall and that they were sort of friends, and he has agreed to..."

He said a lot of other things but I didn't hear any of them.

I was stuck on the friends part for some reason.

That he was my mom's sort of friend.

Who stands before me in the pouring rain right now like a dark, blurry silhouette.

"You," I say, seething.

"Me," he says, quite casually but still making my heart jump in my chest again. "Although I wasn't sure you'd be able to recognize me. Since you can't really see."

"I can see," I say immediately, even though I can't.

It was important.

Now that he's here, I can't let any weakness show.

I need to be strong and confident.

"No, you can't," he counters. Then he raises his hand, his fingers clutched around something. "Not without these."

I squint to see what he's holding — damn it — and after a second or two, with a lot of squinting, I make it out.

My glasses.

He's got my glasses.

I glare at him. "How did you... Did you go into my room?"

He lowers his hand and says, "Yes."

I gasp then, still glaring and still mostly blind. "Oh my God.

How creepy. That's my room. Hello? You're not supposed to go into my room without my permission."

I can't be sure but I think he shrugs.

"First, that's my room," he begins. "Because every room in this house is my room. So I don't really need your or anyone's permission. And second, you weren't there to *not* give me permission."

I keep glaring. "Give them back."

"Sure." Then, "Would you like this too?"

By *this*, he means the umbrella.

He's holding an umbrella. Which for some reason I'm only noticing now.

It's a big blurry blob to my eyes and the sight of it also makes me realize that unlike me, he's all neat and dry.

Damn it.

I want to be the one who's neat and dry. *I* want to be the one who can see clearly. But the thought of accepting any help from him makes me want to vomit. So I weigh my options and say, "I don't want your stupid umbrella. Just give me back my glasses."

"All right," he says casually. "I will say, however, that I don't think glasses and rain go well together. But given that I've never used them — excellent eyesight — don't take my word for it."

I glare harder.

Because he is right.

The rain and glasses don't go well together. So the smart thing to do would be to accept his offer. And as much as I hate it, I do; I need all my bearings and all my senses sharp and intact.

"Fine," I bite out.

I wipe my mouth with the back of my hand and walk up to him, somehow feeling every drop of rain that hits my body. Something that I'd grown immune to after standing here for however long.

A few steps in, he comes into focus.

His chest, at first.

It goes from being fuzzy to sharply defined. Dense and solid. Massive under his dark shirt with gleaming white buttons.

Then his shoulders. They also become sharp and distinct. Muscled and impossibly broad under that tweed jacket that he still has on, in the middle of the night.

He's also wearing a tie.

Still crisp and perfectly knotted as it usually is, first thing in the morning when he leaves for work.

And then come his hands, or one hand that's holding the umbrella; his other hand is in his pocket.

When I can see his fingers, clearly and individually, wrapped around the stick, I come to a stop. Because I've gotten close enough.

I reach out my hand then, ready to accept his offerings.

First he hands me over the umbrella.

Which I make sure to hold at a distance from his very manly-looking fingers.

And then the glasses.

Which I also make sure to grab from him in a way that our fingers don't touch.

And finally, the rain stops beating at my body and I can see.

I can see everything.

The raindrops. The black night. And him.

My new guardian.

Alaric Rule Marshall.

Not the boring older brother or the father or the grandfather of my actual guardian. The son.

My mom's sort of friend.

"What about you?" I ask.

He's only been in the rain for a couple of seconds but he's already drenched. His clothes are already plastered to his body, showcasing exactly how big he is. How large. Larger than I thought.

"I'll be fine." Then, "So what's the plan?"

"What plan?"

"Are you running away to New York tonight? If so, I'd advise waiting for the rain to stop first."

Okay, I'm going to say it. I hate his voice.

I hate how good it sounds, all deep and smooth and quiet.

Even when he's mocking me.

"So what, it's not enough to scare the bejesus out of me by appearing out of nowhere?" I say, narrowing my eyes up at him. "You were also eavesdropping?"

His eyes gleam as he says, "The words you're looking for are *thank you*. Because if I hadn't eavesdropped on your plan, I wouldn't have been able to give you a very vital piece of information."

"What vital information?"

"That it's the wrong way," he repeats what he said in the beginning. But when I frown and swat my drenched bangs off my forehead, he goes on to explain, "To New York." He tips his chin. "Through those trees that you were watching. Or trying to. So desperately."

Lifting my chin, I say, "Oh, so am I supposed to believe that you suddenly care about how I get back to New York then?"

He takes in my belligerent stance before replying, "You don't have to believe anything." Then, shrugging, "But there's nothing out there except for more trees. And some very wild bears."

"Wild bears."

"Yes."

"You're saying that there are wild bears behind your property."

"From what I hear."

I throw him a flat look. "You're bluffing."

His eyes — as dark as his hair and his clothes — flash. "Maybe." Then, taking his hand out of his pocket, he pushes back his hair. "In fact, forget what I said. Wild bears or not, I encourage you to take your chances and wander through the strange woods at midnight. Like any responsible, *badass* person would do. You have my permission."

"Your permission?"

"Absolutely."

"I don't need your stupid permission."

"Actually, I think you do. I have a document in my study that says so."

So there it is.

The reminder. Not that I ever forgot, but still. Of what he is to me.

This man.

Of dark hair and dark eyes.

With the broadest shoulders I've ever seen and the deepest voice I have ever heard. This man with a name that sounded so ancient and boring when I first heard it, but it made sense when I saw him.

When I saw his face, I knew why he was named something classic and vintage.

It's because *he* is classic and vintage. It's because every feature on his face, every line and angle, every plane and crest, is quintessential.

It's because he's the very definition of male beauty.

It's insane actually.

How fucking beautiful he is. It's unreal.

And I've been ignoring that, his masculine beauty, but now

that he is here, I can't.

He's the kind of beautiful that once you set your eyes on him, you can't take them off. You can't look away. You have to stare. Probably *because* it's so unreal and so you want to make sure that you're not seeing things.

You want to make sure that his eyes are really that dark and gleaming. And his eyelashes are really that thick and curled, and dense like a forest. Not to mention his cheekbones. You want to make sure that they're really that high and sharp, and how is it that they so fluidly slant and give way to the most perfectly formed jaw. All square and angled.

It's all about the bone structure with him.

Graceful and arched.

And don't even get me started on his mouth.

His mouth is so plush and curved at the ends. Not too much though. Not to an extent that might make his lips look feminine. But enough to cut through and balance out all the steep angles on his otherwise sharp face.

I don't think I've ever seen a more beautiful man than him.

My new guardian.

On that note and at his casual reminder, I widen my feet. "Right. The document that says you're my new guardian."

His chin dips and his wet eyelashes flicker down to take in my stance. "The very one, yes."

"Does it also say that you should ignore your ward for a whole week?"

He cocks his head to the side as he replies, "You know, I'm not really sure. I'm pretty new at this. Maybe I should give it another read. Maybe I'll also stumble upon what to do with your ward when she spraypaints your wall and drinks your scotch."

"That was scotch?"

"And steals your cigar."

"Well, no need to read the document. I can tell you right here and right now that this is what happens when you ignore your new ward and that new ward is me."

He studies me for a moment or two before saying, "Noted." A long breath later, "So now that I'm fulfilling my guardian duties, what can I help you with?"

"I wanna go back to New York," I blurt out without hesitation.

Ah, it feels so good to say that.

So good.

It took a week and a lot of waiting, a lot of being told, 'he's busy' or 'he's at work' or whatever the fuck, and one successfully pulled prank, but the words are out there. One step closer to my goal. Now all I have to do is convince him and then, I'm home free.

"New York," he murmurs.

"Yes." I nod before diving into my whole explanation. "Look, I'm sorry about the prank. I'm sorry that I put you through all that trouble. But the truth is that I don't know you. I'd never even heard of you before a couple of weeks ago. And I'm sure that the same has been true for you as well. I don't know what Charlie was thinking when she named you — your family — as my guardian. But I want to say that I'm grateful. For coming to my rescue, for bringing me into your home even though you didn't know who I was. But you don't have to. You don't have to keep me here or take care of me or do any of the guardian duties. I know there's a will and all the legal stuff but that's why people have lawyers, right? My lawyer or Charlie's lawyer — I'm sure you know him, Marty — is very good. I'm sure if we talk to him, he can find a way to deal with this. He can add a clause or an addendum or whatever they're called. He can find a way to bring me back to New York, where I've lived my entire life, and you won't have to take care of someone you had no idea existed before two weeks ago."

I'm not a legal expert but I *have* given it a lot of thought.

I know I'm a minor. Which means I do need a guardian in the state's eyes.

But nowhere does it say that I need to be living with that guardian under the same roof, right?

I can still live in my old townhouse on Park Avenue only a couple of blocks from Central Park. That house is still a part of Charlie's estate and from what I understand, it will become mine when I turn twenty-one. Until then, my guardian with the help of Marty will handle all the affairs.

And yes, I do understand that people frown upon minors living alone but the thing is that I've lived alone all my life. My mom was barely home and I was passed down from nannies to assistants to agents even, when Charlie used to be busy with her shoots and overseas commitments. So it's not as if I don't know how to handle myself. We can bring back the old staff and I can still live in New York.

And I open my mouth to tell him all that. To explain so he understands my unique situation.

But he speaks. And he speaks just one word.

"No."

I draw back. Not because he's spoken it loudly but because he's done it so decisively. So clearly and in a way that makes everything final so that I'm left with a stumbling, "What?"

He takes my surprise in, sweeps his gaze over my face before throwing out a short nod. "Glad we had this chat. Now —"

"What, no," I cut him off. "We *haven't* had this chat. You haven't even heard my plan yet."

He gives me a look then. A thoughtful look from what I can gather.

Then, "If this new plan is anything like braving the woods in the middle of the night to get back to New York, I think you should save your breath *and* both our time."

I can say so many things to him.

So many, many things in retort.

But.

This is serious. This is about my life, about me going back to New York.

So I curb all my sharp backtalk and try to appeal to him in a nice and calm and rational way. "As I said before, I don't know you and you don't know me. And it was very nice of you to let me stay in your house, but I don't want to stay here. I don't want to live here. In this town. New York is where I grew up. I've lived my entire life there. My home is in New York and I need to go back. Now, I understand that I'm a minor and I do need some parental supervision. But the thing you have to understand is that I'm not like other teenagers. I'm capable of being on my own. I've spent more than half my life being on my own. So as I said, Marty can come up with a solution. I can bring back the old staff. The cooks, the maids, the driver. My mom's old assistants. I always dealt with them anyway and —"

"I don't think you can," he says, cutting me off.

"What?"

Again, he studies me with his shimmering but unfathomable eyes. "From what I hear they won't come back." I frown as he keeps going, "Because you've got a reputation, haven't you?"

My fingers flex around the umbrella. My heart twists.

"And your reputation is the reason," he continues, his voice all deep and quiet, "why my father was named as your guardian. Because no one else would take you."

My heart twists harder.

Reputation.

Yeah, I have one.

People think I'm a wild child. A problem child. An attention-seeking child. A hoyden, a harpy, a shrew.

A troublemaker.

It's not unearned or undeserved.

I completely and fully accept the blame for it. I've done things, bad things, to annoy people. To bother them, to make their life difficult. And I've done all of this for one reason and one reason only.

To get my mother's attention.

To get her love.

Because she didn't, see. She never loved me and she had reasons.

The first is that I'm the result of a very ill-thought and short-lived affair that she'd had with a photographer who'd lured her in with the promises of making her a model at the age of seventeen but left her with me. He never even knew that the girl he screwed over — again my mom's words — was going to have his baby. And she never bothered to tell him.

Honestly, I've never cared about my dad. If he was asshole enough to leave her and me then he can stay gone.

Anyway, the second reason why my mother hated me is because when her parents found out about her pregnancy, they kicked her out. And she had to crash on a friend's couch in New York. Not to mention, I was difficult even when I was in her belly. I wreaked havoc on her body and when I got out, I wreaked havoc in her life by always demanding attention and care. It was a miracle that my mom became the star that she is — *was* — with a hellion of a daughter like me.

All her words and all true.

I did make her life difficult with my attention-grabbing ways. I did concoct plans and plots; I did throw tantrums and make everyone miserable, sent nannies and assistants away, terrorized her agents and her boyfriends, so I could be closer to her. So she spent time with me rather than at work or with anyone else.

But all I ever ended up doing was making her hate me more, making other people hate me more. And now that I *need* those people, no one will come to my rescue.

Except him.

This man.

Who keeps going, "Now you already know that my father is unwell. Which means," he pauses, his eyes looking into mine, "you're mine."

A shiver runs through my body.

Big and massive.

It rolls through me and makes its way through my spine and my legs, all the way down to my toes.

It's a shiver of dread. Of fear.

Still, I stay strong and say in a clear voice, "I'm not an object."

"Nonetheless, you're still mine and you'll stay here."

"I'm —"

"Now that I've listened to you," he cuts me off, his voice slightly louder than before but nowhere near as hysterical or disturbed as he's making me feel. "I want you to listen to me: I'm choosing to ignore your little stunt yesterday because I realize that it was misguided and an act born out of desperation. We *should* have had this talk a long time ago. That's on me."

I open my mouth to tell him that yes, it *is* on him, but he doesn't let me speak. "So in case I wasn't clear before: you're not going back to New York. I don't care that you grew up there and that you've lived your entire life there. You're here now, in this town. You're going to live under my roof. And when you live under my roof, you show respect. At all times and under all circumstances. I don't tolerate temper tantrums or teenage rebellion. If you break something, you fix it. If you make a mess, you clean it. You steal something, you find a way to pay for it. And if you walk through doors you're not supposed to walk through, I lock the door to *your* room. With you inside. Is that understood?" His chest expands on a deep breath. "Now, I'd like you to go back inside and get out of those wet clothes and get some sleep."

"You hate me," I say then.

I don't know why but the words come right out.

Actually, I'm lying.

I do know why.

I know why I said it. I said it because I have nothing to lose here and I have to somehow convince him. I have to make him see that I can't live here.

Not like this.

Which is the biggest reason as to why I want to go back so badly.

Because the man whose house I'm living in hates the sight of me.

And he does.

Oh yeah, he does.

The proof of that is right here: at my words, his jaw clenches.

The very first reaction that he's shown me tonight.

"Don't you?" I prod, my heart beating so fast that it's bordering on painful. "Marty told me that you were Charlie's friend. Back when she lived here. But that's not true, is it? You weren't her friend. I pick up on things, you know. I pick up on how whenever I talk about my mother, Mo gets this look on her face. Like she's frozen. Like she's in pain or something. Her smiles are strained. Her voice gets all tight. Of course I don't know the reason. Charlie never talked about this place. All I know is that she hated living here. She wanted to get out and so when her parents kicked her out because she was pregnant, she took that opportunity and escaped to New York. So I don't know why Mo behaves that way but there's a reason, isn't it? And then there's you. You avoid me like the plague. This is the first conversation that we're having in a week. You won't even stay in the same room as me. It's because of who I am, isn't it? Charlie's daughter. That's why you hate me."

I pause when a muscle jumps on his cheek.

And I think he'll speak now. He'll say something, either confirm or deny my conclusion. He'll put all these questions that I've had ever since I arrived here to rest.

But he doesn't.

He holds his silence and so I continue almost desperately, "So you can see why, right? You can see why I don't want to live in a house where people hate me. Not to mention, why would you want me around anyway? You should be looking for ways to get rid of me." I swallow thickly. "You don't want me here and I don't want to live in a house where I'm not welcome. So this is as much for you as it is for me. Just let me go. It's that fucking easy."

It is.

Only I'm not sure why but it hurts me.

It stings.

That he hates me.

Which is ridiculous.

Because it shouldn't matter if he does or does not. I don't even know him. So I shouldn't care.

But for some reason, I do and I don't understand why.

"No."

"What?"

He takes a final look at me — at least that's what it feels like — before he steps back. "Have a great rest of your night. If you get the flu, stay away from the staff."

Then he turns around and I'm so shocked that I don't even stop him when he begins to walk away.

Not until he's about to disappear.

"Wait. What… Did you hear what I said?"

No response and no stopping him either.

I run after him. "What are you doing? Are you listening to me? I made the perfect argument here."

He keeps walking.

"Hey, stop, okay?" I call out again. "You can't walk away from me. You can't…"

I breathe out sharply because it's not working.

He's not stopping and he's not responding.

So coming to a stop in the middle of this huge fucking balcony, with the rain beating down on the ground, thunder rolling up in the sky, I almost scream, "This is kidnapping, you hear me? You are keeping me here against my will. It's illegal. It's a crime. You're a fucking criminal. I'm calling 911."

Finally, finally he stops.

At the threshold of the door, protected against the rain, he halts in his tracks and faces me. "Tell them I said hey."

I clench my teeth and tighten my fists. "You're an asshole."

"Tell them that too. May make your case stronger."

"You know what, no. You're not an asshole. You're the devil."

"You sure you want 911 then? Maybe we should call the church."

I shake my head at him. "You don't know what you're starting here."

"And what is it that I'm starting?"

"War," I tell him. "You're starting a war."

"War."

"Yes. Because if you think you've won, then I want you to think again. I'm not going to take this lying down. And let me tell you something about myself, my reputation that you've heard about? It's all true. I am a troublemaker. A problem child. A harpy. And I hold a mean grudge. Very, *very* mean."

At this, his eyes flash. They shine and they take me in.

They take in my heavily breathing form, my clenched fists, my glaring eyes before he murmurs, "Noted."

"Good." I breathe in sharply. "Because I'm about to burn down your life and turn it into hell, Mr. Marshall."

As soon as I say it — Mr. Marshall — a shiver, much like the one I felt when he called me his, runs down my body. I'm not sure why. This isn't the first time I've said it.

In fact, that's what I've been calling him because Mo told me to.

Mr. Marshall.

She told me that this is how Mr. Marshall likes to be addressed. Or Dr. Marshall because of his PhDs. I picked Mr. Marshall because there's no way I'm calling him *Dr.* Marshall.

But anyway. I feel like I should've called him by his first name just to piss him off and I'm about to do that when he does something… unexpected.

And astonishing.

His lips twitch before they pull up on one side. Into a small lopsided smile.

Which hits me in my belly.

Like his voice.

Because I swear to God, it makes him even more beautiful. Like that was even possible or needed.

"Ah, but I'm the devil, remember? My life is already hell and I'm used to burning." Then, "And if we're going to go to war, then we should at least be on a first-name basis. Don't you think?" He pauses, and another shiver rolls down my body. "Poe. So feel free to call me by my name."

And then he leaves.

He disappears right in front of my eyes.

As if he really is the devil.

As if he didn't just make my body shake. My heart. My world.

And then I make a promise to myself.

That I will forever hate him and do everything to make his life hell.

That I will never — not ever, not in this life — call him by his name.

Alaric.

Chapter Three

The Renaissance Man

A knock comes at the door and I look up from an article about humanism, a fourteenth-century cultural movement, that I was reading.

Or trying to read.

"Come in."

The door opens to reveal Mo. She nods at me in greeting and says, "She's out. Finally went down."

My fingers tighten around the papers.

My whole body tightens but I manage to nod. "Okay. Thanks for letting me know."

With sheer willpower, I go back to my article, hoping to finally focus enough so I can get through this paragraph. But Mo says, "She looked tired."

Despite myself, I say, "Can you make sure to check up on her? In case she develops a temperature or something." Then, "She got caught in the rain."

"Sure, of course."

I begin reading. "Thanks."

She'll leave now. At least that's what I'm hoping she'll do.

And then I'm focusing.

I have to.

On top of my own lectures and a paper that's due next week,

I have a talk to prepare. Plus a department meeting about the budget proposal for the next year. Followed by another meeting with the city council. I don't have time to waste and I've already lost an hour.

But she doesn't leave. She hovers at the door, forcing me to look up and ask in a clipped voice, "Is there anything else?"

Looking hesitant, she says, "I just… I was wondering."

I frown, my patience spreading thin. "About."

Her hesitance grows. "She, uh… She looks like Charlie."

My fingers tighten further.

In fact, I'm almost crumpling the paper between my fingers.

"Not in the obvious sense, of course," Mo goes on. "Not the hair color or even the eyes. But the way she carries herself. Her mannerisms and this effortless beauty and grace."

Mo isn't wrong.

She does look like Charlie, and no, not in the obvious sense. Charlie's hair was blonde and her eyes a dark brown, whereas *her* hair's black as midnight and her eyes are crisp blue. Charlie never wore glasses; I guess they were too unbecoming for her, so she had contacts, while *her* glasses are thick and black-rimmed. And Charlie would never let herself be caught in the rain like *her*. From the looks of it, *she* would've stood there all night had I not gone up to bring her back; I saw her through this office window.

And neither would Charlie be so free with her emotions and thoughts. There's a reason why Charlie was able to make a career out of acting; she was good at it.

Not her though.

Not Charlie's fourteen-year-old, rebellious, troublemaking daughter.

I look to the wall where she spray-painted her message.

It's gone now. Mo and the staff took care of it, but I can still see it, stark, bright red.

I force myself to relax my grip on the paper as I reply, "I hadn't noticed."

Her eyes grow concerned and I clench my teeth. "I just want to make sure that you're okay. That —"

"You should go to sleep."

But she's persistent. "But Alaric, I really think that you should —"

"Good night."

For a second it looks like Mo won't listen to me, but she backs down. Nodding, she says, "Good night then."

But as she's leaving, I call out, "Can you," and she turns back to face me, "make sure that," I breathe in sharply, "she's okay? From now on, I mean. Just look out for her. Just… You're in charge of her."

So I don't have to be.

So I don't have to look at her or talk to her or think about her.

So I don't have to think about the past.

I have already made the mistake of giving her permission to call me by my first name when no one — absolutely no one, except for Mo — has the right to call me anything other than Mr. Marshall or Dr. Marshall. Due to this insane and irrational urge to make her feel more comfortable.

Fuck that.

I don't care if she's comfortable.

All I care about is that she doesn't fucking bother me for as long as she's here.

When Mo nods dutifully, I release a sigh of relief, thinking that now I can focus.

But for a long, long time after she's gone, I can't.

For a long, long time I stare at the wall where she spray-painted her message.

Poe.

Part II
The Tyrant + The Siren

Chapter Four

St. Mary's School for Troubled Teenagers Present

It's time.

And everything is ready. Every*one* is ready.

Everyone is gathered around in a huddle, their eyes on the far horizon, pinned on the target.

Everyone is holding their breath, their hands either pressed on their chests or pushing back their hair, smoothing their skirts, pulling up their socks, making sure they all look perfect and pretty in their school uniforms: white blouse, mustard-colored skirt and knee-high socks with black Mary Janes.

Someone breathes out then, "Holy shit, I can't wait."

Followed by someone else going, "I know."

"This is like, the best part of my day," a third someone says.

Which prompts yet another person, the fourth speaker, to reply, "I know. It's only been a week but God, how did we live before this?"

I want to correct her and say that it's been eight days.

So longer than a week, but I keep quiet.

"Do you think today's the day he's going to look over here?" a fifth voice says.

"Maybe. I'm keeping my fingers crossed though," yet another

voice replies.

She should uncross them, her fingers.

He's not going to.

He has no interest in looking over here. He's never had much interest in people. People are beneath him.

Now books, however, are a different story.

He's more interested in what a book has to say than what a bunch of teenagers are giggling about.

At least, this is how I remember it.

But again, I don't tell them that.

"What color do you think his jacket is going to be?" someone asks, probably the very first girl who spoke.

"I don't know. Maybe blue. Like dark blue," another familiar voice answers.

"I would really like to see him in dark blue."

Nope.

Wrong again.

Blue is not his color.

He never wears blue, even dark blue.

There's not a single blue thing in his wardrobe; I've checked. And the handful of times that I've seen him over the last four years, he's always worn either black or gray or chocolate brown like his eyes.

I've concluded that it's because blue is too colorful for him. And he's not a colorful man. He's the kind of man who sucks all joy out of this world and so it makes sense that he'd wear colors that suck all joy out of the world as well.

Besides, if you really think about it, the devil never wears blue.

But as I've done for the past eight days, I'm going to keep this knowledge to myself and sit here quietly on this stone bench out in the courtyard as I read my biology textbook.

Or as I *try* to read my biology textbook.

Okay, fine. I'm not even trying.

Clearly, I'm eavesdropping.

But I'm going to stop now. It's not as if they're saying or doing anything new or even remotely interesting. This has been the norm for days now.

Every morning, a group of girls gathers here in the courtyard before the first bell rings. They are all bright-eyed and rosy-cheeked, brimming with enthusiasm and joy. Their happy eyes are always peeled at the same thing: a row of cottages on the far side of campus, across the massive green clearing.

As they wait for their day to begin.

It's annoying. I'm not going to lie.

Not their enthusiasm.

Of course not. I wouldn't begrudge them even a tiny amount of joy, not in this place.

What annoys me is their reason.

The reason *why* they're so happy and giggly and just over the moon enthusiastic.

And then it happens.

I hear a collective gasp from the group.

He is here. The reason of all the excitement.

Although even if they hadn't gasped, I'd still know.

It's the air that tells me.

It grows hot and heavy.

My skin grows heated. Sweat rolls down my spine. My lungs fill with smoke and I can't breathe.

Four years ago, I told him that I'd set his life on fire but I was wrong. *He's* the firestarter.

He's the flame-thrower. The lighter, the match.

And time hasn't changed that.

And neither has it changed the fact that whenever he's around, my eyes inevitably go to him.

Like they do now.

A dark figure striding across the vast green clearing.

He sports a tweed jacket, a shirt and a pair of dress pants.

All black, all crisp.

All intimidating.

But not as intimidating as he himself is.

Even though he's all the way over there, you can still tell that he's tall. He's probably one of the tallest men you've ever seen. He's also broad. His tweed jacket-draped shoulders, even from this far, look like they would block the sun, the moon, the stars, if he ever stood close enough.

And then there are his thighs.

His powerful, muscular thighs that bulge and strain under his dress pants as he walks, covering twice the distance that you normally would. Or at least, that *I* normally would.

And so very soon, he gets close enough that he comes into focus.

The fine details of him.

His dark hair with curls that shine under the summer sun. They also brush against the collar of his jacket. The duskiness of his skin. His dark tie. The crisp collar of his dress shirt. The shine of his Italian loafers, also black. The briefcase that he's carrying, clutched by his long fingers.

And his face.

That comes into focus as well.

And I have to say that it is — as it was the first time I saw him four years ago —spectacular. It's jaw-dropping and breathtaking. Even more so than before, if possible.

Like his features have become more distinct and sharper over time. Like his cheekbones have honed even more with age. His jaw has become more angled at thirty-five than it was back when he was thirty-one. His brows have gotten more arrogant and his mouth, the one soft thing on his very classically masculine face, has grown softer and more plump. Maybe because it had to, to balance out the increased edginess.

But the most beautiful thing about him is his eyes.

Which I can't see because he's got a killer pair of shades on. As shiny and expensive as the rest of his ensemble.

But even so, I know his eyes are chocolate brown. I know that they're surrounded by thick and sooty eyelashes. They tip up slightly on the sides, much like his lips.

So yeah, spectacular.

And as I predicted, he doesn't look at them. The group of girls in the courtyard that are openly gawking at him.

To be fair though, I wouldn't know what he is looking at since his eyes are hidden, but I know that he doesn't tip his chin or tilt his head or break his stride in any way as he passes them by, that might indicate that he's even aware of their presence.

Their adoration.

He's completely unaware that one of those girls is me.

That I watch him as he passes through the courtyard and reaches the concrete steps, like I used to watch him through my second-story bedroom window back when I lived at his stupid mansion. I watch him as he climbs those steps with purpose, getting up to the landing before he disappears through the big doors that mark the entrance of hell.

Otherwise known as St. Mary's School for Troubled Teenagers.

And he's definitely unaware of the fact I do all that, that I watch him and follow his every move, with the opposite of adoration.

I watch him with hatred.

And let me tell you that there are reasons for it.

Several reasons for the hatred that I feel.

That I've felt since I was fourteen, and now that I'm eighteen, that hatred has only grown.

Much like his masculine beauty.

"Hey."

Startled, I look away from the door through which he disappeared only a few moments ago. And blink. When my vision clears, I notice that the 'hey' came from a girl with honey blonde hair and a kind face, who's sitting at the concrete table, opposite to me.

"Uh, hey," I say unsurely, shifting in my seat. "Sorry, I was… I didn't see you there."

She smiles, setting her bookbag on the table. "Oh, that's okay."

"We know you were preoccupied."

This is said by a second girl who comes to sit beside the first one. She has the most beautiful copper-colored hair I've ever seen. Not to mention the freckles that are sprinkled like cinnamon over her pale skin, especially her nose and the apples of her cheeks. Which also makes me realize that I know her.

I know the first girl too, actually.

Now that my mind isn't clouded by other things, I know they're seniors like me.

Before I can say something though, the copper-haired girl goes, "Do you want some candy?"

I glance down to see that she's offering me a short and twisty black string, flopping between her fingers. Looking back up, I ask, "What's that?"

"Licorice," she says. "Black licorice twist."

I look at the bite-sized Twizzler again. "No, thanks."

"You sure? Sugar is magical." When I shake my head to confirm that I don't want it, she pops it in her mouth and chews. "Wait, I also have gum."

"What flavor?" I ask before I think better of it.

"Uh, let's see." She roots around in her bookbag which is also sitting at the table. "I have licorice, of course. Mint, strawberry. Watermelon. Oh, and cherry."

"I'll take cherry."

What?

No.

I will absolutely not take cherry.

Why did I say that? I don't even like cherry.

Well, I mean I'm supposed to not like cherry.

And the reason is because he likes it.

He.

The devil.

He's quite the fan of cherry pies, actually, and when I lived at the mansion, Mo would make one for him almost every other day. And I'd pray that maybe this would be the pie that might kill him with sugar overload.

"Here you go."

She offers me a strip wrapped in magenta that I want to refuse just on principle. But she's taken the time to look for it so I can't. Besides, why should I deprive myself of my favorite thing just because it's his favorite too?

I take it from her and pop it in my mouth.

"Thanks," I say, tasting sweet cherry on my tongue and loving it. "You're, uh, Jupiter, right?"

She beams. "Yup. And that's Echo."

The first girl waves at me. "Hi."

Right, Echo.

Of course I know these girls.

Because as I said, they are both seniors like me and so we've had a few classes together over the years; never had the opportunity to talk to them though.

Although I have been wanting to.

For the past few days at least.

Because from the looks of it, they're in the same boat as me, aren't they?

"Hey," I say to Echo. "Nice to meet you. Both of you. Although, we have met before. I mean, we haven't talked but I'm sure you know that we've been in some of the same classes over the years."

"Yup. Chemistry, trigonometry, biology and english lit," Echo replies, counting on her fingers.

"Oh, and physics," Jupiter adds.

"Right. I usually don't pay attention in classes, so." I chuckle. "I mean, I'm here, right? Exhibit A."

By here, I not only mean this hellhole of a school but also the fact I'm here over the summer. When we all know that regular school sessions are out, and everyone else is free and having fun on their summer vacation.

Not me though.

Not us.

"Well, we're not good at paying attention either, so," Echo says kindly.

"Yeah, we basically suck," Jupiter goes. "I mean, *I* suck. Echo is better. But biology kinda bit her in the ass."

Echo sighs. "That and math. I mean, how anyone expects us to ace the cardiovascular system while also learning about integration is beyond me."

"Ugh, no. The worst is the law of thermodynamics. Like, what is that? Why do I care about the flow of energy? All I want to do is go outside in the sunshine, wear a bikini that makes my boobs look good and swim in my neighbor's pool."

"Despite," Echo addresses me, "being told numerous times that she is not allowed to."

Jupiter rolls her eyes. "Whatever. My neighbors are control freaky psychos. What am I gonna do, not swim?" Then, to me, "I'm a water baby. I have to swim. And it's not my fault that we don't have a pool in our backyard. Besides, they have a kickass pool. I'd go swim in it even if I wasn't a water baby." She sighs. "I miss it though. God, do I miss it."

This makes Echo sigh as well. "I know. I miss being outside. I miss ice cream. Like, those softies. You know, the kind you get from an ice cream truck? With pineapples. I want pineapples. Like, just give me pineapple on everything."

"Yes," Jupiter agrees. "But mostly with rum and coconut."

Echo shakes her head. "So basically, a piña colada then?"

"Yup." Jupiter grins. "And it's even better when you sip it in my neighbor's pool."

They go back and forth some more, listing things that they miss doing over the summer. The only couple of months that we get to escape this hell. But this year, we can't because we're going to summer school on account of our low grades.

But it's more than that.

It's *worse* than that.

Because we're not supposed to be going to school at all, let alone summer school.

We're supposed to be done with school. We're supposed to graduate.

Or we *were* supposed to. A month ago.

Like the rest of our senior class.

"But anyway," Echo says. "That's not why we're here."

"What?"

After glancing around to make sure we're alone — we are; those girls dispersed as soon as he went inside the school building — Echo leans forward, setting her arms on the table. "To help you."

"To help me?" I look at both of them. "Do what?"

Jupiter leans forward as well, popping a tiny Twizzler in her mouth. "To play a prank on him."

Him.

The fucking devil.

My guardian.

Mr. Marshall.

Or rather *Principal* Marshall now.

Yeah.

Because it wasn't enough for him to just be my guardian and keep me under his thumb like he has for four years, he also had to take the job as the temporary principal of this school. And his first act as the principal: hold my graduation and keep me in this prison-like school for the summer.

Yes, I said prison-like because it *is* a prison-like school.

An all-girls reform school located in the middle of the woods, in the town of St. Mary's.

Meaning, all the girls who go here are troubled in one form or another.

They're the rule-breakers. The rebels. The delinquents. The pains in the ass that everyone around them is fed up with.

And of course, I fit right in, don't I?

Sometimes I think that if my mother had known about this place, she would've jumped at the chance to send me here. As it is, she didn't.

He did though.

My guardian turned principal.

He knew about this place. His family built this place. Decades and decades ago.

So here I am, sent here three years ago to be rehabilitated and restored.

Just one of the many reasons why I hate him still.

Why I hate him *more* for keeping me here.

I take a moment to absorb their words and their expectant eyes before, still confused, I go, "What? What prank?"

Echo's the one to explain. "Look, you hate it here as much as we do. In fact, I think you hate it here *more* than we do. But most of all, you're sad that you're here. It shows. You're always by yourself. You sit in a corner, without talking to anyone. You keep your head down during classes. During lunch even. You hardly interact with the staff when you used to be best friends with so many of them, always asking favors, smuggling stuff in and out of the kitchen. You're never in the TV room anymore, and you used to be the first one there, begging the wardens to let us watch more than our allotted time."

Something pricks my eyes, my throat.

I didn't know my misery was that obvious. That transparent. And I hate that it is.

I don't want anyone to know that I'm struggling. That something is wrong with me.

Not only because I hate breaking down in front of people. But also because I'm Poe fucking Blyton.

I'm the bane of everyone's existence. I have a reputation to maintain.

So I push all my emotions down and go to speak, to lie and deny it, but Jupiter speaks first. "So we're here to offer you our help. I know we aren't close and we haven't talked to each other much but you can trust us." Echo nods to emphasize Jupiter's words. "We'll do everything we can to help you. And maybe playing a prank on him might cheer you up a little bit, you know?"

Again I go to speak, but Echo gets there before me. "It might even make you… miss them less. So if you're up for it, we'd like to help. What do you think?"

I know I can speak now. I know they want my answer but I

don't think I can.

Not after the reminder as to why I'm miserable and having a tough time.

Them.

Not that I forgot. I can't.

It's unfathomable to forget about them. Every day I live here is a stark, brutal reminder that they are not here.

My friends. My girls.

Every girl who goes to this school has this dream of graduating and leaving this place behind one day. It's the one thought that keeps us all going. But in addition to that, I also had my girls — Callie, Wyn and Salem — to keep me going. Especially Callie, who I met my first day here. Followed by Wyn a year later and then, Salem another year after that.

Our friendship with each other kept us sane and hopeful.

We all had each other's backs no matter what and we had so many plans for getting out of here and going back to the real world. From which we had all been banished for one reason or another.

And I am glad that they are out there now.

I am.

I'm just sad that I'm not with them. That I'm stuck here all alone.

"I…" I swallow thickly, my fingers worrying the pages of my book. "I'm…"

"Oh God," Echo breathes, reaching over to grab my hand. "We didn't mean to make you upset."

Jupiter grabs another. "Yeah, gosh, we didn't mean to make you even more sad. We're so sorry. I —"

"No," I cut her off, forcing myself to get a grip. "Please don't apologize. I just… wasn't expecting it. I was… You're both right. I do miss my friends. And yeah, I've been kinda out of it. I just didn't know anyone noticed."

Jupiter squeezes my hand. "Are you kidding? You're the life of the party, Poe. Of course we noticed."

"But don't worry," Echo jumps in. "We're the only ones. Because we're seniors and we know you. The other girls are mostly sophomores and freshman, who are *choosing* to be here by the way," she rolls her eyes, "they don't have a clue."

"Yup, so your badass street cred is safe," Jupiter says.

And I smile, probably my very first smile ever since this shit-show summer school started. "Good. Thanks." And then, before I can stop myself, I ask, "Uh, would you guys like to go out?"

Echo frowns. "Go out. As in off campus?"

"I thought we weren't allowed to go off campus," Jupiter says.

Technically, we aren't.

And this rule only applies to us three, the bad seniors who haven't graduated yet.

Because we have no privileges.

Since this is a reform school where girls are sent to be rehabilitated, they have a privilege system. The thing they give you as a reward if you're good.

If you pass your test, they give you an extra hour of TV. Or if you show up on time for your classes, they let you use the computer for more than an hour. And if you've been really, really good and turned in all your homework or scored an A on your test, in addition to behaving politely, they let you go out on the weekends.

Needless to say, I haven't had very many privileges.

Every student here is assigned a guidance counselor who keeps track of their deeds and misdeeds, and mine had been super busy counting my misdeeds and yanking my privileges left and right.

Anyway, when I said that my girls had my back no matter what, I meant that they really did. Meaning, they knew how miserable I'd be without them. Because they would be too, if they were the ones who had gotten stuck here. So before they parted ways with me, they made a plan.

That we'd uphold our traditions.

Sneaking out to a bar called Ballad of the Bards, every Friday night.

Now that my graduation is once again a dream, I've been counting down the days until I can go see them.

And I get that what I'm proposing to Jupiter and Echo may not be their cup of tea. But I honestly feel good for the first time in a long time. I *smiled* for the first time in a long time, and it's because of them. They've been so nice to me. So I had to.

"Well, we aren't but I was talking more about off the books," I say, leaning forward.

Both their eyes shine at my words.

Jupiter is the one to speak first. "Oh my God, yes please."

"What she said," Echo says enthusiastically. "Please take us."

"Yay! Deal," I tell them and they squeal and high five before high five-ing with me. "We go Friday night."

I was already pretty excited about Friday but now that spark grows. And it makes me feel like myself for the first time in days. For the first time ever since I found out that I wouldn't be able to graduate with my friends.

That *he* wouldn't let me.

That he would keep me here longer, torture me with further time behind bars.

But guess what, I'm taking back my control. At least, some of it.

I'm sneaking out from under his very nose.

And not just Friday night either, nope.

Tonight as well.

Because graduation and my friends aren't the only thing he's taken away from me, has he?

He's taken away something else too.

Someone else.

He's taken away the love of my life.

Chapter Five

In the beginning, there were tears.

Lots and lots of tears.

Tears shed in the pillows. Tears shed under the blanket, in the shower, in between classes. In a quiet corner of the library. In the third floor bathroom that's always out of order, hence empty and a perfect spot for crying.

For the first few weeks when I was sent here, to St. Mary's, all I did was hide out and cry.

But then things changed.

Because Callie found me, befriended me, and the rest is history.

You know, I always say that Callie, and then later Wyn and Salem, saved me from going crazy in this reform school. But they saved me from so much more.

They saved me from heartache.

Because when I was sent here, I wasn't only angry for being banished, I was also heartbroken.

I was also heartsick and devastated.

Over my broken love story.

Yeah, before I was sent here I was in love with a boy.

That's actually the *whole reason* why I was sent here.

Out of all the reasons that could have had me banished, falling in love was the one that got me in the end. And trust me when I say that there were plenty of other reasons. *Plenty.*

Because while I was living under his roof, I did everything that I could to make good on the promise that I'd made to him that night in the rain. Of making his life hell.

I actually had a whole routine back then.

School and boring classes; shooting the shit with Mo; exploring the vast grounds surrounding the mansion; doing things and playing pranks to mess with him.

After a while, I have to admit that I started to… *enjoy* living in that mansion.

I started to enjoy Middlemarch and how peaceful it was. Except for the times when I disturbed the peace myself. I started to warm up to my routine.

And the biggest reason for it was Jimmy.

Jimothy Wilson.

He had blue eyes and blond hair, and a voice that made me forget my own name.

His voice was the reason we met actually.

I followed it one day, on a crisp spring morning in April, into the woods behind the mansion. And found him sitting on a log, his blond head bent and his muscular arms cradling a guitar. He was playing and humming a tune, and I couldn't look away. I stared at him and stared at him until he realized that someone was watching him.

He looked up.

He saw me with his blue eyes.

And he smiled.

I remember that vividly. His soft, curious smile.

Because that was the instant I fell.

In love I mean.

We spent that whole morning talking and laughing. I found out that his name was Jimothy but people called him Jimmy. He was seventeen years old, had left school his sophomore year, and that this spot in the woods was his favorite. He loved coming here in the mornings to be by himself and with nature. And practice his music.

Because Jimmy was a musician. He was a poet too.

He was the lead singer and the lyricist of his band, and he wanted to make it big.

I knew he would because he was phenomenal, and every day since then, he'd shown up in the mornings before school, and we'd meet at the same spot. We'd talk; I told him everything about Charlie and New York and the life that I'd left behind. And we'd laugh and he'd sing me a song that he'd written. I'd even sneak out at night to go see him and his shows with his band.

By the time summer arrived, I was so enchanted by him that I was ready to tell him.

I was ready to tell him that I loved him.

That he was the only boy that I'd ever loved and that he made everything okay. He made living in that new mansion okay. His warm blue eyes made it easier for me to bear *his* dark, cold ones. His affection made it easier to bear *his* hate.

And I even made a whole plan to tell him. I plotted everything down to a T. It was all going to be perfect.

If not for *him*.

My devil guardian.

If not for his sudden, abrupt decision to uproot my life again, and send me away.

After months of trying to convince him, prank him, *force* him to let me go, he *was* letting me go. He *was* sending me away. Only he wasn't sending me back to New York but to a reform school.

And he didn't even have the decency to tell me to my face, no.

He sent Mo as always, to break the news.

To tell me that I was being shipped off to a reform school come that fall because I was being stupid. Because I was chasing after a guy who wasn't good enough for me. A guy who was too old for my fifteen-year-old self and who was a high school dropout with no future for whom I was throwing away my own future by breaking all the rules, crapping on my grades, breaking curfews, missing classes.

So maybe I missed a few classes and got a few bad grades, so what?

That doesn't warrant sending me to a reform school.

Jimmy made me feel good. Jimmy made me feel happy. Jimmy made everything bearable.

Not to mention, I'm still not sure how my devil guardian knew about Jimmy. Yes, I was missing school and breaking curfews and all that but I'm not sure how he found out that I was doing it over a boy. Because I'd been very careful to cover my tracks.

But I never got a chance to ask him.

Because when I demanded to see him — so I could tell him to his face what a fucking asshole he was and that I wouldn't let him tear me apart from the love of my life — Mo told me that he was gone.

Yes.

He was gone.

He'd left for Italy.

For his stupid fucking archeological dig.

Where he remained for the next three years.

Only coming back a couple of months ago as the stupid fucking principal of this stupid fucking school.

And of course now that he's back, he's messing with me again.

Because *again*, I had made all the plans.

For this summer. For my life after graduation. For me and yes, for Jimmy.

If he thought that locking me up in a reform school would keep me away from Jimmy, then he was wrong.

He was dead wrong.

Nothing would keep me away from Jimmy.

So here I am.

Standing in the crowd, watching Jimmy like a distant but familiar dream. Because he looks exactly the same today as he did the day I met him. He holds his guitar the same way. He sings the same way. His voice makes me *feel* the same way.

The only difference is that he's bigger and more muscular three years later, and right now, he's shining and shimmering like a mirage, as all these bright lights fall on him.

As they highlight his sweaty blond hair and his gorgeous face.

His singing lips.

God.

I love him.

I love him. I love him. I love him so *so* much.

Other people love him too, obviously, and I'm happy to share him in this way. They're dancing and writhing and waving their arms in the air. They're singing along with him and I grin and sway like the rest of them until he finishes the set and is rewarded by a loud cheer and a thunder of claps.

And then I wait, biting my lip, my eyes tracking his movements as he thanks everyone in the mic; high fives and hugs the rest of his bandmates. When he's done all of that, he looks at the dispersing crowd. His blue eyes run through the space until they land on me.

And then that smile.

The one he gave me the first day we saw each other.

Actually it's a little brighter than the first time. A lot brighter, and more animated, as he abandons his bandmates and jumps down from the stage, cuts through the crowd to come see me.

"Poe," he exclaims, stumbling slightly.

I catch him though. I grasp his biceps and steady him. He gets this way after shows. All hyper and dizzy. All that adrenaline rushing through your system would do that to you.

And well, I'm pretty sure there are other things in his system too.

I mean, he's a musician. Of course he has things and *substances* running in his system.

"Hey," I say breathlessly, my eyes wide as I look into his shiny ones.

Which I'm pretty sure is because of those substances, but I like them nonetheless.

"You came," he says in a loud voice.

I try not to flinch.

Even though the bar is crowded and noisy, his voice is a little too loud.

But it's okay. I love his voice. I love his shiny eyes. I love *him.*

"Of course I came."

Why wouldn't I?

It's his show. I never miss a chance to catch his show.

Needless to say that the whole point of *him* sending me to St. Mary's was that I'd have to cut ties with Jimmy. Mostly because I wouldn't be able to see Jimmy, given the strict rules of St. Mary's.

But of course, I've improvised.

Of course, I've found ways and loopholes to go see Jimmy.

Not as often as I would've liked, because in addition to me being locked up in St. Mary's, Jimmy now lives in New York. He moved a couple of months after I was banished, to live with a bunch of his friends and make it big in his career.

So yeah, things have been tough.

But still I've managed.

"You like the set?" he asks.

"Do you even have to ask? You killed it. I loved it," I tell him.

I love you.

He laughs then, a brilliant sound, only slightly high and

drugged. "Ah, Poe. You are amazing." He comes to hug me then. "So fucking amazing for my ego."

I clench my eyes shut then. As I get to feel his body.

As I get to smell him after months.

The last time I saw him was over Christmas break. He was back in town with his friends and I snuck out to go see him and his show while I was at the mansion for the holidays.

He breaks the hug — too early in my opinion — and looks at me intensely. "It's happening."

"What?"

His face splits into a grin. A *huge* grin. "We're doing it."

"Doing what?"

His grin gets even bigger if possible before he declares, "We're going on tour."

I freeze then, my eyes going wide.

But he doesn't have that problem. He's high and he's animated so ignoring my shock, he pumps both his hands in the air and jumps up and down, screaming, "Woohoo! We're going on tour, baby!"

Which elicits a similar reaction from a number of people.

I'm still frozen though. I'm still immovable.

And I only move when he lowers his arms, wraps them around me and says, "And I want you to come with me."

"What?"

"I want you to come with me on this tour, Poe."

My heart thumps. And thumps and thumps again.

Before my own lips stretch into a wide smile. "Oh my God." My arms around his body tighten and I exclaim again, this time louder, "Oh my fucking God." Which makes him chuckle and I burst out laughing as I hug him, and keep chanting, "Oh my God. Oh my God. Oh my God. I can't believe this. This is…" I pull back so I can look at him. "I'm so proud of you. I'm… I knew you could do it. I knew it. I fucking knew it, Jimmy."

I did.

He's phenomenal.

His voice is amazing. I knew someone would recognize it. I *knew* someone would see all his talent and give him a chance.

High school dropout with no future. Oh please.

Take that, you devil guardian. My Jimmy did it!

"You haven't answered my question yet," he says.

At this, my heart thumps again. "Y-you want me to go with you?"

"Yeah." He smiles.

"Really?"

He gazes into my eyes, *gazes* as he responds in a low, husky whisper, "Who else, Poe? Only you."

Oh my God.

Oh my fucking God.

I can't believe this. I absolutely cannot believe this.

Okay so here's the thing: I'm in love with Jimmy, okay? I wanted to tell him three years ago that *I* loved him. *Me.*

But.

I didn't know what his response would have been. Because I didn't know if he loved me back or not.

We were friends, yes. Great friends, and I knew he liked me as one. But I didn't know if he liked me the way *I* liked him.

And so this summer, when I got out of St. Mary's, I was finally going to tell him. I was finally going to confess my feelings to him and I had made all the plans to make him fall in love with me. I'd made all the plans to convince him to be with me.

So this summer was going to be my summer of dreams.

Until all my plans were destroyed, but…

The fact that he's inviting me on tour. The fact that he's gazing into my eyes. He's *gazing*…

"It kicks off in four weeks," he tells me and I freeze again.

"What?"

He nods. "In four weeks, we're gonna be on a bus, traveling cross-country, and I want you with me, Poe. I want you by my side."

"I…" I shake my head. "F-Four weeks?"

"Yeah."

"But I —"

"No, listen," he says, cutting me off, his voice sounding oddly sober as he puts his hands on my cheeks and tilts my head. "I know. I know quitting school isn't ideal. But you don't need that shit, Poe. You don't need a fucking diploma. I mean, look at me. I don't have one and I turned out okay, yeah?"

"Jimmy, I —"

"No, don't say no," he says, his eyes intense and clear. "Just please, come with me."

I grab his wrists. "I… It's about more than the diploma, remember? I told you. If I don't graduate high school, I don't get —"

"You don't need that shit either," he tells me. "I can take care of you."

"But –"

He comes even closer to me. "Look, I know there's something here. Between us."

My heart thumps harder and I whisper again, "What?"

"I like you, Poe," he says. "I liked you three years ago when I saw you in the woods and I like you now. I think this could go somewhere, you feel me? We could be something, you and me. And I've waited enough. That fucking douchebag guardian of yours has made us wait enough. I'm not letting him control me or you. So you're coming with me."

Holy shit.

Holy *fucking* shit.

There's something here, he said. We could be something.

He has *waited enough* for me.

Oh my fucking God.

This is all very surreal. This is all very dream-like.

This is exactly what I wanted.

Exactly.

How is this even possible? How is this even *happening*?

"Hey, Jimmy."

At the voice, feminine and soft, I wince.

And look to the left. Where the voice came from.

A girl — a few years older than us — with blonde hair and pretty features is standing a few feet away, looking at Jimmy. Who steps back from me, taking his arms away and turning toward her.

"Hey," he greets her, and she approaches him with a pleased smile.

Immediately, I know that she's like me. That she loves him.

Or at the very least, is strongly infatuated with him.

She has that look, the kind that I get when I glance at Jimmy. A look of wonder and awe. And all the happiness, the lightness that I've been feeling for the past however many minutes, starts to evaporate.

It evaporates completely when she puts her hand on his arm and says, "Great set tonight. You absolutely killed it."

Grinning, Jimmy bends down to hug her. "Thanks, E."

'*E*' turns to me then. "Who's your little friend?" Then with a little condescension, "Nice glasses by the way."

Nice glasses?

Seriously? She doesn't even know me and she's being catty.

I try to school my features though. I try not to show how her proximity to the boy I love is making me feel. Especially when Jimmy is smiling at me with such happiness.

"*This* is Poe," he tells her, pointing toward me. "Remember I told you about her? I said I want her on the tour with me. The girl who got away." Despite my jealousy, I blush at his words and he continues, "And this is Erica. Our tour manager. She's the one who discovered us, back in New York. She helped us get signed and she'll be going on tour with us."

Tour manager.

Her?

In my experience, tour managers are supposed to be obnoxious middle-aged men. They keep a tight leash on everything. *And* they don't touch the talent because it's against the company rules.

So why is this Erica touching him?

And how can I make her *not* do that?

My nails are on the verge of breaking skin with how tight my fists are clenched at my sides as I smile and say, "Uh, tour manager. That's wonderful."

My words get Erica's attention and she comes back to focus on me, but her eyes depict a shrewdness that wasn't there a few seconds ago. "Yup. I'll be there every step of the way. Jimmy is amazing." She turns to Jimmy for a second, who's looking at her like she holds the secret to all the questions he's ever asked. "He's going to be a star. And this tour is only the beginning."

"It is," I say, sort of urgently and loudly, so Jimmy focuses on me, which he does. So I smile at him and continue, "I always knew that. He's amazing."

His blue eyes — now clear after our intense talk — soften and a private look passes between us, putting a balm to my jealousy.

"So I hear you've known Jimmy for quite a while," Erica says.

I shift my gaze to her. "I have. Three years now."

"Wow. That's a long time."

"I know." I lift my chin and before I think better, I continue,

"And I plan to make that a *very* long time in the future."

Yes. Take that, Erica.

I'm here to stay.

Her eyes narrow slightly but her smile stays in place. "Well in that case, I hope you can join us on tour. It should be fun."

I open my mouth to respond but she looks away and focuses on the guy I love. "Can I borrow you for a second? There are people I'd like you to meet."

"Yeah, just a sec," he says and Erica leaves with a nod.

Then it's just me and him.

"Jimmy, I —"

"No, don't answer yet," he says, reaching up and putting his hand on my cheek. He caresses my skin, my jaw, going super close to my lips. Which is where his brilliant blue eyes drop as he whispers, "Just think about it, okay? You and me."

Somehow I manage to nod.

With one last swipe of his thumb that comes very, *very* close to my lips, he lets me go and walks away.

As soon as he does, my own hand comes up and I touch the spot he was touching. I trace my jaw, the side of my lips as I watch him up ahead, meeting up with Erica in the crowd. Erica rubs her cheek on his muscular shoulder, and winds her arm around his waist.

And I know I don't have to think about it.

I know what my answer is.

Yes.

It's yes. A thousand times yes.

I'm going on that tour with him.

I *am.*

And my devil guardian won't stop me.

Not again.

Chapter Six

A few weeks before my finals, when Mo told me that he was coming back, I didn't know how to feel.

First, it's not as if he hadn't come back from Italy ever since he went away three years ago.

He had. Multiple times.

Well, three to be exact.

And all of those times, I was at St. Mary's.

Which means, by the point Mo told me that he was coming back for good, I hadn't seen him for three years. I hadn't seen him ever since he decided to tear me apart from the love of my life, and hadn't cared enough to actually be there to tell me that he had done that.

Suffice it to say, I wasn't happy about the news.

But strangely, I wasn't angry either.

I can't say why.

Especially because I'd spent the last three years cursing him out. And hating him and telling anyone and everyone who would listen that he'd ruined my life.

What I was, however, was curious.

To see him again. After such a long time.

I was curious whether *he* was curious or not. About me.

And as much as I want to deny it, I crazily wanted to know if anything had changed.

Not just looks-wise. I mean, I was definitely curious about that. About how he looked. If he had aged and how he had, if so. If he was still as masculine and commanding and beautiful as he had been before.

But mostly I was curious to know if something had changed between us.

I was curious to know if he still felt the same way about me. If he still saw me as an unruly, troublemaking fourteen-year-old who made his life difficult that one year we lived under the same roof.

I wanted to know if he still saw me as an extension of Charlie.

If he still hated me for it.

I mean, *I* did — I had reasons to hate him — but I wanted to know if his reasons were gone or not.

But then I got this *second* piece of news: that I wasn't graduating on time and that the new principal was responsible for making that decision, him, and I got my answer.

Nothing has changed.

Not between us.

We're still enemies, him and me.

He's still my devil and I'm still his harpy.

And if there was any other way to do what I want to do, I would do it. I would steer clear of him. Like I have for the past week, ever since summer school started.

I can't though.

Because I have a goal. An urgent goal, and I'm going to have to face him in order to make it happen.

That's why this morning, I'm sitting on the concrete steps that lead up to the entrance of hell or, you know, our school. The girls are in their usual places, the ones who watch him stride across the field. Jupiter and Echo are in their places as well. Although they're watching me rather than the row of cottages he's going to emerge from any second now.

I also have a book in my lap.

I'm not sure why. It's not as if I'm reading it. It's simply open to a random page and I'm worrying the corner of it, my eyes unfocused.

I'm nervous.

It's strange because I'm very rarely nervous. I make other people nervous actually.

But the thing is that a lot is at stake here.

A lot.

If my plan — yes, I have a plan; finally after *days*, I do have a plan and it feels *amazing* — doesn't work, I could lose everything.

I could lose my one chance at love.

I could lose Jimmy.

There's something here. We could be something...

God.

God.

I can't believe he feels the same way. That he *waited*. God, he fucking waited for me.

And so I have to.

I have to go on that tour. I have to go on the road with him.

There's no other choice.

Especially when I know Erica is going to be there.

I'm not losing Jimmy to Erica.

Because this is it. This is my dream. I could have it, you know.

I could have someone to love me. Finally.

After eighteen years of my life, I could finally be loved.

I could finally break the curse.

The curse of a troublemaker.

We're unloved, see. Troublemakers like me.

Girls like me are chaotic and complex and difficult. Girls like me are restless. Our souls are filled with fire and volcanoes. No one wants to love us. No one wants to care for us. No one wants to burn with us.

Which means it's important that today goes well. It's even more important that *he* not only agrees to my plan but also that he doesn't find out, under any circumstances, that my plan has anything to do with Jimmy.

No way.

Because if he does, I'm sure he'll try everything to keep me apart from the love of my life, and for good this time.

Just as the thought flashes across my mind, he appears.

The devil.

Not in the distance, coming out of the cottages, but right in front of me.

Holy shit.

Because there's that heat.

His signature.

It has gone up, making my skin both sweat and shiver.

And then there are those Italian loafers of his that are in my vision. Black and shiny, right at the bottom of the steps. And his dress pants, dark gray. Slightly above that, his leather briefcase.

But what gets my heart racing and thumping in my chest is the shiny thing on his hand.

On his left pinkie, to be specific.

A silver ring with a black stone.

It adorns his finger and practically glows on his dusky digit.

I finally look up and there he is.

In all his tall and broad and tweed jacket-wearing glory.

His chin is dipped and his eyes are pointed at me. Or rather his sexy sunglasses.

And in them, I see myself reflected back as I come to my feet while I study something else.

A little bump on his nose.

Which indicates that he must've broken it in the past. The slight imperfection on his otherwise perfect face.

That only gives him an edge. A roughness, a danger.

A mystery.

"Hey, Mr. Marshall," I say, my voice chirpy and his name in my mouth tasting like cherries.

Mr. Marshall.

Four years ago, I made another promise up on that roof, of never ever calling him by his first name. Just because he asked me to. And I haven't and neither do I plan to, ever.

But every time I call him by *not* his first name, I begin searching his face.

I begin looking for a reaction from him.

To see if my deliberate defiance affects him.

I've never been able to find anything, and I still don't.

His gorgeous features are cool and blank. His clean-shaven jaw hasn't moved nor have his arrogant brows twitched. And I'm pretty sure if he took off his sunglasses, his chocolate brown eyes will be as calm as ever.

Well, moving on.

I correct myself and go, "Well, Principal Marshall. *Principal.* Since you're the principal now." I hug the book tightly. "Things have changed, huh."

Okay, that was a dig.

Because I know they haven't.

He might be the new principal and somehow even more gorgeous than he was three years ago, but he's still the man who hates me for who I am.

Not that he's going to show me.

His features are still carefully blank but he does speak. "They have, yes."

And for a second, all I can do is clutch the book in my arms really tightly. Because his voice, like all the other things, is the same as well.

Deep and smooth and quiet.

So patient sounding.

"Although, you're still a student," he murmurs, breaking my wayward thoughts, his chin dipped toward the book in my arms, the only indication that he's looking at it.

A dig by him now.

After mine, it's fair I guess.

So I forge ahead, "Long time no see." Then, "Well, I mean we do see each other. Since you're here now. But you know, not really. We haven't talked. In a while."

He keeps staring at me with a neutral face. "Yeah. But that's the thing about luck."

I frown slightly. "What thing?"

"It runs out." Then, he repeats my words, "In a while."

I bite the inside of my cheek then.

To stop myself from chuckling. It's a thing I'd somehow forgotten about him.

That he has a dry, very killer sense of humor.

"So, how's it hanging?" I quip, completely forgetting my nervousness from before. "Kicked any puppies yet today?"

This time, I let my chuckle loose.

He is as serious as ever though as he replies, "Not yet, no. I was planning to but a wildcat is in my way."

Ha. Ha.

Very funny.

I raise my eyebrows. "You do know that wildcats are called that for a reason, don't you?"

"And what reason would that be?"

"They're known to bite."

"Are they also known for their incessant chatter first thing in the morning?"

"Not particularly, no," I tell him. "Although I do hear that in addition to sharp teeth, they have killer nails." Then, to emphasize, I scratch the air with my nails and say, "Meow."

He notices my gesture with a straight, bored face, before he hums, "Well, now I know why I'm allergic to cats." Then, nodding, "A very good impression by the way. You almost had me sneezing there for a second."

I shrug, completely unbothered by his sarcasm. "What can I say, I have many talents."

"But alas, getting to the point isn't one of them, is it?" he deadpans.

"What?"

Then, his chest moves. It expands under his dark gray dress shirt as he breathes out and says, "You were sitting on the stairs."

"I was."

"Instead of over there." He jerks his head to the side. "On one of those benches where you usually sit in the mornings."

"You know where I sit in the mornings?"

"I'm guessing there's a reason for it," he says, ignoring my words.

"There is."

Another breath. "So let's hear it."

He knows where I sit.

That's the first thing.

It's not as if I hide myself or anything but still. I sort of sit in the back and usually I'm partially hidden by his thick group of fans. That I honestly didn't think he paid much attention to. He certainly acts like it.

Even now, his fans are watching us. They're watching this exchange.

I can feel their eyes on me and if I were even remotely hesitant about being the center of attention, I'd be running for cover. As it is, I'm the daughter of a famous soap opera actress. I know how to handle the limelight.

And second, I wonder if he knows that like his fans, I watch him too.

With all the hatred in my heart, but still.

Who cares though?

It's not important.

I'm here for something else and so I push aside every wandering thought and say, "Well, I'm here because I wanted to talk to you."

At this, his frame tightens.

Only slightly but it's there.

His shoulders go even more rigid and I notice a tautness in his jaw. And even though I can't see it, I somehow know that his eyes behind those sunglasses have grown alert as well.

I really wish he'd take them off though.

I really wish I could see his eyes right now.

Not being able to is making this thing even more difficult.

"Regarding," he asks, his voice all business now.

I swallow. "Uh, regarding my classes."

I know I should keep going but I have to pause here for a second. I have to rehearse it in my head one more time. The plan I made last night in my bed as I watched the stars through the bars of my window and imagined a life with Jimmy.

I clear my throat. "So I was thinking that there might be a way to —"

"Make an appointment."

I flinch. I actually freaking flinch at his interruption. "What?"

"If you'd like to discuss your classes, you're welcome to make an appointment with my assistant," he explains in his most business-like and formal voice.

"But…" I hesitate, completely taken aback. "I mean, we're talking right now and —"

"And I'm going to need you to hand it over."

I open and close my mouth as I stare at him, flabbergasted. "What? Hand *what* over?"

This time I definitely know that he's glancing down. And he hasn't even dipped his chin or made any outward movements. It's just that I can feel his gaze. I can feel it on my hand, my fingers actually, where I'm hugging my book, and I look down as well.

"You're not allowed the use of any cosmetic products," he tells me. "School policy."

I jerk my head up. "Um, what?"

"So I'm going to need you to hand over whatever it is that you're using to paint your nails."

Oh my God.

Oh my *God.* Oh my *fucking* God.

"Whatever it is that I'm *using*?" I parrot his words. "It's not drugs, you… ancient, fashion-hater *dinosaur*. It's called nail polish."

"Whatever the term might be," he says, still all formal and bored. "I'm going to need you to hand it over to my assistant. She'll take care of it."

"No, she will not," I say, shaking my head. "I'm not handing over my Purple Durple to anyone, least of all to your assistant, okay? So you can forget about that."

I swear he blinks. I *swear* it.

And I also swear that I'm going to rip off his sunglasses and stomp on them right here and right now.

"Purple Durple," he repeats.

"Yes. That's the name of the shade, you genius. And it's organic."

"What's organic?"

"My nail polish." I lean toward him, clenching my teeth. "It's made of organic products."

He stays in place however as he asks, "What are organic products?"

"Products that are…" I think about it for a second or two. Then, "…*Organic.*" Damn it. I wish I knew but I keep going, just so he doesn't focus on my lack of knowledge. "Not to mention, it glows in the dark."

"Why do you need it to glow in the dark?"

"Because I do."

"Are you hoping that it will light your way to the treasure chest?" he deadpans. "Hidden at the bottom of the sea."

I stab my finger at him. "You know —"

This time he does dip his chin to look at my purple-painted fingernail before saying, "As intellectual and fashion forward as this conversation is, I'm afraid I'm going to have to cut it short." Then, "Have your Purple Durple on my assistant's desk by noon."

"You're being completely unfair. This is a stupid rule and —"

He takes a step back. "Have a good day."

"No, wait." At least, he does and I go on, "Look, we both know that I'm not just a student now, don't we?"

"Do we?"

I am this close to growling but I refrain. "Yes. I'm also your ward, remember?"

A slight frown appears between his brows as if he's really trying to remember. "Ah, right. My ward, yes." Then, pinning me with his gaze that I feel even from behind his sunglasses, he adds, "I still have that document in my study that says so."

A shiver rolls through my spine at his words from so long ago.

The rage I'd felt that night. The anger. The frustration.

The helplessness.

I'm on the verge of feeling all that now as well.

Plus there's more at stake now than it ever was back then.

But somehow I still keep marching on. "Yes, I'm sure you do. And I'm sure you look at it every night and laugh evilly like the devil you are, but —"

"Not every night, no," he interrupts. "I'd say every weekend or so."

Ugh.

Can I please kill him?

"And you can have my Purple Durple if you like, but don't you think that seeing as I'm also your ward, I deserve a little special treatment?"

"A little special treatment."

"Yes. For example, how about we talk *now* rather than me having to make an appointment for later?"

He hums. "Intriguing concept."

"It sure is." Then, "Besides, look, everyone is watching. Everyone knows you're the first principal in a long time to ever stop someone's graduation. Not just one someone but *three* someones."

He so is.

In all the history of St. Mary's, there have only been a handful of cases when students have been held back like this. In fact, we don't even talk about not graduating. We call it The Unspeakable because it's awful enough to be going to a reform school that no one even wants to think or talk about not graduating on time.

Which means that he's not exactly popular. Yes, girls watch him because he's oh so handsome, but his interpersonal qualities leave a lot to be desired.

"I didn't know that I was that infamous."

"Well, you are," I tell him. "So maybe now's your chance to,

I don't know, redeem yourself a little. Don't be such a hardass, okay? This is your school now, for however long you stay here. How about you play nice and talk to me and inspire some warm sentiments toward you?"

"No."

"What?"

"I don't think I'm interested in inspiring warm sentiments. I'm quite comfortable making students shiver and quake in their boots."

"I can't —"

"And I'm irredeemable."

"You —"

"Have a good day." Then, tipping his chin at my book, "If you're attempting to read that, might I suggest having it right side up? Instead of upside down. Like you do right now."

With that, he dismisses me and leaves. And I'm so shocked by the turn of events that I let him leave.

I even *watch* him leave.

I watch him climb the stairs with the same authority and purpose that he exudes every day. And when he reaches the landing and disappears through the doors of hell, I clench my fists around my book, finally coming out of my stupor.

Fucking asshole.

Fucking devil.

I could smack him right now. I could climb these stairs, go through the same door, run after him and slap his fucking face as soon as I catch up. And then I could scratch it too.

With my purple-painted nails.

You know, our old principal — Principal Carlisle — was no picnic in the park to deal with. I know; I've had to deal with her a lot over the years, being the troublemaker I am. But she wasn't even remotely this crazy. There are a fuck-ton of rules in the St. Mary's manual and while she enforced ninety percent of them with an iron fist no less, even she understood that some rules are just super fucking cruel.

Like taking a girl's makeup away.

So everyone was allowed to use some. Definitely not heavy but *something*.

But not him.

Not the new fucking principal.

It's okay though.

I already knew what a douchebag he is.

If he wasn't, I wouldn't be here.

And if I want to get out, I need to play by his rules. So that's what I'm going to do.

I'll hand over my Purple Durple. I'll make an appointment to talk to him.

And I'll try to not kill him in the process.

Because I was right. Nothing has changed at all.

Chapter Seven

I'm going to kill him.

I am.

That's the only way out of this hellhole.

Because the plan that I came up with, he isn't ready to listen to.

It's been two days since I intercepted him on the stairs and he dismissed me by saying that I needed an appointment to talk to him. Since then I have gone to his office five times — yes, *five* — to either make an appointment or to simply catch him if he's there.

Twice, I was turned away by his assistant, Janet, with the excuse that he *has* no time to meet with students. Once, she did say that he had some time but when I got there, that time vanished because he had to run out for a meeting. And then, the other two times, I hung around the office during lunch and after school to see if I could run into him.

I didn't.

Because somehow he was nowhere to be found.

He didn't even take his usual route to the school building like he has in the past.

Needless to say, I'm not the only one disappointed. His legions of fans are too.

But I'm the only one who's angry.

Angry enough to do this: break into his cottage in the middle of the night.

Because I'm done with this shit.

I'm done with him jerking me around. I thought we could be mature about this but apparently not.

So here I am, walking through the row of cottages.

Not going to lie, I'm not thrilled about making this excursion in the middle of the night. Mostly because these cottages have been abandoned for decades and it shows. Once upon a time they used to be housing for teachers, but now they are scary looking and shabby and are creepily adorned by overgrown ivy.

I hate that I have to enter one when I'd rather stay away from this whole gothic vibe-y area. The only consolation is that he isn't home. Because when I was hanging around the office, hoping to run into him, Janet told me that I was wasting my time. He was back in Middlemarch for a city council meeting and then he was running back to New York for a lecture and he'd be gone for the rest of the evening and well into the night.

Which means that whenever he does return, I'm going to be waiting for him in his stupid cottage.

And this time, he's going to listen to me.

I know I'm breaking a million rules doing this. If a little nail polish sets him off, I'm pretty sure this might blow his head right off. But I don't care anymore.

When I reach his door, I get out a hairpin from my skirt pocket with firm, determined movements. I pick the lock expertly and then I'm inside his silent and dark cottage.

And I immediately know that I'm in the right place. I already knew that, but still.

It's the air, see.

It's hot. And it smells like him.

Leather and cigars.

The scent I once lived with for a year.

And I remembered it *exactly* right.

Only it's more potent now.

Thicker and real.

Just like this heat.

It makes my fingers tremble as I fish a tiny flashlight from my skirt pocket. And my trembling fingers are joined by my heart that trembles also, when I switch it on.

Because it's as if I'm back in his study.

Wall to wall bookshelves filled with thick leather-bound books. Leather couches and chair. A coffee table covered with loose papers and documents and notebooks. A long table by the wall carrying his favorite things: scotch and a box full of cigars.

And further up, there's the reason for his broken nose.

Or at least I like to imagine that it is.

Because it's a heavy punching bag.

Hanging down from the ceiling, just behind the leather couch. It's brown and weathered, well used.

Just like that bump on his nose on his otherwise perfect face, this heavy bag is a contradiction too. A great contradiction to his scholar-with-two-PhDs persona.

I personally never would have guessed that he likes to punch things.

And the fact that he does, that he actually has a dedicated room at the mansion for his workouts that includes a heavy bag like the one hanging here, gives him an edge. Much like the bump on his nose.

I turn my attention to the kitchen adjacent to the living room. To the fridge, specifically.

Because I know what I'll find in there.

A cherry pie.

Mo must have sent some. She knows how much he loves it, and I'm right.

It's there. Sitting on the very first shelf.

Like the most perfect thing that I've ever seen.

And it sure is, especially as compared to the stupid cafeteria food.

So I don't hesitate to dig in.

I find a fork and polish off at least one fourth of the pie in like five minutes. I wish I could finish it all by myself so there's none left for him, but even I can't eat that much. I debate just throwing it away but I can't do that to Mo. No matter how much pleasure it might give me to deprive him of his favorite thing.

I do leave my used fork in there though. Just to annoy him.

And then I look for something that I can actually mess up.

I would've rearranged some books on his bookshelf but he's already plenty messy when it comes to his books and notes. So it's not very useful. I do find a knife sitting on the butcher's block on the island so I grab that and move on.

Down the very short hallway lies his bedroom and I go inside.

Much like the bedroom in his mansion, this one holds a king-sized bed with a large wooden headboard and a nightstand with a lone lamp. While his room used to be all clean and put together thanks to his staff, here it's messy. Sheets are wrinkled and unmade. Books and documents adorn the nightstand *and* the floor as well.

Sighing, I open the door opposite from his bed.

Ah, his closet.

Meaning a long row of tweed jackets. All gray or black or brown in color, and all of them with elbow patches made of leather. I've always thought about messing with his jackets but I've never been able to bring myself to do it. As old-fashioned as they are, they suit him. They fit him so well, like his body was made for them.

Actually, no.

They were made for his body.

Like someone invented them back in the day with him on their mind.

I reach out a hand so I can touch them.

But suddenly I find that I can't.

Suddenly I find that I'm restricted.

Because someone is touching *me*.

Actually not just touching me. Someone is *grabbing* me.

My wrist.

Someone has their fingers wrapped around it. And everything happened so abruptly, so unexpectedly and jarringly, *Jesus fucking Christ*, that I drop my flashlight, which falls to the floor with a clatter, and my mouth opens.

But the only sound that comes out of it is a gasp.

A broken, hiccup-y gasp.

Instead of a loud scream.

But before I can gather enough steam to make a second attempt, I hear a growl. "Let go."

Holy shit.

Holy *fucking* shit.

What… How… That growl.

It's him.

He's here.

He's behind me.

In the dark. With my stupid fucking flashlight on the floor

casting eerie shadows on the closet wall.

But more than that, *more than that*, he's touching me.

He's *touching* me, the hand that's holding the knife, and I can't breathe.

I absolutely cannot breathe right now.

And then that hand of his tightens around mine, his fingers digging into my wrist. When his rough thumb mashes into my pulse, my whole body jolts and my fingers holding the knife loosen, and he swipes it.

He takes it away from me and along with my knife, he's gone too.

He steps away, and my breath comes rushing and slamming back into my body. And then I'm breathing like a hurtling train, all noisy and fast. My chest is heaving and I grab hold of my wrist — the one he'd grabbed — with shaking fingers.

A moment later, the space floods with light and I spin around.

It takes my eyes a second to adjust and then there he is.

The man who came out of nowhere. Who shocked my breaths out of me just now.

My devil guardian.

He stands at the threshold of his bedroom, looming like a threat, dwarfing everything around him with that knife in his hand.

And he's not just holding it, he's toying with it.

His thumb — that dug into the pulse of my wrist — is flicking the shiny edge of the knife softly.

"What the…" I still can't catch my breath. "How did you… What are you doing here?"

His face is a study of harsh lines as he stares at me. And through my shock, I realize that I can see them.

His eyes.

For the first time in days, I can see his dark, chocolate brown eyes.

Crazily, I think that they remind me of chocolate chip cookies. Especially the ones that Mo makes, with shiny, melted chocolate chips. My favorite thing ever.

Not that anything about his eyes can be called melted, but still.

They're hard just like his face.

Just like his jaw, which moves when he replies, "I live here."

"I —"

"Which I guess you know," he goes on, a muscle jumping on his cheek. "Don't you?"

"But you were…" I swallow. "You were supposed to be out and —"

"Is that what you were counting on?" His thumb digs into the sharp end and I tighten my own body, afraid that he might cut himself. "Me being out."

Yes.

I was.

That was my whole plan. I was going to do what he just did to me.

I was going to lie in wait until he came back and then ambush him. Or rather, confront him and force him to talk to me.

But for the second time this week, he ruined my plan.

"How did you even… come up behind me like that?" I ask, slowly getting my wits back together. "You scared me."

His chocolate chip eyes glitter at my words. "I think I should be the one scared." He presses his thumb on the knife again. "Don't you think? Given that I found this knife in your hand when we both know about your history."

I flinch.

It's slight but it's there and I hate it.

I hate that he's bringing it up to taunt me for all the things I've done to him.

Yes, I haven't been an angel to him. In fact, I've been a downright menace. I've done everything that I can to make his life hell, like I promised him four years ago.

But it's not as if he didn't deserve it.

It's not like *he* was an angel to *me*.

Even now, the fact that I broke into his cottage and I was looking to mess with his things is *only* because he wouldn't give me the time of day.

So I raise my chin and shoot back, "Yes, we do. And given that *you* are the history expert between the two of us, you should know why my *history* is the way it is, shouldn't you?" Then before he can say anything, I add, "And my hand that was holding the knife? You didn't have to manhandle it."

His eyes flick to my wrist.

I still have it clutched between my fingers. And it's as if his gaze is so potent, I feel it.

I feel his touch again.

It was searing.

I couldn't figure it out in the moment but I realize now. I realize that his devil fingers, his *devil touch* was hot.

It burned me.

"That wasn't manhandling," he says, his voice low, his eyes coming back to me.

"It was." Then, staring into his eyes, "It hurts."

He stares back. "No it doesn't."

No, it doesn't.

I realize that too.

Because as hot and burning as his touch was, it didn't hurt.

It *doesn't* hurt.

"It's going to bruise tomorrow," I lie again, keeping my eyes on him.

He keeps them on me as well. "No it won't."

My voice shakes a little when I say, "I don't ever want you to touch me again."

Finally a truth.

Isn't it?

Of course it is.

Of course.

His jaw clenches for a second before he goes, "That we can agree on."

I feel the clench of his jaw in my chest for some reason and I say, "I was —"

Whatever it was I was going to say is interrupted by him. "I'm going to need you to hand it over as well."

"Hand what…"

I trail off because I know. I know what he's talking about.

My purple lipstick.

I wore it in rebellion. I wore it knowing he'd notice and well, he has.

I bring my fingers up to my lips and he asks, "Does it have a name too?"

"Yeah."

"What is it?"

I swallow, bringing my hand back down. "Wild Child Bad Child."

Something flickers across his features, something as dark and mysterious as him. "Perfect for you, isn't it?"

"I —"

"You pick the lock?"

I hesitate for a second before replying, "Yes."

He stares at me for a moment, his jaw tight, his thumb still on the sharp end of the knife, not flicking though, nor digging, simply there. As if waiting for something. Then, "How'd you get out?"

"What?"

"*Out*," he clips, "of your dorm building."

My heart thumps at his sharp tone. But it's more than that. There's an underlying danger in it, in his voice, in that poised thumb. "W-why?"

His eyes flash at my stumbling tone. "This isn't the first time you've done this."

"Done what?" I ask, clutching my skirt.

Which I don't think I should have done; it's a sign of nervousness.

But the thing is that I *am* nervous.

Given how crazy quiet he's gotten right now. How he's watching me, my every little move. My fists clutching the skirt. The pulse thrumming on the side of my neck.

He looks and studies all of it before he brings his eyes back to me and continues, "Sneaked out like this."

"I'm not sure why we're talking about that," I say, trying to infuse steel in my voice. "I got out. I picked the lock. And now, I'm here. You can punish me if you like but —"

A very large audible breath from him steals my words.

That and a muscle jumping on his cheek.

Taking his thumb off the knife, he commands, "You're going to sit down with Janet tomorrow and tell her *exactly* how you got out. I'm going to assume that you have your ways. In fact, you have multiple ways. In and out of both the dorm and the campus." He pauses and my throat goes dry at all his right assumptions and guesses. "Don't you? Because you're not breaking out of your dorm just to go cavorting around campus at midnight. So I want you to tell all those ways to her in as much detail as possible. Meanwhile, I'm going to fire the warden on duty tonight." Then, "No actually, I'm going to fire every fucking warden we've got on duty *and* the security guards. Because this is worse than I thought."

After issuing that angry, ominous statement, he leaves the bedroom.

I'm so shocked that for a few seconds, I simply stand there.

I mean, I knew he'd freak out about me sneaking out like this, but come on. This is an exaggeration. I thought he'd be pissed but then he'd get over it and we'd talk.

This is insanity.

I force myself to break out of my stupor and rush out of the room. Back in the living room, I blurt out, "You can't fire them. That's crazy."

I say all this to his back because he's facing away from me.

He's standing at the table that holds his vices and from the clinking of glass, I assume he's pouring himself a drink. I'm proven right when I watch him throw it back in one gulp, his head tilted up to the ceiling, his back rippling with his actions.

"Don't you think you're being a little extra?" I prod when all he does is pour another drink as if the first one was simply a warmup, something to take the edge off. "Getting so crazy over a little sneaking out and lipstick and nail polish. I mean, when Principal Carlisle was here —"

Finally he turns to face me, glass in hand.

His eyes are still as dark as before, his jaw still tight as well. Making me think that the drink hardly helped. "That's precisely why she's not here and I am."

"What?"

"She wasn't doing her job right and I'm here to fix that."

It takes me a second to understand his meaning.

I know that our old principal left because she was retiring. And he came in as a replacement because he's on the board and he's a good friend of hers. At least, that's what we have all been told in the announcements and school newsletters. But now I'm thinking differently.

Now I'm thinking...

"Oh my God, was she fired?" My eyes go wide. "Did you fire her?"

"We took a vote."

I gasp. "Oh my God, I thought she was your friend. You voted against your friend? What kind of an asshole are you?"

"The kind you don't want to piss off right now."

"So what, you're here to correct her mistakes? Whatever they might be. You're here to make more rules or something?"

"And fix the old ones."

Oh holy God.

I stare at him for a few seconds then. At his formidable demeanor, his intimidating and yet somehow gorgeous features. His glittering brown eyes, his harshly angled jaw.

His dark jacket. That dark tie.

He *is* the devil, isn't he?

He's the king of devils. The lord. The tyrant.

All dark and dangerous.

He's here to make this hell more hellish.

And I'm here to beg for my freedom from him.

"You have five minutes," he says, pulling me out of my thoughts.

"What?"

"To talk. That's what you're here to do, correct?"

I swallow. "Yes."

My answer makes him move.

It makes him walk — no, prowl actually — to the overstuffed armchair adjacent to the couch. Where he puts the amber liquid down on the side table and proceeds to divest himself of his tweed jacket.

I'm not sure why but the view of his big shoulders rolling and his gray dress shirt coming into view is somehow even more intimidating.

Like he's getting ready to fight. He's getting ready for the main show, whatever that might be.

Then throwing the jacket aside, he takes a seat in that overstuffed armchair. He sits back, his thighs wide and sprawled, his elbows on the armrests as he wraps his large fingers around the tumbler, his silver ring clinking against the glass.

It's a small, barely-there sound and yet it makes me jump.

Then he takes a small sip while keeping his eyes on me and says, "Better make it count."

Chapter Eight

After his command, I think I lose twenty seconds of the allotted time.

At *least.*

Because all I can do after he's gotten comfortable in his chair and issued the order for me to speak is simply stare at him.

While I search deep inside my core for my strength, my confidence.

My courage.

Now that the time has actually come, I find that I'm extremely nervous. And the bomb that he's dropped on me, about being here not to help out his friend but to correct her alleged mistakes, is not helping at all.

God, what an asshole.

But it's okay. It's okay.

I can do this.

In my most confident voice, I go, "I have a proposition for you."

Is it me or does that word — proposition — sound not right?

His eyes flash and he takes another sip of his scotch. "Proposition."

Which is when I realize that no, it was not right.

The word, I mean.

It has… innuendo. Of a certain kind.

The kind that makes a shiver go through me when he repeats

it in his low voice.

So I clear my throat and begin again, "Well, more like an idea. A bright idea."

Another sip. "And what is this bright idea?"

Gaining another drop of confidence that he's at least receptive to hearing it, I forge ahead. "So usually when a student is falling behind, teachers are willing to, you know, work with them and give them projects for extra credit and things."

Which is what I'd been doing before finals in the hopes that it would be enough for me to graduate, and it *was* until my guidance counselor called me into her office and told me that I wasn't graduating after all.

"So I was hoping that maybe I could do something like that now," I continue, keeping my hands straight at my sides and not curling my fingers into nervous fists. "You know, to move this process along, uh, faster."

This time he doesn't take a sip.

He simply twists his glass tumbler gently back and forth on the armrest as he watches me. "Faster."

"Yes." I nod, my heart pounding. "I talked to my guidance counselor. She said that as long as I complete all my assignments and projects plus stuff for extra credit to make up for my grades, I can be let out of here early. As early as in four weeks instead of the whole two months. She said that it's a lot of work to be packed into such a small interval but if I'm willing, she has no problem with it. But of course, the principal has to okay it."

That's the whole problem, the principal.

But I'm telling the truth. I did go talk to my guidance counselor, and she did tell me all these things. Well, after she told me that it's going to be hard and it's not a very common occurrence. Usually it's better to just go through the two months and have the process happen naturally.

But of course I don't have two months, do I?

I only have four weeks before the tour starts and I need to be out of here by then.

I *need* to.

Hence this whole by-the-book legitimate plan.

I mean, this should impress him, right? This should work.

It's a plan he's bound to like, this fucking rule fiend who's here to make *more* rules, apparently.

"Four weeks," he repeats yet again, breaking my thoughts.

"Yes."

His ring clinks against the glass as he picks it up to take another sip, his eyes never leaving mine. "That's a lot of work."

My belly tightens at the clink and I shift on my feet. "I'm willing to do it."

Another clink as he lowers his glass. "You're willing to do it."

"Yes," I say, my toes curling this time.

"You must be very desperate then."

"What?"

"To get out of here," he explains. Then, "In four weeks."

"Yes, I am. *Of course* I am. I've been desperate to get out of here since the moment I was trapped here." I raise my eyebrows and inch up my glasses. "Three years ago."

Which is obviously the truth and is not a mystery to anyone.

I've been quite vocal about my hatred of this place.

And so I'm counting on that. I'm counting on the fact that he'll buy it as the reason.

As the *whole* reason, I mean, as to why I want out in exactly four weeks.

God, please let him buy it.

Something flickers in his eyes and he murmurs, "But if you've been trapped here for three years, what's another two months?"

"You're not seriously asking me that, are you? *Seriously.*"

He's unbothered by it though. My snippy tone and my glaring eyes.

He takes another sip of his scotch, his ring hitting the glass again, and I swear if I have to go through the chaos his stupid silver ring is causing in my body, I'm going to do something drastic.

Like march over there, wrestle that drink out of his hand, and throw it in his arrogant face.

"I guess not." He throws out a short nod. "But that's not what I'm asking."

"So then what the fuck are you asking?"

His dark, penetrating eyes narrow in warning. But I don't care.

I mean, how can he even ask me that? How?

When he knows how much I want to get out of here.

"I'm asking," he says at last, "why is it important for you to leave in four weeks? *Exactly* four weeks. And why is it *so* important that you're willing to work for it? Something that you've never really done. For anything, actually."

Jesus Christ, why does he have to be so difficult?

Why can't he just make it easy for me?

Just this once.

"Are you saying that I'm a spoiled little princess?" I snap out.

"No."

I'm slightly taken aback by his negative answer. When he clearly implied something else. And maybe that's why I launch into this long monologue. "Good. Because I'm not. I'm not fucking spoiled, okay? Look at where I am. Where I've been living for the past three years. How I've been living. Every joy in this place comes with a price. Every happiness is attached to a million rules. Not to mention, I'm not some freeloader. And you know that. There's a trust set up in the will that pays for my upkeep. And before you call me a trust fund baby, let me also tell you that I have talents of my own. I have my..."

I come to a halt though. A screeching halt.

Because... what do I have really?

What *talent* do I have?

I mean, I have my...

But can I really call that talent? They are silly... doodles.

They're not even doodles actually. They're just...

They're nothing.

It's nothing.

"You have your what?"

My breaths — that were rapid, I realize now — stop at his prodding. They halt and somehow get tangled up in my chest, and I can't believe I'm thinking about something so inconsequential right now.

Something that has no bearing on my goals, my plans.

Throwing him a belligerent glance, I say, "I'm not spoiled. And even if I am, it's none of your business. It doesn't concern what we're discussing right now."

His eyes flick back and forth between mine for a few moments and I'm hoping that he accepts this and moves on from this topic.

And somehow, miraculously, he does.

Although there's still a thoughtful hint on his features. "Maybe not." Then he drains his scotch in one go and goes, "How about I do you one better?"

I'm instantly suspicious. "What?"

He sets the tumbler down and says, "Instead of making you wait for four more weeks, how about I let you go now?"

"N-now?"

He nods. "Yeah. You've already been here for three years and now I'm trapping you for another eight weeks. It's not really fair to you, is it?" Tipping his head to the door, he says, "Tell you what, you can walk out of here right now and leave. You can quit school, quit your classes. No one will stop you. Least of all me."

I watch him for a few moments, my heart racing in my chest. "I can walk out of here right now."

"Yes."

"You're joking, right?"

He shakes his head slowly. "I'll even call you a cab."

"Hilarious, isn't it?" I glare at him, my nails digging into my palms. "You know I can't leave."

Something akin to satisfaction flickers through his features. "No, you can't."

"Not until you give me my money."

And that's the whole point, isn't it?

That's the whole point why I haven't left yet.

Why I'm trying to chase him down and convince him to let me graduate.

Why I didn't leave the moment I found out about not graduating on time.

I might have needed a guardian when I came to him at the age of fourteen, but I don't need one now.

I'm eighteen years old. An adult.

I don't need someone controlling my life. I can pack up and leave and no one will come after me. Not the law, not CPS or whatever bullshit organization.

But.

Charlie, my mother, in her infinite wisdom drew up a will that stipulates that I need to be a high school graduate in order to receive the first chunk of my money. And the other chunk, along with a bunch of other stuff like properties and whatnot, will be handed over to me when I turn twenty-one. There are a bunch of strings attached to that as well. Namely, that the final decision will rest with the guardian, whether or not I can receive what rightfully belongs to me.

I'm pretty sure it was Marty's idea; I don't think Charlie was even thinking about all the legal technicalities. So Marty drew up a standard will that he probably does for all the other celebrity kids.

So yeah.

I'm tied to him, my devil guardian, until I turn twenty-one.

I know that I'll have to jump through hoops three years from now as well to get his fucking approval. But for now, I'm concerned about the first half of that money. Which is why I've been a good girl for the past week. I've been attending all my classes, doing all my homework. Which is why I haven't been causing any trouble — not that I've felt any inclination to pull a prank or create a disturbance just for the heck of it — because I don't want to put one toe out of line and jeopardize my graduation. *Again.*

Showing up here tonight is an exception, of course.

Which obviously is going to bite me in the ass tomorrow when I list all my secret pathways out of the dorm building to Janet. Who already has my Purple Durple, by the way.

"Your money," he says.

"Yes."

"Because you're not *just* a spoiled little princess, are you?" His lips tip up in a very small smirk. "You're a *rich* spoiled little princess."

That was over the line.

That was way, *way* over the line.

My nostrils flare with a sharp breath. "Do you know why I want my money?"

"To buy more organic nail polish that glows in the dark and lipstick with weirdass but surprisingly accurate names."

"No." I lean forward. "It's because I don't want *you* to control it. I don't want you to control any part of me. Not a single part of me. I want out of your fucking tyranny, do you understand that? Do you understand hating someone so much that you'd do anything to be free of them? This is it. That's why I want my money. I want my money so nothing that belongs to me can *ever* belong to you. Not even for safekeeping. That's how much I hate you. That's how much I've hated you since I met you. That I'm ready to dance on my fucking toes. I'm ready to jump through all the hoops, go to summer school, sit through all the boring fucking classes, so one day I can be free of you. So one day, you can be a distant fucking memory. So one day you have to give up all, every inch of your control. On me. *One day.*" Drawing back, I shake my head. "I told you I hold a mean grudge, didn't I? And I'll be damned if I don't hold it until the day I die. So I'm not a rich spoiled princess, I'm a harpy, Mr. Marshall. *Your* harpy, and I want my fucking money. And I want out of here in four weeks."

Truth.

Every single word.

I didn't want to say it, didn't want to divulge the depths of my hatred for him — although I'm pretty sure he knows — but there you have it.

This is why.

This is why I won't leave with Jimmy. Not without my money. I can't.

I know he said, so sweetly and lovingly and God I love the fuck out of him, that he'd take care of me. But I don't want him to. Mostly because I can take care of myself.

I can.

Despite what my devil guardian thinks.

I'm not afraid to work for it, to get a job — *any job* — to earn my money. But I'm not leaving here without the money that he has under his control.

But a second later, I regret my truthful rant.

Because he unfolds himself from his overstuffed armchair and comes to his feet.

And as soon as he does the room shrinks.

I'm not even lying. It fucking shrinks.

He dwarfs the big walls, the massive wall-to-wall bookshelves with his intimidating height, his impossibly broad shoulders.

While I'm watching that, watching his body take over the freaking building, he strangely goes for his cuffs.

He unbuttons them and, while keeping his eyes on me, proceeds to fold the sleeves up, one by one.

And for a few moments, all I can do is watch him do it.

All I can do is watch him expose his forearms.

No, he is exposing his very tanned and muscular and hair-dusted forearms.

Which makes me realize that I've never seen them before.

As crazy as that sounds.

Yeah, I've never seen his forearms and I'm losing my breath

over them. Because they're so masculine and pretty and distracting.

My focus comes back though when he takes a step toward me. Making my eyes jerk up to his face. "W-what are you doing?"

"Telling you how to earn it."

I have enough presence of mind to step back. "E-earn what?"

"Your money."

I open and close my fists. "What does that… What does that mean?"

"It means," he says and comes another step closer, "that unfortunately for you, my tyranny hasn't ended yet." Another step closer. "I'm still the devil. And you're still mine. I control every little inch of your life, every little inch of you." Another step. "And it means, Poe, that if you want your fucking money," step four, "you're going to have to do exactly as I say."

"What do you want me to do?" I ask, licking my dry lips.

His chocolate chip eyes flicker down to my mouth and I curse myself for bringing his attention to my lips. They tingle and shiver under his gaze.

Looking up, he says roughly, "I'm pretty sure we'll figure something out."

And then he takes another step closer and I know I should move back but I can't.

I'm frozen.

First, because his eyes are glittering more than they ever have, and there's a flush — dark and crimson — on his extraordinary cheekbones. And second, because I think all of that, the flush, the glitter, even the way his lips are parted and the way his chest moves as he breathes, makes him look… predatory.

Jesus Christ.

What is *happening*?

What is he *saying*?

In blind panic, my arms shoot out and I grab the first thing within my reach, a throw pillow.

Then without thinking I throw it at him as I take a step back.

No, *two* steps back.

"Don't come near me," I warn. "Do *not* come near me."

The pillow hits him with a thump — hardly even ruffling his dark curly hair — and drops to the floor, and I hate the fact that in a room full of thick leather-bound books, the only thing I could find to attack him with was a stupid feathery pillow.

"Or what?" he asks, *of course* coming near me.

I keep backing away. "If you're saying what I *think* you're saying..."

I trail off because I can't even.

I can't even complete my own sentence in the face of this. This crazy, absurd, incomprehensible turn of events.

He obviously does not have any problem being coherent though.

In fact, his voice is all breezy and casual as he asks, "What am I saying?"

Oh my God. Oh my *God*.

He's saying… the most despicable things, isn't he?

He's *saying* that I do something in exchange for the money.

That I earn it by doing physical favors.

"My answer is no, you hear me?" I say, stabbing my finger at him. "A thousand fucking times no."

"I thought you were ready to do anything," he says in that same casual tone. "Including working for extra credit."

"No," I snap, moving back; the wall is near, I can feel it, *God*. "Not that. I'll *never* do that."

"Well, you're eighteen now, aren't you?" He cocks his head to the side. "It's a perfect age to work for extra credit." Then, "*Legal* age."

"Oh my God, no. *No*. I swear to God, Mr. Marshall, I'm going to fucking scream."

"It's Principal Marshall now," he corrects, his features growing more predatory by the second, and more beautiful too. "And I very much encourage screaming."

My eyes almost bug out of my head at the innuendo. "I'll throw up then. I'll throw up all over your fucking Italian loafers."

"Well, I hope you're a better cleaner than you are a student. Because if you make a mess, you're the one who's going to clean it up."

"I —"

My words evaporate when my back thumps the wall and I have nowhere else to go as he descends on me like the devil he is.

I fully expect him to put his hands on the wall and cage me. I expect him to get even closer to me, lean over me so he can box me in, trap me like he's always done.

But he doesn't.

He does none of those things.

He comes to a stop a couple of feet away from me and stands tall and broad. He even thrusts his hands down into his pockets.

And it's worse.

Because I'm still caged.

My feet are still glued to the spot and my spine is still stuck to the wall. I'm still all trapped and pinned and he didn't even have to move a muscle.

My chest heaving, I whisper, "I'm not… I'm not *that.*"

A whore.

His jaw moves back and forth as if he heard the word. "And if I wanted you to be *that*, I would've found a way to make you one."

"I —"

"I'm the one with all the power here, aren't I?"

My nails dig into the wall behind me as I jerk out a nod. The only answer I'll give him.

"I can do whatever the fuck I want with you," he says, his eyes heated. "And by your own admission, you'd do it, wouldn't you?"

"Yes."

"Because you hate me so much."

"I do."

His eyes shimmer with something before he rasps, "So if I wanted the clumsy fumbling of a wild child bad child, who's barely eighteen and spends her days in a school uniform and raising hell in a classroom, I would've taken it. And trust me, by the time I was done with you, you'd be hating yourself *more* for loving it than me for doing it to you. Not to mention, you'd be cleaning a different kind of mess from a lot of different places *in addition* to my Italian loafers. As it is, my tastes run to sophisticated, much more experienced women. So your teenage virtue is safe tonight."

I know I should be relieved.

I should breathe easier. But my breaths are even messier now.

My skin is thrumming at his words.

My thighs are clenching involuntarily and my wide eyes become even wider behind my glasses. I inch them up jerkily and say, pushing everything aside, "So then… What do you want?"

He watches my features for a few seconds while his own become all serious, hard. "What I want is for you to tell me something."

"Tell you what?"

"The truth."

"The truth?"

"Is it him?"

"What?"

He grits his jaw. And he does it so hard and intensely that it lasts for a couple of seconds before he explains, or rather drops the bomb on me. "Your fucking boyfriend."

"My b-boyfriend?"

His eyes have violence in them as he rasps, "Yeah. All this begging and working for extra fucking credit. He doesn't happen to be involved in this, does he? Your piece of shit stoner boyfriend."

For a few seconds, I can't say anything.

I can't even breathe. I can't make thoughts let alone words.

My heart doesn't beat.

But I guess that's an exaggeration because I'm alive, aren't I?

And I'm not sleeping either, no. So this can't be a dream.

Or a nightmare really.

That the man who broke my heart three years ago, is *somehow* asking me about the boy I love.

That the man who tore me apart from the love of my life has *somehow* figured out that that's why I'm doing all this.

"He's not a piece of shit," I blurt out the first thing that comes to mind.

Which was the wrong thing to say, because his eyes narrow suspiciously. "Yeah, he is."

Even though I know this is a dangerous road to take, I still say, "No, he's not. And he's not a stoner either."

Well, he kinda is but still.

"Yeah, he is," he repeats.

"Okay, so yes, he's a stoner," I say. "So what? Like you're so perfect. In fact, he's better than you *even though* he smokes pot."

And does other illegal substances.

But so what?

I love him and he waited for me. That's all that matters.

A muscle jumps on his cheek. It jumps and pulses.

And somehow my heart that felt like it had stopped before beats to the rhythm of it.

"He smokes more than pot and you know it," he clips. "And I'm not looking to compete with a high school dropout whose IQ is probably less than my shoe size."

"I —"

"And it *is* because of him," he cuts me off and concludes, "because nothing has changed, has it? You sneaked out to see him before you were sent to St. Mary's and given what I found out tonight, I'm assuming you've been doing the same since you got here."

Holy shit.

Holy shit.

Why does he have to be smart?

Why does he have to be such an asshole?

He's going to ruin everything again, isn't he? He's going to break my heart again.

I can't let him do that. I cannot let him do that.

I need to derail him.

I need to make him forget about Jimmy.

"No, it's not," I say with a firm voice, my neck craned up to look at him, my features schooled. "Yes, I've been sneaking out but not to see him."

"Yeah?"

"Yes. Because he doesn't even live here. He lives in New York."

That gives him a pause. "New York."

Good.

"Yes," I say, nodding. "My stoner boyfriend who isn't really my boyfriend because you took that away from me by the way, is in a band. So he moved to New York years ago, okay? He lives there." Then just because I couldn't resist it, I add, "And from what I hear he has hit it big."

"He has."

"Yup," I say proudly. "He's not just a high school dropout anymore. He goes on tours. He's quite a big deal." I sigh sharply. "So no, Mr. Marshall, I haven't been sneaking out to see him. Rest assured I've been truly trapped here. Like you wanted. So congratulations. You successfully broke my heart *and* caged me in a reform school."

He studies my face for a few seconds, I'm sure to check whether or not I'm lying.

Thankfully, he buys it and clips, "Good."

A pain stabs my chest then, at his *good*.

Like he's so happy.

So ecstatic after ruining my life.

And I can't help but scratch the walls with my nails as I bite out, "You're not my dad, you know that, don't you?"

His eyes flash then. "No, I'm not."

"You had no right. To do what you did. You had *no right* to tear me apart from him. From the boy I loved."

That muscle shows up on his cheek again, pulsing and drumming. "Haven't we had this conversation before? About how I have a document stating my rights."

"I —"

"Which makes me," he says as he leans forward slightly, "worse than your dad, doesn't it? Because I'm here and I'm in charge of you. And I'm standing between you and not only him but also every other guy out there."

And then I can't stop it.

Then I can't stop myself from blurting out the question I've been waiting to ask for three years. "Is that why you didn't do it to my face? Because you're worse than my dad."

"What?"

I look at him through a sheen of anger and tears. "That's what you did, didn't you? You didn't even have the decency, the *fucking humanity*, to break my heart in person. You sent Mo to do it. You sent Mo to threaten me, to put me in my place, to break me. To deliver the news that I was going to St. Mary's. And then you left. Just like that. You left like you didn't even care. You didn't even care to stay behind and see your handiwork. To see the broken pieces of my heart lying on my bedroom floor. Because it didn't matter to you, did it? It was inconsequential to you that you ruined my love story. As long as you did it. As long as you flexed your power and played the whole control game." I shake my head at him. "Well, I hope you enjoyed Italy. I hope you get to go back soon. And this time, I *hope,* and I mean this very fucking sincerely, you choke on some pasta."

My heart is beating in my ears. It's beating in my belly.

No, it's booming.

It's thundering.

When I thought that it would calm down. Finally. I thought that if I purged my anger, if I confronted him about what he'd done, it would give me peace. It would bring me much needed satisfaction to say all these things to him.

But there's no relief.

No peace.

And my angst, my restlessness only grows when he moves.

When he comes closer and at last takes his hand out of his pocket, the one that sports the ring — I don't know why I notice that but I do — and sets it on the wall, up above me.

I shift against the wall, my spine bowing as he leans down, his eyes all heated and molten, his jaw all hard and scruffy, "You'd like that, would you?"

"Like what?"

"Me," he says with clenched teeth. "Breaking your heart. To your face."

I swallow. "I… I'm…"

"Is that what you want?" he rasps, his eyes penetrating. "You want me to threaten you to your face. Like I should have."

"I wanted you to care," I whisper, despite myself.

Despite not knowing where it came from.

Where *did* it come from?

But I don't have the time to analyze it or take it back because he says, his voice rough and a touch above a whisper, "Fine. Consider this as me *caring*: if I find out that you're lying about not seeing your piece of shit boyfriend, I'm going to make sure that I be personally present to give you the news that you're never getting out of here. I'm going to make sure that I personally break your heart into tiny little pieces and look at them lying on the floor. Instead of sending in the person you trusted the most. I'll personally count them too, those pieces, to make sure that I did a good enough job breaking you this time so you'll stay away from him. And then, I'll drag you behind bars myself and lock you in there. Before I throw the key away — *personally* — while you watch. Is that good enough for you or would you like me to be more graphic and detailed?"

"Nothing has changed, has it?" I whisper, shivering now.

Trembling under his intense, heavy scrutiny.

"What?"

"Not one thing has changed," I say, studying the terrain of his features that have turned harsh with hatred, the brown of his gaze that has turned black, again with hatred. "You still hate me as much as you did four years ago, don't you?"

He clenches his jaw in response.

"I don't know why I thought that time and distance might

change things. I mean…" I swallow thickly, blinking my eyes as I try to keep my tears at bay. "It didn't change things for me. I hate you just as much. Even more so, after what you did when you found out about Jimmy. But I… I don't know. I don't know what I expected. I… You'll always see me as an extension of Charlie, won't you? No matter what. And that's why you won't let me go, isn't it? That's why you've been jerking me around these past couple of days. That's why you're not willing to listen to any of my ideas. Because you hate me. Because I'm Charlie's daughter."

I can't read him ninety-five percent of the time but *this*, I can read.

I can read him when I mention my mother.

A shutter snaps down when I mention Charlie. His face takes on a mask, a wooden, feelingless mask, where all his features look like his but they have no animation. They look… dead.

Even his movements are wooden when he goes to take his hand off the wall and steps back, taking away his heat and his scent.

I still burn though. I still smell him.

As he says, "I'd like to see you in my office on Monday. At five. For detention. Bring a notebook and a pen. And I suggest you settle in because you're not going anywhere for the next eight weeks."

Chapter Nine

The Renaissance Man

If there's one thing I'm good at, it's tuning out the world.

Shutting it off. Pushing it away. Either withdrawing into myself or losing myself in my work so that things can't touch me.

It's a technique I developed when I was a kid.

I had to.

Or I wouldn't have survived.

Back then, I was also good at hiding.

I was good at cramming myself into small spaces, jamming myself in nooks and crannies, curling myself into a ball to protect myself. Since then I've learned better ways to do that.

To protect myself, I mean.

Like beating the shit out of a heavy bag for an hour every day.

Works like a charm when you want to intimidate people with your size.

But that's not the point here.

The point is that I can't intimidate or tune the world out right now. As much as I'd like to.

"So how are you finding the school?"

We're in a board meeting and I look at John Thompson who's asked me this question. He's my father's age and used to be good friends with him when he was on the board.

"It's good," I reply.

"Are you settling in well?"

There's no malice in that question and since it's him, I believe that. John Thompson, even though he's my father's friend, isn't a complete piece of shit. Which is a surprise because almost everyone here, on this board, is my father's friend and a complete piece of shit.

And were opposed to me joining in my father's stead.

"Yes, I think so."

"Because if you're not we're always here to help."

That comes from Robert Bailey.

Now *he's* a piece of shit.

Old and arrogant and yes, one of my father's friends.

"Well, I appreciate the help but I think I can manage," I tell him as politely as I can.

"Are you sure?" he asks, his bushy eyebrows raised. "We're happy to help. I mean, you just got back from Italy. You must still be getting over the jet lag."

People chuckle and I clench my fists under the table.

Because the other option is to take that fist and plant it on his face.

But I'm not going to do that.

Mostly because it would be grounds for getting fired from the board.

Which is exactly what he wants.

"It's a six-hour time difference. Which I got over last month. Because that's when I came back from Italy. But thanks for your concern. It's very touching."

"Of course," he continues. "We're always here for you. You're our dear friend's son. We've watched you grow up."

My body tightens for a second. "You have, haven't you?"

He chuckles. "Yes. And that's why we're all concerned. Given your…" He gestures with his hands as if he's too polite to say it.

"Given my what?"

"Well, I mean, your history and health."

People shift in their seats, looking all kinds of uncomfortable.

Anger burns in my chest and it's a wonder that I can say the next words calmly. "Again, I'm fine. Thanks for the offer, but I think I'm capable of handling my family's responsibilities."

I am.

And I've proven that many times over in the past. But I know that in this town, I'm going to have to keep proving it for a long, long time.

It's okay though. I can and I will.

After the initial bullshit chitchat, we get down to business.

We discuss all the plans for St. Mary's for the summer and the upcoming year. I'm thinking of hiring new staff, putting some money into the library and a new science lab.

Usually work is something that calms me down. It cools down the rage in my system, but not today.

Maybe it's the 'given your history' comment that got me. Or it was the way that asshole stared at me with condescension all throughout the meeting, I don't know.

But by the time the meeting gets over, I'm all antsy.

So much so that I can't focus.

So when I get back to the cottage, I decide to work out at the heavy bag.

It works like a charm when you want to get your focus back.

It also works when you want to intimidate people with your size.

And it's something I've always wanted.

To intimidate.

Anyway, as sweat drips down my face and as my knuckles chafe to the point where I can see the crimson blood blooming under the white tape, I can't say that it's helping.

I can't say that my focus is coming back and anger is going anywhere.

It's still beating inside my body, my anger.

Rushing through my veins and pulsing in my fucking temple like a headache.

And I have a feeling that it's only going to grow.

Not just tonight but for as long as I have to live here.

In this place.

In this tiny cottage on the campus of a reform school that my family had built decades ago.

Which is why I'm here in the first place.

Because my family built it decades ago, something they took great pride in. But apparently, in the past year the glory of this place has been tarnished.

And so it's my job to restore it.

When I got the call about the situation, needless to say I was surprised.

For years, Leah Carlisle has been a favorite of the board members with her ruthless pursuit of rules and reformation. But apparently, last year a scandal broke out involving her son — Arrow Carlisle — who was on the faculty at the time, and a student. And then immediately after that was another breach of conduct when a pregnant student was allowed to stay on. Not to mention a faculty member getting arrested on the grounds of having a relationship with a student.

The board wasn't happy and they asked her to step down. Since Leah has been a friend for a few years now — as astonished as I am at her behavior and her sudden lack of leadership — I insisted that the board make it look like she's leaving of her own accord.

And needless to say again, since this school belonged to my family, I asked to take over personally. I also asked to stay on campus to keep a closer eye on things.

Yes, I'd miss teaching summer classes at the college and my other departmental responsibilities, something that I do enjoy, but it's fine.

This is more important.

Protecting and furthering the family legacy.

Because when you've lived half your life falling short of your family's glorified name, protecting it becomes vital.

Although as important as restoring my family's name is, I realize that I've made the biggest mistake of my life.

In coming to St. Mary's.

And here I thought that I'd already made it, my biggest mistake. Four years ago.

When she came into my life. And when I *forced* her to stay.

Poe Blyton.

Poe Austen Blyton.

Four years ago when Poe Blyton came into my life, I saw her as an extension of her mother.

And I hated her for it.

I'm not going to delve into why or how.

It's not something I like to think about. It's something I'd rather forget.

It's something that I *had* forgotten about.

But then she barged into my life and forced me to remember.

Forced me to relive all those things because every time I looked at her, Charlie's face stared back. Even though there's very little that they have in common, lookswise.

And so, I'm not proud of how I handled it.

I'm not proud of how I acted and how I trapped her.

Let's just say that it was the biggest mistake of my life. Or rather the first biggest mistake, now that I've made the second one.

Which is why I left for Italy the moment I got the chance. To remove myself from her presence. Probably the best thing I could've done at the time as her guardian.

But then I came back.

And things changed.

Things changed because now when I look at her, I don't see Charlie; I don't even think I remember what Charlie looked like.

Now when I look at her, I only see her.

I only see her thick, perpetually overgrown bangs, the color of midnight. I see her cheekbones that have sharpened over the years, the lines of her face that have matured and fucking blossomed.

I see her fucking body.

That has grown and filled out, somehow becoming both slim and curvy at the same time.

But most of all, I see her crisp blue eyes and those black-rimmed glasses. Glasses so thick that they should hide the shine of those eyes, but they don't.

I realize that I shouldn't be thinking about her in these terms.

She's the girl I'm responsible for. She's my troublemaker of a ward.

The harpy.

Who, when I came back from Italy and took over this school, also became my student.

Whose graduation I stopped.

To be fair, I stopped her graduation because her grades weren't there and I came here to fix things. To make students take the rules seriously. Hence, I stopped a couple of other graduations too.

But.

She was right when she said that I'm not willing to let her out early. I'm not willing to listen to her plans and propositions. That's why I've been jerking her around this past week.

And that's because all I can think about is how I can barely recognize her, let alone see Charlie in her.

So she was right when she said that I'm not willing to let her go. But she was wrong about the why.

She was wrong when she said that things haven't changed.

They *have.*

Because when I look at her, I don't see Charlie.

When I look at her, I see her.

I see someone who went from being a fourteen-year-old burden that I couldn't look at to an eighteen-year-old girl that I can't look away from.

Chapter Ten

Friday nights are sacred at St. Mary's.

Or at least, they used to be. When my friends were around.

Almost every Friday at midnight, we would all get dressed up and sneak off campus to go to this dance bar called Ballad of the Bards in Bardstown. Even though it's a dance bar, their music is super unusual. They're known for their sad songs and songs about tragic, unrequited love.

Callie's brother Conrad used to work there once upon a time, and so she knew the bartender, who allowed us entry even though we were [illegible] are — underage. As long as we promised not to drink. Which was fine. Because it wasn't so much about the drinking as it was a way for us to be free and act as if we were normal high school students rather than students of a strict reform school.

And so as much as I was looking forward to seeing them tonight, I was also dreading it.

Because I was going to do it alone.

And *that's* because for me, Friday nights are about more than being carefree and normal. It's about being with my friends and getting dressed up together. Or rather, dressing them up.

It's not a secret that I'm into clothes and shoes and makeup.

Dress me up in anything purple and suede and I'm a happy kitty.

I'm an even happier kitty if I get to dress someone else up.

I love, love, love to dress other people up. I love to mix and match their outfits, share my own outfits with them, do their makeup and hair, and find pretty shoes for them to wear.

It's an obsession, dressing other people up, and I've had it ever since I could remember.

So when all my friends went away, I thought I wouldn't get to do it anymore. But guess what, I have new friends.

Two new friends.

My partners in crime.

I dress Echo up in shades of pink. Because of her rosy skin and honey blonde hair. A rose pink satin dress with a draped, one-shoulder bodice, and a simple slim fit skirt with a small slit in the back. I had a killer pair of Gucci silver sandals to go with it, so I used those to complete the look.

Which turned out to be very good girl-ish but sexy.

Echo reminds me so much of Callie, actually. Not only because of her good girl persona but also because the reason she's here is a boy. A boy she, like Callie, absolutely hates.

I haven't been able to gather much information because she's reluctant to talk about it. But from what I know, there's two boys: one she loves and is pining over. He's a soccer player and her ex-boyfriend. And the other whom she loathes. Who also happens to be a soccer player and best friends with her ex-boyfriend.

And somehow her ex-boyfriend's best friend is responsible for her being here.

And then there's Jupiter, who is more or less like me. A troublemaker.

Meaning people around her have always seen her with wary eyes, specifically the neighbor whose pool she'd sneak into. In fact, it was that very neighbor who got fed up with her antics and threatened to press charges against her, making her family choose between juvie and a reform school; her parents picked the lesser of the two evils. So she came here in her junior year, same as Echo.

And because she's a redhead, I dress her up in red.

Because I'm so over the stereotype that redheads can't wear red. If it's the right shade of red, they can fucking wear it. So I give her a red dress with more purplish tones than orangish, and complete her look with brown strappy sandals from Prada that I have.

As for me, I'm dressed up in my Friday best: a short fit and flare dress with a V-neck. It has black denim and purple suede patches on the skirt and adorable short cap sleeves, one made of denim and the other made of suede. I've paired that with my Prada suede heels.

Oh, and let's not forget my purple lipstick.

Tonight's shade is called Young and On Fire.

I know sneaking out tonight, specifically after what happened last night and what I now know about why he is here, is risky. Plus I had to sit down with Janet for over thirty minutes while I described all the ways that I've been able to sneak in and out, which means all my pathways have been compromised.

Well, except for one.

Because obviously I didn't reveal all of my secrets.

Obviously.

But I'm not letting him control me any more than he already does.

So risky or not, we're going.

Callie's blinding smile is the first thing I see as soon as we step in through the door at Ballad of the Bards. That and her blonde hair flying behind her as she rushes to hug me. Tightly.

I do that too.

In fact, I think I hug her back even more tightly.

And then we break apart, only for me to get enveloped by another set of arms. This one belonging to my second best friend, Wyn, and her hug is just as tight.

"God, Poe," Wyn says, still hugging me. "I missed you so much."

I clench my eyes shut at her words.

Because if I don't, I'll start crying.

And I don't want to ruin the mood. But I do want to tell her that I missed her too. So somehow, I manage to push past the lump of emotions and whisper, "I missed you too."

That gets me a squeeze like she understands what I'm feeling. Because she's feeling it too.

Then moving away, she grins. "You're here. I can't believe you're here."

Callie chimes in from beside Wyn, "I've honestly been counting down *days* to Friday."

"Me too," Wyn adds.

"Now if only Salem were here," Callie says and my heart twists.

Because our third best friend is the only one not here tonight.

Wyn frowns. "I know. I miss her so much. And California is so far. I really wish she hadn't had to leave so soon."

"Well, it was either us or her hunky soccer player of a boyfriend," I quip. "Of course she had to leave."

Even though we all miss Salem with an ache, we understand why she had to leave so soon.

Because of a guy named Arrow Carlisle.

Who also happens to be a pro soccer player who plays for the LA Galaxy, and even though I have zero knowledge of soccer, I still know he's one of the best players in the country. But more than that, Arrow is the love of my best friend's life.

Has been for nine years actually.

So of course she had to go.

And both my friends agree with me as we stare at each other with sad, understanding smiles. Before breaking down and falling into another group hug.

Because holy fuck, this is the first time we're seeing each other since school ended.

While Callie had moved away from campus in the middle of our senior year — she had reasons — Salem and Wyn still lived on campus with me. So when they found out that I wasn't going to graduate with them, they made sure to linger — even Salem — as much as they could after school ended.

As a sign of solidarity.

Eventually, Salem had to move to California though. And Wyn had to leave her dorm room as well. I had the option of going back home for a few days before summer school started last week but I refused. Because I knew he was back and I was so angry at the time — still am — that I didn't want to be under the same roof as him.

So I chose to linger at St. Mary's until classes restarted.

When we're all done hugging and laughing and crying, I step back to introduce the two new friends that I've brought with me. I clap my hands and point to them one by one. "Okay, so I come bearing gifts. This is Echo and that is Jupiter. They're both unfairly stuck doing summer classes with me. So I brought them here tonight because we all need to become best friends and live together happily ever after."

Wyn smiles and waves in her usual shy fashion. "Hi. So nice to meet you both." Then, "Although, I think we were in a lot of classes together, right?"

"We were," Callie confirms, pointing her finger at Echo first. "Geography. You lent me your notes once. I remember. You have such amazing handwriting. Did I ever tell you that? Geography felt like fun for once."

Echo blushes. "Oh, thanks. I love taking notes so I try to do my best." Then, "It's so nice to meet you all. Officially."

"And you're Jupiter," Callie continues, pointing at my copper-haired new friend. "I'm so sorry that we've never gotten a chance to talk before. But can I just say that I've always loved your hair? It's the perfect shade of red and —"

A second later, she gets cut off because she's engulfed in a sudden hug.

It happens so quickly and so unexpectedly that it takes me a second to realize that it's Jupiter.

That Jupiter is hugging Callie.

That her arms are wound around my best friend, her copper-colored hair that Callie was just admiring flouncing behind her back. And now we're all staring at them, at Jupiter particularly, because she's clutching Callie like a long-lost friend. When we all know for a fact that they haven't spoken to each other before tonight.

Um, okay.

Weird but okay.

Callie thinks so too because her eyes are startled and confused, but I know my friend. She won't be unkind or make Jupiter feel embarrassed so she hugs her back, although slightly awkwardly. "Uh, hey. Nice to meet you too."

It's as if Callie's words pull Jupiter back to the moment; she breaks the hug and steps back. "Sorry. I don't know what happened." She tucks her hair behind her ear. "I swear I don't randomly attack people like that."

Callie shakes her head, smiling. "No, it's totally fine. You didn't attack me."

"Well, it's still weird. I know. I just…" Jupiter laughs self-consciously before looking at Callie intently for a second. "It's just that I've seen you being so friendly and so approachable and I've always admired that about you and…" She pauses to look down, at Callie's stomach, I realize. "Things happened last year. With you. And I was so angry about them. I was so angry at how people treated you and I…" She shrugs, blushing. "I just wish I could've helped."

At the mention of last year, Callie blushes too.

But she's quick to recover and smile. "Thanks. I appreciate that. It was hard, yes. But I had my girls. They helped me through it."

Wyn gives her a side hug and I do the same.

Because last year *was* hard for her. And that's because the biggest, the most life-changing thing that could happen to a girl, happened to her.

She got pregnant.

While she was eighteen and at St. Mary's.

A school that is known for restoring and reforming bad girls. Meaning getting pregnant is not the thing that is going to win you any favors and privileges. It not only ruffled teachers' feathers, but also the students', and so all throughout last year, Callie was a major target for gossip and censure and judgement. And as scary as all of that was, it was even worse because the guy she got pregnant by was the guy she never wanted anything to do with.

Reed Jackson.

Her first love and her ex-boyfriend.

Who broke her heart three years ago.

So it was a shock to her — to us too even though we always suspected there was more to their heartbreaking and painful story — when she ended up getting pregnant by the same guy.

And for a while there, we thought things wouldn't turn out as well as they have.

But they did and now they have a baby together — a gorgeous girl named Halo. More than that though, they're married. In fact, they got married only a week ago and every time I think of it, just like when I think about Salem and Arrow, I can't stop smiling.

Which reminds me that I want to see pictures.

"Show me all the Halo pictures," I tell Callie. "I'm dying to see what I missed."

Soon we're huddling around the high table and ooh-ing and aah-ing over Halo, because she has to be the cutest, chubbiest six-week-old baby ever. And with Reed's dark hair and Callie's blue eyes, she's also the prettiest.

"Oh my God, look at Reed," Wyn chuckles over a picture where Reed has Halo in his arms and she's reaching up to his face with sticky, frosting-covered tiny little fingers. Actually, she *has* reached already because his jaw and cheeks have pink frosting on them and he's gazing down at her like she's the love of his life.

"He's so adorable in this," she continues. "Not a word I thought I'd say when it comes to him. Hot, yes. Sexy, double yes. But not adorable."

I bump her shoulder with mine. "Sexy, huh? Don't let your man hear you say that."

Blushing, Wyn ducks her eyes. "Shut up. You know what I mean."

"Poe is right though." Callie winks. "I don't think my brother's going to like you calling someone else hot."

The color on Wyn's cheeks grows deeper even as she says, "Well, your *brother* knows that he's the only one for me, so."

Well, he'd better.

Because Wyn has been in love with Callie's brother — the oldest brother, Conrad; Callie has four older and very hot brothers — for two years now. And he loves her just as much.

Echo leans forward then, addressing Wyn. "Can I please ask you something? I'm dying to ask you something."

"Sure."

"Okay, so I had like the biggest crush on Coach Thorne last year," she divulges. "Is he like, totally romantic? You know, when he's not glaring at you."

Coach Thorne, yeah.

He used to be our soccer coach, which means that Wyn and Conrad's love story was full of hurdles as well.

Wyn chuckles.

No, actually my best friend *giggles*.

A sound I've never heard from her, but it's adorable just like her.

"I love it when he glares at me," she confesses, her cheeks pink. "But yeah, he can be totally romantic when he wants to be."

Echo bites her lips. "Yeah? Oh my God. I'm blushing." She presses her hands on her cheeks. "Why are athletes so hot though? Especially soccer players."

"I know," Wyn agrees. "Like, the other day he'd just come back from practice and he was all sweaty, right? And so he was in the bathroom, taking his t-shirt off and the drops of sweat were rolling down his shoulders and back and I was like, drooling and —"

"Ew. No." Callie covers her ears. "That's my brother. I don't want to hear this."

Everyone bursts out laughing, teasing Callie and Wyn, asking more questions about Coach Thorne and Reed and Halo, and I know I should participate as well. I should laugh and be merry.

I know that and so I try.

I really do.

But suddenly it becomes impossible and instead of laughter, my tears shake loose and stream down my cheeks. And even though I'm horrified by them, *horrified* that I'm ruining everyone's fun, I can't stop myself.

"Poe," Callie says, grabbing my shoulder. "What happened? What's wrong?"

Wyn leans toward me as well and squeezes my other shoulder. "What's going on, Poe? Talk to us."

I shake my head, hiccupping. "N-nothing. I'm fine."

"You're crying, Poe," Callie insists. "You're definitely not fine."

"Tell us what happened," Wyn says. "Please. So we can fix it."

Their kindness and concern make me cry even more.

Because I missed it. Their undying support and friendship.

I missed being with them. I missed talking to them, their company. And even though I know I'm acting like a moron and ruining everyone's fun, I can't help but blurt out, "I love him."

My declaration is met with silence.

As much silence as you can get in a bar where violins are playing overhead and people are chattering and laughing around us, but still.

Suffice it to say that I've shocked them all.

I've shocked myself even.

I didn't know I was going to say that until I did.

"Uh," Callie begins. "Who?"

Wyn's eyes widen. "Him? Mr. Mar — Principal Marshall?"

I jerk back. "What?"

Wyn opens and closes her mouth before stumbling. "Well, I just… I mean…"

"No. God, no. What?" I clench my fists on the table, my tears forgotten. "Why would you… What?"

Distress is clear on her face as she leans forward to cover my fists with her hands. "I'm sorry. I'm sorry, okay? There's no excuse. I don't know why I said that. I'm an idiot." She squeezes my fists. "It's just that you said *him* and my stupid brain just made that connection and damn it, I'm so sorry."

My heart is racing like a freight train.

A freight train that's about to crash against something. Something big and potentially deadly.

But it's fine.

It's okay. It was an innocent mistake.

So I open my fists and grab her hand, and sighing, I say, "It's okay. It's fine. I love you. I should've been clearer." I squeeze her hand then. "But please, never ever say his name, my name and love in the same sentence."

"Right. Okay. Never," she agrees, her eyes still slightly remorseful. "I promise."

With that settled, Callie asks, "So then who is it?"

Well, okay.

So I did plan on telling them tonight.

Mostly because I need their help.

Because my old plan has hit a wall.

Which was amazing, by the way. It was faultless and seamless.

But he's an asshole who wouldn't listen.

So now I need a new plan because I'm not giving up. Not so easily.

And for that to happen, I'm going to have to tell them everything. And by everything, I mean every single thing: My mom, my relationship with her, her death. Middlemarch, Jimmy. The only reason I haven't yet, in all the years we've been friends, is because it's too painful to talk about.

Too jagged and hurtful.

But with a long breath, I do.

I tell them everything.

Right from the beginning. About how my mother died in a car crash and how I was sent to live with him, someone I'd never even heard of until then. Someone who seems to hate my mother for some reason. And someone who hates me because of her, and how he now has control over my life.

After I finish, there's silence.

This one is longer than the last.

And maybe I should be embarrassed about things. Maybe I should feel awkward because I don't think I've been this vulnerable in front of anyone before. This cut open, but I'm not.

I'm weirdly calm and relieved even.

Maybe because it's finally out there. I've shared my burden.

And I've shared with the people I trust.

My girls.

"That douchebag."

That's Callie.

Her words trigger Wyn's response. "I can't believe he did that. I can't believe he sent you away."

"What a fucking asshole."

This comes from Jupiter.

"Wow, I have no words," Echo says, shaking her head. "I mean, we all knew that he was a major dick for not letting us graduate, but this is..."

"This is cruel," Jupiter finishes.

"This is villainous," Callie adds.

"This is outrageous," Wyn adds in turn before asking, "Why didn't you ever say anything?"

"Yeah, why didn't you ever tell us what he did?"

"We all knew you hated him, Poe." Wyn shakes her head, squeezing my shoulder. "But this is crazy. This is unforgivable. That he'd do that to you. And all because of your mom."

Callie shakes her head. "And you don't know what happened between them?"

"No. I have no clue. And..." I swallow. "No one would tell me."

And I've asked.

Not directly to him, because even when we lived under the same roof, we'd hardly run into each other. He would always be busy with his work and all the other city stuff he's involved in. And honestly, I think us not running into each other was more or less by design.

So I've asked Mo about Charlie and him, about their history, about how Charlie knew him. Aside from the usual surface answer that they were classmates and family friends, she's never told me anything. And as much as I wanted to push her, I didn't. I had a feeling that she was guarding this secret out of loyalty to him, and I didn't want to put her out.

That's not to say that I didn't snoop.

I did.

Mostly in his study and his bedroom when he wasn't around.

I never found anything though. Although I'm not sure what I was hoping to find anyway, but still.

I'm as clueless as I was four years ago.

"But you know what," Jupiter says. "It doesn't really matter. What happened between them."

Echo nods. "Yeah. Whatever may have happened, you didn't do it. It wasn't your fault."

"Exactly." Wyn nods too. "You're not responsible for your mom's or his actions."

"Yeah, you shouldn't have to pay the price of whatever may have happened," Callie says. "He had no right to do those things to you. To take away your love. To send you to St. Mary's and screw up your life like that."

They are right.

They are absolutely right.

But the thing is that I know my mom.

I mean, she's my mom and I loved her to pieces. I wanted her to love me back and so I did everything I could to get her attention. But I also know that she could be… mean.

She could be cruel, my mother.

I saw her use people to her advantage, and then discard them. I saw her make friends and then give them up all in the name of getting ahead. I saw her use *me* when it suited her — especially with men who liked vulnerable single mothers, trying to do it all in the biz — and then cast me aside when she got the job done.

But it was needed in the business she was in, and so I never held her actions against her.

She had to be cunning.

Sometimes, though, when I think about what my mother must have done, I sympathize with *him*.

With the devil.

I sympathize because it must have been terrible, right? Whatever she had done. Because he's so angry and so hateful.

Even after all these years. Even toward me.

But then at the same time, even if she did something, I'm not responsible for it.

I don't deserve his hatred.

His cruelty.

I don't deserve to be kept away from my dream: Jimmy.

Which prompts me to say, "Jimmy's going on tour in four weeks. And I need to be on that tour with him. I need to go with him. He invited me and I intend to go. I have to find a way to go. And I need a new plan."

I look at all four of them as I continue, "I need a plan where I can leave with Jimmy *and* get my money. Because I'm not sacrificing either of those things. I need to get out of that asshole's control. I *need* to win against him. For once, Jesus fucking Christ, I would love to win against him. I would love to tell him that he can't control me. In fact, I would love to control *him*." I sigh, shaking my head. "Only I don't know how. I don't know what to do to make that happen. What *do* I do? I tried going the route that I thought he'd like. I mean, I offered to do the extra work. Can you believe that?" I throw my hands up in the air. "Can any of you believe that I offered to do work for extra credit? Even I can't believe I did that. But I did it. I did offer. And he fucking threw it in my face. So I don't know. I don't know what to do."

For the third time tonight, silence descends over us.

This one is more about us thinking and mulling over stuff than being shocked.

Then Callie says, "So you want to win against him, correct? You want to control him, get your power back."

"Yes. That's what I dream about."

"And you've tried the right way. The decent way."

"I have, yes."

"Well then, there's only one way left," she says.

"I'm listening."

She smiles, her eyebrows raised. "The wrong way."

"O-kay," I say slowly, squinting my eyes at her. "But what is the wrong way?"

Wyn chimes in at this point, gasping as if in wonder, "Oh, that's genius, Callie. I love that idea."

Wyn and Callie high five, as Callie practically squeals. "Right? Me too!"

"How did you even come up with that?"

"I know." She shakes her head, smiling. "It's extremely diabolical. It's so unlike me."

"I know," Wyn cries out in excitement. "I love it."

"You know, I think it's Halo. Because I'm a mama bear now

and I just can't see one of my own in pain. So I just go a little crazy and —"

"Oh my God," I cut her off. "Can someone please tell me what the fuck is the idea?"

Wyn looks at me, her eyes dancing with excitement. "Look, everyone has a weakness, right?"

"Right," I say.

"So you find that out."

Jupiter gasps now, as if finally catching onto it. "Oh my God, yes. And you use that."

Echo nods too because apparently, she's understood it as well. "Yes. *Against* him. Like leverage."

I look at all four of them, one by one, before I repeat, "Okay, let me get this straight: everyone has a weakness. Which means he has one too." All four of them nod. "So I find his weakness," this time their nods are a little more enthusiastic, "and use it against him."

Callie grins. "Yup. As blackmail."

"Exactly," Jupiter confirms happily. "You want to get the power. That's how you get the power."

"You've tried the right way and he didn't go for it," Echo says. "So now's the time to cause some trouble."

Trouble.

Finally I think I get it. I get what they're saying.

Again, I look at all four of them, this time in awe. "This *is* genius. This is super fucking genius. I can't believe I didn't think of this myself."

Wyn raises her eyebrows. "It's okay. You taught us well."

I go to smile but then stop because something occurs to me. "But wait, how do I do that? How do I find out what his weakness is or his secret or whatever? How do I get dirt on him?"

They all look at each other before Callie says, "By getting closer to him."

"Closer to him," I repeat.

At this, all four of my friends, two old and two new, smirk. There's something dangerous in their eyes and Wyn explains, "Keep your friends close but your enemies closer, remember? So you need to get close to him. You need to pretend to be his friend and somehow win his trust. And then you need to make him tell you all his secrets. And you have four weeks."

Chapter Eleven

Blackmail.

It's a neat concept. It's also an evil concept.

But I'm focusing on the neat part.

The part when I finally, after years, get my freedom. When I get to graduate from this place and go on tour with the love of my life. Oh, and also get my money. And if in the process, I get to flex my power over him a little, make him taste his own medicine, then so be it.

Although I have to say that for all my pranks and plotting in the past, I don't think I've ever blackmailed anyone.

It's sort of surprising really. But there you have it.

First time for everything though, right?

So here I am.

With my bookbag at my back that contains a brand new notebook and a blue gel pen, I stand at his door for my detention. I take a deep breath and paste a small smile on my face as I knock.

Two short, *friendly* knocks.

That's important. Being friendly.

I need to come off as friendly, trustworthy, someone he'd want to confide in when the time comes, and smiling is the first step. Being polite is the second.

All of this wisdom is courtesy of my friends.

After they gave me the idea Friday night, we spent the next couple of hours brainstorming how to make it all happen. How to get him to trust me. Because I only have a limited amount of time to do it in.

The general consensus was that I need to be friendly.

And since it's hard for me to do that where my devil guardian is concerned, they all helped me practice my smile *and* my tone. Because apparently, my tone is sarcastic and smartass-y.

"No, you need to stay calm, Poe," Callie explained. "You can't talk back to him. Or say provocative stuff. And you can't glare at him or roll your eyes at him or let your feelings show on your face. Or this is never going to work." She pointed a finger at my face then. "Like you're doing right now."

Needless to say, I was.

But after a lot of discussion, I caved and I promised everyone that I'd give this my best shot.

Which is what I'm doing when after my friendly knock, the door swings open. I also have a polite greeting ready to go.

But the man who stands at the threshold doesn't let me get in a word. "You're early."

"What?"

His jaw is set firmly and there's a light frown between his brows. "It's not five yet."

I look at him for a second, which seems to irritate him further so I say, "Well, yeah. I mean, I thought… being early was a good thing."

At least, that's what my friends taught me when I told them about the detention thing and we all agreed that that's where I'll put my plan into motion. Go to the detention early, they said. To make a good impression.

Which I'm clearly not making because he sighs sharply, impatiently at my response. Then, "Wait outside."

"But —"

I see his arm move and realize that he's got a cell phone in his hand, which he puts to his ear before snapping the door shut in my face.

What?

What just happened?

Did he… Did he really just shut the door in my face?

Is he serious?

What the…

Fucking asshole.

I have half a mind to barge in there to tell him that he can't shut the door in my face. That I won't wait outside.

I won't wait, period.

I'm here, so let's do this detention thing. And besides, he can't tell me what to do.

But that's the problem, isn't it?

He can.

My guardian turned principal.

Who holds my graduation and therefore my money and the fate of my love life in his big stupid hands.

So I take another deep breath — deeper than the last one — and keep standing in my spot, and *wait* like he told me to. And when a few minutes later, the door opens again, I say with a smile, "So is it five o'clock now?"

He gives me a cool stare. "No. But you may come in."

And before I can help it, the words slip out. "Oh joy. How wonderful. I've been just dying to start this detention and reflect on my life choices."

Sarcasm.

That was sarcasm.

What the fuck, Poe?

He watches me for a second before saying, "Given that it's your very *life choices* that have led you to detention today, I should hope so."

I get a serious urge to narrow my eyes at him but somehow I don't, and say, with as little sarcasm as possible, "All right then. Let's begin."

We don't.

Because he watches me some more, his eyes roving over my face that I'm really hoping looks serene and anger-free.

Only when he's done with his perusal, does he step aside in a clear invitation to come in, and I enter.

In my three-year stay at St. Mary's, I've been to the principal's office countless times for countless transgressions. And so I know every nook and cranny of it. I know the large window overlooking the concrete courtyard, right behind an equally large wooden desk. I know the wall-to-wall bookcases on either side, the little sitting area adjacent to the desk.

Only now everything is much different.

But also familiar.

Because everything is his.

Leather chairs and couches. And of course, books. That are leather-bound and thick and towering and covering every available space, in addition to notebooks and papers and journals.

When I hear the door shut behind me, I spin around and words just come out of my mouth. "Who was it?"

Okay, so that was a little abrupt.

And loud.

But I'm going to cut myself some slack here. This is the first time I'm doing something like this. I can't expect myself to be perfect, right? Besides, I'm really itching to know for some reason.

Not that he's going to tell me so easily.

He stands at the door, partially turned, his hand on the knob and his eyes on me. "What?"

I swallow under his suspicious gaze but force a lighter tone. "Uh, on the phone."

Those eyes narrow slightly at my words. But other than that, there's no response from him, nor any reaction.

"You know, because you shut the door in my face just now," I keep going nonetheless. "Was it someone important?"

"No."

"So you shut the door in my face for fun?"

"Yes."

I realize that it's my turn to narrow my eyes at him *again*. But just as I did before, I curb the urge and go for a breezy tone. "Right. I know what you're doing. You're trying to provoke me. But I won't take the bait."

He lets the knob go and turns completely toward me. "You won't."

I shake my head. "Nope. Because I've had an epiphany. Over the weekend, I mean."

"An epiphany."

"Uh-huh. Would you like to know what it is?"

He leans against the door then and folds his arms across his chest. "I'd like nothing more."

For a second, all I can do is stare at the way his biceps have bulged under his dark brown tweed jacket. How his shirt — a lighter shade of brown — stretches across his chest.

How tall he is.

The top of his dark-haired head almost reaches the top of the doorjamb. Oh, and his shoulders aren't far behind in the size department either. They span the breadth of the door.

How can he be so large and masculine and beautiful and yet so cruel and mean?

Anyway.

"So as you know, I'm stuck here," I begin. "At St. Mary's. For the next two months, I mean."

"You are."

"And nothing I can do will change that. Correct?"

He stares at me for a beat or two before confirming, "Correct."

"Not even if I'm willing to do the extra work and expedite things or something similar."

"Not even that."

Asshole.

"So there's no point then," I say in conclusion.

"Of what?"

"Of arguing with you," I explain. "Or bickering with you or fighting with you. Or sneaking into your cottage to convince you to let me go. Because you'll just give me more detention. And quite possibly threats too."

His eyes gleam then. At 'threats.'

Maybe at the memory of all the things he said to me last week in his cottage.

I'm pretty sure things are flickering in my eyes as well. Things that might not bode well for this mission that I have, things like anger and frustration and hurt. So I blink and go on, "So if I'm going to be stuck here, then I might as well not make my life more difficult, right?"

He takes his time absorbing my words.

Which I understand.

I mean, this may be the very first time I've said something to him without any hint of sarcasm or anger or belligerence. He might be a little thrown. A little suspicious.

Although I can't tell by just looking at his face.

It's as always carefully arranged into neat, sharp, emotionless lines. Then, "So this is you waving the white flag then."

I jerk back. "No."

Again, that was loud and abrupt but also instinct.

A knee-jerk response to his comment.

Because there's no way I'll ever wave the white flag and surrender. I declared war four years ago and I'm not backing down.

But he doesn't need to know that. Or he doesn't need to know everything about it.

"Of course not," I say in a much calmer tone. "I never wave a white flag."

"Because you hold a mean grudge."

I'm not sure why but his words — that were mine four years ago — make me blush.

They make me feel… childish.

Although back then, I had every reason to say them. I had every reason to be mad at him, to hate him.

But in any case, I inch up my glasses and go on. "Yes. I do. But I also take breaks."

"From all your war waging and strategic plotting."

Don't narrow your eyes, Poe.

Do not narrow them.

"Yes. It can be tiring."

"I don't blame you. All that work to make someone's life hell can be a great burden," he deadpans.

I spend the next four to five seconds trying not to clench my teeth. Then, "So this is me saying that I'm tired and taking some time off." Before I can stop, I add, "This absolutely does not mean that our war is over in any way, shape or form. We're just on a break."

For the life of me, I couldn't lie about that.

I won't.

It just goes against everything I believe in and stand for when it comes to this man.

"I see," he murmurs.

"So?" I ask, exhaling. "Are we? On a break then. A temporary truce, if you will."

For a second, I think I should hold out my hand for him to shake but I decide against it. Because that would be too much and completely unbelievable. There's no way I am ever going to let him touch me.

There will be no touching between us.

Ever.

So I simply stand here, in the middle of his office, and wait for him to respond.

And when it comes it's completely anti-climactic. "Take a seat."

"What?"

He unfolds his arms and stands up straight, his expression still cool. There's no hint at all that he's heard me or that we've been talking about something important these past few minutes.

"I'd like you to do some lines," he says, walking toward his desk, his polished loafers coming closer.

The sight of them makes me clench my thighs for a second before I say, "But what about what I said?"

He rounds the desk and I turn to follow his journey. Again, ignoring me completely, he commands, "I want you to write a one-line apology."

"What apology?"

"For breaking into my cottage last week."

At this, I forget about what I said and focus on what *he's* saying. "You want me to write a one-line apology for breaking into your cottage last week?"

Standing by his leather chair, he gives me a dispassionate look. "And keep writing it until you fill ten pages with it."

My voice is loud. "*Ten pages*?"

"You'll do this every day, for an hour, until the end of the week," he finishes.

"I'll do this every day, for an hour, until the end of the week," I repeat his words, in a voice louder than before.

He throws me a short nod. "You can begin now."

I don't.

I *can't.*

I stand there staring at him, my mouth open, my hands worrying the strap of my bookbag. Which makes me realize that *that's* why he wanted me to bring them. A pen and a notebook.

Because he wanted me to do lines.

I should've known. It's obvious. Why else would he ask me to bring them if not to do lines?

But I was so engrossed in all the plotting and the planning that it didn't occur to me. Then, "You do know I'm not a child, right?"

He stares down at me from across the expanse of his large desk. "Yes."

"So I don't —"

"But you act like one," he cuts me off, his tone severe. "And if you act like a child, I'll treat you like one."

Right.

Okay.

So breaking into his cottage because he wouldn't talk to me about my *fucking life* like he promised he would was childish.

As always, it makes me angry.

It makes me feel rage-y and helpless.

Which is *exactly* why I don't have to tell myself to calm down. To not roll my eyes at him.

Because for the first time ever, I think I have a real chance of doing something about it. I have a real chance of taking my control back and having *him* helpless for once.

So my body relaxes on its own and the smile I give him takes very little effort.

"Fine," I say, nodding. "Lines it is then."

With that, I take a seat.

All gracefully and politely.

I cross my legs and brush the tail end of my braid that's slung over my shoulder, trying to appear the very picture of civility and friendliness as I fish out my things and poise my pen over my notebook.

I'm sorry I broke into your cottage, asshole.

I'm sorry that you're such an asshole that I had to break into your stupid cottage to talk to you.

I'm sorry that your assholishness brings out my childish behavior.

While trying to come up with a version of an apology for him, I hear the screech of his chair as he pulls it out and takes a seat of his own. Then comes the crinkling of papers, the creak of a book opening, the uncapping of a pen as he probably settles in to do his work.

And I realize that this is the very first time I'll get to see that.

I'll get to see him at work.

Among his books.

That first year when we lived under the same roof, before he went to Italy, there was never an occasion where I saw him working. I saw his books. His papers and documents. His office. His leather couches. But I never got to see him among them.

Now I can though, and before I even tell them to, my eyes

snap up.

And there he is.

Bent over a book.

Well, not really. He's more dipped over it, or at least his face is.

His face is tilted down, and his eyes are lowered as he reads something on the desk. He looks… peaceful.

I really have no other word to describe it.

Sitting back in his chair, with his impossibly broad shoulders relaxed, his thick eyelashes casting shadows on his sharp cheekbones, his chest moving up and down in a slow rhythm, he looks the most tranquil that I've ever seen him.

If not for the movements in his eyelids, going from left to right, I'd think he was sleeping.

And the fact that his lips are slightly parted and his jaw is tension-free completes the restful picture.

So is that what he feels then? When he's among his leather-bound books.

This untroubled and soothed.

I don't think I've ever felt that before, and definitely not when I'm reading.

When I'm... doing my thing, my doodling, though, on the other hand, yeah. Sometimes I feel that way.

When I'm absorbed in my own world.

When what I've imagined is coming to life on paper. And then what's on paper is coming to life in my hands.

That gives me peace.

I look down to *his* hands then and freeze.

I stop breathing as well.

Because his hands are torn.

His fingers, his knuckles specifically, are busted up. They are chafed and bruised, colored an angry purple. And with his fingers gripping the pen as he takes notes with broad and rapid strokes, his knuckles jut out in stark relief.

"What happened to your hand?" I ask, gripping my own gel pen tightly.

His pen — it's a black ink pen with a gold nib — stops scratching and with his face still dipped, he looks up. "Did you need something?"

Still staring at his fingers, I lean forward in my chair. "What happened to your hand? Why does it look all busted up?"

His fingers around the pen flex. "Shouldn't you be writing me an apology?"

I ignore him and glance up. "Is this because of your punching thingy?"

He gives me a flat look. "Punching thingy."

I shake my head. "Your heavy bag, whatever. Is it because of that? Is that why your knuckles look all swollen and torn?"

His jaw that was dipped and relaxed before has now inched up and hardened a little. "You only have an hour to finish your ten pages. If you can't, the pages roll over to the next day."

Maybe I should be worried about this new rule, pages rolling over. But I'm not, and pressing a hand to my chest, I lean even further in my chair. "Oh my God, does this happen every time you punch that thing?"

No answer is forthcoming from him.

Or that's what I think until his fingers flex around the pen again and he clips, "No."

"So then what happened?

His face has a resigned look on it, like he knows I won't let it go until he answers. So he does. "Just went a little harder on it."

"Why?" I ask, exasperated.

I'm not sure why I care to be honest.

But his knuckles really look awful. They must hurt like a bitch too. And I just have to know.

"It's just a workout. It happens."

I study his face then.

For a second I think something lurks behind his tightened features. Something dark and troubled, but I can't be sure. Because it's so subtle and quick, that something. Here one second and gone the next, leaving his beautiful face blank.

"It happens," I repeat suspiciously.

He doesn't like my suspicion and it's obvious in his tone. "Yes."

Why don't I believe him?

Why do I feel like there's more?

And again, why do I even *care* if there's more?

But wait a second, I'm *supposed to* care. I'm supposed to act like it at least.

That's the whole point, right?

This is how I gain his trust. This is how I get him to spill all his secrets to me.

By *caring*. By being friendly and nice.

"Well in case you didn't know," I say with raised eyebrows, "there are other ways of working out. Ways that aren't this…" I glance down at his hand again that's still clutching the pen before looking up. "Painful and injurious."

His eyes rove over my face. "I'll make a note of that."

Then he goes back to his reading.

I don't, however.

I keep staring at him. "Why do you do it?"

He resumes writing on the notepad, his strokes fast and efficient like before. But I don't get deterred.

"You know, the whole punching thing," I add.

He flips a page of his book.

"I've actually always wondered about that," I keep going, setting my own pen down. "Your whole punching hobby. Like, it doesn't make sense, right? I mean, on the one hand you have your books. You have two PhDs. In history and art history. Like, how interesting does history have to be, for someone to get two PhDs in it? It's… *incredible*. And then…" I pause as he flips another page, his pen at rest for the moment as he reads, his eyelids flickering. "You have your heavy bag. Which you occasionally hit so hard that your hand looks like that. Like someone ran it over with a truck or something. So how does it all go together? Books and violence."

I wait for him to say something.

Although I don't think he will because in the middle of my whole monologue back there, he'd started to write. His pen had started to move, noting things down, his eyes swinging back and forth between his book and his notebook.

But I'm nothing if not persistent.

So I forge ahead. "Okay, tell me the truth: you have issues, don't you?" I squint my eyes at him; a few strands of his dark hair have fallen on his forehead. "Like, major issues. You have to. To do something like that. Not to mention, I have never seen you laugh. Like ever. And I've known you for four years. *Unfortunately*. I mean, forget laughing. You never even smile. What's up with that? What's *up* with Mr. Marshall?"

Exactly.

What *is* up with him?

Why is he so serious all the time? So intimidating and grave.

I gasp, stabbing a finger at him. "Is it because you're a professor? And you think that no one will mess with you if you're scary all the time? No student will ask you to bump up their grades. Or give them an extension on their homework assignment."

No reaction from him whatsoever.

If anything, he looks even more engrossed in whatever he's reading. There's a light frown between his brows and his other hand, the one sporting the silver ring — which also looks dark and busted; so much so that his ring gleams even more today — reaches up and he scratches his scruffy jaw with his thumb.

My throat grows dry for a second. At the sexy gesture.

But I continue. I have to.

Because now it has become like a challenge between us, him not talking.

"Oh, or it could be because you don't want a student of yours to break into your cottage at night and ask you to let her graduate early from summer school. That's it, isn't it?"

Nope.

Apparently not. He still gives me nothing.

Damn it.

Then, "Oh! I got it. I know why." I settle back in the chair with a grin. "It's because you wanna look intimidating when you kidnap a puppy. Oh my God, it's so obvious now. I mean, it makes so much sense —"

"I thought my thing was to kick puppies," he says then, cutting off my words.

My air even.

With his sudden words. With his gaze too.

Because finally he lifts his eyes from the book and looks up at me.

And all I can say is, "Hi."

His chocolate chip eyes flash. "Not kidnap them."

A warmth suffuses my chest at the fact that he was listening to my stupid ramblings.

I bite the inside of my cheek to keep myself from smiling. "I thought you weren't listening."

"It's called multi-tasking." Then, "And it's impossible not to listen to you."

My eyes go wide. "Is it?"

"Yeah," he rasps. "You're as loud and as screeching as a lawnmower."

I frown. "You're mean."

"Never said I wasn't."

"And you could do both," I say. "Kick puppies *and* kidnap them."

A moment or two passes with our eyes locked with each other. Then, "Yes."

"Yes what?"

"I don't want a student breaking into my cottage in the middle of the night."

"But what if that student also happens to be your ward?"

"*Especially* not if that student also happens to be my ward."

I lick my lips. "But doesn't she get a little special treatment?"

His gaze follows my action. "No."

My lips tingle for some strange reason then as I say, "Right. That's why I'm stuck spending my whole summer here. With you."

"Yes. Eight whole weeks."

"Eight whole weeks."

Then his eyes turn penetrating as he says, "Because it's not as if you have anywhere else to be now, do you?"

My heart skips a beat. My palms sweat.

And I cross my fingers and my toes, hoping that it doesn't show on my face.

The fact that I do have somewhere else to be.

I do have *someone* to be with.

"No, I don't," I say, somehow managing to keep my voice from wavering.

He studies my face for a second before accepting my answer. "Good."

My belly tightens at how satisfied his response sounds, like he's won something, before I prod, "You can tell me, you know."

"Tell you what?"

"About your punching thing."

"Can I?"

"Yes." Then, I can't help but add, "I can keep a secret."

"Secret."

"Yes. I'm actually very good at it," I whisper, again hoping that it's not obvious on my face.

That I'm lying.

That I have no intention of keeping any of his secrets. Or rather, I have no intention of keeping them *if* he doesn't give me what I want.

"Besides, we're on a break," I finish by reminding him.

He nods slowly, his eyes going back and forth between mine. "Yeah. We are, aren't we?"

"So?" I ask again. "Why are you into punching a heavy bag?"

"Because I have issues."

"What kind of issues?"

"The kind that require me to punch a heavy bag."

"Does it have anything to do with what happened to your nose?"

I frown at my own blurted out question.

I wasn't expecting to say that at all.

Even though for some reason, I think it's obvious. That they are connected.

His busted nose and his penchant for a heavy bag. And the feeling only gets stronger when his jaw hardens.

Not only his jaw but eyes too.

They have been glimmering and flashing but now they go flat. Then, "I think you should really go back to writing that apology for me."

This time I know that I have to. I know that I can't push him any more than I already have.

So I nod and agree, "Okay."

And then I go back to my apology writing. Although now I'm even more curious. Which is saying something because I've always been super curious about him. About the way he is. His past. His history.

His relationship with Charlie.

A shrill noise fills the silence then.

Even though it makes me flinch, I'm grateful for the interruption to my tangled-up thoughts.

It's his phone.

It's ringing.

It's sitting on a pile of papers close enough to me that I see the caller's name: Cynthia March.

My stomach pitches and rolls for some reason and I snap my eyes up at him. He's not focused on me though. His entire attention is on the phone as he reaches for it. He answers it and stands up in a split second.

"Hello. Yeah," he says, striding over to the door and leaving his office.

I sit in my chair for a few seconds, feeling oddly at a loss now that I'm alone.

Before I spring up from my seat as well and follow him.

I only go to the door though, which is slightly ajar, and peek through the gap.

I can see his broad back. His dark hair, curled and brushing against the collar of his jacket, listening to whatever this Cynthia March is saying on the phone.

My heart thumps in my chest as I stand there, glued to my spot.

Spying on him.

Not that I haven't done this before. But today, it feels wrong. It feels nerve-wracking.

Maybe because my intentions are way more dangerous than they usually are.

I'm not sure why I'm suddenly feeling guilty but I am.

But I tell myself that he brought this on himself. That he's forcing me to do this. If he'd just gone for my original, non-threatening plan, I wouldn't be doing this. Besides, if my plan is successful, I'd be doing everyone a favor. He's here to make this place even more hellish. Maybe I can blackmail him into easing up a little.

So I force myself to listen.

Although all I really get are his clipped one-word answers: yes, no, all right. It goes on for another couple of minutes and I never get any clue as to what they're talking about. And then at last he says, the longest sentence he has said in this phone call, "Fine. Tonight at nine then. My place."

And then he switches off and I rush back to my seat.

I duck my head and with trembling fingers and a shaking heart, I start writing. I have no idea what I'm writing though. I have no idea what letters and words are flowing through the tip of my new gel pen but I keep at it. Even when I hear him come into the room, his footsteps muted by the carpet, and as he settles back in his chair.

And then I keep at it until he says, "Your time's up."

I actually jump at his voice.

Looking up, I find his chocolate chip gaze on me, all intense and penetrating. It immediately makes me squirm in my seat, guilt churning anew at what I did. "Uh, I haven't finished all the pages."

He lets a beat pass before he replies, "So you'll finish them tomorrow."

I study him for a second, trying to solve the mystery of the call.

More like, the caller.

But I can't say that I see anything different on him. He looks the same as he did when I walked into the room.

Swallowing, I nod. "Okay. So I'll go then."

He doesn't respond to that, simply keeps his eyes on me, his elbows settled on the armrest, his fingers gripping the pen. Under his steady gaze, I somehow manage to come to my feet. I sling my backpack over my shoulder before I take a last look at him — he's still watching me — and turn around.

I feel his heavy gaze on me as I walk to the door with trembling knees.

I reach out my hand to open the door but hesitate. I don't want to leave, I realize.

I want to ask him about the phone call. I want to know who this Cynthia is.

I just do and I don't care how it affects my plans.

With that stupid, reckless thought, I begin to turn around but find that I can't.

Because he's right there.

Right behind me.

Like the night in the cottage, I feel his heat at my back, his scent in my lungs. And oh my God, he's touching me again.

His fingers are wrapped around my hand, the one that's touching the knob.

And before I can stop myself, I whisper, "You're hurting me."

"No, I'm not."

No, he isn't.

God, he isn't.

Even though his touch is just as hot and rough as that night.

It doesn't hurt.

"It's going to bruise tomorrow," I lie.

"No, it won't." Then, letting my wrist go, he adds, "Turn around."

My belly clenches at his command and I drop my hand from the knob.

Before I know what I'm doing, I obey him.

I turn around and press my spine to the door when I see how close he is. I hug my backpack to my chest when I realize how his impossibly broad shoulders are blocking out the room behind him.

My heart is so loud and fast that it's beating in my ears.

Reaching up to adjust my glasses, I ask, "What are you doing, uh, four feet away from me?"

"I want you to tell me something."

"What?"

He doesn't answer right away. He studies my face for a few seconds before asking, "Where are your contacts?"

I realize that he's looking at my hand that's still on my glasses.

Lowering my arm, I reply, "Oh, uh, I don't wear them."

"Why not?"

For some reason, his question — so abrupt and intimate — makes my own words stumble. "B-because I can never get them in. And if I do, I always forget to take them out. So it's just easier." Then I add, "I hate it though."

"Hate what?"

"Wearing glasses." I lick my lips. "They're always clashing with my bangs."

He looks at my bangs. A thick hunk of them is tangled up the side of my glasses like they always are. Glancing away and into my eyes, he nods. "They are."

"Sometimes I think I should just get rid of them," I add, hugging my backpack even tighter to my chest. "My bangs, I mean. Can't get rid of my glasses. I won't be able to see."

"No."

His answer is immediate and also confusing. "No what?"

"No to both." When I still frown, he explains, "Getting rid of your glasses or your bangs."

"Oh."

This is strange. This conversation.

It's even stranger that we're having it in lowered tones, just a touch above a whisper.

"Is that what you wanted to ask me?" I ask then.

"No."

"So then what?"

He chooses to hold his silence again.

And my own impatience gets the better of me so I ask a question of my own. "Tell me who Cynthia March is."

"Why?"

"Because I'm asking. Was she the one who called before? When I first came in."

"Yes."

"Great. You shut the door in my face for her. So who's she?"

"And I should tell you because we're on a break."

I swallow. "Yes."

He leans in a little. "Because you had this great epiphany over the weekend, yeah?"

"I did."

His lips tip up slightly, not in a smile but maybe in a flicker of it, as he takes in my messy bangs and glasses, my flushed cheeks. "Hell of an epiphany though, isn't it? Makes you wonder."

"Wonder what?"

"How much easier my life could've been, how calm and undisturbed, how structured and peaceful. Like it always was before you came into it with your little plots and plans and pranks. With your peanut butter sandwiches and your poison ivy shampoos. How none of those things would have existed, if only you'd had this epiphany sooner."

I can't believe he's bringing that up.

I can't believe he's bringing up my peanut butter sandwich fiasco right now. *And* my poison ivy shampoo.

"I wrote you an apology letter for the peanut butter sandwich," I say. "And I left you the ointment for the poison ivy shampoo."

I did. Both of those things.

Look, I admit that both of those things were bad, especially the peanut butter sandwich. Because I knew that he was allergic. In the heat of the moment, I smeared a little peanut butter in the sandwich that Mo had made for him — she'd used almond butter — when no one was looking. But as soon as I did that, I regretted it. I went back to the kitchen to admit my mistake but by then he'd already eaten it.

And so the next time when I did something similar — switched out his shampoo with one that had a little poison ivy in it — I did leave him an ointment. Under his pillow even, with a cute little note that said, 'let the girl go or I won't be here next time.'

In all the pranks that I've played on him, those two have been relatively serious, and I completely regret them.

But I cannot believe that he'd bring that up right now.

"You did, yeah," he says, his lips twitching with amusement. "As a courtesy."

"Yes. So I cannot believe that we're talking about this right now."

His amusement grows. "Well, allow me to do the same then."

"Same what?"

I think he'll answer me.

With words I mean.

But he doesn't.

Instead, he leans down further. He bends toward me and if I could, I'd press myself harder to the door.

As it is, I can't since I'm already stuck to it.

So all I can do is crane my neck up and watch him come closer.

So much so that I can see his thick eyelashes tangled up with each other. I can see the dark fine bristles of the stubble on his sculpted jaw. I can feel the epic heat of his body turning into sweat on my skin.

When his face is right above mine, I ask, "W-what are you doing?"

"Giving you the same courtesy."

"What?"

"By getting the door for you."

I glance down then. Only now realizing that he's got his arm reached out and his fingers wrapped around the knob. Jerking my eyes back to him, I continue, "Uh, I'm…"

"Since that's the thing we're doing now, aren't we? Because you're stuck here for the next eight weeks and since no matter what you do, I won't let you go. So we're taking a break, yeah?"

I swallow. "Yes."

"Good." He turns the knob. "I'm glad we're on the same page then."

"Okay. I —"

"Because I'd hate it if we're not," he continues, his voice soft but somehow threatening, making me swallow again. "I'd hate to think that somehow this wonderful epiphany that's going to change our lives is another one of your little plans. Or one of your plots to get out of detention or to sneak out or maybe to get out of summer school altogether. I'd hate that, Poe. For you. Because then I'd have to make good on my promise. The one I made at my cottage last week. About breaking your heart and counting pieces of it. Personally. Before I lock you in a cage and throw the key away. So yeah, very glad that we're on the same page." With that, he opens the door. "See you tomorrow."

Chapter Twelve

She has blonde hair.

Not my friend Callie's blonde. But more like Echo's blonde. So honey blonde I guess.

Cynthia March.

And she has a svelte figure that's tightly swathed in a slim professional skirt with a red blouse that shows off a hint of cleavage. I have to admit that it's nice cleavage. And she isn't missing any opportunity to thrust it at him.

Him being my devil guardian.

Yes, I'm watching them.

I'm spying on them.

And quite potentially risking my entire life and future.

Because if he finds out that I snuck out of my dorm room as soon as I could and that this very second, I'm crouched under his window, he'll likely go through with all his threats.

But I had to come.

I *had* to.

I had to know who this Cynthia is and if she could be useful for my plans.

That I'm also curious about her in general is something I'm not focusing on right now.

So far the only piece of detail I've gathered is that Cynthia has a huge crush on him. She keeps touching him, smiling at him, thrusting her chest at him, batting her eyelashes.

But he doesn't really notice.

They are sitting on that big leather couch right in front of the window. She's more or less perched at the edge, her legs crossed and her body turned toward him. And wearing the same brown shirt that he had on during detention earlier this evening, Mr. Marshall is sprawled, his thighs spread wide and relaxed. He's got a drink in his hand and he's looking at some papers in front of him on the coffee table.

Until she touches him again.

This time on his thigh, not really high up but not somewhere that I'd call innocent either.

That's when he looks away from his papers, and at her.

She preens at finally getting his attention and that hand of hers on his thigh moves up slightly. At which point, he completely abandons those papers on the table and his drink before putting his large hand on hers.

A smile breaks out on her lips. A small, dare I say sexy smile, as she says something to him.

He leans closer to her then.

And I lean closer to the window.

So close that my nose bumps the glass.

Especially when it's his turn to speak.

Is it me or do his chocolate chip eyes look hooded? His high cheekbones look flushed as well.

But I don't have time to focus on his cheekbones or his eyes when I notice his other hand. It was simply resting on his thigh but now it reaches up and goes to the nape of her neck. Before I can even draw a breath, I watch those fingers grip it tightly. So tightly that her neck cranes and her face tilts up. And my hands go up and plaster themselves on the glass because I know what's about to happen.

I know he's going to kiss her.

Before it even registers what I'm doing, I do it.

I clench my fists and bang on the glass.

Causing them to break apart.

Which is fine really. Which is what I wanted to do for *some* reason.

But what is not fine is the fact that now I've ruined everything. I've fucking ruined everything by giving myself up. Because the moment they break apart, they both also turn to the window.

To me.

And his chocolate chip eyes that were hooded until now grow alert.

They grow sharp and they trap me in my spot.

That trap only tightens its teeth around my ankles when, detaching himself from her, he slowly comes to his feet.

He also slowly moves toward me.

One step, two, three.

That's all it takes. He covers the distance between the leather couch and the window just by the door in three very long and very prowling steps — it's a considerable distance though, requiring way more than three steps — and all I can do is watch him do it.

And then, I hear a click.

Which feels so loud — louder than my earlier bangs on the glass — that it manages to break this strange spell I'm under. I manage to tear myself away from the window to notice that he's opened the door and he's now standing on the threshold.

A few moments of silence pass between us where he stares down at me with a ticking jaw, and I open and close my fists, trying to stand still under his scrutiny.

Then, "You're here."

"I'm…"

I'm not sure what I was going to say but his tone — low and dangerously soft — demanded that I speak. Demanded something from me.

My non-answer answer pisses him off even more.

I can clearly see that on his face.

But before I can say anything, someone else speaks. "Who is it?"

That shrill, feminine voice belongs to Cynthia. Who appears on the threshold, her brows slightly bunched and her eyes curious.

"Uh, hi."

She greets me back warily. "Hello." Then, to him, "Who is she?"

He doesn't reply.

He doesn't even pay her attention.

His entire attention is on me. His entire menacing and threatening attention.

Feeling awkward and nervous, I rub my hands on my skirt.

"I'm sorry for, uh, crashing the party. I didn't know that someone was here."

Lies.

Of course I knew. That's why I came.

But it was never my intention to make my presence known.

"That's okay," Cynthia says, her tone still wary but sweet enough to be called cautiously friendly. "Alaric and I were just hanging out."

I suck in my belly when she mentions his name, something that I never call him.

Something that I've promised myself that I won't.

I just don't know how to feel about *her* calling him that though.

"I'm —"

Finally, he speaks. "I think it's time for you to go."

For a second I think he's talking to me, because his eyes are on me. But then he glances away and looks at Cynthia.

Who appears slightly distressed at his command. "Oh, but…" She glances at me for a second before saying, "I thought we were going to spend some time together."

I go to say something, I'm not sure what but he speaks before I do. "And we did." When she seems confused, he explains, "Spend time together."

"Yeah, but I mean…" She chuckles nervously. "I drove all the way out here and…"

"And you can drive yourself back. Although if you need," he sighs, frowning, as if searching for words, "gas money or something like that, I'm happy to provide you with some."

"What?"

That's me.

I said that because I think Cynthia looks too horrified to utter even a word.

When he glances over at me, I continue, "Did you… just offer her money?"

His jaw goes back to ticking for a few seconds, alerting me that I'm already on dangerous grounds, before he commands, "Stay out of this."

He's right.

I should.

I should think about my own ass. Which I don't think is going to survive whatever he's planning on doing to me right now.

Which apparently warrants Cynthia leaving.

That's why he's sending her away, isn't he?

"Does a hundred cover it?" he asks Cynthia, and no.

Just no.

I *cannot* stay out of it. I have to speak.

"What are you doing? Stop offering her money."

His eyes narrow and he begins, "What did I —"

I take a step toward him and going up on my tiptoes, I cut him off. "She doesn't want your money. What is she, a hooker? What..."

Then something occurs to me.

Something monumental.

I go back down on my feet and my eyes go wide. "Oh my God, is she?" I turn to her. "Are you?" Before she can reply either way, I raise my hands and continue, "Not because I judge you. Please don't think that. I'm the least judgmental person in these cases. I grew up in Hollywood. I've seen everything. My mom was an actress. Charlie Blyton?" I nod. "Yeah. She was my mother and she was *very* progressive. I am too. It's your body and you can do whatever you want with it. In fact, I think me and everyone in my generation is very pro sex work. Hashtag support sex workers. And I really think it should be legalized and I'm pulling for you guys. But if you are... then he is... And he's the principal and you're meeting him on school premises and..."

Holy fucking shit.

Is this it?

Is this the break that I've been looking for?

Could this be one of his weaknesses? Is that why he wouldn't tell me who Cynthia was?

Oh my God.

If so, then I've hit the jackpot. I've hit the fucking *jackpot*.

A principal of a *reform school*, no less, meeting up with a prostitute on school premises. Oh my God, it will create a scandal so bad that...

"You're Charlie's daughter."

Cynthia's words pull me out of my musings and I blink. "I'm sorry?"

She looks at me with something very similar to hostility. "You're Charlie Blyton's daughter."

"Um, yeah." I press a hand to my chest, my running thoughts coming to a halt. "Did you… Did you know her? I mean, personally?"

She takes a moment to study me before she goes, "Yeah. I knew her. I knew her very well, actually."

I'm taken aback. "Oh, I —"

"Leave," he commands, cutting me off.

Again, I think he's talking to me. But his eyes are firmly and very dangerously pinned on Cynthia.

She doesn't look fazed, however. "What is Charlie Blyton's *daughter* doing here?"

"Cynthia."

That's his only answer. A warning, I feel like.

But she doesn't heed it because again, she goes, "Why is Charlie's daughter in your house right now?"

His jaw is clenched and it's clenched so tightly that I don't think he'll be able to speak.

So I do it for him. "Uh, because I go to school here." She whips her eyes over to me. "And because, uh, Mr. Mar — Principal Marshall is my guardian."

"As I said, it's time for you to leave," he says.

She watches him with disbelief for a second or two. "You're *Charlie's* daughter's guardian." Then, shaking her head, "I can't believe it." Her disbelief has hardened into something harsh and cruel even. "After everything. I really thought that we could be allies."

"We could be," he agrees. "If it was a real thing. But unfortunately, we're not in high school anymore."

"I thought I could trust you."

"Your two divorces should've taught you not to trust men. Although, you were the one who screwed them over so maybe not."

"You're —"

"Now get out."

She doesn't.

Not right away. She looks him up and down, her head shaking. "You're still the same, aren't you? You might have changed on the outside but on the inside, you're still the same fucking loser."

He stiffens.

Not that he wasn't already all stiff and tight.

But Cynthia's words turn him into a rock. Hard and barely breathing.

Wooden and feelingless.

Me, on the other hand, I'm breathing really fast. I'm breathing like a hurtling train. And I'm all ready, I swear to God I am, to do something drastic.

To maybe lunge at her and smack her face.

For calling him that.

In his own home no less. At his own school.

What the fuck is wrong with her? How dare she?

I even take a step toward her but then she focuses on me and says, "And I'm not a hooker."

With that, she moves. She turns around and walks toward the couch. She picks up her handbag, spins on her heel and then strides back to the door, before walking out and leaving.

Leaving both of us alone.

And maybe I should be afraid right now. Maybe I should be panicking because he's back to staring down at me with a ticking jaw and his voice is so low and rough that it sends shivers down my spine. "Inside."

But I'm not afraid.

As I step inside his cottage, I'm seething.

I'm angry.

As soon as he slams the door shut, I spin around. "Who was she? And what the fuck was she talking about? How dare she call you that? A loser." I'm so angry that I don't let him get in a word as I keep going. "How fucking dare she? Doesn't she know who you are? I mean, you're the principal of this school and that's the least of your achievements. I can't believe it. I'm so mad right now and —"

He moves then, stealing my words. He strides over to the couch and picks up his tumbler of scotch before draining it in one go. And then he turns around, his eyes darker than before and his jaw tighter.

Which finally makes the situation sink in.

Which finally makes my fear seep through my anger.

He looks at the empty glass, moving it back and forth in his hand. "You know, ever since I got here, I've been quite taken with this particular piece of literature. This manual. With all the rules and regulations of St. Mary's. I have to say that my family thought of everything." He looks at me then. "I specifically like this clause about bed checks."

"You're kidding."

"No, I actually do find it interesting."

"Y-you're…" I lick my dry lips. "You're thinking about bringing back the bed checks."

He lowers his glass and puts it back on the coffee table. "The thought had crossed my mind."

"You can't do that," I say, loudly. "You absolutely cannot do that. That's cruel."

He shrugs then, all casually. "But then I do so enjoy being cruel."

I can't believe this.

Having me list all my secret spots and pathways is one thing, but now he wants to bring back the stupid bed check rule? It's an ancient, cruel rule that was banished many years ago, where a warden would conduct regular bed checks during the night to account for all students.

Which means sneaking out would be next to impossible.

What *is* it with him?

Why is he so hellbent on sucking every ounce of joy and life out of this place?

"You're a tyrant, you know that? You're a big fucking bully."

My insults make him tip his mouth up in a small smirk as he says, "And yet you keep messing with me."

"I —"

"I told you what would happen if you sneaked out of your dorm again, didn't I?"

I take a step back then. "I'm not afraid of you."

He looks at my retreating feet that are basically making a liar out of me. "Then I highly advise that you start now."

I keep backing away. "Why are you like this, so mean?"

His chest expands on a breath. "Why do you make it so easy for me? To *be* mean."

"What happened to you?" I ask, shaking my head. "Something happened to you, didn't it? To make you this way."

He shakes his head, barely affected by my words. "Yeah and it's a very tragic tale."

My back hits the wall and I have nowhere to go.

And then he's upon me in a flash.

Just like that night last week, he stands a few feet away from me, his hands thrust into his pockets. And again just like that night, I'm glued and trapped to this spot.

With his head bent, he asks, "But first why don't you tell me what you are doing here."

I swallow, my fingers digging on the wall. "Was she your girlfriend?"

He breathes sharply at my non-answer. "No."

"So then why were you kissing her?"

"Because she's not my girlfriend."

"She was awful," I say truthfully.

"Beyond."

"How did she know my mother?" I ask, fully expecting him not to answer. "What did my mother do to her?"

But he surprises me and replies, "She stole Cynthia's boyfriend. Back in high school." Then, "Or something similar."

"What?"

"And since those were the best years of Cynthia's life, she's still not over that."

"Oh my God," I breathe out. "Charlie stole Cynthia's boyfriend?"

"It's okay. She survived."

Did you?

Because from the looks of it, he didn't.

He hasn't.

He's still living that, whatever it is that my mother did.

"And what did my mother do to you?" I ask, this time *knowing* that he would never tell me.

And he doesn't.

Instead he asks, "How about you answer my question now and tell me what you're doing here?"

I'm here to know all your secrets.

I'm here to ruin you.

"Is she your fuck buddy then?" I ask. "Cynthia."

His jaw hardens at the F word.

"What," I ask, lifting my chin and inching up my glasses, "you think I don't know the meaning of a fuck buddy?"

His nostrils flare. "Start talking."

I don't. I keep pursuing this for some reason.

"You think I'm too innocent and young to know about these

things," I provoke. "For your information, I'm not. I'm not too young or innocent to know about these things. I know what fuck buddies are."

His jaw begins ticking again.

But I don't stop. "I know what kissing is."

Another tick.

"And I also know what fucking is."

Another tick, this one harder.

"In fact," I add, craning my neck and going up on my tiptoes, "I've done it myself."

Wrong thing to say.

So very, very wrong.

I'm not even sure why I said it.

Except I couldn't not.

I couldn't not bait him in this moment. I couldn't not mess with his control.

With his ticking jaw and flaring nostrils.

But now that I have, he's awake.

I've awoken the beast and his chest expands on a wave of a breath. He takes his hand out of his pocket and puts it on the wall up above my head, hanging over me, pushing me down on my feet without even laying a hand on me.

Then, hanging there, looming, he rumbles, "You've been fucked."

I wince, clutching my skirt. "I have."

"When?"

"M-many times."

"Where?"

"A lot of places."

"Who?"

This question is growled.

This question has been ripped out of his chest. I can tell.

I can feel the vibrations of it in my own chest, and it makes lying to him even harder.

Because I am lying.

I haven't been fucked. I haven't even been kissed yet.

I've been waiting for it.

For my first kiss, since I was fifteen. Since I fell in love with Jimmy.

But in this moment, it's imperative that *he* knows, that my devil guardian knows, that I've been fucked and I've been kissed and I've been around the block many times.

So I say, "A lot of guys, okay? A lot. I have experience. I'm not some naive little girl who doesn't know anything."

Now his fingers are vibrating, the ones on the wall.

I can see them in my peripheral vision.

And his voice goes even lower. "Is that so?"

"Yes." I swallow. "You didn't think that you'd tear me apart from the love of my life and send me here, and that would be it, did you? That I'd sit in a room, all trapped and crying. No. I went out. I did things. I met guys and I seduced them all. I'm quite the seductress."

"Seductress."

"Yes, and guess what, I liked it, too."

"You liked what?"

"Seducing them," I say, although I have no idea now what I'm saying. "I loved seducing them. I loved bringing them to their knees. I loved it when they begged me and cried out for me. Yes, I did and —"

"Shut up." My breaths are all jumbled up now, all scattered as he leans in further. "Shut the fuck up, Poe, or I'll make you. And I'll do it in a way that requires you to be on your knees in front of me. Because I don't like girls who run their mouths, who tease. I like my girls wrecked and ruined. I like them to soak my shirt with their tears and my sheets with their juices. So if you know what's good for you, you'll stop talking bullshit and you'll start telling me what the fuck you're doing here."

My heart is beating in my ears.

My heart is beating on my tongue.

And the words are right there.

The truth.

That I came here to find out things about him. That I came here to spy. That I'm plotting something, planning something.

That I'm going to blackmail him.

"I came..." I lick my lips and his jaw clenches. "I came because I had a nightmare."

What?

A nightmare?

Where did *that* come from?

Except maybe it was self-preservation. It was an attempt to

save myself from his wrath, and so I said the first thing, the *very* first thing, I could think of. Or rather, I said it *before* I could even think of it.

And somehow, it works.

It fucking works.

Because at my lie, his anger breaks.

It leaches out of his tight features and something else takes its place.

Something that I've never seen from him before and so I can't say what it is.

I can't say what it means when his chocolate chip eyes go from being harsh to slightly liquid, and his clenched jaw loosens up and he says, "A nightmare."

"Yes."

A few seconds pass in silence.

Then, he says, "Been a long time."

My heart clenches, and I can barely get the words out. "Yeah."

"Years."

"Yes."

He studies my face, his eyes roving in quick but thorough circles over my features, and I swallow. Then he takes a deep breath and takes his hand off the wall.

He steps back too.

While I stay there, glued to my spot still.

Because even though I lied to save myself from his anger, I didn't think that he would buy it.

I didn't think that he would… look like this.

Concerned.

Oh my God, he's concerned.

This is *concern*.

I can't believe it.

In those initial months when I came to live with him, I used to have nightmares. Which I think was obvious. My mother had just died. I'd moved to this new town to live in this new house, among strangers. And one of those strangers had a history with my mom that caused him to hate me.

So much so that he wouldn't let me go.

Of course I had nightmares.

If I didn't know better, I'd say that he didn't even know about them. Because it's not as if I told him, or even *wanted* to tell him. He was the reason for them, wasn't he?

But he knew.

Even though it was Mo who always came into my room after I'd wake up screaming and crying, I know he knew.

"Was tonight the first time?" he asks, breaking my thoughts.

"What?"

"That you had your nightmare."

"I… Yeah."

"I'm calling Dr. Rover in the morning and making —"

"What, no," I cut him off.

He breathes out sharply. "You need to go see him."

"No, I don't. I'm fine."

"You're not fine. You had a nightmare."

No, I didn't.

At least, not tonight.

I did have one last week though. When summer school started and I was super depressed at being left behind and all alone. It was before I got to know Echo and Jupiter. Since then I've been in much better spirits.

"Yes," I say, nodding, deciding to tell him a version of the truth so we can move on from this. "I did have a nightmare. And that's because I'm stuck here, all alone. Without any friends. When for the past three years, ever since you so generously sent me here, I had plans to graduate with them. Which means that I'm in a stressful situation. So it's not really a surprise that I had a nightmare, is it? I don't need Dr. Rover to check me out. Not again."

The reason I know that *he* knew about my nightmares is because after Mo had to come into my room to calm me down a few times, she told me that Mr. Marshall had made an appointment for me.

With a doctor.

A psychiatrist.

Of course I refused to go. I wasn't going to see a psychiatrist; my head was fine. It was him — my new devil guardian — who was the problem, not me. But when I kept refusing, the doctor came to see me. So there was no escape.

Although I have to admit that it did help.

He recommended medication and outpatient therapy with

one of his colleagues. Which I also refused in the beginning, but then the therapist grew on me and my nightmares did recede after a while. All of that being said though, I have no desire to repeat that experience.

"I want you to tell me."

His voice brings me out of my thoughts and I focus on him.

Still standing in front of me, he appears even more stiff than before. Even more statue-like and still than when Cynthia said those things.

"Tell you what?"

Somehow he unclenches his jaw to say, in a rough voice, "The next time you have a nightmare."

"W-what?"

"I want you to come find me," he says in the same voice.

Maybe in an even lower voice.

Which hits me in my belly. But not more than his words.

His words not only hit my body but bruise me too. The meaning behind them.

"You want me to come find you when I have a nightmare," I say, both because I want to make sure that I heard him right and because I don't really know what to say to that.

"Yes."

I frown, my fists clenched. "I don't... I don't understand."

His jaw pulses at my confused words; his eyes flash. Then, "You have them because you're stuck here, yeah?"

I jerk out a short nod. "Yes."

"And before, it was because you were stuck in a strange mansion."

"Yes."

Another pulse runs through his jaw. "And all of those things are because of me. I'm responsible for that."

I look into his intense eyes. "You are."

They grow even more penetrating than before. "So I want to know. All the things I'm responsible for."

I don't know what's happening.

I really don't.

I gather words to say, "But you didn't before. It was always Mo. She came to me. She talked to me."

We study each other in silence for a few seconds before he

says, "She's not here. So all you have is me. Which means you'll come to me when you have a nightmare."

"And what will you do? If I come to you."

A slight frown appears on his brows, as if he thinks my question is asinine. Well, tough luck.

I think this whole situation is asinine.

"Calm you down. Talk to you," he says.

"But you never talk to me."

He breathes out a sharp breath. "So I'll just listen to you then. And make you tea."

My eyes go wide. "You'll make me tea?"

"Yes. Chamomile."

My heart races. "But Mo used to make me chamomile tea."

"She used to make you chamomile tea because it's good for relaxation."

"And you know how to make it?"

"Yes." Another sharp breath. "I know how to boil water and put tea bags in it."

My heart races harder. "And what about curfew?"

"Fuck curfew."

"But you said that I'm not supposed to be out of bed, sneaking out in the middle of the night."

"Fuck what I said."

"So you're not gonna punish me for sneaking out tonight?"

"You promise to come to me and I won't."

"Even though you're here to make this hellhole even more hellish. And you think every student should follow all the rules."

"You're also my ward."

My belly tightens. "So this is special treatment?"

"Yes."

Again, I'm not sure what's happening right now.

How we went from where we were only a few minutes before to this.

This whole bizarre exchange where he looks concerned about my nightmares.

And even though I'm not sure if this is real or if I'm dreaming, I find myself nodding and whispering, "Okay. I promise."

Chapter Thirteen

The Renaissance Man

I look away from my computer when I hear my phone ring.

It's Mo.

Saving the latest draft of my paper on the Spanish Inquisition and its severity against Jews and Muslims, I settle back into my chair and pick up the call. "Mo. Hey."

The line crackles at the other end. "I was just calling to ask if you're planning to come home this weekend."

I frown, rubbing out the kinks in my neck after working on my computer for the whole afternoon. "What's this weekend?"

"Your birthday."

Right.

Forgot about that.

Even though Cynthia came to the cottage to remind me of that. And she's been blowing up my phone all morning. Something that I knew she would do despite what happened last night. She's a fucking piranha with a one-track mind and apparently, her next target is me. Something about making a big mistake and ignoring me in high school. And no matter what I do and how much I push her away, she doesn't get deterred. And since she's on the board of St. Mary's — newly appointed because her dad chose to retire — she has excuses to come find me.

Pushing thoughts of her away and resting my head against the backrest, I look out the window of my office into the summer afternoon. "Well, you can have the day off, if you like."

"Actually, the whole staff is getting the day off."

"Are they?"

"Yes. It's your gift to them."

"My gift."

"Yes, and they're all very happy about it."

"I should hope so," I drawl, watching a group of students sitting on the concrete benches with their textbooks open. "Given how generous I am. Giving gifts on the day I should be getting them."

"Well, that's what happens when you're a dick the rest of the year," she quips.

A surprised chuckle escapes me. "That's because I sign everyone's paychecks."

"And that's the tragedy, isn't it?" she murmurs. Then, "So are you sure you're not coming?"

I rub my forehead as I reply, "No. I've got deadlines. I've got two papers due next week and I'm guest lecturing at Columbia this Friday."

"Fine. As you wish," she says pleasantly.

Almost a little too pleasantly.

Which makes me frown with suspicion.

Mo has been a constant presence in my life for as long as I can remember.

She was with me when I was a boy, singing me lullabies at night when I couldn't sleep, feeding me dinner when I was too weak or too sick to eat, looking for me when I'd hide – she knew all about my hiding places. She's also bandaged up a lot of my scrapes, growing up. And she was there when I left Middlemarch as a sixteen-year-old boy, and came back after completing my studies and travels at the age of twenty-eight.

Which basically means that she knows everything about me. Including the fact that I don't do birthdays.

Not even when I was a kid.

My birthdays have never been very joyous occasions in my house.

That has never stopped Mo, though.

Every year since I was a kid, Mo has not only remembered my birthday but also celebrated it by making me a cherry pie — my favorite — and a birthday card.

So this is surprising.

Her backing off so easily.

And I think I know the reason why and since I don't want to talk about it, I choose a neutral topic. "How's your knee?"

"It's fine."

"Any difference in the swelling?"

Mo's left knee has been bothering her for years and despite my insistence that she get it checked out, she's always been reluctant. Until I put my foot down a couple of months ago — told her I'd fire her nephew who works with the groundkeeper and isn't very good at his job anyway, if I saw her limping around one more time — and she finally went to the doctor. I knew if I'd threatened her job, she wouldn't have taken me seriously or even cared. But threatening her loved one did the trick.

People tend to do stupid things when it comes to love.

Not that going to the doctor was a stupid thing, but still.

The doctor suggested surgery to alleviate the pain, and here we are. Two months post-op, and while she's still going to PT, her pain has been much better than before.

"Yes, the swelling has gone down some."

"And the pain."

"That's fine too."

I'm about to ask another question but she says, "But thanks for asking, Mr. Marshall. I'll be going now."

Jesus. Fuck.

Mr. Marshall.

She's bringing out the big guns.

To the world, I'm either Mr. Marshall or Dr. Marshall or Professor Marshall.

I wasn't always, however.

Before I left Middlemarch, I was Alaric, the disappointing son of the town's mayor and a greatly celebrated family of Middlemarch. But when I came back from grad school and postdoctoral studies — with my father out of the picture — I was upgraded to Mr. Marshall.

I made sure of that.

I made sure to live up to that name. Made sure that everyone knew that the new Mr. Marshall was as intimidating as the old one.

Except to Mo.

While she knows that there are certain lines even she can't cross, she's the only one I've given the freedom to call me by my given name. Only in private — I wouldn't tolerate such disrespect in public — but still.

She's not the only *one though, is she?*

I clench my teeth at the thought.

I don't need this right now. I don't need to be thinking about *her.*

Sighing, I rub my forehead again. "How long do you think you're going to keep this up?"

Silence.

She wasn't expecting me to get into it.

Which is fine, because it wasn't my intention to get into it either. I have better things to do with my time. But let's do it.

Let's get into it and get it over with once and for all.

"I don't know what you're talking about," she says.

That's what does it.

That's what ends my patience with her.

Because even though she is allowed some liberties, I'm still her boss. I'm still the man who signs her fucking paychecks and it may upset me to fire her but I absolutely fucking will, if need be.

Turning away from the window, I begin in a stern voice, "All right. This is what we're going to do. You're going to stop with your passive aggressive bullshit because I've tolerated it for weeks now. I've given you time to get it out of your system and that's only out of respect for our relationship. But that time ends now. Now, you're going to start talking so we can discuss it like two adults and move on. *Now* do you know what I'm talking about?"

When I finish I realize I may have been harsher than I intended.

But that's okay.

It's always better to be perceived as cruel and hard than as weak and soft.

And it always works wonders.

Because in the next second, I hear a sigh and Mo says, "I apologize. You're right. I have been passive aggressive with you for the past couple of months. I shouldn't have been. And not because you're my boss but because I've always considered you as my own. I've always cared about you, loved you. I've watched you grow up. And I know this will upset you, but you're the same boy to me who left as a sweet, intelligent teenager but came back as this harsh, intimidating man."

She takes a few moments of pause. As if giving me time to absorb her words.

And she's right to do that.

I do need time to absorb her words. To get past her statement about who I was, who I pathetically used to be, and who I am now. Whom I've changed into.

And whom I have changed into is the man I was always supposed to be.

At least that's what I've been told all my life.

"So I should've been direct. Because I owe it to you to tell you this," she says after a few moments.

"And what is it that you want to tell me?"

She sighs and despite myself, I brace. "What you're doing is wrong. It's wrong." Then, "You need to do the right thing, Alaric."

In my most curt voice, I reply, "I *am* doing the right thing."

"Keeping her trapped is not the right thing."

At her words, the very first words she's spoken to me on the subject, I shake a little. My chest vibrates at the impact of them even though I'd braced myself.

Trapped.

I have done that. Kept her trapped and firmly under my control.

Since the day she came into my life.

And the thing is that Mo doesn't know the half of it.

"You didn't ask for this, Alaric," Mo continues. "Four years ago, you didn't ask to be put in a position like that, to be a guardian to a fourteen-year-old. And not just any fourteen-year-old but her. I remember being so angry on your behalf, you know. When we heard the news, when that lawyer called, I was so furious. I have to admit that I wanted you to say no. I really did. I wanted you to refuse the responsibility. Something — yet another thing — that your father put on you. But you didn't. You kept this promise like you always have. You've kept up the name of this family, kept up its reputation, its legacy."

"Yes," I grit out. "Because it's my responsibility."

"I know, and sometimes I wish it wasn't," she says. "Sometimes I wish you'd refuse. At least, refused this responsibility. Responsibility for her. But you didn't."

Mo is right.

I never refuse my family's responsibilities.

In fact, I embrace them all.

I've not only embraced my family's name, but I've done everything that I can to elevate it by doing even more than what my father would've done, by going the extra mile, by getting involved with all the right town projects, by achieving excellence in my own work, by getting not just one but two PhDs, countless grants and papers and whatnot.

And it wasn't easy.

Given my history, I've had a lot of naysayers. I've had a lot of critics. People who have watched me, underestimated me ever since I took over for my father. People who think I might still screw up. And going away to Italy for three years didn't help that judgement against me.

Anyway, that's not the reason that I said yes to taking on responsibility for *her*.

In fact, she wasn't. My responsibility, I mean.

And *this* is my greatest mistake. Or rather my first biggest mistake, before I took this job at St. Mary's.

My first biggest mistake was that four years ago, I lied to keep her at the mansion.

The night she wanted me to contact Marty and see if he could do something, I told her that he couldn't. When he already had some measures in place, a new family — some acquaintance of Charlie who came forward at the last minute — which was ready to take over in my stead. But I told him no. I told him that I'd take care of her and that she'd stay in Middlemarch.

And I did all that because I was angry.

Because as I said back then, whenever I looked at her, I saw her mother. I remembered what she did and what had happened. And so I trapped her against her will.

Not that Mo knows anything about all this. I never told her why I do the things I do. It's none of her business. It's none of anyone's business.

And I'm not about to start now.

Doing heart-to-heart chats.

"If the point of this conversation is to tell me how much you pity me, then I'd ask you to spare me. I don't want your pity and you don't know why I do the things that I do."

I hear her sigh again. "You're right. Maybe I don't. I don't know what goes on in your head anymore. You're not the same boy I took care of, who would just light up whenever I brought him my cherry pies. I haven't known that boy in a long time. But you can't tell me what to feel either. What you think is pity is my anger for you. My anger for that boy, my sadness. I miss him, and you can't tell me not to miss that boy, Alaric.

"Which is why I haven't said anything. I didn't say anything or argue with you when you told me to watch over her. When you refused to have to do anything with her. When you buried yourself in work and were hardly home, that first year. Even when you went to Italy. Even when she thought that you hated her. I know you didn't. You just hated what she represented."

Mo is right.

I never hated her.

I hated that she was her mother's daughter. I hated that she reminded me of my past.

I hated the fact that I punished her needlessly for something that wasn't even her fault.

And that's why I kept my distance.

That's why I removed myself from her presence, from her proximity, and left for Italy.

"And just as you asked me to do, I made sure that I was always available for her," Mo continues. "I made sure that I became her friend, her confidant. I even kept my mouth shut at your decision to send her to that awful school."

"You know why I sent her to St. Mary's," I snap, my body getting even tighter.

Why I had to.

It was because of my own mistakes and crimes that I'd committed against her.

Because of them first came the nightmares.

For some very strange reason, she has always been able to make my chest burn. To set it on fire.

Initially, it was because of who she reminded me of and so the fire inside me burned in anger. But once her nightmares started, that fire became something else. It became one of guilt and self-recrimination.

It became one of *protection.*

I wanted to make it go away, whatever it was that was haunting her. I wanted to make it… better.

Even though I knew I was the cause of it.

That's why I'd send Mo.

Because Mo was her confidant, and I'd pace the hallway until Mo would come out and tell me that she was okay and sleeping. And I sent her to a doctor for that very reason as well. And it helped, I think.

But while her nightmares abated, other things started.

She was failing all her classes and she was doing it on purpose. She would stay out late, way past her curfew. She'd cut school; get into fights with students and teachers. Not to mention her pranks and little revenge schemes at home. And though I could handle — sometimes even ignore— all of the above, there was one thing I couldn't tolerate.

One thing that pushed me over the edge.

Her boyfriend.

First, she shouldn't have been dating back then at all. She was fucking fifteen and running after a seventeen-year-old douchebag. And second, fuck being fifteen. She shouldn't be anywhere near a *douchebag* with a guitar, period.

She tried to keep him a secret for the longest time and she was fucking smart about it too. Took me a few months to figure it out. Where she was disappearing off to when she cut school; why she'd stay out past her curfew.

But when I did, I knew it was time to fix the damage.

It was time to fix what I had done.

Because it was me, wasn't it?

She was doing it all, spiraling out of control, because of what I had done to her. How I took away her choice. I'd already sent her on a path of rebellion, I wasn't going to stand there and let her ruin her whole life for a stupid fucking boy.

Hence St. Mary's.

"Yes," Mo agrees. "I knew why. And that's why again, as much as I hated that school, I didn't say anything. I even agreed to break the news to her myself. But it's enough now, Alaric. As I said, it's time for you to do the right thing. It's time for you to let her go."

I knew this day would come. When my guardianship would be over and she'd leave.

In fact, that's why I came back from Italy. Because it was time.

To not only get back to my own responsibilities but also to settle everything with my guardianship, hand over the money, send her to New York, plan for the future.

But then I had to take on the job of fixing this school. And in pursuit of that, I had to stop her graduation.

And now we're both stuck here and she has changed and how I look at her changed and…

It makes me so angry that I grip the phone tighter. "I can't. It's school policy."

But you can still expedite things, can't you?

"But you're the principal. You're on the board, Alaric," she tells me, unaware of the turmoil inside of me. "You can help her. You can do something to let her graduate."

"I'm not going to ignore or bend the rules for her. She's just like any other student here."

What a fucking joke, isn't it?

Bending the rules.

When I've already done it once before, with her lawyer.

When I'm ignoring them now by not listening to her and letting her graduate early.

"But she's not like any other student, is she?" Mo insists. "She's your responsibility. Not to mention, she's Charlie's daughter."

"Oh, is she?" I snap out, sarcastically. "It makes so much sense now. Why my life has been such a shitshow for the past four years."

Why I made *her* life such a shitshow by punishing her for things she never did.

By holding her responsible for the crimes her mother committed.

"Yes," she says firmly. "And how do you think that was for her? Being Charlie's daughter."

That gives me pause. "What?"

"I don't think it was easy, Alaric," she says, her voice serious and low. "Being Charlie's daughter. I don't think they had a very good relationship. I don't know everything, or anything really. Because she never told me, and whenever I tried to ask, she always evaded the question. But I don't think Charlie was a very good mother to her. And then Charlie passed away so abruptly and she had to move to a different town. Live with strange people, with a new guardian who hardly looked at her, let alone talked to her. And yes, you had your reasons but I think it's time to let her go. Maybe her grades or whatever it is you want her to have aren't there but she's survived a lot. She deserves a second chance. And whatever your reasons may be for taking on responsibility for her four years ago, you deserve to be free of it as well. And you have the power to make it happen. To set both of you free. Promise me that you'll think about it, please?"

"I will," I reply but I don't even hear my own voice.

I don't hear her hanging up the phone either.

Because I'm hearing something else. I'm *listening* to something else.

Laughter.

Streaming in through the barred windows.

Before I even turn to confirm, I know who that laughter belongs to.

I've heard it numerous times in the past. Ringing through the dead corridors of the mansion, my childhood home. Before every time I heard it, I would feel a sense of relief. Even though I didn't deserve it. After what I did to her. But I would be able to go on about my day with a lightness that she was laughing. Maybe she was happy, in that moment, on that day.

Now I don't think I'd be able to go on about my day like before.

Now it sounds like something musical, that laughter — no less happy though. Something that I would have to stop and listen to. Something… seductive.

Fuck.

I'm not supposed to think about her that way.

She's my ward. My student.

She's fucking eighteen years old.

But despite myself, despite the fact that I hate this uncontrollable urge, I turn back to the window.

And there she is.

Out in the courtyard.

Laughing.

Her midnight-colored hair blowing in the wind, her bangs fluttering. That's the first thing I see.

The second thing is her hat.

A big purple hat with floppy sides that's fluttering in the wind as well.

As she flies paper airplanes.

And every time it hits the target, usually another girl sitting either on those stone benches or on the ground, she throws her head back and laughs, clutching her hat.

She laughs with her whole body.

Her mouth, her hands, her bowed spine, her legs as she hops up and down with joy.

I don't think it was easy, Alaric.

I hear Mo's voice and I have to admit that I never thought about it.

About her life before she came to live in Middlemarch.

At first because I was so blinded by rage that I didn't want to think about her. And then, because my guilt had sent me to Italy. The only solution that I could think of for what I'd done.

But if I had, if I had given it a little bit of thought, I may have figured it out.

I may have sensed that she didn't have it easy with Charlie.

And if anyone knows about difficult things and relationships with one's parents, it's me.

So Mo is right.

I have all the power.

Something that I never had for the first half of my life. I never had control, respect, power, all the things that came naturally to my father, other people even. But never to me.

But now I have all of it in abundance.

So I should use it. For some good finally.

Especially when I know that her nightmares are back. That she's all alone here, without friends.

Not to mention, that fucking boyfriend of hers. He's out of her life now.

He is, isn't he?

She can't be that stupid.

Not after my warnings.

So yeah, there is no reason for me to keep her here. I can bend the rules for her. I can let her graduate today, give her the money as per the will so she can go wherever she wants to go. So she can do whatever she wants to do.

I owe her that.

After everything I've put her through.

I watch how her hair flows down her back, flies around her pale face. She's the only one in the courtyard with her hair down and loose in the air. She's the only one running around and not doing her work as she should be. She's the only one disturbing other people's peace.

She's a fucking menace.

Her purple hat is a fucking menace.

And for some reason, she's the only one who's ever held my attention like this.

Fucking fuck.

Look away from her.

Let her go.

I'm the worst guardian in motherfucking history.

Because I'm not going to.

Not because I'm angry or hellbent on some twisted revenge.

But because for some reason, I can't.

I can't let her go.

Not yet.

Chapter Fourteen

He made me tea.

Chamomile.

Like he told me he would.

He boiled the water for me in his tea kettle — he has a tea kettle; it's steel with a black handle — before pouring it into a white ceramic mug and plunking a couple of teabags in it.

He not only plunked them and left it at that, no.

With his big, busted fingers, he clutched the delicate bags and dipped them in and out as well. Until the water turned a thick brown, only a few shades lighter than his chocolate chip eyes, and the air around us turned aromatic.

And then I drank it. Again, like he told me I would.

And it was the best chamomile tea I'd ever tasted. Somehow even better than Mo's.

Then I went back to the dorms and went to sleep.

I'm really not sure how I managed to do that after what had transpired between us last night.

The very extraordinary turn of events.

His extraordinary concern.

What *was* that?

But you know what, I've decided that I can't dwell on it.

I have other things to dwell on.

Things like my plan. My blackmail scheme.

My freedom.

Whatever it was, let's call it an anomaly and move on.

Cynthia, who also happened to be my mother's rival, was a bust apparently. So I need to find something else. Some other piece of damning evidence that I can use against him.

With that determination, I go in for my second day of detention.

I arrive at five o'clock sharp, and this time when he opens the door, he doesn't make me wait outside. He simply steps aside to let me in. I barely throw him a glance as I enter, keeping my mind focused on the task. Maybe I could…

"You sleep okay last night?"

I jump at his voice coming from behind me and whirl around.

Like yesterday, he's standing by the door, his large frame filling the doorway both length- and breadth-wise.

But *unlike* yesterday, he's all settled over there.

As in, completely turned toward me and leaning against it. Even his arms are folded across his chest, his biceps looking like small hills under his dark gray tweed jacket.

He looks the very picture of relaxation and patience.

As if he has nowhere else to be right now except where he is, propped against the door and watching me.

As strange as that development is, I'm not even thinking about it right now though.

Because there's something else here that requires my attention.

The fact that he's not wearing a tie.

Instead, the top two buttons of his gray dress shirt are open and they are two too many because I can see everything. As in, I can see the triangle at the base of his throat. I can see a little bit of his chest as well. Like, very *very* little of his chest. Maybe even less than an inch, but still.

Because the thing is that I've never seen it.

I've never ever seen that dusky patch of skin on his throat or that micro-inch of his chest.

And that's because I've never ever seen him without a tie.

Ever.

In all the four years that I've known him — granted that he was away for three of them, but still — he's never *not* worn a tie in front of me.

And I realize that this is even worse than that forearm thing from last week. That display messed up my breathing.

This one stops my breathing altogether.

And makes my belly drop.

Staring at the triangle of his throat, I blurt out, "Where's your tie?"

"What?"

I swear I can see his chest vibrate with his clipped word, or maybe I'm just losing my mind. "Why don't you have your tie on?"

There's a moment of silence then.

Which makes me jerk my eyes up to his face. To his confused face actually.

A small frown between his brows. His eyes slightly narrowed as he watches me.

I admit that I might have sounded a bit abrupt, but I want him to put a tie on. I *need* him to.

I can't afford any distractions from my grand scheme of blackmail, and so I say, clenching one fist and clutching the strap of my backpack with the other, "You're violating the dress code."

"The dress code," he says finally.

"Yes." I nod. "You're the principal, aren't you?"

"Last I checked."

"And you wear tweed jackets with elbow patches."

"I'm aware."

"Well, are you also aware that tweed jackets went out of fashion back in the fifties?"

Not true.

They're still very much in fashion.

As in, they're usually featured in most fall collections. Wherein sometimes they catch fire and then you have everyone from LA to London to Paris wearing them. In fact it happened just last year.

"No," he says, his tone dry, bringing me out of my musings. "I'm afraid my tastes run more toward the moral dilemmas of the mid-Victorian imperial state than the great vagaries of the modern fashion industry."

I open and close my mouth for a few seconds. Then, "Moral dilemmas of what?"

An emotion flickers through his gaze, lighting up his chocolate chip eyes. "It's okay. Even though tweed was a popular fashion choice for upper-class British men back in the nineteenth century, you're not missing much."

I narrow my eyes at him, ignoring everything he just said. Mostly because I didn't understand it; it all sounded very intelligent though.

"You're the principal. And you're the principal of a reform school who wears tweed jackets with elbow patches and who's here to make this place even more prison-like. So just wear your tie, okay? Just do it."

It's the stupidest, most pointless thing I've ever said.

But I'm flustered, okay?

There. I admit it.

I'm flustered.

His tea has *flustered* me and now his stupid throat is flustering me also. And I can't have that.

I have a mission to focus on.

So I want him to wear the fucking tie so I don't have to look at that sliver of his exposed skin. Because I've looked at it at least fifteen times since we started this asinine discussion.

I've looked at it. I've analyzed it.

I've even imagined dipping my finger up there, at the base of his throat.

And my nose.

Because I have a feeling that his scent of leather and cigar would be the thickest there.

He watches me with amused eyes. "Are you okay?"

"I'm fine." I blow my bangs. "Can we please just get back to the detention?"

"As long as we're talking about dress code violations," he begins with his face dipped, his eyes strangely intense. "Let's talk about your floppy purple hat."

For a second, I don't get his meaning or what exactly he's talking about. But then it clicks.

My floppy purple hat. That I was wearing over lunch.

It was the first time in days that I'd worn it, feeling all light and carefree. Because even though I still don't know how I'm going to accomplish the impossible task that I've set forth for myself and what the hell that tea was about, I'm not quite as alone as I thought I'd be.

But I'm not light or carefree right now.

I'm pissed. Also a little breathless that he was watching me, but more pissed. "No. We're not talking about it."

"I —"

"No, no, no." I stab a finger at him. "No. We're not talking about it. Because you're not taking away my hat. It's purple and it's suede. It's fucking fantastic, okay? It's my favorite. You've already taken away my Purple Durple and my Wild Child Bad Child, *and* sucked *all the joy out of my life*, I'm not giving you my Lady Gaga Over Purple too. Specifically named as such because it's purple and because Lady Gaga gave it to me when I was eleven. So you can just forget about that. And guess what," I continue, widening my feet, "I don't care that you made me tea. I don't care that you looked concerned about my nightmare last night. Because you're the reason for all my nightmares in the first place. *You*. So where do you get off being all concerned, okay? Where? So I don't want your tea and you're not taking away my hat. You could give me a hundred fucking detentions over it and still I wouldn't hand it over to you. You could keep me here until the end of time, locked up in your stupid school —"

"You're right."

I draw back at his interruption, heaving, pulling in large amounts of breaths. "What?"

He's calm but I can see the gravity, the seriousness in his eyes as he says, "You're right. I'm the cause of all nightmares. And so," a deep breath, "I'd like to hear about it."

I stare at him for a few seconds then.

Shocked at first.

But then afraid.

That he's asking me about the one time I *didn't* have a nightmare.

"You want to know about my nightmare from last night," I say finally.

His expression appears contemplative as he replies, "Last night. Any other night before that."

Again, I stare at him for a few seconds.

This time I'm not as afraid as before, but I am still as shocked.

That he's asking.

That like last night, he looks… concerned right now.

God, no.

I don't want him to look concerned. I don't want that frown between his brows and I don't want that molten look in his eyes.

"Why?" I ask in my most stern voice.

"Because I'd like to know," he says in his most polite voice.

I lift my chin. "Well, you never tell me anything about yourself, so."

He stands there for a few moments, his expression and demeanor the same.

But then he shifts on his feet and exhales a long breath.

A really long one that not only swells his chest but rolls his shoulders as well. Then, "It's an old high school injury."

It's a testament to how much I've been dying to know things about him that he doesn't even have to explain what he's talking about.

I already know.

I already know he's answering my question from yesterday. "Your nose."

His jaw clenches as if he's gritting his teeth before he throws me a short nod.

It's enough for me, however.

It's enough for me to glance at the bump on his nose and ask, "What happened?"

Again, he clenches his jaw and I know that he doesn't want to answer. He doesn't want to divulge anything regarding this and my heart twists in my chest.

My heart wants me to tell him to stop.

He doesn't have to if he doesn't want to.

But then he goes, "I walked into a fist."

"Someone *did* this to you?" I gasp. "Someone beat you up?"

Because that's what people say when they get beaten up, right? Not 'I got into a fight' but 'I walked into a fist or a door.'

Again, a jerk of a nod to confirm my theory.

And holy shit, I did not expect that.

I absolutely did not expect that someone *beat him up*.

Him.

With all that he is. With all his muscles and bulk and the punching thing.

"But you punched him back, didn't you? You beat him the fuck up for doing this to you," I ask, because that's the first thing I could think of.

That I fucking hope and wish that he beat that asshole up.

Whoever he was.

I already hate him.

"Given that I was laid up in the hospital at the time, no."

At this, I have to press a hand on my belly. I have to press it really hard because what the fuck?

What the… Is he serious?

"He put you in the hospital?" My voice is loud, screeching almost. "I can't… I… What happened? What… Who…"

In this moment, I don't even *know* how to string words together.

I *don't.*

My head is filled with all these images of blood and fists and broken noses.

The hospital.

I try again. "I don't understand. H-how did it even happen? Who was he? What —"

"Nightmares," he cuts me off, his features calm.

Which is totally insane because how can he be so calm right now?

How can he not be angry?

Enraged and shocked and all the fucking things that I'm feeling right now.

"But I want to know. What —"

"Your turn," he says.

All calm and still.

But no less commanding and authoritative.

This man. My formidable devil of a guardian. Tyrant of a principal.

Whom I've hated for as long as I've known him but for the life of me, I cannot bear the thought of him lying beaten up and injured in a hospital.

A *hospital.*

God.

I give him what he wants then. I give it to him because I don't think I can deny him anything right now. I don't have the energy when all my attention is tied up in the fact that someone put him in the hospital when he was a teenager.

"It's…" I take a deep breath. "It's always the same thing. It's… In my dreams, Charlie is still alive but somehow, I'm in Middlemarch. And I'm up on that roof, in the pouring rain like I was that night. Four years ago. And I want to leave. I want to get out of this town. I want to go back to New York. To Charlie. To my old apartment. Sleep in my own bed. I'm… I'm thinking that I'm wasting my time here. I have to get back because I have things to do. I have to... but…"

"But you can't," he finishes.

"No."

"Because I won't let you."

I look into his eyes that at once look molten and hard. As hard as the muscles and bones of his face.

Hard with something akin to regret.

And like his concern, I don't get that either.

Why is he regretful? Why's he concerned?

When he hates me.

When he's done all these things to me.

"No," I say. "You're never in my nightmares. As much as I like the thought of that. Because it would be poetic. Since you're the one responsible for triggering them. So it's only fair that you should be in them as well. But it's not you. It's Charlie. She doesn't want me there."

I hold his gaze for about two seconds after that, after my big confession, and drop it to the floor.

It's a shameful secret, see.

All this time, I let everyone believe that my old life in New York was amazing. Yes, nobody wanted to adopt me because of my troublemaking reputation, but that's okay. That's reality. Because every celebrity kid is a little bit of a diva. No one wants to deal with them. But in reality, my own mother was included in that 'no one.'

It's not something I like to talk about. How unloved I was by the one person who's biologically designed to love me.

But because I have told him this much, I go ahead and tell him everything.

"Because she never wanted me there. She never wanted me anywhere. Not at her shoots or award ceremonies. She'd only take me to interviews if she knew it would get her the front page or the ratings or whatever. She never wanted me at her charity functions, or on her vacations that she took with her friends or boyfriends. And I'd try so hard to impress her, you know? To do things that would make her wanna be around me. So I'd participate in like, school plays or art competitions. Why did I think she'd be impressed by art competitions, I don't know. School plays I understand. I mean she was an actress but art competitions? Anyway, I did them nonetheless. I also learned everything about makeup and hair because those were her favorite things. I'd paint my nails the exact same color as hers. Wear the same style clothes and shoes so we could have something in common. I even learned to *make* clothes."

I chuckle. "Yeah, I did. Can you believe that? I was always so fascinated with her costume fittings and all these designers who would hang out at our apartment, using her as a model to design new clothing lines. And so one day I just started doing these little sketches in my notebook. I always hated homework, right? Anything to get out of doing it or studying. So I'd spend hours doing these little sketches of dresses instead of completing worksheets. I'd think of colors and fabrics and whatnot. And then one day I just grabbed a few of my clothes and started cutting them up, mixing and matching fabrics and then sewing them up. And just like that I made a skirt for myself. Of course it was silly. I mean, I was what, ten? Or something. My mom saw it and said it was hideous. So I just threw it away.

"But can I tell you a secret? I really didn't. I kept it. Because I loved it so much. Even though it was shoddy work. But that was the first thing I remember loving to that degree. And since then, I've made sure to hide everything that I ever made. I even hide it from myself, if that makes sense. Because I didn't wanna give her any more reasons not to love me."

And then I blink.

Because I realize that I'd gone into a trance. A sort of hypnosis.

But now I'm back.

In reality and into myself.

I told him everything.

Every fucking thing that there is to know about me.

About my mom. About my thing.

My *thing*.

I told him about my *thing*.

Holy God.

What did I do? What the fuck did I do?

I've never told this to anyone. I barely acknowledge it to myself.

I barely, *barely* think about it even. Think about the fact that most of my notebooks and textbooks are filled with little sketches of dress designs. Mock-ups of colorful skirts with tiny little notation marks about the fabric and stitching. Things I learned from Charlie's designer friends.

Not to mention, I barely give it a thought that I browse through thrift stores, looking for clothes and fabrics to buy that I can later cut up and make into pretty dresses.

But now he knows.

Him, of all people.

And why? Because he *asked.*

Because he *barely* showed an interest and I blurted out my entire life story.

What the fuck, Poe?

What did you do?

"You make clothes."

His voice makes me jerk up my head and I find him standing up straight now, pushed away from the door and his arms unfolded.

"I want to leave," I tell him.

Yes because I need to regroup and think about what I just did.

"You sketch dress designs," he says, this time taking a step toward me.

I shake my head and move back. "I just want to leave, okay? Can I leave?"

"And you hide the clothes that you make."

Oh my God.

Oh my fucking God.

I keep backing away until my ass hits something, the chair, and I blurt out, "What are the chances of you potentially forgetting what I just said?"

His response is to take my breath away.

Because one second, he's standing at the door, slowly approaching me and the next, he's here.

Where I am.

He's standing right in front of me and I don't even know how he got here. How he moved so fast and how is it that I'm staring up at him, my neck craned, my hands gripping the back of the chair and my backpack lying on the floor.

"You *hide* the clothes you make," he says again as if that's the most objectionable piece of information in all of this.

"I did. Before. But not anymore," I answer despite myself.

It's his tone, I think. Also his eyes.

It's the look in them.

All harsh and liquid somehow.

"So what do you do with them?"

"Wear them. Or, uh, give them away."

"Give them away."

"To friends." Then, "But they don't know."

"That you made them," he guesses correctly.

I nod. "Yes. I just tell them that I bought it."

I do.

Whenever I give them birthday presents or Christmas gifts and stuff. I usually sew everything over the summer holidays, well in advance, so when the time comes, I can just gift wrap them and tell them that I bought it for them.

So I try again to steer him away from this conversation. "No one knows about this, okay? I'm not even sure why I told you. But please can you just… can you forget about what I said? I'm —"

"No."

"But I —"

"Because I've never felt this kind of rage before."

"I-I'm sorry?"

His jaw moves back and forth and I swear his eyes, even though looking at me, turn unseeing as he continues, "And trust me, I've felt a lot. I've felt a lot of rage, a lot of fury. To the point where I thought I was suffocating with it. I thought I'd die with it. With my rage. But I've never felt this kind of violence, this kind of fire. This kind of hate."

His eyes come back into focus. "So no, I'm not going to forget this, Poe. I'm not going to forget that you come up with your own dress designs and then sketch them all over your notebooks. You not only sketch them and color them, you also bring them to life. You fucking sew the clothes together. And instead of handing you the scissors and buying you a goddamn sewing machine, she made it so that you had to hide it from her. And not only from her, but also from the world. From your friends. From yourself. She *made* you hide your talent from yourself. But that's not the worst part. That she was a fucking idiot. An undeserving fucking idiot. That's not what pisses me off the most."

"So then what?"

"That I did the same."

"You what?"

"I underestimated you. I underestimated you at every turn. I refused to know you. I *refused*… And I did it because of her. I did it because…" He grinds his teeth again. "And I thought I was doing the right thing. By leaving for Italy. By leaving the fucking country after what I did, but…"

"But what?" I ask, my heart beating furiously. "What are you talking about? What about Italy?"

What is he saying?

Why did he think it was the right thing to leave?

I don't get it.

I don't…

"You're not hiding anymore," he says, determined.

"What?"

"You have a sewing machine?"

"What? I'm —"

"How do you sew your clothes? The ones that you make for your friends."

"I'm… I have a sewing machine."

"Where is it?"

"Back at the mansion," I tell him, swallowing. "Mr. Marshall, I —"

"I'll buy you another one."

"What?"

"And have it delivered here."

"To the dorms?"

"Yes."

I'm so flabbergasted at this.

So fucking astonished right now.

More so than I was last night.

It's like I've entered a different dimension. A parallel dimension.

Where things look the same but they don't act the way they should.

He is not acting the way he should.

He is not acting like he hates me.

"But I…" I shake my head. "But I don't think we're allowed to have stuff like that. I mean, I've never tried to bring it here before. Because I didn't want anyone to know, but —"

"Now they'll know."

"But —"

"You're not hiding."

"But, Mr. Marshall, I don't —"

"You're not," he pauses, leaning down further, "*hiding*. Anymore. You're not allowed to."

I swallow, my toes curling in my Mary Janes. "Okay. But what about the school rules?"

"Fuck the school rules."

"But you're supposed to make this place worse."

"And I will. But not like this."

I swallow again. "But I'm a student here too."

"You're also my ward."

"So this is special treatment then?"

"Yeah."

I look into his eyes. I look at his whole face then. His dense curly eyelashes. As curly and thick as his dark hair. His beautifully high cheekbones that still look flushed with his earlier anger.

I even look at the triangle of his throat.

Before whispering, "I told you a secret."

An unknown emotion flickers through his face. "Yeah."

"My biggest secret."

How did that happen?

How did I end up telling him something that I've never told anyone before?

But more than that, how did I end up spilling my secrets to him when I'm here to find out his?

God.

"You're the last person I wanted to tell this to," I continue.

He winces slightly. "I know."

"I hate you."

"I know that too."

"Tell me a secret of yours."

Now he takes his turn studying my upturned face. My messy bangs and my glasses. My trembling lips. Before he whispers, "I don't. I never did."

What?

He doesn't what?

Before I can figure that out, he goes on to say, "And I want you to know that no matter what I've done," a harsh clench of his jaw, "no matter how I've acted in the past, I'll guard it with my life. Your secret."

Chapter Fifteen

My plan isn't going well.

Not at all.

It's been a week since I came up with it and I have made exactly zero progress.

It's like he has no weaknesses. Like he's impenetrable.

Every morning he emerges from the cottage at the same time. He walks over to the school building with the same purposeful strides and always without sparing a glance for the group of giggling teenage girls who gather around in the courtyard to watch him. He then spends his entire time in the office before breaking for lunch that he gets from the cafeteria. He brings it back to his office, where he eats in solitude while working.

And that's it.

That's all he does. All day.

Well, he does one more thing: he keeps his promise.

Of buying me a brand-new sewing machine.

Purple and way more advanced.

Turns out, there's no specific rule in the St. Mary's manual about owning a sewing machine. Although even if there was, I don't think it would matter much. Because he's the principal, isn't he? The lord and the king. The devil. And I'm his ward. So if he wants to buy me a sewing machine and have it delivered to the dorms, then he can and he does.

As promised, the sewing machine arrives at the dorm reception one afternoon and everyone goes crazy over it. They ask questions and gush over how sleek it looks.

I'm too busy to gush.

I'm busy being all breathless and restless and thoughtless even, to do anything else.

At the fact that he actually followed through.

Not to mention, I told him something so personal. Something so sacred about me.

Him, of all people.

The man I hate. The man I'm supposed to destroy.

How did that even happen?

"I can't believe he did that," Jupiter breathes, sitting beside me on my bed, staring at the pretty purple machine on my desk.

"I know," Echo agrees, also staring at the machine.

"Wow," Jupiter goes. "This is actually a very cool thing to do."

"I think it's more than cool," Echo says while all three of us still stare at the machine. "I think it's epic. Because he did it."

"I think you're right." Jupiter nods before spookily adding my own thoughts, "Him, of all people. *Him.*"

Yeah, him of all people.

"And he told you to not hide," Echo reminds us both.

They're both talking in reverent whispers.

As if taking in the enormity of the gesture. The enormity of what I shared with them just now.

About how I spilled my secret to him when I'm supposed to be working on getting his.

Everything aside, it *was* a very cool thing to do.

It was also a freeing thing.

I've never experienced this kind of freedom before. This kind of weightlessness.

Or relief.

Yeah, I'm relieved.

That I can share this with people. That I can acknowledge the presence of all the sketches in my notebooks and texts. I can acknowledge that I spend almost all of my allowance on thrift stores, and now I have a brand-new sewing machine that's going to make my life so much easier.

"Uh, so," Echo begins, still looking at the sewing machine, "we're still doing it, right? We're still following through with the plan."

"I mean, if you don't want to," Jupiter begins cautiously, "you don't have to."

I know that.

I know I don't have to.

But the thing is that I *do* have to.

"I'm doing it," I tell them firmly even as my heart twists in my chest.

Because it's not as if things have changed now. After our accidental heart to heart.

It's not as if he's ready to let me go.

He hasn't even let go of my detention.

I still go to his office at five every day and I still write that apology while he works on his things — conference papers, guest lectures, presentations; I asked and he told me.

The only difference is that at the end of every detention session, he asks to see my notebook. Every time he does, I get up from my seat, walk around the desk under his scrutiny and hand it over to him. Then I stand there, my hands folded primly in front of me, as I stare at him while he stares at my notebook.

And not at the apology-filled pages, no.

But at my dress designs.

The little doodles on the margins.

Well, they're not little. They're elaborate sketches, but still.

And they're not in the margins. They're at the front and center of mostly every page because I hardly ever take notes in class.

I remember my friend Wyn, who is an artist and has probably hundreds of sketchbooks, told us that her boyfriend, Conrad, likes to stare at her sketches all the time. And she has always felt extremely shy about it. Even now.

I never understood that.

Because I've never really been shy about anything in my life. The more outrageous I am, the better.

Except right now.

Except when I watch him flick through the pages, giving my sketches cursory glances, before settling on one randomly and staring at it for several minutes.

When he does that, I feel my cheeks heat up and a shiver roll through my body.

As if he's staring at me and not at the dresses.

As if those fingers of his, now not as busted as before but still as large and masculine, are running over my skin instead of the sketch. Like he's skimming his ring-sporting pinkie over my collarbones and my shoulders instead of the ones on the piece of paper.

As if he's imagining *me* in those dresses.

And as shy and heated and shivery as I get, I still bring in different notebooks every time so he has more of my dresses to look at.

More of my dresses to touch and imagine.

"So this one is…" I swallow, standing beside him, my toes curled in my shoes, my belly tight. "Sort of like a prom dress. The bodice is fitted as you can see and… these little dots here are sequins. And this skirt here is long and full and shaped like a bell almost. And these little furry things are feathers. See the curled, uneven hem at the bottom? It's because the skirt is going to be lined with feathers. Dark purple. So it's like a dress made of feathers."

He stares at it for a few more moments before lifting his eyes up at me. "What's it called?"

Now in addition to curling my toes and tightening up my belly, I also have to clench my thighs. Because not only are his eyes a deep dark brown, but also he always asks me that.

"Miss Light as a Feather."

Those eyes of his become even darker and deeper and more liquid.

And it happens every time I tell him the name of my dresses — Miss Yellow Buttercup; Miss Pink Me Lemonade; Miss Oopsie Daisies; Miss Tempest in a Teacup — that I know, down to my core, that he loves it.

I may not know anything else about him but I *know* that he loves my dress designs and he loves that I name them.

And all the shyness that I always feel melts away.

My body becomes looser and more relaxed as he keeps staring at me there at the end.

It's the strangest thing.

Like he can *do* things with his chocolate chip eyes.

"I love chocolate chip cookies," I blurt out one day, looking into them.

Those eyes of his narrow slightly. "What?"

"What." I shake my head. "No. I mean, I… I didn't say that."

"I think you did."

I adjust my glasses and accuse, "But only because your eyes look like chocolate chips."

This gives him pause. It gives me pause too.

Because why would I say that?

What was I thinking?

"My eyes look like chocolate chips," he repeats.

I fist my folded hands and decide to ride it out. "Yes. Because they're, you know, brown. Like deep brown."

"Deep brown."

"Chocolate brown, you can say."

"Chocolate brown."

"So it's only a logical connection to make." I shrug. "Your eyes and chocolate chip cookies."

A second of silence passes between us. Then, "My eyes and chocolate chip cookies."

"Stop repeating everything I'm saying."

"But you're saying the most logical things," he says, without missing a beat.

I narrow my eyes at him.

His eyes on the other hand flash and something flickers through his features. Something soft and amused and I'm so awestruck by it that I have to say, "Also I hate you. Just so you know."

"I know."

I lift my chin. "Good. Don't forget that just because I'm being nice to you right now."

"I won't."

"It won't last. This is just the 'break' talking," I insist, even going as far as to do the air quotes around the word *break*.

Exactly.

Because I'm not going to stay this nice when I blackmail him later.

And I don't care.

I don't.

Even if my heart twists every time I think about it.

"A car will come to pick you up this Friday after school," he says out of nowhere. "To bring you back to the mansion."

"What?"

I see his chest move under his tweed jacket on a sigh. "You can spend the weekend with Mo. She'll be happy to see you. She was disappointed when you chose to stay here before the summer session started."

I stare at him, confused.

But only for a few seconds.

After that I'm not confused anymore.

I'm restless and speechless like I have been ever since he gave me the sewing machine.

"But I'm not allowed to go out," I say instead, every part of my body clenched once again.

"Fuck what's allowed."

I stare into his chocolate chip eyes. "Because I'm also your ward."

He stares back.

His perusal lasts longer than mine. And every second that passes while he takes in my face, his features grow sharper, tighter.

Until his jaw becomes clenched and he shuts my notebook with a snap without taking his eyes off me.

Then, "Yes."

With that, he offers me back my notebook. And I take it.

In fact, I snatch to take it from his hands so I can leave.

So I can get out of here.

So I don't blurt out all the things that are going through my head right now. Things like, I hate that he's doing this. I hate that he's making things so difficult.

So hard.

Why can't he just go back to being his old self?

His old devil, tyrant, asshole self.

Why does he have to be so nice to me?

I hastily make my way to the door but before I can open it and get out of here, I turn around. My fingers flex around the handle when I realize that he's watching me.

Sitting in his throne-like chair, glowing in the summer sun that he is actually blocking with his impossibly broad shoulders, he looks like the most beautiful man I've ever seen.

The most beautiful and the most powerful man.

God of a man.

And he is that, isn't he?

At least for me.

Because he holds my fate, my stars, my destiny in the palms

of his hands.

I just wish that my god wasn't a devil.

"Are you going to be there?" I ask, my voice breathy. "At the mansion."

Something moves across my devil's features. Something dark and troubled. Mysterious.

Like all the things about him.

It stays there for a while before clearing off and in the end, he says, "No."

And then I get out of here.

Trying to feel relief about his absence.

But I can't.

I feel a strange disappointment.

But a second later, I forget all that. My brain doesn't have the room for it.

Because I realize that I've made a huge mistake.

By agreeing to go.

Not that he asked me. He simply told me what's going to happen this weekend, but still.

It's a major mistake.

Because this weekend, I'm also meeting Jimmy.

And if *he* found out that I'm sneaking out to see the guy he's forbidden me to see, it's going to be a disaster.

Chapter Sixteen

Can I just say that I hate this bar?

I've always hated it.

It's dark and loud and I don't like the area — dingy and lonely and just straight-up filled with creepy vibes — of Middlemarch it's in. Plus ever since I was sent to St. Mary's, it's also super far away and honestly by the time I get there, I'm so sleepy and tired.

But.

It's a bar where the love of my life is super popular so I suck it up. Plus I'm always so happy to see Jimmy that I try not to think about all the stuff that makes me uncomfortable.

Tonight, however, it's very hard.

Very, very hard.

First is the fact that I'm wearing this ridiculous dress.

Okay, let me backtrack: it's not so much ridiculous as not really my style.

I don't wear such tight dresses. Or such short dresses.

Or dresses that show off so much of my cleavage.

It could look really cute on either Salem or Jupiter. Even Callie I think. Mostly because they have the body type for it, slim and petite. Not Wyn or Echo though. They have a bigger bust.

Not as big as mine, but still.

My breasts are big, yes. My ass too. I have an hourglass figure, with a tucked in and slim waist, which sounds really good in theory but it's so hard to find jeans and skirts that fit both my waist and my curvy curves.

So this isn't the dress for me.

The only reason I bought it is because of its frills adorning the plunging neckline and the hem, which hits me way above midthigh, and *just* under my butt, and large polka dots. I really like large polka dots because mostly I find small ones and I thought it could look good on a skirt that I wanted to make. I never got around to it though. So it's been sitting in my closet and I thought tonight's the night I should wear it.

Because, well, I'm trying to get Jimmy to notice me.

I know he already has — he wants me on the tour and he doesn't want to wait for me anymore — but ever since I found out that he has a tour manager named Erica who commented on my glasses and who also happens to be a beautiful blonde with a huge crush on the love of my life, I have been feeling insecure.

And I thought dressing up like a sex kitten might be a good idea.

I also have gone a little heavier on my makeup and my hair is all poofed up and curled.

Although I do not like how people are staring at me, especially drunk old men.

It's icky, and so instead of being front and center and swaying with the crowd and pumping my hands up and down in support of my musician boyfriend, I'm staying back here, at the far end of the bar, stuck to a wall.

Two walls, actually. I'm tucked away in a corner.

And I have half a mind to leave.

Not only because of the dress, but I can't get rid of the feeling that I'm betraying him.

Him. The other him in my life, my devil guardian.

By being here.

It's ridiculous. Super duper ridiculous.

It's not as if this is the first time I've snuck out to see Jimmy against his wishes. In fact, I've made sure to go see Jimmy as much as possible just because *he* doesn't want me to. It's also not the first time I've snuck out of *his mansion* in order to do so either.

That was the whole reason he sent me to St. Mary's, remember?

And so it doesn't matter that he gave me a sewing machine

which is fucking fabulous and works like a dream, and a weekend worth of freedom.

Plus chocolate chip cookies.

Mo had them ready when I arrived earlier this afternoon and I knew — just *knew* — that he was the one who told her to bake them for me after our stupid, embarrassing conversation.

So this guilt — for the past week and tonight — is ridiculous.

When Jimmy's set is over, I take a deep breath of determination. I'm going to enjoy my time with him and not think about *him*. Besides, Jimmy is leaving for New York in a couple of days so this may be my last chance to see him before I go on tour with him.

Oh, did I mention that I said yes to him? Already?

Yeah, I did.

The very next day after my girls and I came up with the blackmail plan.

I snuck up to the third floor bathroom that's always out of order and so where I hide my cell phone — that I specifically bought to keep in touch with Jimmy — and I texted him yes. I told him I'd love to go with him and that yes, I've always felt what he has felt and I can't wait.

He was so excited about it too.

Since then we've been texting and emailing here and there, whenever I could, and I've decided that tonight, I'm going to kiss him.

Yeah, I'm going to get my first kiss.

The kiss I've been waiting for since the moment I saw him three years ago.

Although he's in rare form tonight: all exuberant and charming. He's high and maybe drunk too, and so I'm not as enthusiastic about my first kiss with Jimmy — or anyone else for that matter — as I thought I'd be.

But it's okay.

It's also important.

Now that we've both sort of acknowledged our feelings for each other, I want to seal the deal. I want to give him something to remember me by until we actually go on the road together. Especially with Erica hanging around.

With that thought, I take a step toward him.

But only a step because I see a wall.

A massive wall of a chest.

Of impossibly broad shoulders.

A wall that's sporting a dark tweed jacket and a dark tie.

And that dark wall is moving toward me.

It's coming, barreling closer, and my eyes jerk up.

Only to clash with another dark thing: his eyes.

Not only dark in color but also of dark intentions.

Angry and dangerous intentions.

So much so that my skin starts to heat up. It starts to sweat and burn.

And then I move back.

As if that will stop him from charging over.

It won't.

I don't think anything can stop it or him.

But even so, I retreat. I go back because holy God, how is he here?

How the fuck is he here?

In this bar.

But more than that, how is he here *for me*?

How is he single-mindedly hurtling toward me like he knew I'd be here?

Just as my spine crashes with the same wall I've been standing against, he reaches me.

He stands a few feet away, like a tower, tall and broad, blocking the entire bar behind him, darkening this corner even more.

Both with his body and the look on his face.

He even mutes all the sounds around him.

"I'm… What…"

A ripple goes through his features, tightening them up, making them even more severe than they were. "Where are your glasses?"

His voice, even though quiet, is like a gunshot, making me flinch.

And also blink.

Because of his odd question. But in the face of his absolute wrath, I answer immediately, "I-I'm wearing lenses."

My answer angers him further and I swear he mashes his teeth together before he asks, "Why?"

"Because I'm… I…"

He takes a step toward me, or at least it feels like it.

Because the corner grows darker, smaller, claustrophobic. The only reason my lungs aren't starving is because the air around us is filled with his scent of leather and cigar, and my body can't breathe it in fast enough.

I can't eat up his scent fast enough.

"Because what?" he asks, his voice low and threatening.

"Because of him," I blurt out. "Because I wanted to impress him."

It's the truth.

I wanted to impress Jimmy.

At my answer, he, my guardian, grows darker. His very skin grows more dusky and flushed.

"Because of him."

I fist my skirt. "Yes."

This is it, isn't it?

This is where it all goes to hell.

My plans of turning the tables on him. My dreams of being with the love of my life.

This is the moment when everything comes crashing down. Everything falls apart.

He knows.

That I've been lying about Jimmy.

I've been found out and God only knows what he'll do to me. God only knows that he'll do every single thing he said he would and I have no chance now.

"And this lipstick," he goes on in the same tone.

I swallow, hiccupping. "A-also for him."

"Name."

"Handmade Heaven."

It's purple but more on the pink side of it, to match my dress.

Which he looks at next.

His eyes lower and I thought — stupidly — that maybe it would give me some relief. To not stare directly into his wrathful devil eyes. But I was wrong.

This is worse.

Because now his devil eyes are taking me in. They're taking in every part of my exposed body.

My collarbones, the slopes of my exposed shoulders in the strapless dress. My deep cleavage. The fitted bodice leading down to a fitted skirt that leaves almost all of my thighs bare.

He's staring at each and every inch and it's making me squirm.

It's making me want to hide myself.

Not because he's the one who's staring at me, no. It's because of *how*.

It's the opposite of how he stares at the dresses I sketch.

I can feel it.

He stares at my design sketches with sort of an awe, with reverence even, and it melts me. It melts all the things inside of me.

Right now though, it's the opposite.

With his face dipped slightly, he's watching me with anger, with hatred and I'm freezing. It's making a chill run down my spine. And I wrap my arms around my waist.

Which makes him jerk his eyes up.

"You make it?"

I shake my head adamantly. "No. I didn't. I don't…" I swallow, fisting the fabric on both sides. "I don't like dresses like this."

"So this is for him too then," he says, a muscle jumping on his cheek.

I nod, unable to say anything.

He stares at me a beat, all tight and angry. Then, "Let's go."

"What?"

"I'm taking you home."

He steps back then, ready to leave.

But I can't.

Not yet.

I'm still struggling to understand how he is even here in the first place, and I want… I want to know what he's going to do to me. I want to know what my punishment is.

"But wait," I call out, stepping away from the wall. "I —"

My words halt when he stops and looks directly at me. I even jerk back, crashing into the wall.

He doesn't say anything though, simply stares at me. Either waiting for me to speak or to snuff out all the words I was going to say with his dark eyes.

But I still forge ahead. "What… What are you going to do?"

It's as if my question triggers something inside of him. Something big and drastic.

Something that really makes him inch closer to me.

That really makes him shrink this corner to the point where

it's just me and him and the two brick walls that I'm plastered against. And we're encased in shadows, shut away from the world where all I can see is him and all he can see is me.

All I can breathe is him and all he can breathe is me.

And all I hear is his words and nothing else.

"What am I going to do," he begins in a soft, rough tone. "You mean, now that I know."

"Mr. Mar —"

"That you've been lying."

I wince, not because he's raised his voice but because he's lowered it. To the point that each word scrapes against my skin. "I-I'm —"

"You were lying, weren't you?" he cuts me off again, inching even closer, dipping his head further, as if trying to box me in. "That night. When you said that you hadn't seen him in three years."

Oh God.

Oh God, I'm going to throw up. I'm really going to throw the fuck up.

"I… Yes."

His chest shudders with an angry breath. "When you assured me that I'd already taken care of it all. That I'd successfully torn you apart from that worthless cocksucking son of a bitch."

My arms have come back around my waist again and my nails are digging into my skin now. "Yes."

"So you really don't want to know what I'm going to do to you," he says. "Or to him."

My eyes go wide.

And without volition, they skirt away from him and go to the boy I love.

Or at least try to but can't.

Because the man in front of me is so massive that the extent my eyes can travel to is his right pectoral. And also because he tells me to.

"Eyes on me," he growls.

A thick animalistic growl.

Which grabs hold of my entire body and squeezes, taking my breath away.

"I… I was —"

"You don't want anything happening to him, do you?" he asks in what I'd think is a casual tone except his words are growled and his eyes are shooting fire.

"No."

"You don't want me to go over there and take his guitar from him, do you?"

"N-no."

"And then break it into pieces."

"Oh God..."

"Before I grab those useless fucking strings and wrap them around his *useless fucking* scrawny neck."

"God, please, I —"

"And when I've really got a grip on it, you don't want me to squeeze and squeeze until his useless *fucking eyes* pop out while you watch, do you?"

At this, I let go of myself and grab his jacket.

I clutch his tweed jacket and look up at him, craning my neck, stretching it to the point of pain. "Please, stop it. I'm begging you, okay? Please."

My pleas make his nostrils flare. "So then you'll keep your eyes on me when I'm talking to you."

"O-okay. I promise. I promise I won't look at J-Jimmy."

He inches closer, pushing his massive body against my fists. "*And* you'll never say his name again."

My knuckles are digging into his boulder-like abdomen as my heart is squeezing and squeezing in my chest. "But I love him. And I just wanted to make him love me and wanna be with me. I've never had that before. And I think he..."

Loves me too.

And I was so close to getting everything that I wanted.

But now he is here.

The devil.

And he'll take everything from me.

"Yeah," he responds to my statement. "Which is why you're dressed like a whore."

This time when I flinch, it's so big and violent that crazily, I'm thankful that I'm holding onto him, to his jacket, for support. Or I would've lost my balance.

As it is, I keep standing and staring up at his furious face, speechless and in pain.

"Isn't it?" he goes on, his own hands fisted at his sides. "For him."

"I'm not…"

"Tell me something," he says, inching closer again, pushing me up against the wall without even touching me. "Does he know?"

"Know what?"

His jaw tics. "About all your men."

"What?"

"That's what you told me, remember? That one night," he reminds me. "That you're quite the seductress. It's all coming back to me now, but it doesn't make sense. If you never stopped seeing your boyfriend here then who were those men, Poe? Does your piece of shit boyfriend know about them? About what you do behind his back. About how many men you've fucked. Or was that a lie too?"

I know he knows.

I know that he knows I was lying.

He's only doing this to humiliate me, to mock me.

He's only doing it because he's angry.

"I was lying, okay? I was lying about that too. I —"

"Right," he cuts me off. "Because you're a stupid little *lying* virgin, aren't you?"

"Mr. M —"

"A stupid little lying virgin dressed up like a whore," he says with clenched teeth.

I flinch again, and again I'm as thankful as I am miserable that he's here.

He's here to save me from falling.

While he keeps kicking me down.

"Actually, not just dressed up," he goes on, mocking me, his eyes flicking up and down quickly, and I grab on to him harder because my knees are shaking. "This stupid little lying virgin fucking went to town and came back looking like handmade heaven."

My lips part then.

When he mentions the name of my lipstick.

And he leans down further, his eyes now on my mouth, making it tremble as he rasps, "Didn't she? She looks like handmade heaven. Like some kind of a goddess that every man wants to worship at the feet of. Every man wants to cause a riot for. But you know what, I don't think you're a goddess. Oh, you definitely look like one, trust me. But I don't think you're as pure as all that. I think you're something else."

He looks me up and down again. "I think, Poe, that in this dress, you're a vixen. You're a fucking siren. Who lures men in with her angelic looks and spreads her thighs to lead them to a kind of hell that feels like heaven. You're that innocent looking librarian, yeah? With her black-rimmed glasses and fan-fucking-tastic tits and a tight skirt. Every time she passes by, you have to look at her. Every time she climbs the ladder to reach up for a book, you have to take a peek under that skirt. Or if she bends down, you have to crane your neck to look at her curvy ass while adjusting yourself under the table. And when it happens over and over and over again, you lose your patience. You lose all your good judgment and abandon your fucking homework or that book you were so engrossed in. You grab your dick and you rub one out under the table. Like a sick, deranged beast of a man. You're that librarian, Poe. Who tempts men astray and turns them into fucking criminals. And all because of your stoner, piece of shit boyfriend."

My whole body is shaking by the time he finishes.

My heart is shaking and I can barely stand up.

I can barely gather my breath after what he just said.

I know his words were supposed to scare me and humiliate me and embarrass me and I am all those things. And I want to smack his face for that. But then I also want to curl up against him. I also just want to hide myself in his impossibly broad chest and sob and sob.

I'm not sure why.

And this urge only grows when he continues, "This ends tonight, you understand? You're not seeing him again. You're not sneaking out. You're not fucking dressing yourself up like a whore and going to a bar where you shouldn't be in the first place because you're underage. Not to mention where guys stare at you like they're waiting to get you alone and tear into you like hungry wolves. Do you understand? Because if you don't and there's any confusion, I want to make it clear that I'll not only deal with you, I'll also deal with him. Which I probably should've done the first time."

My breath catches in my throat. "No, please. Don't."

His eyes turn into slits.

"I understand. I do. I won't see him again. Just don't… Don't do anything to him." When all he does is stare at me silently, I tighten my fists in his jacket. "Please, Mr. Marshall, don't hurt him. I promise I won't see him again. I do. Please."

His features remain so tight and for so long that I don't think he'll ever loosen up again.

I don't think he'll ever lose his anger again.

But he does.

He takes a deep breath and he goes on, "Remember that then."

I jerk out a nod.

"And now," he continues, "I'm going to give you my jacket and you're going to wear it. You're going to walk out of here, all covered up like you should've been in the first place. And then, I'll drive you back and you'll apologize to Mo for making her worry."

That gets my attention and I say, "Mo was worried?"

His jaw clenches. "Enough to call me in the city, yeah."

So she was the one who called him. And he came here.

Which is still extremely unlikely and strange to me. Like, how did he even…

It's as if he can hear my thoughts, he explains in that same growly voice, "This is his regular haunt, yeah? This bar. This is where you used to sneak off to, years ago. So when Mo couldn't find you anywhere and called me in the city, I put two and two together. Thereby chasing after a rebellious teenager and ruining my fucking night."

My breath is coming in and out in bursts and puffs as I absorb his explanation. It all makes sense. Except…

"B-but how did you… know," I ask, my wrist still in his grip. "That this is where I snuck off to."

His abdomen tightens again before he breathes out. "Tracker."

"Tracker?"

"On your phone."

I guess my mind is still too slow to understand him. So it takes me a few seconds of blinking up at him, breathing haphazardly to finally get it.

He put a tracker on my phone.

The one I had when I lived with him.

I left it behind, in Mo's care, when I went to St. Mary's.

So that's how he knew.

About Jimmy and my nightly excursions back then.

I'd always wondered about that. Because like tonight, I'd always been so careful back then as well. So it was a jarring shock when Mo came to me with the news of going away to St. Mary's. But I know now.

It was the tracker on my phone.

I study his features. His carved in stone jaw that makes him look so dominant and authoritative, and his pretty harsh eyes with which he's studying me back.

I want to fight with him. I want to argue but I can't.

I don't have the strength.

Dazed, I watch him take a step back and my hands fall to my side.

He takes his tweed jacket off, revealing his gray dress shirt, starched and stretching against his arched pectorals.

I know that I should reach out for his jacket now.

I should gather enough strength to take it from him and drape it around myself.

But I'm so tired. So exhausted right now.

I can barely stand here or even keep my eyes open.

And maybe it's all clear on my face, my exhaustion, my misery and humiliation, that I don't have to do any of those things.

He doesn't let me.

He steps forward again and then before I can form a thought, he swings the jacket behind me, with tight and snappy movements, and settles it on my shoulders, jerking the collar up.

When he's done, I hunch my shoulders and tighten his jacket, his warmth, around me.

I want to say thank you because I *am* grateful for the cover he's provided.

But the words that come out are totally different.

"Happy birthday."

It's his turn to flinch.

Maybe it was a stupid thing to say.

But it *is* his birthday.

Mo told me this afternoon after *I* told her that it was his idea that I come and spend the weekend at the mansion with her. She also told me that he doesn't like celebrating his birthday. But when I asked her why she did what she always does: shut down, telling me that it's his story to tell and not hers.

I didn't push her but I've been wondering about it ever since. Like I wonder about all the things related to him.

"I know you don't care about your birthday," I continue, "but no one should go without a happy birthday on their special day, so." Then, "I'm sorry I ruined your night. I'm sorry that I've been lying to you for three years. But I only did it because you left me no choice."

That's when I duck my eyes and burrow even further into his jacket. Because that's all. That's all the energy I have.

Now I just want to go home and curl up into myself and disappear.

But he's not done yet.

"You can spend the weekend with Mo as planned but on Monday, we'll talk about your future at St. Mary's."

***

"Are you sure?" Echo asks on a whisper, her eyes wide and concerned.

Which I completely understand.

"Because if you aren't sure, I don't think you should do this," Jupiter adds, her voice equally quiet and her eyes equally wide and concerned.

And again, I understand that.

I understand where they're both coming from.

"I think you should really think about what this could mean," Echo insists.

"This could have really dire consequences. Not only for him," Jupiter explains. "But also for you."

"Yeah." Echo nods urgently. "What if he doesn't go for it? What if this whole plan backfires? What if —"

"Okay, stop," I tell them both in a firm voice, but only a touch above a whisper. "Both of you."

Like the good friends they are, they do.

But their concern is another matter altogether. It doesn't go away and it squeezes my heart.

It shakes my resolve. It makes me think — for the hundredth time since I came up with the plan in that mansion, up in my room, three days ago — that I shouldn't do this.

That this is not only foolish but also dangerous.

This is evil.

This is even more evil than the blackmail plan we'd come up with. More evil than finding his weakness and using it against him.

Because I'm not looking for an existing weakness, I'm creating one.

It's like planting evidence rather than discovering it.

"Look," I begin and they both throw me expectant looks. "I know everything. I've thought about everything. I've run all the scenarios through my head, okay? All the pros and all the cons and…" I sigh, closing my eyes for a second. "There's no other way. I have to do this. I have to take the risk if I want to be… free."

Because in a few hours, he's going to do what he told me he would.

He's going to lock me up here and this time, Mo won't be there as a buffer.

He'll deliver the news personally and break all my dreams forever.

That's why he's called me into his office at five o'clock today.

Hasn't he?

He'd said that we'd talk about my future on Monday — which only means one thing — and Monday is here. Well, for that and also for detention.

Which, according to his note that he had delivered first period, will last until he decides otherwise.

"Okay. Yeah. Yes. I get it," Echo whispers, pulling me out of my thoughts.

Jupiter says, "So what, ten minutes then?"

For a second I can't speak.

Because I'm so overwhelmed.

By their support and easy agreement.

It means more than I can ever say.

I nod, blinking my eyes and getting rid of the moisture. "Yes. Just keep him occupied for ten minutes or so. Make sure that he stays with you. I'll just get in and get out."

Jupiter nods her head with determination. "Okay. I can do ten minutes."

Echo nods. "Yeah." Then sighing too, she throws me a tiny smile. "Good luck."

Then they both get out of the bathroom where we've been huddled in a group and walk in the direction of the cafeteria; we saw him go in for his lunch. And I go in the opposite direction.

Where his office is, and where I'm going to plant a little camera and begin the end.

Chapter Seventeen

I got the camera from Lucy.

Lucy works at the soup counter. And she has always loved my Himalayan crocodile Birkin from Hermès. Or rather, Charlie's Himalayan crocodile Birkin from Hermès that I was bequeathed. I mean, who wouldn't? It's arguably the most expensive handbag to ever exist and was gifted to Charlie by one of her producer boyfriends.

Another thing about Lucy: she has a brother with connections.

The kind that I knew could score me a tiny camera that can stay hidden behind things such as leather-bound books on a bookshelf. And if that bookshelf is haphazardly arranged with no rhyme or reason, that's even better. Because I can then move and arrange things on it to place that tiny camera for the best view and angle without getting caught.

So I put all of these things together: Hermès Himalayan crocodile Birkin in exchange for a camera that I've hidden at a perfect spot on the bookshelf.

I'm not sure why I'm thinking about the camera and its origins when I have other very important things to think about, but I am. I'm also looking out the window directly in front of me.

Or rather looking *at* it.

Because it's all covered up in mist and thick rivulets of rain so all I can really see when I look through it is a blur. And *that's* because it's raining.

Hard.

And ragingly.

It started two days ago. Sometime Friday night when I was asleep.

And it hasn't stopped since.

In fact, it has grown worse.

So much worse that every time the sky lights up with thunder, the whole ground shakes. The windows vibrate and the roof almost caves in. I can hear the wind howling, smacking against the windows right alongside the thick rain.

There has been only one time when something like this has happened.

Up on the roof of his mansion four years ago.

Maybe that's why my heart is thumping right now and every breath I take is shivery and trembling, and I can't stop thinking about that night. The night I had my very first conversation with him.

My devil guardian.

The man who has since trapped me, tormented me. *Controlled* me and left me powerless.

The man who's probably getting ready to do it all over again.

I don't know yet.

He hasn't said anything.

And it's almost time. One hour of detention is almost up, and he has yet to say one word to me.

He sits on his office chair, his head dipped, his eyes lowered and on a book. He looks the same as he always does. Dark curly hair, thick on the top and cut close to the scalp on the sides, pushed back. His eyelashes are curled and so long that they cast shadows on his high and mighty cheekbones.

That bump on his nose that gives him an edge but has such a sad story.

That I'll probably never find out now.

After I do what I've come here to do, I'll lose that chance.

I'll lose any chance of ever getting to know him, getting to know all his secrets.

I'll never know what my mother did to him. Why he doesn't celebrate his birthday. Why he's so angry and grave all the time.

So cold and aloof.

It makes me sad.

But I guess it's just nerves. That's why I'm feeling so strange.

But then again, I've always felt strange and nonsensical things around my guardian.

"Time's up."

His voice breaks my thoughts and I wince.

I clear my throat, grabbing the corner of my notebook. "Uh, would you… Would you like to see it?"

"Yes."

There's no hesitation in his reply.

In fact, it comes even before I finish my question and it makes my heart pound faster. His eagerness.

And it also brings relief.

That he still wants to see it. He still wants to see my sketches after everything.

After he dropped me off at the mansion and I ran up to my room still wearing his jacket, he disappeared. He wasn't there the next morning or throughout the entire weekend. It isn't out of the ordinary, him disappearing whenever I'm around.

But this time, it felt more visceral. More hollow and heavy.

And the fact that Mo was giving me pitying glances wasn't helping matters. She kept telling me that she would talk to him. That she wouldn't give up. Not until he listened to her and promised that he would go easy on me. And I kept telling her that it wasn't her problem.

It was mine.

It *is* mine.

And I'm going to take care of it.

So I ignore the relief, the euphoria that comes with the fact that he still wants to see my designs. It's probably because he's the only one who's seen them, who's made me come out of my shell and share my hobby, my passion even, with the world. And in the past week, I've gotten addicted to showing them to him.

After today, I won't be able to.

But it's okay because I'm gaining so many other things.

Slowly and keeping my eyes on him at all times, I go around the desk and approach his chair. I reach out and offer him my notebook.

But he doesn't take it.

Instead, he turns the chair toward me and, tracing his silver ring-sporting pinkie over his bottom lip, he orders, "Show me your favorite design."

"M-my favorite design."

"Yeah."

I'm not sure why he's asking me this. Or why he's looking at me, watching me with such intense eyes.

But still I glance down at my notebook, ready to do his bidding.

Before I even open it and flick through the pages, I know which one I'm going to pick. It's purely by luck that I brought this notebook with me today because it holds my most favorite dress ever.

When I find it, I give it to him and this time, he takes it without hesitation. When he dips his face to look at it, I go closer as well.

So much so that the toes of our shoes touch.

And for some reason, it feels like such an illicit thing, such a forbidden thing, our shoes touching, that I have to grab my skirt.

I have to fidget with my glasses as I say, "So this is an evening gown and it's all dark purple. It has netted full sleeves and a deep V in the front. That's also covered by this thin netting and…"

I have to take a pause here because he runs his pinkie over the deep net-covered cleavage — it's even deeper than the dress that I wore on Friday, going down almost to the belly button and all covered by this thin gossamer-like netting — caressing the hills, the valley between the breasts.

And I swear to God, I feel it on my own skin.

I feel his finger skimming the valley between my breasts.

I even arch them up as I stand here, all shameless and restless. My breasts feel heavy, my nipples all tingly.

"Matches what?" he prods, still staring down at the dress.

It's hard to pull myself away from these rioting sensations and his phantom fingers but I do it. "It, uh, matches the back in the same way. It plunges down all the way to the small of the back and it's covered by netting also."

There's another sketch depicting that and he takes his time absorbing that as well.

To banish the tingling that is now in the small of my back, I keep pushing forward. "And then the bodice is studded with sequins and —"

"Your favorite," he murmurs.

Making me swallow. "Yeah."

"Along with polka dots." I go to confirm that but he continues murmuring, "And suede." Another pause for a second before, "And of course, purple."

And now I can't even make myself nod to confirm.

That yes, these are the things I love. These are my favorite things.

Things that I've never shared with anyone before.

Except him.

My enemy.

He somehow knows me more than anyone else in my life. He knows me the best.

"What's it called?" he asks, his dark head bent, his chocolate chip eyes on the page.

"Troubled Sweetheart," I whisper.

At this, he finally lifts them, his eyes. "Troubled Sweetheart."

"I named it after a lipstick shade," I tell him because I want him to know, because he's already proven that he'll understand. "Purple, of course. I love how it's tight all the way down but then the hem spreads out like a train. Only in a big wavy circle. Not to mention, it's sexy with all these deep plunges and Vs but then the netting gives it more of a classic, understated, innocent vibe."

And as always now that I've started talking about it, about my design, I find that I can't stop. I go even closer, the tips of our shoes pressing against each other as I lean over and put my finger on the page myself.

"Oh, and this matching headpiece? It's sort of like a dark halo, you know? So it's angelic but not really because it's dark. So it's a play between a troublemaker and a sweetheart. Hence Troubled Sweetheart." I smile slightly, staring at my own design. "I haven't decided on the fabric yet. I'm torn between something super smooth and silky, and something more shimmery. So organza or chiffon, maybe? But yeah. It's my dream dress. Because I think it's my most daring design yet. I'd love for someone to wear it one day. Somewhere." Then, "Like on a runway or something."

I freeze as soon as I say it.

Also, blush.

I don't even know *why* I say it.

I guess it's already been established that I say the most outrageous things to him, but still. This is beyond that.

This is beyond outrageous and fantastical.

I mean, yes, I love designing dresses. And the joy of designing dresses lies in the fact that one day someone will wear your creation. Which is why I gift most of the dresses I make.

And okay, so maybe I've thought about having other people — people who aren't my friends — wearing these. While they catwalk on a runway.

But.

It doesn't mean that I have an active desire to do so. Mostly because it's crazy hard. It's crazy hectic. It's crazy *crazy*. And I don't have it in me to accomplish something like that when I can barely sit through a class or graduate high school without butting heads with my guardian turned principal.

"You will."

His firm words make my eyes snap up to his and I realize how close we are.

How close his chocolate chip eyes are to me.

With me bent over him like this, we're breathing each other's air. Or rather I'm breathing his. I'm breathing whatever he gives me through his parted lips.

I suck it in, all his oxygen laced with leather and smoke, and fill my lungs with it.

With his uncanny belief in me. I've never had that before.

It's addicting.

He is addicting.

Drugged, I whisper, "It's raining like it was that night. Four years ago."

His jaw clenches for a second, something flickering in those eyes. "Yeah."

"I was praying for a miracle. Up on that roof," I tell him. "I was praying for a god maybe."

Another clench. "But you didn't get Him."

"No, I got you."

"The devil."

With dark hair and dark eyes.

Standing there with an umbrella and my glasses.

My newly appointed guardian.

And now he sits here, his eyes just as dark and pretty, his curly hair still rich and thick. Only somehow he's more powerful.

He's more potent and all-knowing.

Somehow, I'm more trapped under him than I was before.

"I thought," I continue, looking into his intense eyes, "that if I made my argument well enough, you'd see reason and let me go."

"But I didn't."

"And then here at summer school, I thought the same. I thought if I came up with a solution, you'd have to let me out early."

Dark things flicker through his features before he says, "You were naive."

"I was."

"So now what?"

"It's Monday."

"It is."

"You said we'd talk about my future."

"I did."

My heart thumps. "So what's my future?"

"Whatever I want it to be."

My heart thumps harder. "And what do you want it to be? What will you do to me?"

He takes a few seconds to answer. In those few seconds, I both live and die, and melt and freeze.

Waiting and waiting for him to say the words.

To deliver the verdict so I can retaliate.

"Is it over with him?"

My fingers flex at his sudden question and I realize that the notebook is still open between us and my fingers are still pointing at things, things we're both not looking at or caring about right now.

I want to move away then but I can't for some reason.

So suspended over him, breathing his air, I lie, "Yes."

"You sure about that?" he asks again, his voice low.

"Yes." I nod, my heart heavy. "I don't want you to do anything to Ji —" His eyes narrow at my slip up and I correct myself. "Him."

My assurance — even though that's what he wanted — makes his body go tighter. It makes his features grow meaner. "What a perfect girlfriend you are, huh." Then, slowly and roughly, with clenched teeth, "What a perfect *fucking* girlfriend."

My heart twists in my chest at the bitterness in his tone, and I whisper, "I don't wanna talk about that."

"Yeah? Then what do you want to talk about?"

"About you."

"What about me?"

My heart in my throat, I whisper, "I want something from you."

"You want something from me."

"Yes. Before you lock me up here." My fingers flex on the page again, the toes of my Mary Janes pressing against his Italian loafers. "That's what you're going to do, aren't you? You're going to lock me up here, at St. Mary's, for a long, long time."

This time, he pushes back.

I feel the hard, sharp tips of his loafers pressing back against the softly rounded toes of my Mary Janes. And it makes my thighs clench, that pressure.

"For all your lies, you mean," he rasps.

"Yes. So I want you to do something before you put me away for a long time. Sort of like my last wish."

Again, he leaves me hanging for his response. And again, in those few seconds I live and die a thousand times.

Then with a ticking jaw, he asks, "And what's your last wish?"

This is it.

This is fucking it.

This is the moment. This is how I get back my freedom and my control.

This is how I trap him.

"A kiss," I say. "My last wish is for you to give me my first kiss."

And when he does, the camera sitting on his bookcase will record it.

It will record Alaric Rule Marshall kissing Poe Austen Blyton.

But that's not all, is it?

It will record Mr. Marshall, the guardian, kissing Poe Blyton, his ward.

Not to mention, it will record Principal Marshall kissing Miss Blyton, his student.

And that's evidence.

That's the weakness that I've been searching for for the past week, and it's a weakness that I'm going to use against him when the time comes.

Chapter Eighteen

He could lose everything.

He could lose his conferences, his papers, his research, his entire reputation that he's worked so hard for. Not to mention his city council duties and everything else that he's involved in.

It makes me want to take my words back.

And that urge only grows when at my words, he licks his lips and glances down to mine.

But that's not all.

That's not all that happens.

There's more.

Right alongside this surge of guilt, I feel a surge of something else. Something fiery and tingly.

Something that makes my thighs clench again, and my belly throb, and then he moves and I lose all my breaths and thoughts.

At first it feels like he's leaning into me, his Italian loafers pushing against my Mary Janes, making me step back. And I think he's going to do it.

He's going to grant me my wish and kiss me.

And everything is going to be captured by the camera and oh my God, I should warn him.

I should fucking tell him that he shouldn't.

He should not kiss me.

He should absolutely not kiss me or he's going to be in so much trouble.

But then I realize that he's not leaning into me, it only looks like it because he's coming to his feet. He's leaving his chair and he's standing up. And because I'm so close to him, I get pushed back.

I get pushed further back when he takes a step toward me.

When he keeps doing it.

And suddenly, I've found myself, my ass, at the edge of his desk.

At which point, I'm thinking and assuming that he'll stop.

But he doesn't.

He backs me up even more. To the point where I have to make room for him, for his large muscled body and something mysterious that's dripping from his dark eyes as he watches me.

And the only way to do it, to make room, is to get up on the desk. To actually sit on his papers and things.

To even lean back a little because he won't stop coming at me.

Not until he's got both his hands splayed wide on his desk and on either side of me.

Not until his eyes are right there, staring at me from this close.

So close that I'm drowning in them.

That I actually taste the sticky, sugary and bitter chocolate on my tongue.

But then he takes away all my thoughts *and* my glasses in the next second. I didn't even know he was going to do that until things behind him become all blurry.

"W-what are you doing?" I ask, looking back at him.

He's not blurred out though.

He's clear. He's the only clear thing right now in fact.

"Taking away your glasses," he replies.

"But I-I can't see anything."

"You don't need to see anything."

"What? I —"

"Anything other than me," he rasps, his eyes penetrating.

I swallow.

Feeling trapped and dominated. Feeling… thrilled.

Stupidly.

"So your first kiss, huh," he rasps again, and lightning flashes in the sky behind him.

Making me realize that the sky is falling just outside this office.

That the rain is coming down even harder, battering against the windows like my heart is battering against my rib cage.

But I don't care.

All I care about is him. All I can *see* is him.

And what's more, all I want to see is him.

I lick my dry lips and grab the edge of the desk. "Yes."

"Because you can't get it from your boyfriend now, can you?"

"No."

"Because it's over with him."

"Yes."

He takes me in with those bright eyes of his. "And because you're going away for a long, long time, you want me to do the honors."

"Yes," I whisper, hiccupping. "Because I've waited for it. I've waited three years for it and every time I think I can get it, you do something. You stop it from happening. You steal it."

"I steal it."

I nod, my nails digging into the wood. "Yes. I wanted to kiss him three years ago but I couldn't. Because you sent me away. And I wanted to kiss him last Friday but you —"

Something akin to satisfaction, cruel and dark, flashes across his features. "But I came in and ruined all your plans."

He did.

"So you owe me that kiss," I tell him. "You owe me my first kiss."

His lips pull up sharply in a mockery of a smile. "The devil owes you a kiss."

"Yes."

My nails dig into the wood harder.

Because I've thought about that. I've thought about the devil kissing me.

How could I not?

I've been waiting for my first kiss for three years now. And I never thought that I'd be getting it from someone else, someone other than Jimmy.

So yeah, I've thought about it and I'd decided that I would make this sacrifice. For us.

I'd make the sacrifice of getting my first kiss from someone else if it meant getting to be with Jimmy.

But God, *God*, now that the moment has arrived, this doesn't feel like a sacrifice.

It doesn't feel anything like a sacrifice at all.

He hums. "I suppose the devil could arrange that." A pause, then, "For his harpy."

At once, my breath freezes and my heart skips a beat. "So you're… you're going to do it? You're going to kiss me?"

He cocks his head to the side as if studying me from a different angle. "On one condition."

"What?"

He glances down at my lips and I have to lick them under his scrutiny. "That I get to do more."

"More what?"

He looks up at my question, his eyes turned dark in a split second. "More than kissing."

Lightning flashes again and lights up the room, which makes me realize that it has gone dark. That the black clouds have overtaken the sky and turned it all gray and menacing.

Exactly like he's done.

Exactly like how his rough words and his black eyes have suddenly turned this principal's office into some kind of an underground lair.

So much so that despite myself, I lean further back and whisper with wide eyes, "What's more than kissing?"

He notices my fear — God, does he — and that plush mouth of his pulls up in a small smirk that hits me right in my belly. And it hits me so hard that I clench it and grip the desk even harder so I don't fall down.

Although I don't think he'll let me go anywhere.

I think he'll pull me back, give me some anchor to hold on to so I stay here.

Where he wants me.

And I'm proven correct in the next breath when he steps even closer to me and *really* gives me something to hold on to.

His thighs.

His powerful, muscular thighs that he settles between my spread ones, opening them up further. And like a magnet, my limbs attach themselves to his. My thighs go flush with his and hold on.

The very first touch between us. Or rather the very first intimate touch between us.

It should feel wrong.

It should feel inappropriate for so many, many reasons. I didn't even want to touch him.

But it doesn't.

"What's more than kissing, Poe," he rasps, making me dig my heels in his thighs harder, "is fucking."

I lose my balance then.

Or at least it feels like it.

That my stomach bottoms out, my heart tips and I'm free falling, and my hands fly away from the desk and grab his tweed jacket to find purchase.

But in reality, I'm here.

I'm sitting on his desk, my thighs wrapped around his body. And he's right in front of me, leaning over.

So clear, so close.

So much so that if he comes any closer, our eyelashes will tangle with each other.

Our noses will bump.

And God, my fucking God, if they do, if our noses bump against each other, I'm going to kiss it.

I know I'm going to kiss that little imperfection on his nose. I'm also going to lick it.

I have to.

"F fucking," I whisper.

"Yeah," he says, his breath wafting over my mouth. "You know what that is, don't you?"

I taste his scent on my tongue. "Yes."

"Yeah, I figured. Since you talk about it a lot."

"I —"

"Which makes me think that you must be really hard up for it."

"I'm not."

"No?"

I grip his jacket tighter. "No."

He takes in my face with glinting eyes. "Liar." Then, before I can say anything to that he whispers, "Poor little Poe. Can't stop lying, can she?"

It makes my body jerk.

His words, both tender and derogatory, make me arch up

against him even more. "But you…"

"But I what?"

I draw in a hiccupping breath. "You can't fuck me. You can't."

His eyes flash. "You should've thought of that when you asked the devil to kiss you. Because a kiss is never just a kiss." He inches ever so close and I swear the tips of our noses touch. "At least, a kiss is never just a kiss, Poe, when *I'm* kissing you. So too late now. You're also getting your first fuck before I let you walk out that door."

"But it's wrong," I say, shaking my head vehemently.

"Yeah? Why?"

I can't think of a reason.

Why can't I think of a reason?

I know there are a million reasons why he can't. I knew them all just a moment ago.

But for the life of me, I can't think of a single one right now. And the fact that I'm clinging to him like he's my lifeline is not helping.

"Because you're my guardian," I blurt out then, the first thing that comes into my head.

Even though as I say it, I know I really don't care.

Who *cares*?

His eyes flash again. "You're eighteen now, aren't you?"

"Y-yes."

"So you don't need a guardian," he rumbles. "Do you?"

"No."

"So problem solved then."

"You're also my principal," I say next, again knowing that it doesn't matter to me.

Not at all.

Why doesn't it matter?

What the fuck, Poe?

Why doesn't anything matter right now, except him and his eyes and his words and his scent and heat.

"Yeah," he whispers, nodding slightly. "That could be a problem."

I tighten my thighs around him as if I don't want him to move away. "It c-could?"

"Uh-huh. You don't think so?"

No.

That's the first thing my brain screams.

But my mouth is still catching up and all that comes out is some sputtering and stumbling that even I can't make any sense of right now. "I'm… I-I… You —"

"Actually, you're right," he says, cutting me off, as if he understood everything I just said. "It shouldn't be a problem. Plenty of principals fuck their students, don't they?" He doesn't seem to want my answer though because he goes on, "They do. All the time. In exchange for better grades, extra credit, no detention. Now, we both know that I'm not going to give you a better grade or let you out of detention, let alone let you out of summer school. So how about I promise to give you more privileges and let you out of your cage every other weekend."

Again, words fail me and all I can do is sputter and stumble upon them. And again, he doesn't need me to be coherent as he continues, "The door is closed and I can find a way to shut your mouth and keep you quiet. Because if my assumptions are correct, then you, Poe, are going to fucking purr like the wildcat you are. So we're safe here. In my office."

And that's it.

That's the reason.

Because we're really not.

We're not safe.

I've made it so. I've made it so that even inside these four walls, in his office that's essentially his sanctuary, there's a threat looming over him.

And that threat is me.

That's why he can't. Not because he's my guardian or my principal or any of those stupid reasons. It's because I'm planning to ruin his life.

I need to tell him.

I need to. I have to.

I can't let this go on. I need to stop this.

But for some reason, words get stuck in my throat and I say something else altogether. "H-how will you keep me quiet?"

At my question, I feel a shudder going through his body.

I feel his chest jerk slightly and I hear the papers crinkling. Making me think that he may be clenching his fingers around them like I'm clenching mine around his jacket.

Making me think that he may need as much purchase in this

moment as me.

So I scoot down even more and tighten my thighs around his hips to give him that.

To keep him with me.

"I'll stuff your mouth with something that'll shut you up," he rumbles.

"Something like what?"

He gazes down at my trembling lips. "I know what I'd like to plug your mouth with. But since I'll have a better place to stick it, I'll just use your panties."

"My panties?"

"Yeah. I'll wad them up real nice and put them in your mouth so no one can hear you scream."

I squeeze my thighs again, actually feeling the fabric of my panties against my skin. My core.

That's pressed up against him so snugly.

"I'm —"

"You're wearing them, aren't you?"

"I am, yes."

Papers crinkle again.

"Good. Because you know what they call girls who don't wear panties to the principal's office, don't you?"

"What?" I whisper, already knowing the answer somehow.

And he knows that I know. He *knows* it and so his voice turns all soft and tender as he replies, "Desperate little whores."

I jump at his filthy words.

At his *gentle* words.

Not like the ones he said to me back at the bar when he was all angry and enraged at seeing me wearing a tight dress for Jimmy, no.

These words are endearments.

Or at least that's what they feel like in this moment.

An endearment that we share and God, I love it.

How is it that I love this?

"You know that, don't you, Poe?" he prods.

And I nod. "Yes."

"Only desperate little whores wear nothing underneath their school girl skirt as they sit and writhe in front of their principal."

"I-I wasn't writhing."

"Good. That's good too." He nods. "Because if you were, Poe, if you were writhing and leaking on my leather chairs, I'd make you clean it up with your mouth. I'm not a big fan of messes, you see."

I swear at his words, I *do* leak.

I feel a drop of my juice sliding out of my core and seeping into my panties, the ones that he's going to stuff my mouth with so no one can hear me scream.

"But your leather-bound books are always strewn about and messy," I tell him.

"And if you ever leaked on them, I'd make you lick that up too."

My eyes go wide and I lick my lips.

Which makes him clench his jaw.

Hard.

As hard as he's clutching the papers because I think I heard something rip just now.

"But you won't, will you?" he rumbles.

"No."

"Because you're not a whore."

"I'm not."

Oh God, but I am. I so am.

I so want to be.

"You only act like one," he says, and then his eyes narrow. "Like you did Friday night."

I jerk again.

But this time it happens because I remember something.

Something that I shouldn't bring up but is probably written all over my face because his narrowed eyes turn into slits and he growls, "What?"

"Nothing."

He leans closer, pushing me with his body and I arch up even more, my toes curling in my Mary Janes. "Poe."

"You'll get mad."

"I'm already mad."

"But I —"

"Spit it out."

"I wasn't wearing any," I blurt out, my voice high. "Friday night. I wasn't wearing panties. O-or a bra."

He stills.

His chest stops breathing and I tug on his jacket.

I pull him closer with my thighs, realizing that in the process I've hiked up my skirt and now my thighs are shamelessly exposed. But in the face of all the other things, I don't pay it more than half a second of attention.

My entire focus is him.

And this anger radiating out of him.

Before I can soothe it or do something about it, he growls, "For *him*."

I shake my head again. "No. It was just the dress. It was super tight and not made for panty lines or —"

"You're right," he cuts me off, a vein standing on his temple. "I'm mad."

"But I swear it wasn't for Ji—"

"If you want me to keep my promise," he cuts me off again, "the one I made to you Friday night about not touching your punk-ass boyfriend, you'd better never say his name again. Not in front of me."

"Mr. Marshall, I —"

"You know what, fuck it," he growls and this time when I hear a page rip, I can see his biceps vibrating. "Fuck promises. I'm going to fuck him up regardless. I'm going to break every bone in his body even though I know it won't be enough. It won't be *fucking enough* for all his crimes. For looking at you. For making you lie and sneak out and break all the rules for him. For making you fall in love with him and giving up your purple polka dot heart to him. Even though he doesn't fucking deserve it."

My heart has never raced as hard as it does in this moment.

My breaths have never been this choppy and uneven and frantic.

And there's never been a stinging pain in my chest, behind my eyes.

And all of it is because of him.

Because how he looks right now, all angry and tight, vibrating and pulsating. "Mr. Marshall, I think —"

"And once I've taken that, once I've taken your first kiss and your first fuck, I'm going to send you to him," he bites out, "with your mouth all swollen from my kisses, and your thighs covered in blood."

I twist my hands in his jacket. Only I realize that it's not his jacket anymore. It's his shirt.

Somehow my hands have migrated from his tweed jacket to

his dress shirt and now my knuckles are digging into his abdomen. His tight and ridged abdomen, and only a layer of clothing separates my skin from his.

Only a layer of clothing separates my skin from his fiery heat.

"There will be blood, won't there?" he asks then.

I rub my thighs against his hips, his soft tweed jacket, as I nod. "Yeah."

He looks down then.

At my hiked-up skirt, my naked thighs.

It's not all the way pulled up but it's enough to know that the hem is there.

Right where if it got pulled up even a micro-inch, he'll get a peek at my panties.

And I so want him to.

I so want my skirt to hike up even more so he can see.

The panties he was going to put in my mouth.

He lifts his eyes. "Because you're a virgin."

"I am."

"You were saving it for him."

"Yes."

A flash of violence on his features. "Not anymore, you're not."

"Mr. Marshall, please."

"Because I'm the one who deserves it, don't I? I'm the one who's given you a roof over your head. I'm the one who's been keeping an eye on you for the past four years. I'm the one who's running around town, going to dingy bars to fucking chase you down. I'm the one ruining my goddamn nights because you don't know how to fucking follow a *fucking* rule. So you're wrong, Poe, you owe me. You owe me because you dressed up for some other guy, looking like handmade heaven on *my* godforsaken birthday."

"I'm sorry."

He grits his teeth. "Not as sorry as I'm going to make you now."

I believe him.

I absolutely fucking believe him when he says he's going to make me sorry.

But it's okay.

It's okay because…

"It's for your birthday," I say my thought out loud.

Something moves over his features. "Yeah."

"And you never celebrate your birthday."

That something thickens over his features, casting a shadow over them. "It's not worth celebrating."

My hands leave his abdomen and fly over to his face. I sink my fingers in the stubble of his harsh jaw, my whole body sighing, breathing as if I was holding my breath all this time.

All through four years.

I never took a breath.

But now I am.

I'm breathing. My fingers are breathing.

My heart is breathing because I'm touching him.

Unabashedly. Without reservations.

I move my thumb over his sculpted jaw, memorizing the feel of it, the heat. "Everyone's birthday is worth celebrating. *Everyone's.* Even yours."

His jaw moves under my palms. His nostrils flare as he says, his tone low and belligerent, "So what, you'll let me do it then? You'll give up your virginity as your birthday gift to me?"

Yes.

My heartbeats explode at the thought. At what I'm feeling right now.

All these tumultuous emotions.

All this longing and these urges that I've never felt before.

I don't know what to do with them. These feelings.

I mean, I'm in love with someone else and now I want…

Oh God.

Oh my God.

No, no, no. I can't.

And even as these conflicting feelings are filling every space in my body, my fingers won't stop touching him. My fingers travel up and touch that bump on his nose. "I… I'm…"

He shudders at my touch.

Violently and savagely.

So much so that his forehead finally drops over mine and he growls, "Time's running out, Poe."

I roll my forehead against his. "M-Mr. Marshall, I —"

He shudders again. "Will you or won't you? Will you let me send you to him or not? Will you let me send you to your punk-ass boyfriend with your thighs bloody and dripping so you can tell him? So you can tell him who got there first."

"I'm —"

"Who got in there first. *Who* got in your pussy first," he growls.

My channel spasms, making a mess of my panties. My heart spasms too.

Because I know what he's asking.

He's asking what he did four years ago.

And back then I was this fourteen-year-old girl who was so angry at him, so hurt by his actions that she just wanted to hurt him back, and so I'd refused. Now though, I'm an eighteen-year-old girl who is still angry and hurt, yes, but I find that I can't hurt him back.

I don't know how or why this happened but it did. Maybe it happened in the past week when I'd show him my designs and he'd give me this space, *this safe space*, to talk about them. Maybe it happened when I realized how much he believes in me and my work that I never even thought was work.

Or maybe it happened when he made me that tea.

Things changed.

I was wrong before.

They *have* changed between us, and so I have to give him the answer he wants.

I press my fingers on his face, his sharp bones cutting into my palms as I whisper, "Alaric. Alaric got in my pussy first."

His eyelids flutter closed, almost as if in relief.

A gusty breath escapes him. Even his shoulders loosen up a little.

And I dig my fingers harder on his face, relieved myself.

So relieved that my four-year-long stupid stubbornness is over.

But the hard part is only beginning.

Because I'm going to have to tell him. I'm going to have to confess what I did. So I begin, "I won't though."

"What?"

"I won't tell him. I won't tell anyone what we do in here," I say, shaking my head. "What you do to me. I can't. Because Alaric, I —"

"Doesn't that defeat the whole purpose though?"

"What?"

He studies my face for a second, his eyes shimmering.

With something mysterious.

But then it goes away and instead, a shutter falls in them. It falls on his face as well.

And in the next second, he moves back.

I don't even know how it happens.

Because I was all wrapped around him. I was touching him and holding him close with my body.

But now he's standing at a distance — not so much where I can't see him without my glasses but still at a point where there's no touch between us — looking all aloof and harsh.

Untouched.

As if my fingers weren't feeling him, tracing his skin, his face, reveling in it, after four long years.

"That's the whole purpose of this, isn't it?" he says, his tone strangely formal and cold.

"Purpose of what?" I ask, somehow having enough presence of mind to close my thighs and push down my skirt.

Not that he glances at my actions. His eyes — devoid of anything really — are planted on me.

"This whole charade," he explains. "Your camera."

At this, I once again think that I'm falling. My stomach bottoms out and my heart tilts and pitches. But in reality, I'm still sitting there, on his desk, my hands back to gripping the edge of it.

"W-what?"

"I'm assuming showing it to people is a part of it," he says, his voice low but again like his eyes, devoid of any real emotion. "The purpose of planting the camera."

"H-how…"

"How did I find out?" He guesses correctly. "You're not as smart as you think you are. Neither are your friends."

I slide down the desk then. I'm not sure if it's the right thing to do because as soon as my feet touch the ground, my knees buckle. But I have to.

I have to stand and bridge this three-step gap between us.

But his next words stop me.

"And you're not the first girl to try to make a fool out of me." Then, "Although I do have to say that your mother was a better actress than you are."

All my breaths freeze. My heartbeats freeze.

A chill runs down my spine, making my skin coarse with

goosebumps.

"What?"

The clench of his jaw is the only indication that he's feeling something. That there's something going inside of him.

That he's not dead or wooden.

"There's a thing in acting called committing to the moment. Well, it's a general term and can be used for just about anything. But in acting it means giving yourself to the role you've signed up for. It means committing to it, taking it to the end, seeing it through." Another jaw clench. "Next time, when you play a part, try to stick to it. You want to seduce the principal, then fucking seduce the principal. You want to play him, you fucking play him. Next time, Poe, smile at the fucking camera when you spread your legs for me."

I shiver.

My legs throb.

I open my mouth to say something but he keeps going, "So it's more convincing to people, yeah? That the tyrant principal of a school is seduced by a siren of a teenager. As it is, if I didn't know about the camera already, your bad acting would've given you up."

"Please, let me explain, okay? I —"

"So what was the plan?" he asks, cutting me off. "Get me to kiss you, record it and then what? Show it to the world?"

He waits then.

And I know this could be my chance to explain things to him. Not that it would make anything better at this point, but I realize that I can't speak.

I realize that I'm too shaken, too shivery, too fucking miserable to say anything.

To *do* anything but stare at him through my tears.

"Or maybe not," he goes on in the face of my silence. "Maybe you wanted to keep it. As evidence."

I flinch and give myself away.

"So that was the plan then," he says, his voice still wooden and without feeling. "To use it against me as blackmail."

At this point, I'd rather have him angry.

I'd rather have him screaming at my face, snapping at me, punishing me and hurting me.

But he doesn't.

He simply stands there, all shut down and apart.

A tear streams down my cheek and I jerk out a nod. "Yes." At my lonely yes, more tears come and I say it all. "I was going to record it and then use it to get what I want. To get my money. All of it, even the chunk I was going to get when I turn twenty-one so I didn't have to deal with you anymore. So I could just get out of your life and have you out of mine."

It's true.

I wasn't going to stop with only getting half of my money. I was going to demand all of it so I never had to see his face again.

Just the thought makes me ache so much that I have tightened up my whole body so I can keep standing.

Because there's more.

"But that's not all," I say, tears streaming down my face. "I also wanted to run away with him. To go on the road. He's going on tour in a couple of weeks and… I wanted to go with him. And I knew that you wouldn't let me. So I came up with a plan. I came up with a plan to befriend you. To make you trust me. That's why I came up with the whole 'taking a break' idea. So you could tell me all your secrets. So you could confide in me and I could use your secrets against you. But then I couldn't find anything. I couldn't… So I came up with this idea. Of creating evidence against you. I was going to convince you to kiss me. And then when you did, I was going to blackmail you with it. But the thing is…"

I take a deep breath, or try to, but it turns into a broken sob. "I couldn't. When the time came, I couldn't make myself do it. I couldn't…" Another sob. "No matter how much I hate you and how much you control me and take all the things away from me, I could never ruin your career. I could never ruin something that I know you've worked and you *work* so hard for. I've never met anyone like you, Alaric. So dedicated and hardworking. I don't even know how you do it, all these things that you do. So yeah, I've never met someone like you. Someone so fucking alone and tortured and mysterious. Someone with so many secrets. Someone so intelligent and smart and so fucking intellectual. But more than that I've never met someone who believed in me. Someone who made me feel so confident in my own abilities. Someone who set me free. You set me free, which is…"

I chuckle and sob as I go on, "Which is fucking ridiculous because you're the one who trapped me here, but I've never felt this free in my entire life. This past week, I… I got so addicted to showing you my designs and talking about them and making them. I've never sketched so much in my life before and it's all because of you. And I… I could never ruin you. I could never ruin the man who gave me myself. Who changed things for me. Because you did. You *changed* things. Between us."

I wish I could stop crying so I could look at him.

So I could see him clearly.

But I just can't stop my tears. I can't stop feeling so stupid and foolish and so fucking evil for even thinking about doing this to him. Not to mention, what he said about Charlie back there.

I don't know what it means but I know that it doesn't sound good.

It sounds bad.

Very, very bad.

"Get out."

At his low command, my breath seizes and I stare at his blurry form, my chest heaving.

"Get the fuck," he repeats, his voice laced with so much venom that I feel it dripping over my skin, "out."

And then I'm leaving.

I'm running out of there.

Because I've never felt this kind of hate before.

I've never felt this kind of anger.

Not even from him.

***

I pound my fists at the big brown door urgently.

I think I'm hurting myself, my fists, my knuckles but I don't know how to stop.

I don't know how to stop crying either.

So I keep going until the door flies open and Mo's sleepy, concerned face stares at me.

Immediately, a frown appears between her smooth brows and her eyes go wide. Stepping over the threshold, she asks, "Poe? What are you doing here? Why are you crying?"

I hiccup. "M-Mo."

Her concern grows at my broken voice and in the next breath, I find myself surrounded by her arms. "What happened, sweetheart? What's wrong?"

I clutch onto her warm, motherly body. The kind that I've never known before and say, "I-I did a bad thing."

"Oh, honey." She squeezes me. "What happened? What did you do?"

I burrow my face in her neck, clutching her harder as I confess, "I made him hate me even more."

Part III

The Guardian + His Doe-Eyed Diva.

Chapter Nineteen

I watch Mo pour tea in a white ceramic mug and dunk the tea bags.

It reminds me of the night when he made me tea and it causes such a pain in my chest that I whisper, "You don't have to be so nice to me."

Standing across from me at the small island in the kitchen, she smiles. "I know." Then she looks up and winks at me. "But I like doing it." I give her a small smile as she pushes the tea toward me with a stern order of, "Drink."

Sniffling, I bring my legs up on the barstool and wrap my fingers around the warm mug.

After I showed up at the mansion crying like a lunatic, Mo ushered me in. And as soon as I stepped in, my knees gave out and I dropped to the ground with Mo's arms still around me. So we sat there for a while in the foyer while I sobbed on her chest.

When I calmed down, I told her the first pressing thing as to how I got here: I snuck out of school, got a cab and asked to be driven out to the mansion. Which led me to tell her all the times that I have snuck out in the past, and how I have a cell phone and a credit card that I sometimes use, petty cash from my allowance that I'd saved up over the years and whatnot.

After confessing those crimes and making her sigh and shake her head with worry, I confessed the one that had really brought me here.

The one that wouldn't let me sleep. The one that would probably haunt me for a long time, for the rest of my life even.

How far I'd fallen. How far I was willing to go to hurt him.

I told Mo everything. And I didn't mince my words or gloss over any detail. I told her how long I'd been planning this blackmail thing. I told her why I'd been planning it, and how it came to me last Friday that I could create evidence instead of discovering it.

I expected her to kick me out by the end of it.

I really did.

I know Mo loves him. She loves him like her own son and it's very apparent to see. And I'm not going to lie, I've felt jealous of him for it. For the fact that there's someone who loves him like that.

Moreover, I'm also not going to lie that I've felt happy for him too.

I know what it feels like to be unloved and despite everything, I have felt happy seeing their dynamic these past four years.

Anyway, for this very reason though, I kept her at a distance in the beginning. Even though she was nice to me and I really liked her, the fact that she was so close to him made it harder for me to trust her in the beginning. But slowly she wore down my defenses and we became friends. I started to trust her with my thoughts — not all of them, of course — but most.

So yeah, I was expecting her to kick me out or at least have words with me about it.

She did neither.

She right away sent me upstairs to my room so I could take a shower that she ordered me to. She also ordered that I change into comfy pajamas and come right back down so she could make me tea and also something to eat.

Now, she takes a seat across from me while also pushing a piece of cherry pie in front of me.

Which only makes me want to start crying again.

Because it's his favorite.

"Oh no, I'm not hungry but thanks," I tell her, taking a sip of my tea only out of respect for her.

It's good but I stand corrected. His was better.

"Eat," she tells me nonetheless with a stern look.

Normally I'd argue, but I don't have the energy or the fight in me so I dutifully pick up the fork and take a bite, trying not to let tears well up in my eyes at the burst of cherries on my tongue.

"Good." Mo nods approvingly before taking a sip of her own tea and pinning me with her warm brown gaze. "Now, I want you to promise me something." I nod eagerly, setting my cup aside, but she goes, "No, don't nod your head, Poe, if you're not going to listen. If you're going to keep doing it and lying and sweetheart —"

I reach out and grab her hand. "Mo, I'm not going to lie. I'm not. I'm…" I swallow down the emotions pressing against my throat. "I know that I do that. A lot. I lie and I plot and I do… bad things but…" I squeeze her hand. "I'm not doing it here. I realize how hollow that sounds since I'm sitting in front of you right now, after having snuck out, but I came because… Because I wanted to tell you. What I did. I wanted to confess and I…"

Wanted you to hate me for it.

Yeah, that's why I came to the one person who's close to him.

Who would take his side. Who would condemn me for what I did.

Echo and Jupiter were sympathetic when they saw my face after I ran back to the dorms from his office. I didn't tell them what had transpired but they both could tell that something bad had happened. But since they're such good friends, their concern was for me and not for him.

That's why I came.

Because I need that.

I need condemnation. I need to be hated in this moment.

Like he hates me.

"You what, Poe?" Mo prods.

I blink back my tears, sniffling. "I just wanted to tell you. I wanted you to know what I almost did. To hurt him. And I hate myself for it. So I guess, I just wanted you to hate me." I chuckle sadly which sounds similar to a sob. "But you're giving me tea and pie. I don't… I don't understand that."

Mo's eyes grow even warmer if that's possible. "I'm giving you tea and pie because I don't hate you. I could never hate you, Poe. And I could never blame you for what you did."

"But —"

"No, you did what you thought you had to do, and we all do that sometimes. The important thing is that you didn't. That you pulled yourself back at the end. That's the important thing, Poe."

Still gripping her hand, I squirm in my seat. "I just… You didn't see his face. His face was…" My heart squeezes and squeezes in my chest. "It was like he wasn't there. He was but not really and God, I…" I try to breathe through the pain. "I never want to see that again. I never want him to go to that place again. Wherever he went. He was all gone. Like, there was no emotion there. And he's got the best poker face but that was… something else. Something painful."

You're not the first girl to try to make a fool out of me…

Chills race down my spine again.

Something that's been happening ever since he said those words to me. Something that I think will keep happening for a long time. Because it's not good.

Whatever it is he meant by those words, it's not good.

It's awful and terrifying and just the thought of it, what it could potentially mean, is enough to make me want to throw up.

Mo sighs, her grip on my hand tightening further. "I know. And that's why I'm going to tell you a story."

I jerk back in my seat. "What?"

"About him."

"Mo, no," I protest. "You can't."

"I should've done this a long time ago but —"

"Mo, no, listen." I pin her with a meaningful gaze. "Don't do this. Please. I'm begging you. Don't break his trust, okay? Just… He's had enough of that for one day. For a lifetime I think. Just please, don't. As much as I'd like to know, I don't *need* to know anything. Because it wouldn't change the fact that I still did it."

She smiles at me then.

A sad smile that makes me want to bawl my eyes out because I know that that sad smile of hers is as much for me as it is for him.

For everything that I don't know about him and want to.

But not like this.

Not when the price is breaking his trust.

But Mo doesn't share the sentiment because she goes on, "If he wants to see it as betrayal, then that's up to him. But I think you need to know because it's as much for you as it is for him."

And then we both grip each other's hands harder than before.

As if we both know that we're going to need it.

"So," she begins, her eyes on me but with a faraway look. "I guess to understand it all, I'd have to take you to the beginning. The very beginning, the day he was born. I remember that day for two reasons: one, it was the hottest day we'd had in decades. Temperatures were through the roof. We were sweating our butts off. The air was so thick and still and heavy. There was no relief to be had. It was like we were living in an inferno and we were, both literally and figuratively. Because Mr. Marshall, the old Mr. Marshall, was angry. He had a temper, you know. A very bad temper. He was impatient and testy most of the time but on that day he was particularly so because Mrs. Marshall, Mara, was in labor. And it wasn't her time yet and it was painful. She'd been in the hospital all night and she'd lost so much blood, and we were all walking around on eggshells, dreading that we'd be getting bad news soon. We thought we'd lose both the mother and the child. We didn't though. By some miracle, the baby was saved. Not the mother, however. But as sad as we were, because we all loved Mrs. Marshall — she was the only one who could calm Mr. Marshall down — we were also happy, you know. We were thankful that one of them was saved.

"But not Mr. Marshall. He wasn't thankful. I guess he didn't want the baby to begin with. He wasn't ready to be a father, but Mrs. Marshall insisted and he loved her so much that he gave in. But now his wife was dead and there was this baby in his arms that he apparently didn't want. And on top of that, this baby was weak. This baby was premature and needed so much care and attention. He was underweight. He had problems with his lungs, his heart, his kidneys. And when we all saw how precarious his life was, we thought we'd lose him after all. But somehow we didn't. Somehow that baby survived and lived through all the atrocities that were visited upon him so early. Because that baby was a fighter.

"He had to be, see. Not only because he had to push through those first few months of his life but also because he had to survive his father's neglect. His hatred. His downright abuse. Because there was a lot of that. At first we all thought that he'd grow out of it, you know. That he was mourning the loss of his wife, so we thought it was grief. But that grief never ended. The grief made a home in him and turned him into something else. And he took it all out on his son.

"I'd find him, you know, Alaric. Hiding and crouching and just trying to make himself smaller whenever his dad was around. I'd find him under the bed or in his closet or in the woods behind the property. He'd tell me that he wanted to disappear. He'd read stories about it. Those were his favorite kind, where people had magical powers to disappear. But then I think he grew up a little and he realized that there's something even better than disappearing. And that was being strong.

"Because he wasn't, see. He was not a strong child, Alaric. Because of his early health issues, he was smaller for his age. Thinner and sickly. He'd get sick often. He'd be in and out of the hospital so much. Which frustrated his dad even more, that his only son, who killed his wife, was weak. He'd never visit Alaric in the hospital. It went on until Alaric was about ten or eleven.

"And by then he knew: his dad hated him. His father wanted nothing to do with him. Not that he didn't already know that. He spent the better part of his childhood hiding from his father, his mean words, his mean fists, his bad temper, so Alaric knew. But by the time he was ten or eleven, I think it was cemented in his brain. It was cemented that he was a hated child. That his own father didn't want him. And when you grow up like that, with that kind of neglect and abuse, you find a way to cope. Books were his escape.

"He'd usually read and keep his head down. He was always at the top of his class, always had his homework done well ahead of time. He was very intelligent and smart. Not strong though. Still not strong. Still smaller for his age. And when you're like that, a scrawny kid with his nose buried in a book, you become a target at school. And he was. Which means he was not only a target at home, he was also one at school."

She pauses here.

And I know.

I just know.

As soon as she said 'school,' I knew.

And by this point, we're both gripping each other's hands so tightly that I think we're both bruising each other. But both of us don't care. Because the pain that the man we both care about has endured is worse.

It's much worse than I would've ever anticipated.

"Target at school," I whisper, my eyes stinging with tears but still dry, as if the tears won't fall until I've heard it all.

Until I've absorbed every single painful word into my body.

Which is when I'll get the relief of letting things out.

But I know already that I don't want it. I don't want the relief. I want to be tortured. I want to be in pain.

Because he still is.

"Yes," Mo whispers.

"H-high school, you mean," I go on and she nods. "Which also means her. Charlie."

Mo nods again.

I press my free hand to my stomach. I dig my fingers into my flesh because it's roiling. It's turning right now. Bile is surging up, stinging my throat as tears sting my eyes.

"What happened?" I whisper thickly.

"It was me," Mo whispers back, her tears already falling. "I encouraged him that night."

"What?"

She lets them fall as she continues, "Charlie was... She was a good girl. We all thought that. We all liked her. Her father was a very good friend of Mr. Marshall. They worked together on the city council. So they hung out in the same circles, went to the same events, parties. Charlie would come to the mansion occasionally but since Alaric was so shy and withdrawn and often sick, they never really had much of a friendship. Plus I think at school, she was part of a different crowd. While Alaric kept to himself, Charlie was a social butterfly. Debate team, theatre, class president. She also ran track. Was a cheerleader, the homecoming queen. So yeah, they were different.

"But then they got paired up for a project their sophomore year. Alaric wasn't happy about that. He never wanted anything to do with the 'cool kids.' They'd always tormented him, made fun of him, called him names. And even though Charlie had never personally done anything to him and they were family friends, she was friends with a lot of those kids. So he was wary. But I encouraged him to give her a chance, and he did. And well, I think slowly he started to see another side to her. They became friends. Not the kind who sat together at the lunch table; I knew that. But the kind where they'd acknowledge each other's presence in the hallway. And after being neglected and hated and ridiculed, he liked that. I could tell. I could tell that he liked her. So when they had a dance coming up, I told him to go ask her. He didn't want to; I could tell that as well. He wasn't into school dances or asking girls out but I wanted him to experience that, you know. I wanted him to experience something more, something good, something that every boy his age wants. To go out with a beautiful girl. And..."

When she trails off, reaching up to wipe her tears off, I know

I've drawn blood on my skin.

I've moved my hand from my stomach down to my thighs and drawn blood. I've raked my nails on the bare skin and scratched myself.

Not only because I know that this story doesn't end well but because I also know that it's my mother.

I know that *she* made it end badly.

"What did she do?" I ask in a low voice.

"She… said yes," Mo replies. "And I remember being so happy for him. So delighted. He was too, I think. He wouldn't say anything but I knew. Even as shy and reserved as he was, I could tell. He was also shocked. Anyway, I spent the whole week getting him prepped, giving him all the tips that I could think of. We all did. I even bought him a new suit. And then the day came and he went to her house to pick her up and… well, it was not as real as we all thought it would be."

Her face takes on a pained look, even more so than before as she goes on, "Turns out it was an ambush. She, uh, had only said yes to make this other boy jealous. I think he was captain of the football team and she was trying to get back together with him or something similar. So she used this opportunity to make him jealous. And so when… Alaric got there, the whole football team was waiting for him. They… they beat him up. And they beat him up so badly that both his arms, four ribs, his jaw, his left knee were broken. Oh, and his nose. They shattered almost every bone in his body, and then they passed pictures of him around. They passed around his bloody and battered photos all through the school, along with the story that he dared to ask a cheerleader to a dance. That he dared to step out of his league and try to get with the most popular girl in school. They weren't happy with just putting him in the hospital for a month, they ridiculed him as well. They made up stories about him, about how small he was, how pathetic, how nerdy, how stupid and desperate to want to be with Charlie. And Charlie supported all of that."

My tears are falling now.

They are.

And I hate them.

I hate how pathetic they are. How useless and such a waste.

They're not going to do anything. They're not going to help.

They're not going to change anything. They're not going to

change the fact that he was in the hospital.

For a month.

God, he was in the hospital for a month. For an *entire fucking month.*

And all he said about it was that he'd walked into a fist.

That's what he said, didn't he?

That day in his office.

He said that he'd walked into a fist and that fist had broken his nose.

But that's not true, is it?

Because his entire body was broken. His entire body was fucking shattered.

And all because of her.

All because of Charlie.

My mother.

All because she wanted to play her usual games.

And I've always known about them, about these games.

But what's more is that I always thought that it was okay. It was fucking okay that she played those games because that's who she was. That was the world she lived in. And she had to do all those things to survive.

But this is not survival.

This is cruelty.

This is pure, undiluted cruelty.

Oh my God.

Oh my *God.*

I've been so naive.

I've been so fucking naive to ever condone that behavior. To ever think that it was okay. For her to treat others like that. For her to treat *me* like that.

To ever think that I *knew* her.

I knew the extent of everything that she did.

I had no clue.

I never — not in a million years — imagined that her casual cruelty and her games could've done this.

That her behavior put someone — put *him* — in the hospital.

"It took me two weeks to convince him," Mo continues, breaking into my thoughts but lost in her own. "Two weeks to push him to ask her. If I hadn't, then none of this would've happened. He wouldn't have..."

I want to tell her that it's not her fault.

It's absolutely not her fault.

It's someone else's. It's my mother's and those assholes.

That school. His father.

This fucking town.

It's their fault, not hers.

But words won't come out of my mouth. They feel tangled up and jumbled in the wake of truth.

Sniffling, Mo wipes her tears, her voice stronger now. "The only consolation was that he moved away after his sophomore year. It's the Marshall family tradition, sending boys out to a boarding school. So at least he was away. From this town, from all the people. And when he came back, he was a different man. He was stronger, for lack of a better word. At least in his body. He'd finally hit his growth spurt and he was... yeah, stronger. Harder too. He'd seen too much of the world, lived too much of it too. And well, now he lives here. At the same mansion, in the same town. Because I think according to him, it would be a sign of weakness. To not live in a place where generations of his family have lived. To not do what his father and grandfather did. To do it better even. I don't think he likes it very much though. I don't think he's happy here. Who would be, after everything that has happened? But he won't admit it. I wish he would. Because I miss that little boy. I miss that he was so sweet and shy and easy to smile, despite everything. He was so easy to please too. Books and cherry pies."

Books and cherry pies.

That's him.

That's Alaric.

And I think that Alaric is hidden somewhere inside Mr. Marshall. He's hidden behind all the violence and all the rage.

All the hate.

"Books and cherry pies," I whisper through my tears.

"Yes." She smiles before going on, "But I want you to know, Poe, that this is not an excuse."

"Excuse?"

"For the way he's treated you."

My heart twists. "I'm —"

"No, listen, he was thrown this curveball, when he was named your guardian. I don't think he handled it well. He doesn't hate you,

Poe. He never did. He only hates what happened to him and you bore the brunt of it."

I don't. I never did…

At Mo's words, I hear his.

The ones he spoke only a few days back when I'd asked him to tell me a secret, but now feels like such a long time ago.

He doesn't hate me.

That's what he meant, didn't he?

That he doesn't. He never did.

Oh God, he never hated me.

"But that doesn't mean that what he did was right," Mo goes on. "What he keeps doing. So I want you to know that there's no reason for you to blame yourself. For what you did today. Was it wrong, yes. Was it taking things to the extreme, yes. But you were pushed into it. You both were. I told you all this because I want you to understand. I want you to know and not wonder why. Because I know you do that. And I wish…" She shakes her head. "I wish I'd told you sooner. I wish I'd made you understand so probably none of what happened today would have happened. And I also want you to know that in the light of these events, I'm putting my foot down. I am, Poe. I know he won't like it because he thinks he's the boss of everything and everyone. But I'm making it clear that he needs to let you go."

"Let me go," I breathe out, freezing in my seat.

"Yes. None of what happened with Charlie is your fault. And neither is it his. But it needs to end now. Whatever he's trying to play at by keeping you here, I'm telling him that it won't fly anymore. It's not fair to you."

I know it's not.

I know that.

But suddenly I don't care.

I absolutely do not care about being fair or unfair.

All I care about is finding him.

All I care about is touching him, talking to him. Seeing his face.

God, I want to see his face.

I want to trace that bump on his nose. I want to sink my fingers in his scruffy jaw.

His thick hair.

Something that I haven't even touched yet.

My fingers are tingling with the need. My heart is clenching and squeezing with the urge to see him.

But I have to do this one thing first.

This one thing, this one weight that I have to shed, before I can go to him.

I guess it's the other reason why I came to Mo tonight. Because I need her to make things right.

"Can you," I ask, wiping off my tears, "do one favor for me, Mo? I have to do this one thing. Can you help me do it, please?"

Chapter Twenty

After I asked Mo to do me this favor, I threw up.

And I kept throwing up for about twenty minutes. After that, I cleaned myself up and put on some fresh clothes and came here.

To the same bar as Friday, because I know Jimmy is playing again tonight.

He's been texting me since last Friday when I disappeared out of the blue. He's been worried and his usual caring and loving self. I didn't tell him what had transpired and why I'd disappeared though, because I didn't want him to worry even more. I didn't want him to think that I wouldn't be able to do the tour with him.

But now I have to.

I want to.

I want to tell him that I won't be able to go. Because the only way that I *can* go is by hurting *him* in the process — Alaric, not Mr. Marshall; he'll never be Mr. Marshall to me now — and I'm not willing to do that.

I've decided to finish summer school instead. I've even decided to stay beyond that if that's what he wants.

Because I want to show him that I'm sorry. That I have remorse. And this is my penance.

Besides, it would be nothing more than what I deserve, so.

Mo is outside waiting in the car, because she insisted on coming. I only wanted her to make arrangements to have the car ready so I could go by myself; if I was going to break his rule one last time, I wanted to do it as gently as possible. Hence telling Mo about it and using his car so it's slightly less rebellious.

I know it's silly — these tiny steps to ensure I'm not going way over the line while still *going* over it — but I didn't know what else to do. I needed to tell Jimmy in person. He deserves at least this much after everything, after my promises that turned out to be false.

But suddenly as I stand here in the middle of the crowd, waiting for him to finish his after-show routine — he just finished his set and is now in the process of shaking hands and chatting with his fans — I'm rethinking this decision.

I'm rethinking this hard.

Because he's…

He's kissing another girl.

One of his fans.

A few seconds ago they were simply chatting, but then he leaned down and before I could blink, he was on her.

He was actually *on* her and now they're full on making out.

There's groping hands and rubbing bodies and clapping and cheering. There's also Erica. Who I thought was the biggest threat to my relationship with Jimmy.

But right now she is stunned. Just like me.

And I actually feel some sort of kinship with her.

I can't believe this.

I can't believe that he's kissing someone else. After everything that we'd promised to each other.

After all the texts and emails these past couple of weeks.

All the anticipation that he'd shown and all the enthusiasm and longing. He even wrote me a freaking song and sent a few lines every day via text so this fucking wait would get easier.

I'm not naive though, okay? I'm well aware of his lifestyle. He's handsome. He's in a band. He lives in New York. Of course he's been with other girls. And while I've never been with another guy, that was my choice. I never asked Jimmy to be loyal to me in that sense. It did piss me off to see girls flirting with him, but I curbed my jealousy and understood.

But what the hell?

What the fucking hell?

Things had changed between us and now he's kissing another girl.

I come out of the stupor and charge over to him. I poke him in the arm as soon as I get there, making them jerk apart. Or rather the girl jerks away, Jimmy is slow to come out of the kissing haze.

Which breaks as soon as he sees me.

His blue eyes go wide and *then* he jerks back.

"Holy fuck, Poe," he cries in his usual way, high and animated, fearful for the first time ever. "What the fuck? What… What are you doing here?"

He goes for a hug but I put a hand on his chest to stop him. "What are you doing? Why were you kissing her?"

As if my words remind him of what he was doing, he snaps his eyes to the girl. Who mumbles an excuse and runs away before I can even properly glare at her.

And now it's just him and me and the dispersing crowd.

"Jimmy." I push him slightly to get his attention because he's still watching the girl go. "What the hell? Why were you kissing her?"

He looks at me, his eyes wide as he swallows. "Well, she came on to me, Poe. I was just —"

I push him again. "No, she didn't. I saw you. You were the one who leaned down and kissed her first."

He swallows again, his drug high crashing right in front of my eyes. "I… I was…"

I shake my head. "I thought… I thought you liked me. I —"

He grabs my arms then. "I do. I do." He squeezes my arm to make his point. "I fucking do, Poe. It was just one kiss. It was harmless. It was… It didn't mean anything. All this, doesn't mean anything. It's just the high from the show. High from the music and people cheering you on. It's… It's nothing."

I look at him, at his face that's been so dear to me. Such a dream that I wanted to be real.

And I did everything that I could to *make* it real.

But we're not.

That's what I came here to tell him. That I can't be with him.

So what does it matter if he was kissing someone else?

I let the tension drain out of my body and sigh. "I can't go with you."

"What?"

I inch up my glasses, feeling an ache in my heart. "I can't go on tour with you."

His eyes cloud over and that ache jacks up. "Why?" Before I can answer though, he tightens his grip and growls, "What, because of this? Because I kissed some slut in a bar?"

I frown up at him.

First, we don't know if she's a slut. Just because she was kissing Jimmy — my would-be and almost boyfriend — doesn't mean she's a slut. I mean, he was kissing her too. So what does that make him?

And second, I can't help but notice that his growl — the first time I've heard it, by the way — was… boyish.

It wasn't as deep or authoritative or rough, so that chills would run down my spine or make my skin rise up in goosebumps.

Like *his* does.

His growls make me clench every part of my body and…

Oh God, Poe. It's not even important right now.

"Come on, Poe." Jimmy's voice breaks my thoughts. "I just told you that it wasn't important. It didn't mean anything and —"

"It's not because of her," I cut him off, swallowing. "I-I can't go. I can't quit summer school."

His fingers squeeze me so tight that it becomes painful. Not the good kind though, and it makes me wince. "Why the fuck not? You don't even like school, Poe."

"I know. I'm sorry, Jimmy," I tell him, fighting through the pain he's causing. "But I can't. I really can't. I-I have to stick it out."

For *him*.

"I know this is disappointing to you," I continue, pleading for him to forgive me with my eyes. "And I'm really, really sorry. I am, Jimmy. It's breaking my heart but you have to —"

"Is it about the money?" he asks then, his blue eyes hard in a way that I've never seen before and it makes me want to cry because I'm doing this to him. I'm breaking his heart right now.

"What?"

"Is it about the fucking money, Poe? Your trust fund. Because I told you that I'd take care of it."

Oh right.

The money.

Something that has been so important to me all this time, but somehow it hasn't even entered my mind while making all the decisions. And now that I *am* thinking about it, I know that I don't care.

I don't care if he controls my money.

It doesn't matter to me anymore.

"You don't have to," I tell Jimmy. "I know you wanna take care of me and all but first, even if I was going with you, I would be taking care of myself. I know I don't look it but I can work. It was never about the money so I appreciate this so much, and second —"

"It is always about the money," he booms and his grip gets even tighter.

Honestly, I don't think I can take this pain now. I think I need to ask him to ease up a bit.

But I never get the chance because he continues, his eyes wild now, "Listen Poe, you can't do this, okay? You can't do this to me right now. I need you to go with me. I fucking need you."

My heart breaks further and I reach up to clutch his t-shirt. "God, Jimmy, I'm so sorry. I'm so fucking sorry but I can't. I really can't. I have to stay here. I have to. For him and —"

"Fuck him," he booms again. "All right? Fuck your fucking guardian. Fuck that fucking loser. You —"

"Hey!" I shake him. "Don't call him a loser. He's not a loser."

"What?"

"And don't talk about him like that. Ever," I growl — first time in front of him — and give him another shake for good measure.

He looks at me, confused, and I understand that.

He knows about my own hatred for my guardian. Which I regret now.

God do I regret it.

But no one calls him a loser. Even *I* didn't call him that back when I hated him with every fiber of my being.

I *hate* that word.

I hated it when Cynthia called him that and I hate it even more now that I know all the things he has been through.

So no, no one and *absolutely no one* gets to trash talk my guardian. Even the guy I love.

I won't tolerate it.

Jimmy shakes his head. "Whatever. I don't even care. Look…" He takes a deep but shaky breath. "You have to understand, Poe. You have to fucking understand and come with me."

"But I told you —"

"Holy fuck. Shit." He throws his head back and looks up to the ceiling, all agitated. Then, coming back to look at me, he says, "All right. Listen. You have to listen carefully."

I wait for him to go on but he keeps looking at me with both wild and serious eyes as if waiting for something. So I tell him, "I'm listening."

He takes another deep, shaky breath. "Big Jack is going to kill me for this, okay? But I want you to know."

"Who's Big Jack?"

He shakes his head again and leans down further. "There's a plan, all right? A big plan, and it involves you coming with me."

"What?"

Another breath. "Look, there's no tour." My eyes go wide and he goes on, "There never was any tour. The whole plan was to get you to go with us and then…" Yet another breath. "And then ask your guardian for your money. And not just the partial trust fund. All of it."

He finishes with yes, another breath.

Meanwhile I'm not breathing at all. Meanwhile I'm frozen.

And shocked. And so fucking confused.

"What?" I ask, gripping his t-shirt tightly. "W-why would… Why would he give you the money?"

He leans down further. "Because we were gonna make it look like you got kidnapped."

"Kidnapped."

His eyes get wilder with excitement. "Yeah. A fake kidnapping. And look, it's a win-win."

"Win-win."

"Yeah." He smiles his usual charming smile but right now it looks more manic than I've ever seen it. "You were gonna get out of your guardian's control. That's what you've always talked about, right? Getting out of his control and being free. And if we get all the money right now, you wouldn't even have to see him after this. And yes, I'll need a little bit of that money myself but it's a very small amount. And once the band takes off, I'm gonna pay you back."

"Why do you need the money?"

He grimaces. "I owe some people. Long story. But Big Jack had been getting impatient. I told him that I'd give him the money soon. I knew you were gonna get out of school and get the money anyway in a few weeks, but the fucker put a date on it and when he found out that you were my friend, he came up with this whole brilliant plan. Of you quitting school now and going on the fake tour with me." He grimaces again. "Full disclosure though, he might have jacked up the loan. For the plan, you see. So we might have to give him more than what I owe him in the first place. But I figured you wouldn't mind because you're finally going to be free."

Free.

He's the second person to say that to me tonight.

And like Mo, he's not wrong.

"So then who's Erica?" I ask, my voice all calm and low.

"She works for Big Jack. He sent her to keep an eye on me." He rolls his eyes. "Like I need to be kept on a leash. I know what I'm doing."

"And Big Jack is a mob boss?" I ask with the same voice.

"What, no." Jimmy looks horrified. "I wouldn't be tangled up with a mob boss. Are you crazy? He's just a drug dealer."

My voice is still the same and it's starting to scare me. "Just a drug dealer. You owe money to a drug dealer."

"Yeah. Nothing to worry about, babe."

"Babe."

He smiles. "Well I mean, I could call you that now, right? You know everything now. Even my bandmates don't know this. Big Jack wanted to keep it a secret, even from you. I told him you'd be cool with this but he didn't wanna take any chances. But now you know. And once we pay off Big Jack, we can finally be together. We can start a life in New York, explore this thing between us. It's gonna be epic, Poe. You and me. It took us three years to get here. But we are here now."

"Three years, yeah."

"And I promise no more kissing other girls," he whispers, grinning. "Not as long as I get to kiss you."

Kiss me.

He wants to kiss me.

I've waited for that kiss for three long years.

And look, it's happening.

It actually is happening right now.

Like literally.

Because he leans forward, his lips puckered, his eyes hooded.

He's going to do it.

Kiss me for the very first time.

And here I was, only a few hours ago, so worried about the fact that I might have to take it from someone else. That I might have to sacrifice my first kiss at the devil's altar so I could be with Jimmy.

I shouldn't have worried.

He should have though. Jimmy, I mean.

He *should be* worried right now.

Because as soon as his lips come a hairsbreadth away from mine, I let go of his t-shirt and ball my fist. I then rear back my arm and fucking lay that fist on his fucking face.

He howls and falls back, letting go of me.

"You fucking asshole," I growl. Then, on a shout, "You fucking asshole! You *motherfucking* goddamn asshole!"

His hands are covering almost all of his face so his words are muffled as he speaks. "What the fuck, Poe? What the —"

And since it's not enough, just punching him in the face, I fucking knee him in the groin too as I scream, "You fucking piece of shit!"

Now his hands are covering his junk as he drops to his knees, howling and moaning in pain.

I bend down and growl again, "Stay away from me, you understand? You and that Big Jack. And stay the fuck away from my Alaric."

And then I'm running out of there.

I'm dashing away and when I see Mo's face through the car's window, I burst out crying.

Chapter Twenty-One

The Renaissance Man

Jimothy Wilson.

I know guys like him.

Blond haired and blue eyed.

Chiseled and athletic with a penchant for smooth talking and flicking their hair every five seconds like they're in a fucking shampoo commercial. Throw in a football or a guitar and you've got yourself a regular teenage heartthrob.

They know how to play a girl. They know how to make her think that she's special and that she's the only one.

Yeah, I've known a few guys like him.

A guy like him — several guys like him, actually — gave me my broken nose.

Two titanium plates in my arms and a bunch of broken bones scattered around my body.

And a fuck-ton of anger.

At myself.

For being so stupid. For being so weak and pathetic.

For being so gullible as to believe that a girl would be interested in me, in the boy that I used to be, completely opposite of everything that my family name was supposed to represent.

So much so that I didn't know what to do with it, my anger.

For the longest time, I didn't know where to put it.

I'd lie there in the hospital bed — like many, many times before — doped up on pain pills but seething with anger.

I went through my PT while seething. I learned to fucking walk again while seething. I learned to make fists, move my fingers while seething. I learned to breathe again without pain while seething. When I rejoined the world as I was before, new and shiny with no broken bones, I did that while seething.

Until I found a way to channel that anger: into my work and a heavy bag.

And then I made it my mission never to be weak again.

I made it my mission to kill all the softness inside of me, all the naïveté, all the gullible things. To gain respect, power, control.

And so far, I haven't slipped up.

But then I got this call from Mo.

I was on my way back from the facility where my father has been living for the past seven years. It's an assisted living home that caters to the elderly suffering from memory degenerative illnesses. My father suffers from dementia and I go up there to see him once a month.

Not that he recognizes me, now that his illness is at an advanced stage.

Which is just as well.

Because I'm not sure what I would do if he did recognize me.

If he did recognize the son he'd hated for ever being born and killing his beloved wife.

If he would hate me still. For being weak.

By the time I completed my studies and got back to Middlemarch, my father was already in the throes of his illness, and since I was his heir, I got everything handed down to me. I bet he was worried about that; other people were for sure. He was worried about our family's legacy going into the hands of a son he never thought was capable or even worthy of it.

But sometimes I wonder, if he could see me now, all powerful like him, what his reaction would be.

Sometimes I also wonder if I wasn't here, would she still be alive, my mother?

Or if she hadn't died, would she have loved me?

Would my father have loved me?

Would none of the things that happened have happened?

But they did.

Everything happened, and now I visit my father who doesn't recognize me, not because I feel any kind of love for him but because like so many other things, it's my responsibility.

I do a lot of things because of that.

Like the board meeting I attended before going to see my father.

As always it was a fucking shitshow.

More so because they – and by they I mean that piece of shit Robert Bailey – wants me to do his bidding. He wants me to bring back some of the more archaic rules of St. Mary's such as the bed check.

The rule I threatened her with a few weeks back.

It was simply a joke because even I think that it's too archaic and harsh to be implemented along with majority of the board. But not Robert Bailey and some of his lackeys apparently.

"If you think you're not up for the job, we can easily find someone else who is," he threatened me yet again.

"I'm sure you will," I told him, my fists tight. "But until then I make the decisions. And my decision is no." Then I looked at the members in general before continuing, "You're all welcome to take a vote if you like."

In short, it's been hell of a day so I'm actually looking forward to this.

I've been waiting — wanting and fucking craving — to do this ever since Mo called. And told me that one Jimothy Wilson had the fucking audacity to make her cry.

Last time, I spared him.

I let him go.

I thought St. Mary's would keep her safe from him. But I was wrong. *Way* wrong.

I'm not going to make the same mistake again though.

I know I promised her that I wouldn't touch him but fuck it.

Fuck that fucking promise.

Tonight, I'm going to end it.

And then I'm going to make damn fucking sure that it stays that way.

So when I see him stumbling out of that dingy bar, I get out of my car. I slam the door shut and I do it hard, so the sound reverberates through the quiet parking lot, making him and his punk-ass friends —

actually, worse; his *bandmates* — flinch.

That my plan is successful and they do, looking around frantically, is hardly a consolation to me right now.

It's hardly cold water over my burning rage.

I stride through the parking lot and in my peripheral vision, I notice his friends staring at me wide-eyed and scared, muttering among themselves, and scattering away from him like little ants. It would be funny if I was in the mood to laugh.

I'm not.

As it is, I don't stop until I'm there.

Where I can wrap my hand around his fucking throat and squeeze.

"H-holy sh…" he squeaks like the fucking rodent he is, his hands flailing in the air before coming to grab my wrist.

I squeeze harder and jerk him up so his feet are hovering above the ground and those pretty blue eyes of his look ready to burst. "What the fuck did you do to her?"

His struggles grow, his fingers digging into my arm as he squeaks again, "What the… W-Who…"

I squeeze again; I'm actually starting to like his squeaky little noises.

Leaning closer, I growl, "What the fuck did you do, you motherfucking shit stain?"

"Jesus, what the… let go, man."

"You know what." I squeeze his throat again. "This isn't working. Let's change tactics, shall we?" Still struggling, he gurgles but I go on, "Stay away from her, do you understand me?"

I ease up a little so he can speak. "H-holy shit, who?"

"Poe Blyton," I snap with clenched teeth. "You know who she is, don't you?"

His eyes widen in recognition and he goes to say something, but since I'm not really interested in listening to his whiny voice, I up the pressure and keep going. "I see you finally know what I mean. Now let's try this again: If I see you around her one more time, I'm going to reach down your fucking throat and rip your small intestines out and wrap them around your neck, do you understand me?"

"I d-don't —"

"Blink once for yes, and twice if you want me to make you taste your intestines right now."

He blinks once.

Fucker.

I'm kinda disappointed.

But I let him go. Not without a last, punishing squeeze that makes him squeak and gurgle like a pathetic buffoon. And as soon as I do that, he falls to the ground, coughing and moaning, his hands clutching his throat.

And she loves *him.*

This guy.

This pathetic fucking weasel.

My anger renewed, I bend down and grab his collar so he looks at me. The sight of his face, though, gives me a little pause.

Disgusted, I growl, "What, are you fucking crying right now?"

He sniffles, his hands still around his throat, trying to stumble back. "Get the fuck away from me, man. She already punched me out, okay?"

"She did."

"Yeah." He sniffles. "She even kneed me in the junk, all right? So get the fuck away from me."

My lips twitch with a smile.

That's my girl.

I still keep a hold of his collar though and shake him. "Stop fucking crying like a pussy." Another shake. "And I will."

Something about my tone might have registered with him because he stops struggling and looks up at me. Although, I'm not sure how much he can see with tears still running down his face and his chest shuddering.

"I want you to understand this very clearly, yeah?" I begin, my fist tightening in his shirt as I look into his eyes. "You need to stay away from her."

His eyes are wide and he stutters, "Y-yeah. I-I —"

"No, don't talk. I don't want to hear your pathetic little voice. Just blink once for yes."

The fucker does it. He blinks.

"You don't try to contact her in any way, shape or form. Meaning you don't text her or email her or write her a fucking letter and send it in the mail. You don't even send her a postcard clutched in the fucking beak of a fucking owl, all right? And then slowly, little by little, you forget about her. You forget her name. You forget where she lives.

You forget what she sounds like. What she looks like. You forget her smile. You forget her fucking laughter. And you forget the color of her eyes. Are you getting all of this down?"

He blinks again.

Although this time it was more like a jerk since his fear is mounting by the minute. I can smell it.

I think he's going to shit his fucking pants in about five seconds so I need to make this quick.

"And then she doesn't exist for you. You don't think about her. You don't even dream about her. If you dream about her, you smack yourself in the face and you wake yourself up, yeah?"

"B-but I don't... How can I control... It's a dream!" he cries out.

I'll let it slide. His breach of conduct about using his voice.

I tug at his collar, pulling him up slightly, making fear dance across his pretty boy features. "So don't fall asleep then. Ever."

"But that's impossible. How —"

"Enough talking. Now blink once if you understood everything, and I wouldn't suggest blinking twice, even by mistake, because you're not going to like what I do to your eyelashes. Before moving on to your eyes and other body parts."

He does it.

And he does it hard.

So much so that I think he almost injured himself right then.

Even though this is the answer I wanted, I'm still not very happy. I would've liked a go at his eyelashes, plucking them out one by one and feeding them to him.

I take one last look at his pathetic face before letting go of his collar.

The look of relief is so big on his features that it pisses me off and I grab his collar again. Before laying it out on his jaw.

He howls in pain and that's when I let go.

But I keep myself bent over him and growl, "That's for making her cry tonight."

And then I'm ready to get out of here but his stupid fucking voice stops me. "What the fuck, man? What the fuck is your p-problem? You're not her d-dad."

I look at his pathetic form for a second. "No, I'm not. I'm worse than her dad. Because I'm here and he's not. And I can put you in a world of hurt if you don't take my advice tonight."

And then I'm striding away.

Twenty minutes later, I'm back at the mansion and Mo is there to greet me at the door.

"She's finally asleep."

I jerk out a nod. "Any nightmares, anything?"

"No," she tells me. "But I made her tea and gave her a sleeping pill anyway. Hopefully she'll sleep through the night."

Another nod. "Fine. Thanks."

"I'm not sure what that boy did. She wouldn't tell me but —"

My fists throb with violence. "That boy won't be a problem anymore."

I'm about to walk away when Mo says, "I told her."

I pause then. And go still.

"Everything," Mo continues, her eyes both defiant and slightly fearful. "I know you might see it as a betrayal. But she needed to know. That child has been pushed to the brink, Alaric. What she did today, she was so guilty and regretful. She never would've done it if—"

"I know," I cut her off, not interested in listening to what I already know.

What she did this afternoon was wrong. It was devious and malicious and it was totally unlike her.

She's played pranks in the past, broken rules and lied, but none of those things were done with an intention of permanent harm or damage. So yeah, she did this because she was pushed to the brink.

And as always, it happened because of me.

I look at Mo, study her distressed face as I continue, "It wasn't a betrayal." She goes to say something but I don't let her. "And she's not a child."

Not anymore.

That's the fucking problem, isn't it? That she's not.

She hasn't been ever since I came back from Italy and I want to fucking break something. I want to fucking tear something apart. Because she does things to me that no one has ever been able to do. She fucks with my control that I've spent years to build.

And she shouldn't be able to.

So how is it that she's the bane of my goddamn life and the fire in my goddamn soul?

How is it that when I walk away from Mo, I'm bounding up

the stairs, taking two at a time, charging to her room? How is it that I want to make sure that she's really okay and really asleep?

And how the fuck is it that when I find her like that, only then am I able to breathe.

Only then am I able to calm this rage that's been bubbling inside of me ever since Mo's call.

I approach the bed with silent steps to where she's curled up on her side under a blanket. Her midnight hair is scattered around the pillow and both her hands are tucked under it. There are tear tracks running down her pale, milky cheeks. Even her curly eyelashes are wet, and every now and then she jerks in her sleep, hiccupping.

She looks so young, so innocent.

Heartbreakingly innocent.

My fists clench as I feel that rage bubbling up again.

I should've broken more than his nose. I should've broken every bone in his body. I should've fucking killed him.

No, I should've found a way to wipe him out of existence so she never met him.

So he never breaks her heart like he did today.

But that's not true, is it?

I did that. I broke her heart. Like so many things, I pushed her into his arms.

So it's me.

I should've let her go.

Four years ago when she asked me to, I should've driven her back to New York and left her there myself.

I shouldn't have trapped her like I did.

I shouldn't have seen her as Charlie's extension. Even in the beginning.

Because she's not.

She never was.

She *is* too unique. She's too original and talented and imaginative and fucking brave to be like anyone else.

Brave enough to fight, to push back, to stand up for herself every time I tried to put her down.

Not only that, she's brave enough to bring things to life.

To create them. To will them into existence.

I can study creations. I can catalog them, analyze them, admire them and write papers about them. But she's the one with a vision. She's the one with style, with the flair and courage to build what people like me study.

Mo was right to tell her.

It's not something I ever would've done myself. I don't like to think about that part of my life. I don't like to think about how I was before I became what I am today. But I'm glad Mo told her.

Not because it's an excuse, but because she needed to know that it was never her fault.

It wasn't her. It was me.

And now it's my turn to do the right thing.

To be the guardian I was appointed to be four years ago.

With that thought in my head, I take one last look at her, her pale moon-like skin, her small body, her midnight hair, that plump pink mouth, devoid of her occasional dark purple lipstick.

As I turn around to leave, all I can hear is: *I want you to give me my first kiss.*

Chapter Twenty-Two

I can't find him.

I can't find him anywhere and I've looked and looked.

I've gone through every concrete hallway, every room of St. Mary's, every inch of the campus grounds. I've also checked the mansion, all the rooms and all the floors. I even looked for him in the woods.

Where is he?

Why can't I find him?

I know something has happened. Something bad. I know he's in danger. His body is all broken and bent and bloody. And he's lying somewhere all alone and I have to find him.

I have to. I have to. I have to.

With that thought running in my head on a loop, I scream out his name. And I keep doing it and doing it until I'm enveloped in warmth.

And strength.

That's when I'm jerked awake and I realize that it was a dream.

No, a nightmare.

I was having a nightmare and I'm shaking and shivering and crying. And I can't stop even though I want to.

Even though I think… I *think* there's someone else who wants me to as well.

Someone who's making shushing noises, deep soothing hums.

Not to mention, I'm clinging on to the warmest and the strongest pair of arms. That are attached to the warmest and the strongest pair of shoulders and chest.

They smell like my two favorite things: leather and cigar smoke.

And I'm staring at a dusky patch of skin.

At the base of a throat.

His throat.

"Alaric?" I say into his throat, my heart pounding.

I feel my body being squeezed. "Here."

Jerking back, I look up at him. "You're…" I swallow, my sleepy vision slowly coming into focus "You're here."

His eyes are dark and shiny as he stares down at me. "Yeah. And you're okay. You were just having a nightmare."

I realize I'm clutching his shirt in my fists.

I also realize that I'm wrapped around him.

I'm not sure how that happened. But we're on my bed and I'm sitting on his lap, my thighs circled around his hips and my body pressed close.

But it isn't close enough for me.

I want to be closer.

So I squirm and shift — and holy God, his thighs are fucking built; his thighs are all hard and muscular and freaking cut —until I'm *really* plastered against him.

Until all my curves are flattened and molded against his rock-hard chest and ridged torso.

When I've situated myself the way I like, I press my palms on his scruffy jaw and look into his eyes, whispering, "I couldn't find you."

"What?"

"In my nightmare," I tell him, hiccupping, the tips of my fingers digging into his face. "I couldn't… I thought something happened to you. I thought you were in danger and so I looked and looked everywhere. At St. Mary's and here and… and in the woods behind the mansion. But I couldn't… And I was so scared, Alaric. I was…"

A sob escapes me without volition and I feel my body being squeezed once more.

Before I can understand how that's happening — the squeezing of my body — he speaks in a gravelly voice. "I'm fine. I'm here, all right. I'm right here. There's no need for you to be scared."

"You're fine," I whisper, tracing his high cheekbones with my fingers.

"Yes."

"And you're here."

"I am."

He is.

He is here. I don't know how he's here but he is.

He's not in any danger or lying somewhere in a ditch, broken and bloody.

He's whole and warm and alive and I'm wrapped around him. I'm touching him. I'm *looking* at him.

His dark, rich hair that looks messy for once, rumpled and spiked, a few strands falling on his forehead. His jaw's scruffy, scruffier than ever, and for some reason, his skin looks even more dusky than usual.

As if sleep colors him at night and leaves him looking even darker and more delicious.

Flushed and heated.

Finally, I sigh. Finally, I let all the tension go from my body and give him a small, tentative smile.

It makes his jaw clench for a second, watching my lips pull up slightly.

I tighten my hold around him. "Did I wake you?"

He lifts his eyes. "I wasn't sleeping."

My fingers make circles around the side of his mouth. "What were you doing?"

I feel my body being squeezed again. "Working."

My fingers leave his face and go back, sinking themselves into his rich, soft hair. "You work too much."

I feel my own hair being tugged, making me wonder why. "I work just enough."

"No, you don't."

"I'm —"

I lean in then and smell the triangle of his throat, cutting him off.

It's something that I've been wanting to do ever since I saw that patch of skin in his office a few days ago.

And now that he's here, I couldn't stop myself from giving in and I was right.

I was so fucking right.

His scent *is* thicker here.

Thicker and headier and I have to open my mouth to take it in.

Leather and cigar smoke.

With a hint of cherries.

That's new though and I wonder if I can lick it too. I wonder if I could take a bite out of it, his throat. Just to see if it tastes the same as it smells.

I feel my body being squeezed again, followed by a tug in my hair before I hear his growled question, "What the fuck are you doing?"

Taking a big whiff of his throat, I look up. "Smelling you."

His brows are drawn together as he looks down at me. "Smelling me."

I probably should be more embarrassed at this.

But I'm not.

I have no space in my body to feel any sort of shame or embarrassment. All my tiny spaces have been filled to the brim by relief and his warmth.

So I rub my nose in his throat — it's hot and stubbled — as I whisper, "Yes. Because I've always wondered about your throat."

"You've always wondered about my throat."

"Yes. How it smells."

"How it smells."

"Yeah. If your scent is thicker here. Your scent of leather and cigar smoke."

"My scent of leather and cigar smoke."

"You're repeating everything I'm saying again."

"Because you're saying such logical things."

I give him a small smile and he stiffens but I don't care.

I even go so far as to put my cheek on his chest and sigh again.

He shifts under me. "I'm going to send Mo in and she can —"

I snap my eyes up, protesting, "No, don't." His scruffy jaw clenches and I clutch his hair. "Don't go anywhere." Then, in a whisper, "Please."

His response is to clench his jaw harder for a few seconds and breathe out as if giving in.

Which makes me relax that he's going to stay, but now that he is, there's something else that I need to think about.

"Did Mo call you?" I ask, my heart starting to race for a different reason now than the nightmare. "I-I mean, about the fact that I was — *am* — at the mansion."

Where I shouldn't be in the first place.

I know it. He knows it.

When I snuck out, I knew I was taking a huge risk. I knew that he was already mad at me — beyond mad — for what I'd done in his office and so I was aware that this might send him over the edge.

But I had to be here and so I guess the time has come to face it, face his wrath.

Which actually is already showing on his features, tightening them up, clenching things, making them go harsh.

Even his voice is tight when he replies, "Yes."

My heart pounds harder.

Because sneaking out is the lesser of my crimes right now.

I have done something else as well. Something worse.

That he's absolutely not going to be happy about.

But I have to tell him so I do.

And I do it without looking away from him. Without hiding or closing up.

"I know that I never should've…" I swallow, my fists in his hair getting tighter, "snuck out of school. But I did and… it's okay if you wanna punish me for it. But I guess you should also know that I did something else too. Something that's far worse and I don't know if Mo told you but I —"

"She did."

I wince slightly, my limbs flexing around his body.

"Oh. I want… I want you to know that it's o-over." I have to take a deep breath here. "Between him and me, and I know that I've lied about that before. Two times. But I'm not lying now and again, it's okay if you wanna punish me for that as well. I-I realize —"

"What did he do?" he growls, cutting me off.

I have to blink.

First, because I wasn't expecting that question.

And second, because a moment ago his eyes were liquid brown, like melting chocolate chips, but now they've gone dark. They've turned into hard diamonds in a split second.

Which somehow makes me realize something else.

Something obvious that my sleepy, overwhelmed brain had

been blocking up until now.

So I guess three things then, and the third one is the most important one. And it's the fact that I've suddenly solved the mystery as to *why* my body felt like it was being squeezed at times and why I felt like my hair was being tugged and pulled on.

It's because it *was.*

By him.

It's because I'm not the only one who's holding on to him. He's holding on to me as well.

His arms are wrapped around me, around my body, and he's keeping me in place. He's anchoring me in his lap with one hand cradling the back of my head, his fingers buried in my thick hair. And his other hand is splayed wide on my spine.

I guess it should've been obvious that he's holding me — I mean, I'm sitting in his lap; of course he's got his arms around me — but it wasn't.

Not until he asked me that growly question and his eyes turned dark.

And they're not dark with rage at me but with something else.

Something else like protectiveness.

This is protection, I realize.

This is what it feels like to be safe. To be tethered and grounded.

A comfortable lap to sit on, a powerful body to wind my limbs around and a pair of muscular arms holding me tight. So tight that every inch of my body is touching his. Every curve of my body has a place on his body to rest against, my breasts to his ribs, my thighs around his slim waist.

Every beat that my heart takes echoes through his chest, and he watches over every breath that goes through my lungs.

This is it, isn't it?

This is what it feels like to be guarded.

"Poe," he growls when all I do is stare up at him in awe.

"I… He… It's not important."

And it isn't.

Not in the face of what I've just discovered: what it feels like to be held by my devil guardian.

No, just my guardian.

Alaric.

His hold around me tenses though and he growls again, "It was important enough to make you cry. In the car. The whole way back."

My eyes go wide. "Mo told you that?"

"And then in your fucking sleep."

"H-how did you—"

"So what the fuck did he do?"

I know he's getting impatient.

But my brain is stuck on the fact that he knew I was crying in my sleep and that instead of Mo, who usually comes in here to help me when I have nightmares, it's him who came.

"Is that why you came when I cried out? Instead of Mo."

"Poe, I swear —"

"Just tell me."

His chest moves on an impatient breath. Then, "Yes."

Things melt inside me at his confirmation. They drip and pool at the bottom of my belly, making me feel heavy and cozy. "If I tell you," I whisper, "you'll get mad."

A muscle jumps out in his cheek. "I'm already mad."

I bite my lip, still hesitating.

He leans in, the tip of his nose grazing mine. "Tell me what the fuck he did, Poe."

"He lied," I whisper finally.

"Lied about what?"

"About the tour," I tell him, holding on to him tightly. "There was never any tour. He was lying to me because he wanted to… he wanted me to go with him so he could…" I grimace but then just come out with it. "So he could make it look like I'd been kidnapped and then ask you to pay him my trust fund as ransom. And that's because he owes money to this drug dealer and that drug dealer, Big Jack, was putting pressure on him so they came up with this whole fake kidnapping idea."

And then I'm glad that he's holding me in his arms.

I mean I already was but now I'm even gladder because I feel a pain in my chest.

I feel a sting.

I guess I've been so focused on how he'd feel and how he'd get angry about me sneaking out of St. Mary's and then going to see Jimmy that I forgot about my own heartbreak.

I forgot about my own pain.

I forgot that my love is gone now. That my love was a lie.

That all my dreams and my hopes that I'd pinned on Jimmy were a lie.

God, it was all a lie.

"But before all that," I continue, my eyes teary and unfocused, "I saw him kiss another girl. I saw him make out with her. I saw him… I felt so stupid. I felt so stupid standing there, watching him, all because I wanted to tell him in person. I wanted to give him the courtesy of telling him that I wouldn't be able to go with him. On the tour. I thought he deserved at least that. I was gonna let him go. I was gonna tell him to not wait for me because I… I didn't know when I was getting out of St. Mary's and so I wanted to say goodbye in person and… As it turns out, there wasn't even a tour. It was all his plan. To get the money. And he made it sound like he was doing me a favor, like I'd buy that bullshit. Like I'd… But I guess it's not really his fault because I bought into his other bullshit, right? That he wanted me. That he had feelings for me. When all this time, it was just a ploy. When he was kissing someone else while I was… I was saving my first kiss for him."

A tear streams down my face then.

A thick, lonely tear that tells me that I'm stupid.

That I'm *beyond* stupid.

That I've been so desperate for love and attention that I was blind.

Blind to Jimmy. Blind to his intentions. His sudden interest in me. The tour.

What a joke.

But it's worse, isn't it?

Because I've always been this way. I've always been this blind and it all started with her.

With my mother.

God, my mother.

My fucking mother.

The mere thought of her brings me out of my self-pity. It brings me out of my stupid teenage angst to focus on other important things.

Things like him.

And the fact that he's gone all still under me.

All stiff and harsh, his eyes blacker than the night and his jaw made of granite.

And I bring my hands back to his cheeks. I press my palms over his hard bones and whisper, "Alaric."

As if me calling his name wakes him up, he breaks his stillness and moves.

He shifts under me but I bear down.

I put all my body, all my power into it and stop his movements. "Alaric, what are you —"

"Get off me," he growls.

"No." I shake my head and keep throwing my weight into it.

"Poe, get the fuck off me."

"No, I won't," I tell him. "Not until you tell me what you're doing."

At this, he stills or at least, he lets go of his efforts to dislodge me from his lap.

Not only that, he also moves his arms.

And then he's not holding me anymore, he's gripping me.

He's clutching me in his palms, my waist at least, and digging his fingers in my flesh.

And this feels even better.

Because now his hold is not only protective, it's also possessive.

It also makes me think that no one else could ever hold me this way. That I could never fit into someone's palms like I fit into his.

"What I'm doing, Poe," he growls, breaking my fanciful thoughts, "is that I'm going back to that bar. I'm going to find him and then I'm going to fucking finish what I started tonight. Which means I'm not going to stop at just breaking his nose like I did before. I'm going to go all the way and fucking stuff him in a body bag."

His chest is shuddering, moving up and down in waves, his nostrils flared. His forehead is pressed against mine as if he's an animal, a bull, ready to charge.

But he isn't going anywhere.

I'm not letting him.

"Y-you broke his nose tonight?" I ask, my own breath coming in shudders.

He watches me a beat, his eyes still dark and furious. "Let me up, Poe."

"Why?"

His response is a gusty breath and his fingers almost fisting the soft flesh at my waist.

I arch my back at the sting of pain but I don't budge. "Why did you do that? Why did you break his nose?"

Another few beats of silence. Then, "Because he deserved it. Because he fucking made you cry."

It's my turn to go still then.

My turn to pause and cease breathing.

My turn to simply study his anger-lined features. They look even more sculpted like this, even sharper and crisper. More beautiful.

So much so that things inside me get all twisted up.

They get all angsty and restless and heated.

And maybe it's a testament of how much that I manage to overpower him.

I manage to put even more of my tiny weight into it, more of my will and my little body, that I push him back on the bed with a growl. With a shout even.

And then he's flat on his back and I'm straddling his torso, bent over him, my hands clenched in the collar of his shirt.

"You idiot," I say into his face.

That looks as stunned as I feel after having accomplished this feat, overpowering his body like that.

But before he can say anything or overpower me back, I go on, "Why did you do that? Why the hell did you have to do that?" I flex my thighs around his body as I practically sit on his abs that have to be at least a six pack. "Don't you know it by now? I'm like my mother."

At this, his hands that are still somehow hooked on my waist even through this sudden turn of events, tighten. They actually mash my top as he growls in a low voice, "What?"

I swallow painfully, tugging on his collar as I say all the things I've been feeling ever since I found out about him and Charlie. All the parallels that I've been drawing, all the conclusions that I'm coming to.

"Mo told me. She told me everything and you can be mad about that later if you want but first I want you to know that you were right. You were right to avoid me. When I first came to live here. You were right to go out of your way to never be in the same room as me. To never pay me any attention, to not look at me. You were right to go to Italy. You were *right.* I don't even know why you took me in. Why you let me stay under the same roof after..." My thighs flex again;

my whole body flexes and spasms at this point. "But more than that I don't even know how you managed to *care* enough to do other things for me."

At this, his body jerks and tenses under me.

His eyebrows snap together and he opens his mouth to say something.

But I put a hand on his mouth.

I clap my palm over his lips to stop him. Because I'm not finished.

Not by a long shot.

"Mo told me that as well," I tell him, ignoring the softness of his mouth under my palm, the heat of his thick breaths. "That you asked her to look after me when I first came here. She told me that you were the one who told her about my nightmares and that you were the one who'd send her in whenever I cried out. And she told me that you were the one who asked her to deliver the news about St. Mary's. Because you knew that she was my trusted confidant. So maybe I'd take it better, the news. So maybe if my heart broke, it would break in front of her, in front of someone *safe*. As opposed to you."

She told me all that.

She told me everything.

So all that care that I saw, back at his cottage, that threw me off, it was already there. It was real.

He *cared*.

He always did. Even though I can't even imagine how hard it must have been for him. To care for me.

To care for someone so tangled up in his past.

"But not only that, you also sent me to St. Mary's, didn't you?"

His eyes darken and his jaw clenches under my palm but still, I keep my hand over his mouth as I continue, "I figured it out in the car. On the way back while I was crying. All this time I thought that you broke my heart when you sent me away. Every time you forbade me to see him, I thought you were breaking my heart all over again. But you weren't. You were saving me. You were saving my heart. You were protecting it, weren't you? You were protecting me from him. You were protecting me from myself. Because I was too headstrong, too rebellious, too fucking desperate for attention and I didn't listen. But the thing is, Alaric," I lean closer, my hand still on his mouth and his fingers still mangling my top as I whisper fiercely, "that you shouldn't have. You shouldn't have done all of that because I'm like her. I'm like my mother. Like her, I've lied to you. I've deceived you. I've hidden things from you. I've played pranks on you. I've..."

My eyes well up again while his narrow, his breaths bursting under my palm, and I lean even closer.

I touch my lips to the back of my hand that still covers his mouth as I whisper, "Like her, I tried to ruin your life. Can you believe that? I tried to ruin your fucking life, Alaric. Can you imagine how bad I have to be to do that? How malicious. How like Charlie. How like all those people who..." I pause as a tear falls down my eye, plopping onto his hard cheek, "*hurt* you."

His abs flinch then.

His face flinches too as soon as the teardrop lands on his skin.

And I hear a rumbling in his chest but I hug his sides with my thighs and hold him in place.

"They hurt you, Alaric. They hurt you so badly. And I never knew. I could never figure it out. I could never even imagine. And I would. I'd try to come up with all sorts of scenarios, all sorts of crimes that Charlie had committed against you but I could never have imagined this. My brain, my tiny stupid teenage brain, could never have come up with something so horrifying, so... painful and life altering and..."

I breathe through my nose. I breathe through my mouth.

I simply breathe.

None of it helps though.

None of it calms this rage in my heart. This fire in my body.

None of it tames these violent emotions slamming against my bones and so my next words are spoken on a growl while my body bears down harder on him.

"It makes me angry. So angry. It makes me *so fucking angry*, Alaric," I tell him, even as my hand presses harder on his mouth. "That I want to... I want to do something drastic. I want to burn this house down. I want to burn it to the ground because of everything that you went through here. Because of how your father treated you. How he made you feel rejected and unloved. I know about that, you know. I fucking know how much it cuts you, how much it hurts."

I do, don't I?

I know how painful it is. I know how it affects you. I know how lonely it makes you feel.

The rejection. The neglect. The very hatred from someone who's supposed to love you.

I *know*.

I just didn't know that *he* knew as well.

That he's lived with it like I have.

"But that's not all. Because then," I continue, "*then,* Alaric, I want to find those people. The ones who dared to hurt you. The ones who dared to put their hands on you. Who dared to torture you. Who for even a single second *dared* to think that they were better than you. I want to find them and I want to burn them alive too. I want to fucking burn them until I hear them scream and beg and fucking shit their pants out of fear. Do you get that, Alaric? Do you understand what I wanna do before I can even think of calming my shit down?

"But before you say anything, let me tell you that I have thought about it. I *have* thought about maybe not resorting to violence. Maybe being the bigger person and letting bygones be bygones. And maybe breaking every bone in *my* body so I know how you felt. How painful it was. How terrifying. And maybe I'll still do that, I don't know, but then I thought that it doesn't matter. It doesn't matter that it happened a long time ago or that I've come to know how it feels to be in that much pain. It doesn't *matter* because it doesn't change the fact that it happened, okay? It doesn't change the fact that it happened to you. It doesn't change the fact that you were lying in a hospital bed for a month. It doesn't And it doesn't take away your pain or give you that one month of your life back. So this is it. This is it, Alaric. This is what I wanna do. I want vengeance. I want to teach them a fucking lesson. Because I don't think I'm ever calming down again. *Ever*. I don't think I can let this go, Alaric. I'm fucking livid right now."

I am.

I fucking am.

I've been livid ever since Mo told me. Ever since I realized that I'm like her.

I'm like Charlie.

And the worst thing is that it's something that I always wanted. I always wanted to be like her so she could love me.

But I'm only now realizing how wrong I was.

I'm only now realizing the truth of *who* my mother was. The truth of all the things she did, all the things that she was responsible for.

And I never ever want to be that.

I never ever want to be the reason someone gets hurt or has scars and wounds. I never want to be the reason that someone has a bump on his nose and a fuck-ton of rage on the inside.

So no, I don't want to be like my mother.

But I guess I am and I don't know what to do. I don't know how to fix that. How to go back in time and undo all the things that I did to him and…

Before I spiral down that hole of misery, I feel things shift and slide.

Because he's moving. Because he's gripping my wrist and taking it off his mouth. Because his abs are bunching up as he jackknifes on the bed, sitting upright and taking me with him.

But he doesn't stop there.

He twists his torso so fast and with such athletic grace that it's all I can do to hold on to him, his shoulders and his hips, as he reverses our position, making me gasp and making my heart whoosh in my chest.

Which means that now *I'm* the one lying flat on her back in the bed and he's the one leaning over me.

He's the one covering me, dwarfing me with his large body, which is settled in between my thighs, his pelvis locked with mine.

With his hands on either side of my head and him hovering over me like he's going to do a push-up, he rumbles, "Are you done?"

"No," I reply back, my nails digging into his shoulders. "Of course not. Didn't you hear me? I'm not going to be done —"

"You're done," he rumbles again, interrupting me, his eyes moving all over my features.

"Alaric —"

"You're a wildcat, you know that?"

I frown. "What? That's not even —"

"No, that's not true. You're not just a wildcat. You're a dragon."

I fist his shirt and squeeze his hips with my thighs. "Alaric, listen to me, okay? I have a very devious mind. I can do things to these people. I've been trained my entire life to do things to these people. What do you think all my plotting and planning has been for? And —"

His lips twitch as his eyes keep roaming over my features that

I'm pretty sure are flushed with anger still. "You're a pocket-sized dragon." Then, as if to himself, "Angry little Poe is a pocket-sized dragon."

My belly swirls with heat.

It boils and surges with heat.

It surges with the fact that I'm all spread out under him and he's looking at me like I'm the most wondrous thing in the world.

With rapidly diminishing breaths, I whisper, "It's not funny."

His eyes change then.

They go a little darker and harder as he says, "No, it's not. It's fucking hilarious that you think you're like her."

"What?"

He keeps studying my features as he continues, "It's downright comic and tragic that you think you could be like anyone but yourself. That anyone could have your fire, your light. That anyone could burn as bright as you. As loud as you. It's fucking laughable to think that anyone could command attention like you do or that anyone is even worthy of utmost focus and devotion and loyalty like you are. Least of all Charlie. You're you and you do the things you do *because* you're you. You fight and push back and stand up for yourself. And then you wait. You wait for someone to see you, to love you, to give you your first fucking kiss. And you do all that because you're a fighter. You fight for the things you love. You fight for the people you love. When in a fair world, you shouldn't have to. In a fair fucking world, people wouldn't be so stupid and they wouldn't be so blind. So no, Poe, you're not like your mother or anyone else. Because you can't be. Because you're too fucking original and because it's the world that's too stupid to understand you. Is that clear?"

By the time he finishes, I can't breathe.

I can't get air into my lungs.

But that's okay because I'm living on his words. I'm living on the ferocity of them, on the ferocity of his features. They are sharp and dark and so beautiful.

So dear to me.

"Now I want you to promise me something."

His eyes look determined and angry now. Not as angry as they did when I confessed things about Jimmy but still it's enough to make me nod right away and agree. "Anything."

His jaw clenches at my eager answer. Then, "Promise me that you won't waste your time on people like that. Promise me that you're done chasing after people like that. People who don't see you. People who are *incapable* of seeing you. People who don't deserve you. Or your loyalty or your fight or your fire. People who don't deserve your love or your fucking purple polka dot heart."

"I promise," I whisper without hesitation, without holding back.

He doesn't believe me though.

Fisting the sheets, he growls, his eyes even more grave, "No lying, Poe. No more fucking lying, you understand? I don't want you to make a promise that you'll —"

"I'm not," I cut him off, twisting his shirt. "I'm not lying. I promise I'll stop. I promise I won't run after people who don't deserve it." Then, "But more than that I promise that I'll listen to you from now on. I'll listen and I'll obey."

"What?"

I dig my heels in the small of his back as I reply, "I-I know I snuck out tonight and went to see him but that was the last time. I won't do it anymore. I won't lie to you or hide things from you. I won't break your trust. I'll finish summer school and then I'll stay at St. Mary's for as long as you want me to. And this time, I'll follow all your rules. I'll do whatever you want me to, Alaric."

He stares at me a beat.

His eyes dark, his jaw clenched, his fingers fisted in the sheets.

Before his eyelids flicker down.

To my throat, my arched-up neck. His gaze settles on my fluttering pulse and I bite my lip.

I bite my lip harder when he moves on from my wildly beating pulse to my heaving chest. And that's when I realize what I'm wearing. Or rather how flimsy my clothes are, how exposing.

It's not as if I didn't know what sort of clothes I had on before this moment.

I knew I was in my purple pajamas with lace trim.

But this is the first time *he's* noticing it. He's noticing me lying all spread out and underneath him. He's noticing how my thighs are entwined with his and how I'm holding on to his shirt sleeves.

Not only that, he notices how disheveled my top is. How my one fragile little sleeve has been pushed down my arm, leaving my shoulder all bare, pulling the neck even lower. And how the hem is all twisted up, exposing a sliver of my pale belly.

And all of that causes a rush in my body.

So much so that I have to arch up against him. I have to move and squirm under him because I can't contain all these buzzing emotions inside of me. I have to squeeze my thighs around his hips, pull at his shirt, rub my pelvis against his so I can expend this energy. This electricity that seems to be rushing up and down my veins.

And all my effort, my shameless twisting, makes his nostrils flare.

A muscle comes alive on his cheek.

And the moment my top hikes up even more, showing my belly button, he stiffens for a second before moving. Before pulling himself up and away from my body in a split second. As if electrocuted.

As if he can't stand to be so close to me.

I lie there for a second or two until I feel a chill rushing down my body, a cold front replacing the fire.

Making me get up myself.

Making me come up to my knees on the bed and go, "What —"

"I haven't been completely honest with you," he begins, now standing on his feet, his hands shoved down into his pockets.

Looking stern and shut down for the first time since I woke up from my nightmare and found myself in his arms.

This is also the first time that he stands at a distance from me, making me realize that I don't have my glasses on.

Not because I can't see him but because I can.

Without my glasses.

He has made it so by standing within the range of my poor eyesight.

My heart clenches in my chest. At the care he's taking. Still taking. At how mindful he always is because he knows about my vision. And that just makes this sudden separation even more unbearable.

Even colder.

But I fist my hands at my sides, trying to give him space. "Honest about what?"

His jaw moves back and forth. "I guess it's pretty ironic and unfair of me to keep punishing you for lying and for hiding things when I've done the same. But that's the thing. That I have been unfair to you. I've been hard on you for no reason other than the fact that you reminded me of a time in my life that I'd rather forget. You reminded me of her. I guess Mo has already told you all that, but…"

His jaw tightens then; his entire body tightens until he makes himself breathe.

Until he forces himself to move his chest up and down.

"I lied to you that night," he says. "When I said that your lawyer couldn't find someone else to take you in. He could. He did in fact. There was a family, old friends of Charlie, who were ready to take you in, but I refused. Because I wanted to keep you here. Against your wishes. Because I wanted you under my power. I wanted you helpless and hopeless. I wanted to punish you for all the crimes committed against me. And when I realized how wrong I was, I ran. I fucking ran to Italy, thinking that that would absolve everything. Thinking that if I removed myself from your presence, all the crimes that I committed against you would somehow be forgiven.

"And yes, I sent you to St. Mary's to protect you from that asshole, but I was the one who pushed you into his arms in the first place. I was the one who pushed you into rebelling and skipping school and cutting classes. If I hadn't, you probably never would've met him and… And then I came back and did the same thing. I pushed you again. I cornered you again. So what you did today is not your fault, it's mine. I made you do it. But it stops now."

He shifts on his feet. "It stops tonight. I can't take back everything that I've done. Every lie I've told, every unfairness that I've dealt, but I can give you back your freedom."

My heart thuds. "What?"

"You are free. From St. Mary's. From this mansion. From me. I'll make arrangements for you to finish your summer classes early so you can graduate and I'll set up a meeting with the lawyers to get the paperwork sorted to transfer funds." Then, "I haven't been a good guardian to you. And I want you to know that I'll regret that. I'll regret punishing you for the things that weren't your fault, pushing you, torturing you, trapping you. I'll regret not seeing you as your own person since the beginning. But most of all I'll regret making you think that I hated you when I never did."

Chapter Twenty-Three

I'm free.

I'm finally free.

I have what I want. What I've wanted for years now.

My freedom. My control.

Or almost, at least.

He's called me into his office this afternoon to talk about it. To discuss my classes and assignments so I can make up for my grades and finish summer school early. He says he also wants to talk to me about meeting with the lawyers. Or rather, Mo told me that that's what he said.

She was very happy this morning at breakfast while she relayed the news to me. She was happy that he was doing the right thing after all. That he was going to let me go and live my life in New York. She said that she'd miss me of course and that I could always come back here for a visit.

I didn't say anything to her. I didn't make any promises.

All I did was smile and finish my breakfast before getting in the car that he'd arranged for me and coming back to St. Mary's. Where all morning, I attended classes and went through the routine. And now I'm here, in front of his office, right on time for the appointment.

I knock at the door and it opens before I even finish lowering my arm.

He's wearing his usual clothes, a dark gray dress shirt, a shiny black tie, and a matching tweed jacket with elbow patches. His hair is combed back, not a strand out of place, and his jaw is clean-shaven.

He's all polished and every inch the history professor slash principal of a reform school.

Unlike how he was last night.

All disheveled with wrinkled clothes and spiky, messy hair.

Without a word and regarding me dispassionately, he steps aside so I can enter. He then closes the door and walks around me, approaching the desk. "Take a seat."

His voice sounds very professional and principal-ish as well and I walk up to the chair, obeying his command. When he's all situated in his chair on the other side of the desk, he begins, "I've discussed your situation with the faculty and we've all come to an agreement that with a few assignments and quizzes, you should be able to make up your grades and graduate." His eyes are on a file in front of him that he opens and flicks through. "Considering your lack of grades over the last year, I'd say math and biology are the ones that require the most effort from you. I've talked to the respective teachers and they both feel that you'd be required to complete three homework assignments and two make-up quizzes. The rest are pretty straightforward. However…"

He says a lot of things after that.

He explains what quizzes I'd have to take and what the assignments would require. All the reading material and whatnot.

I'm not listening to him, however.

I've tuned him out not because what he's saying isn't important but because I have other important things to focus on. Like the fact that when he reads, he has this habit of lifting his eyes while keeping his chin dipped and for some reason, I find that extremely… sexy.

I find that extremely commanding and authoritative.

The way his forehead creases slightly and the way his eyelids flicker as he looks up at you when he's busy doing his favorite thing in the world.

And then there's that pinky finger of his with that silver ring.

While reading, he has a habit of resting that finger right at the corner of a book, right at the edge, and then tapping it, the pages, the binding, whatever, every now and then. Making that silver flash and sparkle like a beacon. I guess he does that when he drinks as well, tapping the glass with his pinkie.

I find that extremely sexy as well.

I find it so sexy that I can't help but ask, "Why do you wear that ring?"

I've always wondered about it but never had the chance to ask. And now, this might be my only chance since he wants me to leave soon.

My question makes him stop talking. It makes him lift his eyes in that sexy way of his and go, "What?"

I tip my chin at his left pinkie. "That ring. Why do you wear it?"

He stares at me a beat, just like that, keeping his face dipped, his forehead creased, before he lifts his face and replies, "It's a family heirloom."

The mention of his family gets me alert. It makes me sit up straight on the chair as I ask, "What does it mean?"

He notices the change in my demeanor with a flick of his glance but shows no outward reaction. "Not much. It's just something every Marshall wears when he assumes his responsibilities."

"So like your…" I pause and lick my lips, "dad gave it to you?"

"No." A pause, then, "It was in the will. He was indisposed at the time."

"What does —"

He sighs. "He has dementia. Alzheimer's. Meaning he doesn't remember anything. Doesn't recognize anything nor is he aware of anything."

My heart is racing. "Where does he… I never saw him. At the mansion."

His eyes narrow slightly. "Mo didn't tell you that?"

Shame pricks my chest that Mo was the one to tell me something intensely private to him. "No."

I wanted to ask her though. But I stopped myself; I'd already broken so much of Alaric's trust that I wasn't willing to add another breach to my list.

He watches me for a beat. "That's because he lives in an assisted facility."

I clench my fists in my lap. "Do you, I mean, ever see him?"

"Every month."

"You go see him every month?"

"Yes."

I swallow. "But he was…"

I don't know what to say here. I don't know how to put into

words what his father was. How he treated Alaric. How he was responsible for making Alaric feel unwanted and hated. I hated him the first time I heard of him last night from Mo, and I hate him now. The news of his condition doesn't change that fact. It does make me feel pity toward him though.

"He was an asshole, yes," Alaric finishes the sentence for me, his shoulders tight. "But he's still my father and hence my responsibility."

"Do you always fulfill your responsibilities?"

His jaw tenses for a second before he replies, "Yes."

"Do you always *like* fulfilling your responsibilities?"

Another few seconds pass in silence as he watches me with a firm jaw. Then, "No."

"So then —"

"But it's necessary, like this one. So can we get back to it?" he cuts me off and glances down at the file. "I have an appointment right after."

I want to prod more.

I want to ask him more. Ask him all about his childhood, his dad, the school he went to.

Even though I know the story now, it doesn't mean I know what *he* felt.

He never told me anything.

In his *own* words.

But I'm not going to. At least not right now.

When he's so determined to fulfill his responsibility toward me.

"I've arranged a meeting with lawyers of both parties at the end of the week. I'd like you to be there so we can go over the terms of the trust fund and what the next steps are." He flicks a page. "While you're under no obligation to listen or to follow those steps, I'd highly recommend that you do so anyway. I think it'll be wise to set some money aside in investments and stocks. Low-yield bonds are a good solution long term and the lawyers can help you with that. And I'm thinking that maybe you should consider applying for a fashion or design program of some sort. Not this year of course, but the next. In the meantime, we should look into community colleges and something similar. While I make no promises, I can talk to a few of my colleagues and see what I can come up with and —"

"You want me to go to fashion school?"

Again, he looks up in that typical way of his. "Yes. If you want your designs to be out there someday, on a runway, you'll need training."

I stare at him in disbelief.

"But that was..." I shake my head. "That was just something I said. And it's freaking crazy and impossible to even —"

"If you work for it, it won't be."

"But I —"

"No," he says sternly then, raising his face, his eyes determined. "I'm not going to hear any excuses, Poe. You're good. You're talented. And I told you that you're done hiding. All you need is a little focus and discipline and you can make this happen. Not to mention, now is the time to get serious about your future. You're about to graduate high school. You're about to go out in the world. You need a goal. And you need a solid plan to reach that goal." He nods as if to emphasize. "I think we should make a list of colleges and then we can divide them into three tiers. Top choices, middle choices, and safety schools, based on their program, how strong and prestigious it is, and their admissions criteria. Although I do understand that you might not want my help, and that's okay. In that case, we can go through lawyers and mediators. But I want you to know that I'll help you in any way that I can. Especially through this whole transition period. And —"

"I don't want to go," I whisper.

Or rather mumble incoherently.

Which makes him frown and say, "Excuse me?"

I clench my fists in my lap and take a deep breath.

Hoping that it might help with my nerves. No such luck though.

My heart is still beating like a restless bird. My heart is still twisting and turning and clenching like it has been ever since he came to my room last night and held me in his arms — his strong guardian arms — to protect me from my nightmares.

And then told me that he was letting me go.

As soon as he left my room last night, I'd made my decision.

I'd decided — firmly and without hesitation — as to what *I* wanted to do.

And all morning, through breakfast and the drive over and through all my classes, I kept waiting for the moment, for the chance, to break it to him.

This decision.

But now that it's here, I'm nervous.

Not because I'm nervous about the decision itself but because I need to convince him of it.

And under his dark, slightly confused scrutiny, I can hear my heart beating in my ears.

I clear my throat, mostly just to hear my own voice over my heart, and sit up straight. I inch up my glasses, and while he watches me compose myself, I say, very clearly this time, "I don't want to go."

Apparently, it's not clear enough for him though because he goes, "I think we've already discussed about you going to a fashion school, and so —"

I clutch my skirt. "No, not the fashion school." I frown. "Although that's super surreal to think about but…" I shake my head. "What I mean is that I don't want to leave St. Mary's. Not yet. I want to finish summer school."

Finally, I've made myself clear.

I can see it.

My words and my meaning have finally registered and they have done it in an impactful way. In a way that straightens his already straight shoulders. That makes his already hard jaw harder and firmer, and his frown much thicker than before.

"What?"

Even his deep voice is deeper and I have to remind myself that I knew this could happen.

I knew it might take him a while to warm up to this turn of events.

Given that he was adamant about letting me go last night. Given how adamant *I* have been about leaving.

"I'd like to finish summer school the right way and —"

"What's the right way?"

His interruption throws me again but *again,* I knew this would be the case so I'm determined. "By staying until the end. Finishing all my classes and then taking the tests."

For a few moments, he doesn't say anything.

He simply studies me, my features. My glasses, my bangs. Then, "Why?"

Finally a question that I have prepared for.

This boosts my confidence a little bit and I begin in a much calmer voice, "Because the reason that you're willing to let me graduate early is because you're my guardian. There are two other girls here who are going through the same thing but they have to stay until the end. So why I should be treated differently just because I have an in with the principal?" I nod for good measure. "So I've decided that it's best for me to finish out summer school and then leave."

Again, he takes me in for a few moments. Then his eyes flash and he rumbles, "You've decided."

"Yes. I don't want special treatment."

"*You* don't want special treatment."

Something about the way he says it makes me blush and shift in my seat. "No, I don't."

His gaze is unwavering as he goes, "And that's why you want to stay here for another four weeks."

"Yes."

No.

Well, kinda.

Okay, so I said that I wouldn't lie to him and I'm not. Not totally.

I'm just not divulging the entire reason.

And the entire reason is that I'm not done.

With him.

Not yet.

And it's crazy. I get that.

It's absolutely fucking crazy when all I've wanted for the past four years is to *be* done with him. All I've wanted ever since he appeared in my life out of nowhere is for him to disappear. To let me go, let me free.

But then, I didn't know him four years ago.

In fact, I didn't know anything about him up until a month or even a day ago.

Yes, things had started to change between us ever since summer school started but up until last night, I didn't know him.

Not really.

I didn't know what he'd lived through, all the things that he'd endured and survived. I didn't know that his story was similar to mine. No, I didn't go through the sheer pain and the torture that he had. But there is this one pain that I know very well.

And it's the pain of being unloved.

Of being hated at the hands of the very people who were supposed to love us.

In that sense, we're the same, him and me.

So I'm not going anywhere.

I can't.

How can I when I've just found someone exactly like me? When I've found someone whose heart, whose very soul matches mine. When there's so much still to discover. When there's so much that I want to know about him.

I'm not going to tell him that though.

I don't want to freak him out.

I mean, it's freaking *me* out.

That the man I've hated for so long, my devil guardian, my tyrant principal, is actually my soulmate.

Soulmate.

Alaric Rule Marshall is my fucking soulmate.

It's insane.

Not to mention, we've just, and *only barely*, gotten on civil terms. We've just cleared out the air between us, shed all our lies and all the things we've done in the past. So this partial reason will have to do.

And on that note — the one where we just cleared the air between us — I have something for him.

"So," I begin, squirming in my seat. "I brought you something."

He was already watching me with suspicion but at my unexpected words, his suspicion climbs. His eyes narrow even further and he goes, "You brought me something."

I nod. "I know we've had our difficulties in the past and —"

"That's one way to put it."

But I forge on. "And what you told me last night, what you did and why you did it, I…" I shift on my seat again, my heart racing, "I don't condone it. I want you to know that. I don't think it was right. You never should've done it. Lying to me and making me pay for something that I never did. But I do understand why you did it. I do understand why you felt like you had to trap me and keep me under your control. And even though it wasn't right or fair to me, I still forgive you for it."

A flinch goes through his body.

A shudder that leaves tightness and granite in its wake.

His fists clench around the file he's still holding and his features go sharp.

"I know you think that you pushed me into doing what I did yesterday and that may be so, but I still did it. I made that choice myself and… And I know that you've forgiven me for it, haven't you?"

His only response is to clench his jaw but I do get the message.

I know he has.

That's why he's letting me go after everything. That's why he sat down with the faculty and came up with all these plans. That's why he's meeting with the lawyers this week to give me back my freedom.

And that's why I can't leave.

Because I know that as soon as I do, he'll disappear from my life. He'll never contact me or see me or talk to me again. While I believe that he will help me through the transition like he said he would, he'll make himself scarce after that. Something he's an expert at. And while that would've been okay with me before — that's exactly what I wanted even — I'm not okay with it now.

Hence I go on, "So I forgive you for all the things that you did as well."

Then, the hardest part.

The part where I give him the thing I brought for him.

Looking away from him and bending down, I retrieve it from my bookbag. Clutching it in my trembling fingers, I look up to find him still studying me, still tight and rigid. "So as I said, I brought you something."

I bring it up to the desk to show him.

For a long moment, he simply stares at me and not my offering, his eyes flicking back and forth between mine, as if trying to know all my secrets.

But the thing is that I don't have any.

Well, apart from that soulmate thing.

So I let him study me. I let him stare at me and pick me apart. I let his penetrating, intense chocolate chip eyes dig deep and peer into my soul. Which I imagine perks up and sighs at being under his scrutiny.

When he's studied me to his heart's content, he glances down.

He stares at the object for a couple of seconds before lifting his eyes. "A phone."

My fingers flex around the cold object — my old phone that I'd left back at the mansion when I was sent to St. Mary's. The one he put the tracker on, but it's not important right now.

"Yes," I say, nodding my head. "But what's on the phone is more important."

"And what's on the phone?"

Right.

Okay.

Shifting yet again, I say, "It's my trust." He frowns and I explain, "In you. I'm giving this to you to show you that I trust you. That I feel safe with you. Despite whatever you did. And I also want you to know that you can trust me. And you can feel safe with me. Despite whatever *I* did." I glance down at the phone then. "This is me wiping the slate clean between us. You know, and putting everything that has happened behind us. This is me waving the white flag."

I nod again.

I also put the phone on his desk and bring my hands back to my lap.

Still staring at it, I continue, "Uh, okay. Yeah. So…" I sigh, rubbing my sweaty palms up and down my skirt. "It's in the photos folder. I'm gonna leave this with you and you can look at it, uh, whenever you have time and if you'd like to discuss something with me regarding this, uh, you know where to find me and —"

"I'd like to discuss it."

I jerk my eyes up. "What?"

He hasn't even looked at the phone; I can tell. Not beyond that half- second glance.

All this time, he's been looking at me. Staring at me, watching me, and my already hot cheeks heat up at the realization.

They heat up because his eyes are shimmering with something. Something that makes me breathless. Something that makes me bite my lip.

At which point, he orders, growling, "Right now."

That makes me breathless too.

His growl.

But I manage to ask, "But I thought you had an appointment right after and —"

"Fuck the appointment."

My toes curl. "But I really think you should see it after I leave."

"I really think I should see it now."

"But —"

"Now."

That growl is the thickest I think. The roughest and the deepest I've ever heard from him.

And it makes me obey him. It makes me go for the phone.

This time, it feels heavy when I pick it up. And when I come to my feet, the weight of it grows heavier.

It only keeps growing with every step I take toward him.

So by the time I reach him — which only takes like five seconds but they are enough — I'm a breathless mess. My phone is too heavy and my fingers are trembling, and it's almost a relief when I offer it to him.

Not that he takes it right away.

Sitting there, in his luxurious leather chair turned toward me, revealing his sprawled thighs and shiny Italian loafers, he first watches me with his dark eyes. He rubs his mouth with his left pinkie while he considers me for a few moments.

I'm not sure what he's thinking but I'd really like him to hurry up.

Because if he doesn't, I'm going to drop the phone.

It's as if he can read my thoughts — which is quite possible, to be honest — so he goes for it. He reaches out and grabs the phone from my hand, his silver ring tapping against the glass.

The dull sound makes me fist my school skirt.

For a second, all I can do is stare at that phone in his large hand. Stare at his big thumb, his roughened knuckles as he holds that device in his hand.

And that's when I relax.

Because it's his hand.

His.

My phone — my trust — is in his hand and what I told him stands corrected.

I do trust him. I do feel safe with him.

It has happened gradually over the course of the last few weeks and it was cemented last night.

So with all the trust in my heart, I repeat, "It's in the photos folder."

And then, I simply watch him tap his fingers on the screen, go to the location I pointed out and… freeze.

Yeah, he freezes.

As in, literally freezes with his thumb hovering over the screen, halted in its track to tap on it.

On the thing I brought for him.

Not to mention, his chest.

That's frozen as well. It's not moving. It's not going up and down.

Oh, and his face. His features. That frown between his brows that's been coming and going ever since we started this conversation is here and is frozen.

See? This is why I wanted to leave the office.

This is why I wanted to be gone when he looked at it.

Or them.

The photos.

My photos.

My *nude* photos.

Chapter Twenty-Four

Yes, I brought him nude photos of me to look at.

And to keep.

That's important. That I brought him my nude photos to *keep.*

I know it's a little extreme and insane but what I did yesterday was extreme and insane as well. I was going to seduce him — my guardian turned principal — and I was going to record it. I was then going to use that clip, where he'd be seen taking advantage of me, to blackmail him.

I was going to bring his character, his reputation into question. Now he could do the same with me. He could very well use these pictures to blackmail *me.*

He could use these pictures to make me do things, to subjugate me, to trap me.

But I know he won't.

That's the whole point here.

That I trust him and that he can trust me as well.

So there.

White flag.

Although I would like to point out that when I say nude pictures, it means nude of course but all the important parts are covered. By my hands mostly, and by the sheets. So it's not as if I'm showing things I shouldn't be showing.

But tell that to him because he's still frozen.

He's still in a trance.

And I can't stand the silence so I break it. "So I know this might seem extreme to you. But I just wanted to give you something that would show you that I trust you. And that you can trust me too. Like, you could use this against me. If you wanted to. You could put these pictures up on the internet or blackmail me with them. But I know you wouldn't. I know you'd protect me and keep me safe. I know you're my guardian. I realize that now. And this should show you that I would never, not ever, bug your office like I did before or do anything to hurt you either. So this is like a token of trust, you know. Because we've both broken each other's trust in the past and I thought that it was important to —"

"You thought it was important to give me naked pictures of yourself."

That's the first thing he's said and I gulp in a huge relieved breath that he's not still as a statue.

In fact, he even looks up.

That thumb of his goes down and taps the screen, bringing up a photo of me.

In this one, I'm sitting on the bed, my legs folded under me and hidden by the sheet. But my torso and my chest are visible, and I'm hiding my breasts with my arms as I look at the camera, my hair all strewn haphazardly around me.

"I know you think that these are just naked pictures but —"

"These *are* just naked pictures," he says, his voice low and his eyes flashing.

"Yes, but as I've explained before, they're also —"

"A token of trust, yeah."

Since he keeps interrupting me, I clench my skirt tightly and lean toward him. "Yes, and I'm giving them to you because I want us to forget the past and move on. I want us to be friends, and I definitely think that we could be because —"

At this, his entire body moves.

It draws up and back, his impossibly broad shoulders rigid and his chest moving up and down with large breaths. But the voice he uses is low and gravelly, almost still, completely in contrast to the way his body is flickering and in motion. "You want us to be friends."

"Yes." I inch up my glasses. "I'd like that very much."

It's not as if my answer was surprising and came out of left field. I mean, I just said that, but still he takes a moment to absorb it. Like he wasn't expecting it.

He takes a moment to absorb *me*, standing there in front of him, clutching my school skirt, curling my toes inside my Mary Janes.

I know he can't see my toes but I have a feeling that he might still know what I'm doing with them.

He might still know that my heart is fluttering inside my chest and my belly is whooshing because of the way he's watching me. And maybe that's why he doesn't move his gaze, because he knows it's affecting me, when he comes to his feet.

And since he was already so close to me, I have to crane my neck all the way up to look at him.

Hiccupping with rapid breaths, I ask, "W-what are you doing?"

He responds by leaning down over me. And before I can ask him again, he backs me up like he did yesterday. And he keeps doing that until I'm up on his desk, sitting on his files, again like yesterday.

"Alaric..." I breathe out, clutching his tweed jacket. "What's happening? What —"

Putting his hands on my waist, he squeezes my flesh with a force that makes me arch up my chest and almost whimper. "When'd you take them? The pictures."

My heart is racing at his rough words. "Last night."

His eyes rove over my face. "At the mansion."

"Yes."

"And that's clearly your bed."

"Yeah."

He lets me rest for a second before he fires off another question. "Did you do it right after I left your room?"

Something about the way he asks me this question makes me blush. "Y-yes."

His eyes narrow for a second. "So you took your clothes off the second I left you alone."

I gasp. "But I —"

"And then you posed in front of the camera while I was right next door."

"You weren't right next door. You were —"

"Down the hall," he interrupts, his hands squeezing my waist again. "Same fucking thing."

"Alaric, I —"

"Actually, I wasn't down the hall," he murmurs then, to himself. "I was right outside your fucking door, pacing the fucking hallway because I wanted to make sure that I heard you if you *motherfucking* screamed in your sleep again."

"What?"

"I was right outside your door, Poe. I was right the fuck outside."

"I didn't —"

He clenches his teeth. "While you were in there, in your room, naked and ripe and flushed. While you were —"

This time I cut him off. "You were keeping an eye on me. You were watching over me."

My breathless voice makes him breathe deep. "Yeah, while you were in your room so fucking eager to be my friend."

"I'm eager right now too."

In fact, I'm even more eager.

I'm dying.

I'm practically dying and writhing in agony to be his friend. To mend our rift. To trust each other.

Because he was watching over me.

My guardian was keeping an eye on me last night and I know Mo told me about that but this is the first time that I've seen it or known about it first-hand and I don't know what to do.

I don't know what to do except everything.

Except every single thing that he wants me to do. Every single thing that I *can* do for him.

At my words, his chest expands on a breath.

His fingers flex on my waist. Then, "You're eager to be my friend."

I nod enthusiastically. "Yes."

"And you take your clothes off and pose in front of the camera for all your friends."

I shift on the desk, crinkling the papers. "N-no. Just for you."

"For me." He scoffs slightly. "How about fuck-me eyes?"

I jump at his words. "What?"

"You give those fuck-me eyes to all your friends or is that something just for me too?"

"F-fuck-me eyes?"

"Yeah," he rasps. "Flushed cheeks and parted mouth. That arched-up back that makes your tits look all bouncy and juicy, thrusting up to the fucking sky. And those big blue eyes, all drowsy and hooded, behind your librarian glasses. Yeah, that's a fuck-me look, Poe. Is that for me?"

I blush hard.

Harder than I've ever done before.

Because I didn't know that he'd notice. I didn't know that he'd catch me.

Actually I didn't even know that I *would* do something like that.

I didn't want to.

This was serious business.

I was doing this for good reasons but then those reasons turned bad.

Then those reasons turned… horny.

The more pictures I took, the more I imagined what he'd think when he looked at them. And the more I imagined him all angry and authoritative, his jaw clenching, his eyes narrowing, the more turned on I got.

"I just… I got horny," I whisper.

A muscle jumps on his cheek.

Before he leans closer and as always, my thighs wrap themselves around his hips.

I'm not even sure when this became a habit because we've only been this close a couple of times and only yesterday, but it has, and I hook my legs around his hips like they belong there.

And he settles himself between my thighs like he belongs here as well.

"Horny," he whispers.

"Yes," I eagerly nod and tell him.

He grits his teeth. "Because you were writhing around in bed, flashing your tits at me."

"My t-tits are covered."

He scoffs. "Fucking barely."

"You can't see my nipples." Then, "Well, not in this one at least."

"Explain."

"There's pictures where you can see them."

He pauses, his nostrils flaring. "There are pictures where I can…"

"Uh-huh." I lick my lips. "Uh, later."

"Later."

"Yes."

"What happened *later*?"

I lick my lips again and he growls. He isn't even hiding it or being subtle about it, about his animal noises.

"I let my…" I whisper. "I let my fingers slip."

"You let your fingers slip."

"Yeah."

A puff of breath. "You let your *motherfucking* fingers slip and flashed me your pink puffy nipples."

I swallow. "My sheet too."

"What about the sheet?"

"I let that slip too."

It takes a second for him to understand. As if his brain is sluggish. As if I'm killing him, his common sense, slowly but surely with all the things that I'm saying.

But when he finally understands, his eyes flare wide and his mouth parts.

He licks it, his mouth, as he rasps, "You… You fucking flashed me…"

"My pussy," I finish for him because he couldn't seem to.

He couldn't seem to do anything but stare at me with such… violence right now. Such thick intensity and belligerence, like I'm ruining his life.

But I'm not.

I did it for good reasons. Noble reasons.

And yes I became a little horny while doing it but so what?

It was for him. My guardian.

For the man who's protected me all these years, who's tried to keep my heart safe. Who was pacing up and down the hallway last night in case I woke up from another nightmare.

And it feels even more right today.

That I shouldn't be feeling this for my guardian or that he's also my principal or even the fact that I was in love with someone else up until last night doesn't even register.

Fuck Jimmy. Fuck the world.

I don't care.

This is right.

This is my Alaric.

"Alaric?"

"So you couldn't stop yourself then, could you?"

"What?"

"You set out to be my friend but along the way, you flashed me your ripe tits and your cherry pie pussy, and you couldn't stop yourself from becoming a whore for me."

I squeeze my thighs around his hips. "God, no. I couldn't. I loved it."

I *love* it so much.

Maybe I shouldn't but I do.

I so do.

I want to be a whore for him. I *am* a whore for him.

God, I am.

"So what did you do?" he asks, swallowing. "Did you clench your thighs? Press them together? Real hard and real tight. When you got horny."

I go to press my thighs together right now but I can't because he's between them so all I end up doing is squirming and squeezing his body as I whisper, "Yes."

"Why, because there was an ache in your belly?"

I can't sit straight now. I twitch and move, ruining his documents on the desk, but I don't think he cares much. I don't care either except to whisper, "Yes."

I bite my lip.

And his gaze hones in on it.

I bite my lip harder.

And his nostrils flare.

"And what about your tits?" he growls.

"W-what about them?"

"Were they heavy, achy too?"

I nod eagerly again. "Yeah. They were all achy and hurt-y."

"Yeah, they were," he rasps, his face dipping closer. "That's why you flashed me your nipples, didn't you? You wanted to show me. You wanted to show how hard they were, yeah?"

"But you weren't there."

"Yeah. Fuck me for that, huh. That I wasn't there. So you had to take matters into your own hands."

"Uh-huh."

"I bet. I bet there came a point when your tits got so heavy, your nipples got so hurt-y that you weren't only using your hands to play peekaboo with the camera, you were also using your tiny little hands to play something else. Weren't you?"

"Yes. I did. I played with my tits."

A shudder goes through him and I wrap my arms around his shoulders to give him strength. "Were you kneading your creamy tits, Poe? Your creamy and milky and ripe fucking tits?"

"Yes."

"Were you jiggling them too, plumping them up, making them all pink and swollen? Making them all big, bigger than they are."

"Yes."

His cheekbones turn crimson. "Because they're big, aren't they? They're so big, they make my fucking mouth water."

"They d-do?"

"Fuck yeah. Always. They make me thirsty, Poe. They make me want to drink from them."

My tits perk up and jiggle with my next breath as I say, "Oh, but you can. You can. I promise."

His chest shudders again. "Let's not talk about it, yeah? Because I don't want to blow in my pants like a fucking teenager."

"W-what?"

"Let's talk about something else. Let's talk about your nipples," he says. "What did you do to your nipples?"

"I-I pinched them."

He glances down at my tits then. They're all thrusting out, shamelessly and proudly. My nipples are scraping against my blouse and I think he can see them.

I think he can see the outline of them.

And I get the proof when he digs his fingers into my waist so hard, I twist and come off the table almost. I moan in a delicious kind of pain and he growls again.

"I bet they're all pink, aren't they?" he grunts. "All pink and puffy, the size of a fucking quarter. I bet they're so sensitive that you twist them a little, you pull at them mixed in with a tug and you go off." He looks up then. "You go off, Poe, don't you? When someone plays with your nipples. When someone flicks them and pulls at them and fucking sucks on them like they're drinking from your tits because they've been parched for a goddamn century."

Somehow my hands are up in his hair now and at his filthy, graphic words, I whimper. "But no one has ever..."

That makes him shudder even more and he takes in a noisy breath. "Yeah. That's right, isn't it? No one has touched your tits. No one has sucked on them, on your ripe little nipples. No one has ever been in there, in your body. I keep forgetting that, like an asshole." Then, dropping his sweaty forehead to mine, he rasps, "I keep forgetting that she only *acts* like a whore, but my cute little Poe is a virgin."

A spasm goes through my body. An earthquake of all earthquakes.

At his *cute*.

Making me think that I came. Making me think that I broke apart.

But I haven't. I'm still whole.

Because I'm throbbing now.

I'm fucking pulsing and buzzing like an electric wire. My nerve endings are so primed. My tits and my pussy are so primed.

Every part of my body is so primed right now and acting exactly like he said.

Like a whore.

Like a whore with no relief.

And I have no shame in begging now. No shame in begging him to give it to me.

"Alaric, please," I whisper.

He has no plans of giving it to me though, because he goes on, rolling his forehead over mine. "So tell me more, Poe. What else did you do to your nipples?"

"But I —"

"Tell me," he insists.

And in a surprising turn of events, I realize that he's the one begging now. He's the one asking me to give him something and I can't refuse. I can't let his needs go unfulfilled, so setting aside my own needs, I bring my hands over to his face. I clutch his jaw, caress his cheeks, and whisper, "I also scratched them."

He shudders again, his eyes liquid and fiery. "Because you're a wildcat."

"I am."

Your wildcat...

I don't say it but I think he hears it anyway because he swallows.

"And then I," I continue, rubbing the bump on his nose, digging my thumbs in the hollows of his cheeks, "I also touched myself."

At this his body stills for a second before his breaths become gusty. His chest rapidly moving up and down, his stomach hollowing out, his jaw tight.

And I hug him with my thighs, soothe him with my fingers on his face. "I played with my pussy. It was so wet, Alaric. So juicy and drip-y. I dripped onto the sheets I think. I think I left a stain. And I kept thinking that if you saw it, if you saw the stain on my sheets, would you make me lick it up too? Like you said you would. If I ever dripped on your leather chairs or on your leather-bound books. Also your shoes too. On your Italian loafers. They're leather too, aren't they? And you said that you'd make me clean it all up, remember? Lick your shoes and God, I –"

"Stop," he growls.

And I do. Not because of his words but because of his hands.

That travel and become fists in my hair. And pull.

They pull my head back and stretch my neck so hard that I gasp.

I gasp at the force. I gasp at the look on his face, all rage-y and angry and tight.

I gasp at his words.

"Stop ruining my fucking life."

"What?"

His eyes are harsh as he says, "I want you to listen to me, all right?"

I grip his shirt, my haze breaking. "What —"

He tightens his fist in my hair. "I don't want to be your friend."

"What?"

"I don't want your fucking token of trust."

"But —"

He pulls my head back further, stretching my neck up. "No, you listen to me, you want to stay here and finish summer school the right fucking way *despite my wishes*, you do that. I've already forced you to do things that you didn't want to do so I'm not going to fucking force you again. So if you want to attend your classes, you attend your classes. You want to do your homework, you do your fucking homework. You take your tests. But that's it. That is it, you understand? You don't come into my office and show me naked fucking pictures. You don't come into my office claiming to want to be my friend. Because guess what, we're not friends. We're not buddies, you and me. We're not going to sit down and gossip and do each other's hair and wear matching fucking friendship bracelets.

"What we are, is guardian and ward. You understand what that means? That means that I'm the one who protects you. I'm the one who keeps you safe. Who watches over you. Who wards danger off you. What I don't do, Poe, is look at your hot plump body. What I don't do is watch you play peekaboo with your big fucking tits like they're ripe juicy melons ready for plucking. And I definitely don't watch you writhe on my desk, on my fucking lecture notes and your lesson plans as you tell me all the ways you played with your pussy last night. I don't do that, Poe. And I won't fucking do that."

His eyes narrow. "After four years of being a shitty guardian to you, a guardian who's ruined your life, who's toyed with it and played with it like it's his own amusement park, I'm not going to be an even shittier one who toys with your body, you understand? So you're going to get down from my desk, go into the bathroom and throw water on your face, rearrange your uniform to look respectable like it did when you entered my office, and then you'll leave. You'll only come to me if you need something your guardian or your principal can provide. Because that's the extent of our relationship, and I want you to remember that."

Chapter Twenty-Five

The Renaissance Man

I'm a guardian.

A guardian is the one who defends.

He is the one who protects and keeps and preserves.

That's from the dictionary.

I believe the dictionary. I believe in following the rules. I believe in doing the responsible thing.

Not to mention, I believe in being strong enough to do the responsible thing no matter how much I hate it.

This is not the responsible thing.

Nowhere in the dictionary or anywhere else does it say that a guardian is supposed to pick up his purple-loving, fire-breathing, *havoc-wreaking* wildcat of a ward's phone and look at naked pictures of her.

Nowhere does it say that he's supposed to not only look at those naked pictures but bring the phone up to his nose and smell the screen like a fucking pervert.

The dictionary, the rule books, all the fucking books don't say that when a guardian smells the screen, he should then get a hard-on. Not that the hard-on ever went anywhere.

It was there five minutes ago when she finally left. It was there ten minutes ago when she was telling me about what she did last night.

And it has been there for longer than that.

Ever since she showed me those pictures, asking to be friends.

Friends.

Fuck friends.

So yeah, it's there.

And it's fucking throbbing.

It's fucking hurting like a motherfucker and I want to bring it out and wrap my hands around it, and fucking jack off until I ruin her phone.

Until I come all over her naked photos.

Until I bring her back and fucking make her lick it all up, for doing these things to me.

For fucking with me, fucking with my head.

Sitting in my chair, I decide that I'm not going to do it, however.

I'm not going to do anything.

Because I'm a guardian. And a guardian doesn't do these things.

A guardian is strong and good and fucking responsible and as I told her, I'll be damned if I don't live up to that.

Not to mention, I'm also the principal.

The principal who's here to fix this school after all the indiscretions — similar indiscretions with students — done over the past year by none other than faculty members.

So I'm going to sit here and focus on my work.

And the first order of business is doing something that I've been avoiding doing for so long: implementing the bed check rule.

As a reminder that I'm here to do a job.

Not fuck around with a girl I should stay away from.

Chapter Twenty-Six

I'm not good at following the rules.

I'm not good at obeying or doing what I'm told or even doing the right thing or taking the high road.

But I'm doing it now.

I'm doing it because I promised him.

I promised to obey him, and I intend to follow through.

Even if it means that we won't be friends. Even if it means that I have to stay away from him, and any relationship between us will be that of a guardian and a ward, or a principal and a student.

Even if it means that I have to watch him from afar when he leaves his cottage and makes that highly popular walk up to the school building. And that I have to sit on the stone benches and listen to all the girls giggle and fawn over him and pretend that I don't want to scratch their eyes out. Not only during that walk but also other times, like when he goes to buy his lunch from the cafeteria or passes by in the hallway.

Without sparing them a glance.

Without sparing *me* a glance.

Besides, it's not as if he wasn't doing that before. It's not as if I wasn't doing any of those things before either.

We've both been following the same routine, the same pattern.

It's just that it hurts now. It makes me ache. It makes me feel a kind of hollowness that I've never felt before.

And it's because he's my soulmate and I've just realized that.

I've just realized that he and I are the same, and now I won't get to know him. I won't get to get close to him.

I won't get to kiss him.

Because I want to.

I want to give my first kiss to him.

I'm not sure when I decided that. Was it the moment Mo told me his story and everything simply clicked inside of me? Or when he confessed to all the crimes he'd committed, his regret so plain to see? Or it could have been even before that, every time I showed him my designs and he stared at them with a reverence that shook me to the core, the day he told me that he'd keep my secret safe.

All I know is that the moment he essentially kicked me out of his office after those photos, I knew.

In my heart. In my bones. In my very soul.

Like a realization that had been living deep inside of me but only now floating to the surface.

But again, I'm not going to do anything. I promised to stay away from him and I will.

And there are plenty of things to keep me occupied.

First are classes.

Now that I'm committed to finishing summer school and I'm not actively trying to plot and plan things, I'm giving classes a shot. And I have to say that they aren't that bad. Or tough even.

I mean, I'm still not a fan of sitting inside a classroom and listening to lectures, but if I pay a little attention, I could do this thing. I could pass all my classes and graduate the right way. And I honestly think that it might be good for me, for my self-esteem and for my confidence in my own abilities.

I'm not shy when it comes to most things but I'm only now realizing that Charlie's rejection of my creativity has hurt me in a lot of ways. It has made me aimless and uninterested. So yeah, taking something seriously and seeing it to the end may boost my belief in me.

Not to mention, now that people know about this secret hidden talent of mine, I'm feeling more and more creative every day. My head is brimming with ideas, with necklines and bodice patterns, with flowing skirts and wavy hems. With sequins and polka dots and lace and silk. I'm constantly sketching and coming up with designs.

In fact, when the weekend arrives I go shopping.

It was actually a pleasant surprise that I even could, because I don't have any privileges in summer school. But my guidance counselor called me into her office one afternoon and told me that in a surprising turn of events, I have my privileges back. That I could go out if I wanted over the weekends.

I wanted to ask her all the questions. Why and how and who. But I guess I already knew all of them.

I already knew that it was him.

He did it.

The new principal.

Who also told me to stay away from him so I couldn't go and thank him even.

But I do take advantage of the freedom he gave me.

I go out and I drag Echo and Jupiter out with me as well. We spend hours roaming around and hitting all the thrift stores. I buy all the clothes that I want to, all the clothes that I want to cut up and use to make new ones. I get all the colors and fabrics that I think might look good on my friends because watch out, I'm going to sew like crazy and shower them with all the gifts.

I also buy a particular kind of fabric: tweed.

A brown color — a couple of shades down from chocolate — with a very particular checkered pattern done in dark maroon.

It's quite beautiful actually. Very masculine. Very commanding.

Very… him.

And yes, I'm aware that I said I'd stay away from him and I will — I am. But nowhere does it say that I can't make him a tweed jacket with his patent elbow patches if I want to, does it?

I can sew him a jacket on the sewing machine that he bought me, and I can still stay away from him.

I could leave it with Mo when I go back to New York at the end of summer school. Or I could just mail it from New York. It could be a parting gift. Something for him to remember me by. Tangible proof that once upon a time, I was here.

I was in his life.

Once upon a time, he was my guardian and I was his ward and we hated each other.

And then we stopped. And it could've meant something but it didn't.

Anyway.

So yes, days pass and I study. I design. I sew. I spend time with my friends.

And I watch him being all principal-y from afar.

Until one day I have to break the promise and I have to go to him.

In my defense, it's a school matter and he told me that I could come to him for that.

It's for my friend. Echo, specifically.

So she's been moping around for a couple of days about something. She heard through the grapevine that her ex-boyfriend, Lucas, is back in town for a few days, and he's going to be at this bar this Saturday. And she wants to go see him.

"I realize that it might sound stalker-ish," she said last night in my dorm room, where we were spread out on the bed and on the desk, doing our homework. "And I'm not a stalker. I promise. I just… want to see him, you know? I haven't seen him in so long and he never comes to visit. Like, ever. And now he's back for a few days and I'm stuck here and I just, I wish I could go see him. Like even from afar. I'm not going to do anything. I'm not going to like chase him or —"

"First," Jupiter interrupted her, rolling her eyes. "Stop apologizing for wanting to see him. Or even stalk him. Like, stalking isn't even illegal."

Echo threw a pen at her. "It is, you dumbass. Stalking *is* illegal."

Jupiter scoffed. "Ugh, whatever. You're only doing it out of love."

Echo frowned. "Um, I'm pretty sure that's not going to hold up either way. In court, I mean. When he slaps me with a restraining order."

"He's not gonna slap you with a restraining order."

"Well, he might. You didn't see his face when he broke up with me, okay?"

That led to Jupiter and Echo arguing for the next few minutes until I put a stop to it, saying that I'd help.

"Help how?" Echo asked.

I shrugged. "Leave that to me."

Jupiter and Echo looked at each other before Echo said, "Does it involve you…" She searched for a word. "Interacting with him?"

My heart raced but I held on to my composure. "It might."

"Then absolutely not."

"But —"

"No," Jupiter chimed in. "Echo is right. As much as it pains me to say it. You absolutely shouldn't mess with him, Poe."

"But he's not gonna do anything. He wouldn't. Not now."

"That may be so," Echo said, her eyes concerned. "But you still walk around with this shadow over you. You still walk around all sad ever since that whole camera thing. I don't know what happened exactly but I don't want you to do something that will only make you sadder."

I had to tighten all my muscles and swallow and blink several times to get rid of all these surging emotions inside of me.

I haven't told them everything that went down in the past few days. Except to say that the plan didn't work and I didn't want it to either. And that I'm staying here till the end of summer school. But I have no anger or bitterness about it. I have no anger or bitterness about my guardian either.

Of course that was shocking.

Especially since I devoted all my time and energy into hating him and letting everyone know how much I hated him.

But they didn't ask questions and I didn't offer any explanations.

And I'm not going to. Because a lot of what has happened — how he behaved; how I behaved — is tied up to his past and that's his story, not mine.

Although I did tell them about Jimmy and his infamous kidnapping plan. And how Alaric was right to keep me away from him, and sending me to St. Mary's in the hopes that I'd be safe under its rules was his way of protecting me.

So they both hate Jimmy now, as they should, and have been listening to me vent about the fact that he wrote me emails.

Yes.

Since I've given my secret phone, the one I used to contact Jimmy, back to Mo — I'd brought it with me the night I ran away to see her — he has no way of contacting me except through emails. And he has. Several times. Most of them contain paragraphs and paragraphs of apology and how he fucked up and how he needs me.

Both to be his friend slash girlfriend and for my money.

Because Big Jack is putting all kinds of pressure on him.

I see them. I delete them. I contemplate my stupid choices and how naive I was and then I move on.

So it's basically my friendly duty to help Echo. For being my friend, for listening to me, for not asking questions and doling out judgements. For simply being there.

Not to mention, I understand her need.

To see him, I mean.

To simply be close to him.

It's a longing that I feel too.

Plus the infamous and archaic bed check rule has been put in place. Yeah, he finally executed it so now every night, *twice*, the warden peeks through the small square window in the door to see if we're in our beds or not.

It did shock me, yes.

Not because I'm planning on breaking any rules but because he did it in the first place. But I guess that's what he came here to do and I know how seriously he takes his responsibilities. Only I'm not sure if he likes this responsibility or not, being the principal. But it's not my place to ask so there you go.

All I know is that this means she can't even sneak out.

So I have to help her.

With that determination, I walk up to his office during lunch and talk to his assistant, Janet, about getting myself an appointment with him. Echo's ex-boyfriend will be at the bar on Saturday and of course at night. And since we only have day passes, they won't help us here. So I will try to get all three of us an overnight pass for the weekend if possible.

Turns out, I shouldn't have bothered with making an appointment because just as I tell Janet about it and she starts looking at his calendar, the door to his office opens.

And he steps out.

Her too.

Cynthia.

The beautiful blonde woman who called him a loser the night I saw her. Oh, and before that, she tried to kiss him.

She tried to put her mouth on him.

On the man that *I* want to kiss.

Even today I think she's trying to do the same thing. Because standing at the threshold of his office, she's turned toward him, looking up at him and smiling.

He, however, is looking down at his phone.

I can see him scrolling before he says, "I'm not sure at the moment. How about you let me look at my calendar, all right? And you really don't have to take the trouble of driving all the way out here for that. Next time, just call." Then, "Or text. Text works just as well."

She smiles at him, her expression starstruck. "Oh, it's no trouble at all. Although are you sure you can't cancel this next appointment? I just —"

"Pretty sure, yeah," he interrupts, still looking down at his phone but now he steps away from her a little.

She looks disappointed. "Okay, well, that's a shame. And why don't we just ask your assistant if you have any openings? That way, we can just make a date right now. I'd love to take you out to dinner to celebrate your grant." She closes that distance that he'd created between them and puts her hand on his arm. "It's truly incredible. I don't even know how you do it all. You handle so many things and —"

"He does it all because he's amazingly and incredibly hardworking," I say from where I'm standing by Janet's desk, propped against it now, my arms folded.

Looking like a picture of serenity.

But I'm not.

One, because I can't stand how she's looking at him with that hungry expression. Two, because I also can't stand how she's touching him without his permission or his desire.

I mean, he looks bored.

The man looks super disinterested. The man moved away.

Hello, lady?

He clearly doesn't want her. So I don't understand why she keeps touching him.

And third, because it's the truth.

He is amazingly and incredibly hardworking.

And fourth, I plain hate her. She went to his high school and she called him a loser.

"And brilliant," I add, now that Cynthia has her eyes on me and her hand off his arm. "I don't blame you though. For wondering. Not a lot of people understand how gifted and brilliant he is."

Her face sours with distaste but she manages to paste a fake smile on her face. "Of course, I know he's brilliant."

I fake smile too. "Just making sure." Then before she can say anything, I wave my fingers at her. "Hey, Cynthia. Fancy seeing you here."

"Hello," she greets me back, as fake as ever. "I was just stopping by to see if Alaric," I clench my teeth when she says his name, "is free for lunch."

"Yeah, he's not," I tell her, tilting my head to the side as if I'm sad about it. "He has an appointment."

"Yes, he told me."

"With me."

That's a lie.

I don't know who his next appointment is, if in fact he has one. I never got that far with Janet but I had to say it. I fucking had to even if it's not accurate.

And it's worth it because her fake smile falls off her face. "Oh, well, I didn't know that."

I raise my eyebrows. "Well, now you know. Who's raining on your parade." I put a hand on my chest in mock distress. "Although I feel like I'm always doing that. I'm always raining on your parade. Like, you had to leave the last time I showed up. You must hate me. Do you hate me, Cynthia?"

Her eyes narrow but all she does is smile tightly and say, "Of course not."

"Then you're a bigger person than I am, Cynthia. You truly are."

Her eyes narrow further. "I'm aware that Alaric has many responsibilities. It's okay."

She really needs to stop saying his name.

Really.

"Oh, he does. He has so many, many responsibilities. Seeing as he's the principal of this school."

"Yeah. I'm so very proud of him. Alaric has really accomplished a lot."

And this is the moment she seals her fate.

Because she not only said his name again but she also did the two things that I hate: smiling up at him and putting her hand on his arm.

"Yeah, I'm glad." Then leaning forward I continue, "Although can I offer you a piece of advice?"

"Sure."

"You might wanna slow down on your PDA there." I nod casually but the anger in my eyes must be apparent. "It's a school. Students don't want to see their principal getting mauled in the hallway in the middle of lunch."

Her hand jumps off his arm. "What?"

I point to Janet over my shoulder, who gasps behind me. "It makes Janet really uncomfortable. But she'd never say anything. So I'm just letting you know."

"What? I'm…" The mask has come off and Cynthia is glaring now. "I don't understand. This is —"

I take a step toward her and she gasps. "Oh, I can make you understand. Why don't you come outside with me? And we'll solve —"

"Poe."

That's his voice.

That's the first thing he's said to me since I interrupted them.

And it makes me clench my thighs.

Because it's also the first thing he's said to me ever since he sent me away.

From his office a week ago.

With my heart pounding in my chest and my belly fluttering, I look at him.

I've been avoiding doing that for some reason. I'm not sure why. My best guess is that if I had looked at him, I would've lost all composure and broken my promise to him. I would've dashed up to him. I would've begged him to stop seeing Cynthia. Not that he was seeing her or he even wanted her here. It was clear by their conversation that he didn't.

But still.

I would've begged him to see me instead. To let *me* see him. To let *me* in his office.

To let me touch him and call him Alaric.

But I don't think I can avoid looking at him now, so I do. I look at him and then, I also have to clench my fluttering belly.

Because he stands there, all tall and broad and beautiful, with his chocolate chip eyes heated and trained on me. The last time they were focused on me was when he was looking at my naked pictures.

When he was watching me give him fuck-me eyes and talk about all the shameless things I did.

"Well, aren't you going to say anything?"

I jerk awake at Cynthia's voice, reality slamming back as to where we are and *who* we are around.

Alaric seems to already know though.

Because nothing changes on his face as he glances over to Janet. "Can you show Miss March out?" Then, glancing back at me, "In my office."

Cynthia isn't happy about how Alaric is handling it because she goes, "I'd like to stay. I'd like to see how students get handled for their rudeness, if you don't mind."

At this, finally Alaric looks at her directly. "I do mind." Cynthia blanches at his stern words but he keeps going. "This is my school and I like to handle my students without witnesses present. I also mind you stopping by without prior notice. So as I was saying, next time please call." Then he adds, "My assistant."

With that, he turns to me and clenches his jaw.

Meaning I should start walking.

Which I do, my heart ten times lighter now that he put Cynthia in her place. I wish I could shoot her a smile of satisfaction but I'm not going to rock the already wobbling boat so I duck my head down and walk to his office.

He enters after me and shuts the door.

I wait for him to walk in further and reach his desk before I burst out, "Before you say anything, let me just say that I hate her."

My voice echoes around the office or at least it feels like it.

But he doesn't seem to mind.

He simply props himself against the desk, folds his arms over his chest and trains his eyes on me as if he's ready for my tirade with all the patience in the world.

Which is actually a good thing, because I have a lot of tirade to get through.

"I absolutely hate her," I begin when he's all settled. "And the more I see her, the more I hate her, and that's saying something because I hated her plenty the first night I met her. And that's because I didn't like the way she talked to you. I thought that was extremely mean and rude. And now that I know she went to school with you," then I wave my hands, "I mean, I already knew that because you told me that first night. But now that I know how horrible and how torturous and fucking cruel your high school was, I can't stand the sight of her and you can't blame me for that. You can't. I'm sorry but you absolutely cannot. And I'm not going to apologize for it."

There. That makes me feel a little better.

But not a whole lot.

He keeps watching me for a beat or two. Then, "I think you just did."

"Did what?"

"Apologize."

I frown and realize yes, I did do that. Lifting my chin, I say, "I take it back then."

A few seconds of staring then, "What were you doing outside of my office?"

The subject change throws me a little bit but still I reply, "I was here to make an appointment to see you."

"Why?"

"Because I needed to talk to you."

His eyes narrow. "About?"

I open my mouth to answer him but then close it. Frowning harder, I point a finger at him. "No." I stab that finger in the air. "*No.* Absolutely not. You're not changing the subject. That's what you did that night, in my bedroom. When I was angry."

"That's because you were breathing fire like the pocket-sized dragon you are and were about to singe off my eyebrows."

My belly whooshes at his pet name for me, but I'm determined to hold on to my ire. "Well, get ready to bust out the fire extinguisher then. Because I'm about to singe off more than just eyebrows." His lips twitch but I keep going, "Because guess what, I'm angry again."

"I know." His eyes take my features in. "You're not very subtle."

I fist my hands at his casual tone. "I'm angry, Alaric."

"I noticed." Then, "Also Janet. And Cynthia. They noticed as well."

"Are you saying I should be ashamed of it? Of creating a scene."

"I'm saying that I'm glad I interrupted you before it became the kind of scene that the whole school noticed."

I fold my arms across my chest then. "I'm not. I'm very upset about that. That I didn't get to create a scene. Not to mention, I'm extremely upset about the fact that she was here to take you out to lunch."

"Because you don't want me to eat lunch."

"I don't want you to eat lunch with *her*," I snap. "And I don't want that because she wanted to congratulate you for your grant. Which, I might add, I knew nothing about."

He watches me for a beat or two. "Next time I get a bunch of money to dig a hole in Italy, you'll be my first call." I open my mouth to retort but he keeps going. "Besides, I didn't tell her. She heard it through the grapevine."

I shake my head. "Fucking stalker. I bet she's your stalker. I bet she just lurks around, trying to watch you, gather information about you, trying to be like, 'Omigod, what's Alaric up to?' I bet she has those telescope-like thingies so she can keep an eye on you."

"No, I don't think they're telescope-like…" His chocolate chip eyes glimmer. "*Thingies*. I think they're binoculars."

"You think this is something to laugh about," I snap, raising my eyebrows. "You're not gonna laugh about it when one night she jumps out of your closet while you're sleeping. She's fucking dangerous."

"Is she going to be holding a knife too?"

I draw back.

I can't believe he's bringing that up. I can't believe he's bringing up what I did that night when I snuck into his cottage a few weeks back.

I narrow my eyes at him to show him my displeasure.

His eyes glimmer harder with amusement.

My nostrils flare at that.

His lips pull up on one side.

"How are you not angry about this?" I insist, my chest heaving. "How are you just standing there all cool and calm?"

"Because she's not worth it," he says then, his tone grave, any amusement vanishing from his features, his demeanor morphing from casual to serious.

To tight and rigid.

And it causes an ache in my chest. A twist. A pull. A longing to go to him. I make myself stand exactly where I am though. "They hurt you."

He flinches.

It's subtle but it's there and I can't help but flinch with him.

I can't help but stare at that bump on his nose.

"I'm fine," he says, his voice tight.

"They really hurt you, Alaric."

"And I survived."

"That's not enough though."

He breathes out sharply. "It was a long time ago and I'm handling it."

"No, you're not," I protest and his brows snap together in a frown. "You're angry. You may not be angry right now. But you are angry in general. You told me that right here in your office, remember? That you're angry. That you have rage. I haven't forgotten that. I mean, your punching thing. That's where it comes from, right? Because you're angry. Because you have control issues. And it's understandable, given what happened. But that doesn't mean that you're handling things."

His breaths are sharp now. Much like his features, which seem to be carved in jagged stones.

"Why don't you let me worry about what I can and can't handle?" he says, his voice low, his eyes angry.

"I can't. I'm going to worry about it."

"It's not your job to worry about me. It's actually the other way around."

"I don't care. I don't care if it isn't my job or if it's the other way around because I'm your fragile little ward. I'll still worry."

He absolutely doesn't like my insistence. He doesn't like my stand on this, and I know I said that I'd obey him in everything but I'm not going to do that in this case.

I'm not going to simply let this go.

He has rage. He has anger. He has issues, period. Mo and I, we had a long chat that night and she told me stuff about him and his work. And as I said, I don't blame him. But that doesn't mean that he has to live like this. That doesn't mean that he can't let the past be in the past and live in the present.

Live *happily* in the present, even.

If he can show me the way to leave my own issues with Charlie behind, then I can show him too. If he can make me promise that I won't run after the wrong things just to be loved and seen, then I can ask for promises too.

Or at least we can talk about it.

But I don't think it's happening because his next words are, "We're done here."

"But I —"

"We are."

I stare at him. At his shuttered expression. At the closed-off way he's holding himself, his impossibly broad shoulders rigid, his folded arms tight to the point where I can see the bulge of his biceps under his tweed jacket. As if his very body, his muscles and his bones are making a fortress around him.

They have built a wall that no one can get through.

Least of all me.

At least not right now.

So I take in a deep breath and ask, "Is that your final decision?"

"Yes."

I nod. "Okay."

This is way too important for me to simply let go. We are going to revisit this at some point whether he likes it or not.

But for now we're done.

His eyes narrow. "So what was it that you wanted to talk to me about." Then, "Given that we're still operating under the assumption that this is a coincidence."

"What?"

"You showing up here, at my office, right when Cynthia was here."

I'm confused. "Um, it is a coincidence."

"Like it was the night you showed up at my cottage."

I'm still confused.

But then something flashes in his eyes. Something like knowledge.

Like he knows a secret, and instantly, I'm not confused anymore.

Instantly, I know what he's talking about.

The night I showed up at his cottage claiming that I had a nightmare.

Holy God.

He knew.

"I..." I look to the side, swallowing. "You... You knew."

A look of satisfaction crosses his features. "That you eavesdropped on my conversation with Cynthia? Yeah."

"But then why did you..."

He shrugs, and like it always does in that lazy way of his, it looks as if a mountain is lifting and moving. "I just needed an excuse to send her away."

"But you made me tea for my nightmare," I say, my voice sounding a little breathless.

With his eyes steadily watching me, he replies, "Because I wasn't willing to take a chance and not. Take care of you, I mean. In case you really had had one."

And then my *little* breathlessness turns into a whole lot.

It turns into restlessness and thoughtlessness and racing of hearts.

So much so that I have to look away from him for a second. I have to pace myself so I don't lose my balance. So I don't lose this determination that I've managed to hold on to for the past week, to stay away from him.

To not throw myself at him.

To not show him all the places on my body that hurt and ache for him so he can make it better.

I mean, it's his job, isn't it?

To make things better for me.

So why can't he do this?

Why can't he touch me and kiss me and make this ache go away?

I mean, he's already seen me all naked. What's a little kiss?

My first kiss.

Biting my lip, I look back at him. "Alaric?"

His chest is moving up and down now, his features tight and determined. "No."

"But I haven't even said anything yet," I say, frowning.

"You don't have to," he growls. "Your fuck-me eyes are saying plenty."

I pout. "But all I want is —"

"No," he growls harder. "Don't say it."

"But —"

"No, Poe."

Things ache in my body at his refusal. "It hurts."

He winces. "You'll get over it."

I shake my head slowly. "I won't. It's going to bruise."

"You'll get over that too."

I fist my fingers. "Why are you doing this?"

He waits so long to answer me that I think he won't.

That I think I'll die with this pain in my chest, in my belly.

I'll crumple at his feet and he won't pick me up.

He won't do much more than flick me a cool glance and move on.

"Because it's better this way," he says finally. "Because I'm your guardian and you're my ward and this is fucking inappropriate."

"Exactly," I retort. "You're my guardian. This is basically your job."

"Yeah, what's my job?"

"To take care of me," I tell him. "To make things better for me."

He clenches his jaw. "No. That's not how I'm going to make things better for you. That's nowhere in my job description."

"But it could be," I argue. "If that's what I want."

"You want to get fucked, is that it?"

He really shouldn't say things like that if he wants me to stop talking.

If he wants me to not give him fuck-me eyes.

Because it's not as if I haven't thought about it. It's not as if in my daydreams and thoughts about him giving me my first kiss, I haven't also thought about him giving me my first fuck, him taking my virginity.

In fact, that's what he said that day.

He told me that a kiss with him would lead to other things.

And God, I want those things.

I really, really do.

With him.

"Well, all I want is a kiss," I say then. "My first kiss."

He breathes out sharply in response.

"But I also know that you said that a kiss from you could lead to other things."

"I'm glad you remember," he bites out. "Why don't you use your excellent memorization skills to stun us all on your tests?"

I ignore his sarcasm and go on, "And I'm open to that. I'm so open that –"

"Enough," he says then.

He bites it out actually, through clenched teeth. Through pursed lips that barely move.

But it's loud and clear. And authoritative.

It's commanding enough for me to do exactly as he wants me to.

Even though I don't want to.

"This is a place of business," he begins, straightening up and uncrossing his arms and clenching his fists at his sides, as if making himself all taller and broader. "I've already explained that I'm not going to entertain talk like that from you. So if that is why you were out there, making a fucking appointment, so you can act like a fucking diva then you may as well leave and go back to your classes. Because this is not up for discussion." He clenches his teeth hard. "*Ever.* And that's my final fucking decision."

I flinch at the end as well and lower my eyes, ashamed.

I shouldn't have done that.

I should not have tried to convince him when I promised that I would obey him. I can't believe I let my composure falter this way. I can't believe I turned into a diva.

Taking a deep breath, I rein in my impulses though and apologize. "I'm sorry. It won't happen again."

"Good."

"B-but that wasn't why I was here. I was wondering if I could get an overnight pass with —"

"Done."

"But you haven't even —"

He moves away from the desk, cutting me off. "It's fine. Just talk to my assistant and she'll set it up with your guidance counselor."

"There's also a party," I blurt out. "Well, a get-together."

That halts him in his tracks.

He was in the process of walking back to his chair but now he's turned toward me and frowning. "What?"

I nod. "There's sort of a get-together and —"

He folds his arms across his chest again. "When?"

"Saturday night."

"Where?"

"Uh, that's slightly tricky."

He narrows his eyes. "How tricky?"

I grimace. "It's at a bar."

"No."

"But —"

"No."

"Please," I plead, swallowing. "Just listen."

He watches me for a couple of seconds before sighing and shifting on his feet.

His silent indication that I can go on.

Relieved, I sigh too and begin, "The whole reason I'm going to this bar is because I'm trying to help a friend. There's this guy she likes, see, and she hasn't seen him in a really long time, like in years. And he's going to be there and I wanna help her out because she loves him. Like really, Alaric. And this may be her only shot for a while to see him. And…"

He studies my face before prodding, "And."

"And I know what that feels like. I know what it feels like when you wanna be close to someone but can't be. So I really want her to have this." His jaw clenches but I keep going, trying to put his mind at ease. "And I know it's in a bar but it'll be totally supervised. In the sense that my other friends and their boyfriends are going as well. My one friend has like four brothers and they're probably all gonna be there. That's how we're getting into the bar. And please trust me when I say that they're very safe and protective. They're probably actually losing their minds like you are. But it's gonna be fine. I promise. I'll follow whatever rules you may have."

My explanation only makes his expression harsher and I wonder what more can I say to convince him. Maybe I should list off the names of all of Callie's brothers and her husband. Because they're all really coming.

"You know what it feels like," he says finally, his voice low. "To want to get close to someone."

"What?"

"Because you were in love yourself, weren't you?"

I don't understand.

But then I do.

I completely absolutely do.

He thinks I was talking about Jimmy. When I said what it feels like to want to get close to someone but can't.

But I wasn't.

I was talking about him.

I was…

"Alaric, I —"

"Fine," he cuts me off. "You can go."

"But I have to —"

"No drinks from strangers though."

My chest heaving, I watch him. I watch his firmly set features, his chocolate chip eyes, and I really, really want him to know that I wasn't even thinking about Jimmy. I don't even care about Jimmy anymore.

I was talking about him.

But I know he won't let me say anything.

He won't let me go there.

So I give him what he wants from me right now. And maybe in my own way I can show him that I was talking about him. That it's all about him now.

"Okay," I whisper, nodding.

A tic starts up in his jaw. "No tight tops."

"Okay."

"No short skirts."

"Okay."

His tic becomes aggressive here, like he's mashing his teeth. "No dancing with boys."

"I don't even like dancing."

"No touching them."

"I don't wanna touch any boys."

I wanna touch you.

"No talking to them."

"I don't wanna talk to them."

I wanna talk to you.

"No fucking looking at them."

"I don't wanna look at boys."

I wanna look at you.

My easy agreement is making him even angrier and I don't know what to do.

I don't know how to melt his ire.

I'm giving him everything that I can in this moment — everything that he's allowed me to give — but somehow it's not enough.

"Be home by 11:30," he says.

"I will."

He breathes noisily then. A sharp, angsty sort of breath.

Then unfolding his arms, he goes on, "I suggest that at the end of the night, when I ask you if you touched a boy or if you looked at a boy, Poe, your answer had better be no. Or you'll be responsible for what I end up doing to that boy."

"W-what will you do?" I ask with my heart in my throat, my skin all coarse with goosebumps.

His eyes flashing, he growls, "Murder."

Chapter Twenty-Seven

The Horny Bard.

That's the name of the bar that we're going to.

It's in Bardstown and it's a regular hangout for all the soccer players. Hence I thought to invite Callie and Wyn, thinking that their boyfriends — well, Callie is married to Reed so technically her husband — either play or have played soccer and so they must have an in.

And as expected, like Alaric, they weren't happy to hear that we wanted to go to a bar.

But when they heard it was The Horny Bard, they almost lost their shit.

"That place is a fucking rathole. The guys who go there are a bunch of horny and hard-up assholes trolling for easy pussy. And there's no way you're going."

That came from Reed, as Callie told me.

"But you used to go there yourself," Callie told him.

"That's not relevant. What's relevant —"

"How is that not relevant?"

"Fae, you're not going."

"That's double standards," Callie reminded him.

Shamelessly, he replied, "Fuck yeah, it is. But my wife isn't going to that bar."

"Your wife won't be your wife if you don't quit being a caveman, Roman," Callie shot back; she calls Reed Roman like Reed calls her Fae.

So yeah, that's how their argument went, word for word, as

imparted to me by Callie.

Until she convinced him to go along with her.

Conrad, Callie's oldest brother and Wyn's boyfriend, had the same stance. Although he simply said, "Absofuckinglutely not, end of discussion."

I'm not sure how Wyn convinced him but she did and now he's going too.

Which is fine.

What is slightly weird is the fact that Ledger, Callie's brother, is also going. And according to Callie, he volunteered for it only after Callie accidentally mentioned that Reed's sister, Tempest, was also going. She lives in New York and visits when she can and since she'll be in town this weekend, she's coming also. And as soon as Callie let that slip, Ledger was like, "I'll go too."

"Why would *you* go?" Callie asked.

"Because," he said, "it's a rathole. Reed is right. And you need reinforcements."

"Well, Con and Roman are enough reinforcements." Then, "And since when is Reed right? You hate him."

It's true.

Ledger and Reed have been enemies for as long as Callie can remember. Some stupid soccer rivalry, and even though Callie is now married to Reed, they still butt heads sometimes.

"I do," Ledger admitted. "But that doesn't mean he can't be right. Besides, more reinforcements won't hurt."

Again, word for word, as told to me by Callie.

But I guess I misspoke. It's not weird. Because there's something between Ledger and Tempest. Something secretive and mysterious that no one knows anything about. I, for one, am dying to know but Tempest is playing her cards close to her chest and Ledger outright denies everything that Callie asks him. So yeah.

But anyway, they're all coming.

Including one of Callie's twin brothers, Shepard. The other twin, Stellan, is staying home to watch Halo.

I'm not sure how that happened but I don't care. The more, the merrier.

And to be honest, things *have* been fun so far. Yes, there were a few hiccups here and there, but nothing major.

The day started with all my girls coming to the mansion to

get ready.

Their first time at the place I've called home for four years now.

Up until now, I felt like this was my prison and I didn't want them to see the cage that I lived in when I got out of the other cage called St. Mary's. But now that I know that instead of being a cage, this mansion was a safe harbor for me, I invited all of them over and it was great.

After the initial oohs and ahs over the size of the mansion, we all got settled up in my room and proceeded to try on every dress that we could. Mo brought us treats — chocolate chip cookies and mini cherry pies — and stayed a while. I know she was happy to chat with the girls and get all the dirt on St. Mary's, a place she hates as well. And then she stayed all through our hair and makeup and last-minute prep before Reed came to get us.

I'd like to point out though that the only reason he did and not Conrad — which apparently was a point of heavy discussion also — is because he has an SUV. He recently bought it for Halo, and so it was the only vehicle that could accommodate six decked-out girls.

And again I'd like to point out that out of all six girls, according to Reed, Callie was the best dressed in an ice blue flowing chiffon dress with lacy cap sleeves. He stared at her for about a minute — we all counted — when she first walked out of the door.

Then we got to the bar, where Conrad was waiting for all of us to arrive. And let the record show that *he* stared at his Wyn for about a minute and a half; we all counted again. She's dressed up in my personal favorite: a shiny silver A-line strapless dress with sequins. Which I think is now Conrad's favorite too.

Oh, before I forget, Ledger — who is only here for reinforcement; yeah, totally believable — stared at Tempest for about the same amount of time as Conrad stared at Wyn. Only he did it from the corner of his eye and with a very harsh and ticking jaw.

Not sure about the presence of his ticking jaw but I think it could be because of her very tight blue dress, and also because she made it a point not to look at him at all.

I noticed, yup.

Anyway as I said, as fun as everything was, there have been some hiccups.

Hiccup number one: Well, this is more of a weird thing than a hiccup.

And it has to do with Jupiter.

As soon as she saw Conrad, she first couldn't talk when all the introductions were made, and then couldn't stop shaking his hand when he made the mistake of offering it to her. She did the same with Ledger, who gave her a weird but distracted look.

As weird as all that was, the weirder thing was that she didn't even touch Shepard.

When his name came up, she simply nodded and backed away. Not that Shepard took notice. He was — still is — busy on his phone, so he didn't bother to give Jupiter more than a passing glance.

"What the fuck are you doing?" Ledger asked Shepard.

Shepard looked up from his phone. "What?"

Ledger swatted him on the back of his head. "Where are your manners, asshole?" He tipped his head to where Jupiter was standing. "She's saying hello."

Shepard clenched his jaw but let Ledger's swat go before turning to Jupiter and issuing a distracted greeting. "Hey."

"Hi," she said, blushing.

And I think I'm going to ask her about it.

I'm going to ask Jupiter what her deal is. With Callie — remember the time she hug-attacked Callie, back at the Ballad of the Bards? — and the rest of her brothers. Because outside of her strange over-enthusiastic meetings with the Thornes and even stranger blush-filled *hi* to Shepard, she's a pretty chill gal. So there has to be a reason for this.

Now, hiccup number two: This one's slightly more serious and it has to do with Echo.

Because of whom we're here.

And who, according to me and the rest of the girls, is actually the best dressed.

I designed it that way.

She was going to see her ex-boyfriend for the first time in ages, she had to look her prettiest.

In a midnight blue suede dress, she looks like this bombshell temptress who has a penchant for strapless corset style bodices with a slit on the side. And her high, strappy heels prove that she likes to have a good time. Pair that with smoky eye makeup and big curls, and this Lucas guy does not have a chance at all.

He's going to cry us a river when he sees her.

Which he doesn't. Not right away.

Because as soon as we get to a little nook that Callie's brothers have picked out for us to sit and hang out, she runs away. She hides herself behind a big pillar, staring at something fearfully. Leaving all my girls, who look concerned, I go to her and ask her what's up.

"He's here," she tells me.

"Who? Lucas?" I clap my hands, turning to look in the direction she is. "Which one is he?"

"No," she whispers angrily. "Not him. I mean, he's here too. But *him*. He's here."

"Okay, well," I raise my eyebrows, "did you hear yourself? That bunch of sentences did not make anything clear to me."

She sighs in irritation. "His best friend. Lucas's best friend. He's here too."

"Oh, and we don't like him."

Lucas's best friend is somehow the reason why Echo is at St. Mary's.

At this point, Jupiter arrives and answers for me. "Nope, not at all. We hate him."

Followed by Wyn. "We hate who?"

Followed in turn by Callie. "Who are we hating on?"

And Tempest. "Because I'm always down for hating."

Echo shakes her head. "Oh God, this is a disaster. I have to go back. I have to get out of here. He goes everywhere Lucas goes. I should've remembered that. I should've freaking remembered. I got so caught up in seeing Lucas again that I forgot about him. And now I'm wearing a dress that I don't normally wear and it's pretty and if he sees it, he's going to say something derogatory about it. I just know it."

Callie is the one to get her under control. "You're not going anywhere. You look pretty and no one is going to say anything to you. Because we won't let them." She looks at all of us one by one. "Right, girls?"

We all nod our heads in affirmation before I speak. "Okay, so now who's he and why's he going to make a derogatory comment about someone as stunning as you?"

Echo bites her lip and then proceeds to point with her chin. "Him. Reign."

We all look in the direction she points and there he is.

The very definition of a bad boy.

Tall and bronzed, with dark hair and a smirk that makes him look all kinds of sexy. But something more too. You know the kind, where you know he's going to break your heart — you just know it; there is no question about it — but it's a price you're willing to pay because you know that he's going to show you a good time before he does it.

"Rain. As in R-A-I-N?" I ask, watching him talk to someone while he stands in a group of guys.

"Oh, I was thinking the same thing," Wyn says. "What an interesting, dreamy name. For someone we hate, I mean."

"That guy is not dreamy," Jupiter says. "I mean, he is but only on the surface."

"Yup, I know him," Tempest adds, nodding. "He's Reed's buddy."

"*Reign*. As in, R-E-I-G-N," Echo finally corrects.

"Oh," Callie says. "That makes so much more sense now. With that whole bad boy thing he's got going." She shakes her head. "And he's Reed's buddy? Figures. Although, he looks worse than my Roman in the bad boy department."

We all agree to that and then suddenly, the group he's standing in becomes bigger.

Because a bunch of guys join in.

Guys we know.

Namely, Ledger, Shepard and Reed.

As it turns out, our guys know his guys — pretty well actually — and then our guys invite his guys to come over to our nook. So of course, Echo starts freaking out again. But after a lot of cajoling and talk of girl power, we manage to convince her.

And now here we are.

We're all sitting in a cozy nook with leather couches and lounge chairs. Girls are sitting on this big couch by the wall and we've made it so that Echo is tucked in the middle and is protected from both sides. And the guys are spread out in the other lounge chairs opposite to us.

They're all busy talking and catching up with each other. Apparently, they're all soccer buddies. Lucas and Reign's school — that also happened to be Echo's school before she got sent to St. Mary's — has played against Ledger and Reed's team. And since Conrad used to be their coach, he knows Reign and Lucas pretty well too.

And so far, there have been no derogatory comments at all.

Which is great, because that has made Echo relax a little bit. And she's doing what we'd talked about back at the mansion in the event of Lucas spotting her in the bar. She's busy talking to the girls and generally ignoring Lucas. You know, to show how okay she is with their break-up and to throw him a little off-kilter because according to her, she did not handle their break-up well.

I'm super proud of her for handling *this* so well.

And it seems to be working, because Lucas — who's this handsome blond-haired surfer type of guy — can't take his eyes off our Echo. The only problem— and I know she isn't aware of it — is that the dark twin of Lucas, Reign Davidson, is also checking out our Echo, because apparently where Lucas goes, Reign goes too.

Oh, he isn't doing it as blatantly as Lucas but he is.

Every time he laughs or take a sip of his beer, his eyes inevitably go over to Echo in a very subtle move. Every time he checks someone out across the bar, beyond our nook, he checks her out too.

And now I'm wondering what *his* deal is.

Why can't he stop looking at his best friend's ex-girlfriend? What did he do to send Echo to St. Mary's?

Maybe if I figure that out, I can help Echo.

Although I know what I'm doing.

I do want to help my friend — I always want to help my friends — but I can't help but feel that I'm also trying to keep myself busy. I'm also trying to keep my mind occupied and my thoughts on the present. On the people around me.

That's what I've been doing all day.

That's the second reason I invited everyone over to the mansion. So I could be around people.

So I wouldn't think about him.

The man who gave me a bunch of rules to follow and who wouldn't let me get close to him because he thinks it's inappropriate.

I can't help but think what he must be doing right now. Maybe he's sleeping.

Although, nah. I don't think he's sleeping.

I think he's working — because he's always working — and I think he's thinking about me. Because I'm at this bar and he must be wondering and seething over if I'm following all his rules. He must be watching the clock to see if I'll come back before my curfew.

I have every intention of following all his rules though. So I wish he wouldn't worry.

In fact, now that everything is settled and Echo's plan is going well, I want to go back home. I want to go back to St. Mary's where I know he is, in his little cottage. I want to knock at his door and demand that he let me throw myself at him. I want to demand that he take me in his arms and make it all better.

The urge becomes so strong that I excuse myself from the couch in the hopes of going outside and getting some fresh air. So I can regroup and be there for my friends.

But then, almost halfway to the front entrance, I come to a stop.

My legs won't move, like I've come to the edge of a cliff, a precipice, and if I take one more step I'll fall, so my body is afraid.

Which I hate.

Because my heart is not.

My heart wants to fall.

My heart wants to leap and jump.

All the way down. All the way across to him.

Him.

Because he's here.

How's he here?

And he's spotted me. Right away. As soon as he entered.

And now he's striding over to me with a single-minded purpose. With dark eyes and shadowed features.

With a determined purpose of my own, I make myself move.

I make myself take the leap and he's there to catch me.

He's there to put his hand on me, on my arm, as air rushes through my body and my belly whooshes at the drop.

I grab onto his shirt. "Hi."

His chest is lifting up and down as he stares at me, his eyes shining. "The Horny Bard."

My eyes widen behind my glasses. "I… You know about this bar?"

"Yeah," he says, his voice low.

Clutching his shirt, I go up on my tiptoes. "I swear I was safe. Remember I told you all the brothers and boyfriends were coming?" I look over my shoulder, searching for them in the crowd. "They're here somewhere. You should —"

I feel a tug on my arm, making me both snap my eyes back and go crashing onto his torso.

All my nerve endings awaken at being so close to him.

Instantly I try to memorize every part of his body that I'm touching with mine lest he remember that we shouldn't be so close. From the looks of it though, his mind is elsewhere.

His mind is on my mouth, as proven by his next words and his thunderous expression. "What lipstick is that?"

"P-Purple Witchcraft," I say immediately, even though I'm a little thrown about the subject change.

He grits his teeth as he stares at my lips. "Yeah, you're that, aren't you? You're a fucking witch."

I press myself even closer, my heart thundering. "I don't…" I lick my lips and his fingers tighten on my arm. "Y-you didn't say anything about lipstick so I wore some."

"I should have."

I clutch his shirt. "I promise I followed all your rules. I did."

"Did you?"

I nod rapidly. "I swear, I did. I've dressed modestly and I haven't looked at or touched any boys. And it's only 10:00 PM. I was going to come back by my curfew."

I *have* worn a modest dress. I chose it carefully too. It's a white flowy dress with purple polka dots and an empire waist, that ends just below my knees. It's sleeveless but not in a way that shows off a lot of skin. It really is conservative but cute. Plus no high or sexy heels; I'm wearing these really cute pair of suede flats from Prada.

But running his eyes over it, Alaric gets even angrier and I ask, "Why are you mad, Alaric?"

His nostrils flare. "I'm fucking mad, Poe, because my rules are no good."

"What?"

"My *rules*," he says through his teeth, "are bullshit. My rules don't protect you. Because the only rule, the only fucking *law*, I should've laid down was not that *you* don't look at boys but that boys don't look at *you*."

I twist my fists in his shirt. "But that's… How can *I* do that? How can I make that happen?"

"You can't, can you?" I know it's a rhetorical question but I can't help but shake my head and he continues, "So then there's only one solution, isn't there?"

"W-what?"

His eyes harden cruelly. "That I hide you from them. That I throw you in a dungeon somewhere and fucking lock you up."

"But I don't —"

"And since I don't have a fucking dungeon, I'm going to lock you up in your bedroom." He straightens up then. "So you're coming home with me right now."

My heart is pounding and pounding. "What, no. Alaric, wait. I…"

"Let's go."

"No, but… You can't." I look into his dark, dark, mean eyes. As mean as his fingers on my arm. "I know you can't. I know you *won't.*"

"Yeah?"

"Yes."

He grinds his teeth, his features sharp, dangerous. "Well, let's see what I can and can't do." Then he bends down slightly. "Besides, it's not as if you can run anywhere, can you? Not anymore."

"I'm sorry?"

"You gave up that chance when you decided to stay here and finish summer school the right fucking way."

With that parting comment, he turns around and starts walking.

With me in tow.

He's dragging me by my arm, pulling me, making me jog after him. And even though I'm wearing flats, I'm no match for his forceful pushing and pulling and so I stumble. And I keep stumbling and stuttering all the way to Alaric's car across the street.

At which point, he lets go of me to open the door before grabbing me again and depositing me inside. And in a flash, we're off. We're driving away and I swear in a flash again, we're back at the mansion.

I don't remember the drive at all even though I just took it myself. I also don't remember him dragging me out of the car and into the mansion. And then all the way up to my room, through the grand foyer and up the stairs and down the hallway.

All I know is that I'm standing inside my room and Alaric is at the threshold.

I know that he's watching me with so much anger and fire that I'm burning.

I'm burning and crying and pining for him even though he's only a few feet away. And then he's closing the door and when I can only see a sliver of him through the opening, I whisper, "Alaric, please."

But he doesn't hear me, or even if he does, he doesn't care. Because the door thuds closed and I'm alone.

Locked up and trapped.

And he's gone.

He left me here.

I can't believe it. I can't.

He wouldn't do that. He wouldn't lock me up. Not now. Not after everything that we've gone through and all the progress that we've made. He wouldn't revert back to his old ways.

So I watch the door with anticipation. I watch it hoping that it will open.

That he'll come back.

But when minutes and maybe even hours pass without the door opening, my heart cracks.

And I begin to sob and then I'm running away from it, from the door.

I go as far as possible from it like it's an animal, vicious and merciless. When I reach the window on the far wall, I slide down and bury my face in my knees, sobbing and whispering, "Alaric, please come b-back."

For seconds after that, I can only hear my own sobbing, my own cries and whimpers.

But then I hear a click.

It's the loudest sound in all the ruckus.

And my head snaps up.

The door is open and there he is.

The devil. The tyrant who locked me up.

Only he's back as the man I've come to crave. He's back as my guardian.

Our eyes clash and lock from across the space.

Chest heaving, he enters the room and on trembling limbs, I come to my feet.

Without taking his glittering eyes off me, he closes the door behind himself and I lose all my breaths.

And then he does something that brings all my breaths slamming back into my body. That gives me wings so I can fly.

He opens his arms, his big and muscular and safe guardian arms, and I take flight.

I run across the room and jump into them.

Chapter Twenty-Eight

The first thing I feel is his arms closing around me.

His arms plastering me to his powerhouse of a body and grounding me.

His arms tightening around my small, shuddering frame and instantly filling me with all the warmth and protection.

As amazing as all of that is though, the second thing that I feel is much more amazing. It's much more noteworthy and life-altering. It's something that I know I'm going to remember for the rest of my life.

Because it's his mouth touching mine.

It's his mouth gripping mine. Possessing it, covering it, taking it.

In a kiss.

In my very first kiss.

In a kiss that sets me on fire. That lights a flame in the center of my being. In the center of my chest, my belly.

In the place between my thighs.

Yeah.

I don't know how that's possible though. I don't know how I can feel his mouth, his hot and wet and demanding mouth, in my pussy when he's only touching my lips.

Maybe it's the way he's kissing me.

Maybe it's the way his lips have closed over mine, all wetly and hungrily. It's the way he's vacuuming both my lips, my top *and* my bottom, inside and sucking on them. As if he first wants to know and memorize the shape of my mouth. As if he first wants to taste me on the outside. Taste my plumpness and my pinkness that I've colored over and made purple.

Oh yeah, he definitely wants to eat that lipstick.

He wants to devour it and obliterate it and mess it up and ruin it. As if that lipstick has ruined his life. As if that lipstick has obliterated him too.

Before taking things inside.

Before forcing my mouth to open and thrusting his tongue in.

So it has to be the way he's kissing me. It *has* to be.

There's no other explanation as to why I'm feeling it all down there. No explanation as to why an ache has started up in my belly. The kind that I feel whenever I'm all swollen and wet and pulsing in my core.

But then I stop analyzing why and how because as soon as he forces my mouth open to get inside, his lips do the same thing that they did on the outside. His lips suck on my tongue. His lips suck on the taste of me. They suck on all my wetness and I wonder what I taste like to him.

Because he tastes like cherries.

Through and through.

Like the sugar and tanginess runs in his blood.

Like the devil — my most cherished devil and my beloved guardian — has veins made of his favorite fruit, and mine.

And once he's sucked all of my taste and absorbed it, his tongue comes out to play. His tongue digs deep, deeper even, where his lips couldn't go, so he can lap up the last of it. The last drops of my taste, my essence.

So he could lick me dry and empty me.

But that's the thing, I'm not empty, am I?

No, I'm full.

My mouth is full of his tongue. My tongue is full of his taste and my pussy is full of my juices.

All because he's kissing me on my mouth but I feel it in my pussy.

All because he's giving me my very first kiss.

Holy God.

This is my first kiss. And I feel it everywhere and not just in my pussy either.

I feel it in my fingers, for example. Fingers that are now all electric and alive and clutching all the things on his strong body. His rich, dark hair. His veined neck. The crisp collar of his shirt.

My first kiss makes it to my thighs as well. That I keep squeezing and rubbing around his hips.

And my hips.

The hips that are twisting and writhing and dancing against his sculpted torso.

So much so that I think I'm making it hard for him. To stand still.

He has to move his arms, one of which was wrapped around my waist to keep me plastered to him, and the other was holding the back of my head in a possessive grip so he could position my mouth however he wants to.

But now both those arms travel down and down and grab my ass.

And oh my fucking God, he should not have done that.

He shouldn't have grabbed my ass and he definitely shouldn't have kneaded and groped and pinched my bouncy flesh as if his fingers are electric as well.

As if he feels this kiss not only on his mouth but in other parts of his body, like I do.

Because now we're both rocking against each other and my clit is dragging against his ridged abs.

And I'm even more restless.

I'm even more slippery and squirmy in his arms.

My pussy is spasming and ripening even more, and now I know why he said that a kiss with him would lead to other things.

A kiss with him would lead to fucking.

Because I want it. I want it right now.

Right *fucking* now.

And maybe he can feel it.

Feel this need that's suddenly eating me up.

Because I swear I hear a growl.

I know that his abs are hollowing out with each breath. I know that his chest is shuddering.

And I know that a second later, he moves, he walks.

A second later, his fingers on my ass knead me the hardest so I arch up and moan, and then I'm lying flat on my back. I'm opening my eyes and dragging in gulps and gulps of air as his kisses really, *literally* move to other places on my body.

As I feel his kisses on my cheeks, my nose, my chin, my arched-up neck.

But more than that, I feel his tongue.

I feel it licking my skin, my tears. I feel him lapping them up and my heart squeezes so hard and in such a vice-like grip at his tenderness that I have to physically translate it into a hard squeeze of his body with my thighs and my arms.

Crossing my ankles at his back and amidst his tender kisses, I whisper, "You came back. You came back. I knew y-you would… I…"

His fingers that have come to bury themselves in my hair shudder and flex, as he looks up, his lips all red and parted, his eyes liquid. "I never should've left."

I dig my heels into the small of his back, trying to bring him closer, trying to lock us together. "It's okay. It's okay. I don't care. I don't —"

His pelvis crashes against mine and his fingers on my scalp tighten. "It's not okay, Poe. It's not fucking okay."

I bring my hands to his harsh jaw. "But it doesn't matter. I —"

"I'm not okay," he bites out gutturally, regret and anguish slashing his features. "The things I do to you are not okay. The things I do to you are not fair. They're not fucking fair, Poe. They're mean and cruel and demented. And the truth is…" He digs his pelvis into mine. He even goes so far as to bring his hands down and grip my thighs, pushing them up, adjusting them so we're entwined even tighter. "The *truth* is, Poe, that I don't know what else to do. I don't know how else to be. I don't fucking know."

My lips are parted now.

My lips have to be parted.

So I can breathe. So I can stay awake and not pass out under the sheer pain that he's inflicting on me with his words.

The sheer pain that I feel at the sight of *his* pain.

"But you're making it better," I tell him. "You always end up making things better. You gave me my first kiss."

He did, didn't he?

My mouth is still tingling with it. My tongue is still alive with his taste. All the parts of my body are still buzzing with it.

Because he gave me a kiss that I not only felt in every part of my body, but I know that whenever I'm alone from now on, all I have to do is close my eyes and think of it and it will come alive on my lips.

He gave me a timeless kiss.

A kiss of magic. A kiss of stars.

A kiss of the devil and his harpy. The tyrant and his siren.

He gave me a kiss that a guardian gives to his diva.

He doesn't think so though, no.

He doesn't think it was magical in the least. I think *he* thinks that it was a curse. Because the loathing, the self-recrimination is so thick in his eyes that his chest burns with it. I know that because mine is burning as well.

He brings his face even closer, to the point where his mouth is hovering over mine as he growls, "That's because I didn't want anyone else to give it to you. That's because I couldn't *stand* the thought of anyone else giving you your first kiss. That's what I kept thinking..."

"What?" I prod when he trails off. "What did you think?"

"This whole time," he rasps as if to himself, his eyes black, possessed. "Ever since you told me two days ago that you were going to that bar. That is all I *kept fucking thinking*. I kept thinking that she wants it. She's asking for it. Which means she's ripe for it. She's so fucking ripe for picking, her mouth is so fucking ripe for picking that it's written all over her pale, creamy face. It's written in her big blue eyes. It's written in the way she laughs, she smiles, she talks. It's written in the way she moves. The way her thighs jiggle, her tits bounce, her fucking ass dances. It's written *everywhere* on her tight little body that she wants a kiss. That she wants someone to fucking give it to her. And what if," he says, his fingers digging into my thighs, clutching my dress, as if he's imagining it right now, "and *what if* someone does? What if some drunk asshole who can't even remember his own name gives it to her? What if some drunk asshole puts his chapped and diseased mouth on my Poe? On my little doe-eyed Poe. What if he dirties her? Sullies her, *scares* her. What if she doesn't like it?

"I kept thinking about that and thinking about that, Poe. I kept thinking that you were crying out for me. That you needed me. You needed me to save you. You needed me to protect you from this imaginary fucking asshole who stole your first kiss that you'd been dreaming about for years. Until I found myself in my car, driving to that shitty bar to bring you back. Do you understand now? That's why I kissed you. That's why I gave you your first kiss. Because I didn't want anyone else to give it to you. I didn't want anyone else to take your virgin mouth."

I'm shuddering under him.

I'm squirming and twisting under him.

I'm both a bundle of nerves and a wave of relief as I whisper, "Thank you."

He pushes his chest into mine then. "What?"

"You protected me. You kept me safe."

He looks at me for a second or two, his eyes first flaring before he narrows them, like he can't believe what I just said. "Are you crazy, Poe? Are you *fucking* insane?"

"W-what?"

"Thank you," he repeats my words on a bite. "You're fucking thanking me for what I did."

"Yes. Not only b-because you protected me. But because I loved it," I tell him, my hands going up to his hair and grabbing the strands. "It was epic. I want more. I want —"

"Shut up."

"No, I won't." I tug at his hair. "I want more, Alaric. I want —"

His hands snatch away from my thighs and come up to my face then. One grabs hold of my jaw, squeezing my mouth, effectively robbing me of speech, and the other makes a fist in my hair as he growls, "Stop talking, Poe. Stop fucking talking. Because you don't want more. Because you're not going to want more when *I* want more." He gives my mouth a shake. "You know what I mean, don't you? You know what I'm talking about, yeah? You *remember*."

At his words, I undulate my hips, rubbing my pussy over his pelvis. But he presses into me even more, stopping my actions, his eyes now brimming with warning and turned into slits.

"I see that you do," he rasps.

"I do, y-yes." I nod. "I know what you want. I know you'll want my pussy."

"Yeah." His jaw clenches. "I will. And then you won't want more kisses from me, Poe. You won't want me to give you *more* when I come for that cunt. You won't *thank* me when you're lying here, in your teenage bed with bloody sheets and a wrecked, dripping pussy."

I shudder. My pussy shudders too.

A drop of wetness oozes out and I whisper, "But it's already dripping. My c-cu —"

He presses his mouth on mine to stop me and I latch on to him. I kiss him back even though I know he's done this on purpose. He doesn't want me to say it. He doesn't want me to say that word and I'm proven right when he breaks the kiss, ordering, "Don't fucking say that word."

"You said it though."

"I can say whatever the fuck I want." I open my mouth, trying to argue, but he speaks. "Am I going to have to watch everything I say or do in front of you? So you don't throw it back at me?"

I bite my lip, feeling both bratty and guilty. "I just want you. Why is that so bad?" Then, with pleading eyes, "Please, Alaric. Just once."

Something moves over his features then.

Something intense and heavy. Something that makes his chest, his abs, the length of his body flex and strain before going lax. I can't say that his body has gone soft; he's got heavy and hard muscles for days but some sort of tension leaves his body. And his chiseled expression loses its edge.

Even his fingers now cradle my jaw rather than holding it captive. His eyes take in my features. I must look all pink and flushed to him. That's how I feel at least.

"How about I tell you a secret, huh?" he whispers then, in a gentle sort of voice.

"What secret?"

"You wanted to know all my secrets, didn't you?" he rasps. "Back then. When you wanted your freedom." I nod and he continues, "You wanted to know something that you could use against me."

"Yeah."

"I'm going to give you something that you can." He nods, caressing my bangs. "Okay? I'm going to give you something that you can throw in my fucking face whenever you want to."

I know what he's doing.

I know he's bargaining with me. He's giving me something that I wanted badly back then so I won't beg him for what I actually want now.

I should be mad.

I should tell him that I'm not a child. I won't be bargained with. I have feelings and I have thoughts. I have the wishes and desires of a grown woman.

But the thing is that I *still* want to know all his secrets badly.

I still want *him* to open up to me rather than me listening to a story from someone close to him. And I think he knows my weakness, and so right now *he* is using something against me.

And I'm so far gone that I don't even care.

He can use whatever he wants against me.

He can do whatever he wants *to* me.

So swallowing, I say, "Okay."

Even though I give him what he wants, he still flinches like he can't believe it. He can't believe that I agreed and now he needs to really tell me a secret. Then, in a grave, low voice, he says, "It won't be just once."

"What?"

He watches me for a thick, heavy, charged moment before continuing, "Four years ago, when I kept you here, at this mansion, against your wishes, it was because I was angry. Because I wanted to punish you for the things that were done to me in the past."

He pauses here.

And simply watches me, his thumb raking over my skin, his eyes caressing me gently, tenderly.

But with a hunger that I've never seen before on him.

On anyone really.

It sends my heart racing. It sends my breaths racing as well as I prepare myself for what's to come next.

"But the second time," he begins, his fingers flexing. "After I wouldn't let you graduate and you came to me with this grand idea of doing the extra work. *That* time when I kept jerking you around, when I wouldn't listen to you, wasn't because I was angry. It wasn't because I wanted revenge or I wanted to make you pay."

My own fingers flex in his hair as I whisper, "So then why?"

My question makes him chuckle. It's slight and low, barely producing any sound and mostly a puff of air. "Why."

"Yeah."

"It's because you were right all along. I'm the devil, Poe," he says, his jaw clenching. "And you're the cute little doe-eyed diva I wanted to trap in my dungeon."

I don't...

I don't understand.

Not for a few seconds.

For a few seconds, all I can do is read pages and pages of regret on his face. Pages and pages of self-recrimination.

And then I get it.

Then I understand what he means.

I understand why he kept me here.

Why he wouldn't listen to me, my grand, legitimate idea of finishing summer school early.

"You want me," I whisper.

He flinches again, this time harder, and I can't help but tighten my limbs around him. I can't help but grasp his face and repeat, "You want me. That's why you wouldn't listen to me. That's why you kept dismissing all my ideas. Because you wanted me. You didn't wanna let me go. You wanted me for yourself."

His jaw is clamped shut but somehow he opens it and rasps, "Yeah."

"How… How long?"

"Since I came back."

"F-from Italy?"

"Yeah."

My mouth falls open. My eyes go wide.

My skin wakes up in goosebumps. My body wakes up with electricity and currents and fireworks.

He has wanted me since he came back from Italy.

He has wanted me for months now.

"I d-didn't…"

"Know," he says, his features a mix of regret and irritation. "Yeah, I know. I know you didn't know, Poe. I *know* you had no clue."

Then some tightness returns to his body as he goes on, "I *know* that you were in love with your fucking boyfriend. I know that. Not only do I know, it's fucking tattooed in my brain. Which means I think about it all the time. I think about it. I dream about it. I fucking see his ugly mug behind my closed eyes. And every time that happens, I want to go back and strangle him. I want to go back and pop his eyes out of their goddamn sockets because you loved him. Because you chased after him. But not only because of that, Poe. Not only because your teenage heart beat for him but also because of what he did to you. Because of what he was planning to do. The only reason he's alive right now is because he never got there. He never got to your mouth, your sweet, sugary, cherry pie mouth. If he had, I swear to God, I would've ended him. I would've killed him with my bare hands while you watched, Poe. While you fucking watched."

Oh God.

Oh God. *God.*

He has fucking wanted me while I was plotting against him. While I wanted to run away from him.

He has fucking wanted me while I wanted someone else.

I don't...

I don't know what to do. I don't know what to fucking do to make this pain go away for him.

To make this jealousy go away.

He's been burning with it. He's been choking with it.

And all this time, I never knew.

All this time, I was so blinded by the wrong things. By the things that I thought I wanted – Jimmy's love, my mom's love, my fucking freedom. While I've been free here.

I've been free at this mansion.

I've been free with Mo, with my friends at St. Mary's. And now with my sewing machine, with my dress designs.

Will it never cease to make me feel foolish, the way I've behaved?

Will they never stop haunting me, all the mistakes I've made?

All the ways that I've hurt him.

Hurt this man.

The man who in so many, many ways brought me this freedom.

My Alaric.

I open my mouth to say something, anything, but he goes on, in a rough whisper, "I'm this close, okay? I'm this fucking close. I'm hanging by a thread."

He grabs my face and lowers his lips even more, as if he wants me to understand these words correctly. As if he wants me to drink them down right from his mouth as they get ripped out of his chest, his heart, his very soul.

"I've said no to you before, yeah? Haven't I?" I jerk out a nod and he continues, "Lots of times. And I've done it out of malice, out of anger. And then I've done it because I didn't know what else to do. How else to make up for it all, for all the damage that I've done to you. But every time I've said no to you, Poe, something has died in me. Something *dies*. In me. Something burns and howls and lashes out. And it weakens me, you see. It fucking gnaws at my bones, at my insides, saying no to you. Do you understand that? Do you understand what I'm saying to you?"

I nod again.

Only because I know he needs that from me.

"So, I'm asking you, okay?" He pleads almost. "I'm asking you not to ask me. I'm asking you to not fucking ask me, Poe. Not again. And I gave you a secret in exchange for that. It's a fair trade, yeah? You can keep it. You can use it however you want. You can fucking throw it in my face.

"And I know I acted like an ass tonight. I dragged you away from your friends. I locked you up in your room. I fucking kissed you, mauled your mouth, raped it all because I didn't want anyone else to have your first taste. While you were fucking saving it for someone worthy, for someone right. But I'll make it up to you. I promise, all right?

"I'll do whatever you want. I'll give you whatever you want, whatever your heart desires. I'll buy you anything. I *will*. I'll go shopping with you. I'll drive you to the mall tomorrow. You like ice cream, huh? I'll buy you ice cream. I'll buy you all the clothes that you want for your designs. A new phone, a new computer, a new sewing machine. All the makeup. All the lipstick shades with weird-ass names. Your glow-in-the-dark nail polish. Chocolate chip cookies. Cherry pies. I'll fucking buy you diamond fucking tiaras and drape you in suede and sequins and polka dots. Okay, Poe?"

His voice vibrates with intensity as he continues, "Just don't ask me that. Don't fucking ask me to fuck you. Because I'll do it. And if I do it once, I'm going to do it twice. I'm going to do it three times. Four, five, six. I'm going to do it a million times and in a million ways, and I'll keep doing it. I'll keep coming back into your bedroom when everyone's asleep, when Mo's asleep and the whole staff is asleep, and has no clue about what goes on when Mr. Marshall walks into his ward's room at midnight and closes the door. And doesn't fucking leave until he's wrecked her and ruined her and turned her into his cute little whore. So this is not a game. Just let me leave, all right?"

I should listen to him.

I know that.

I can see that. He's all torn up and agitated. He's really at the end of his rope.

And he's right. This is not a game.

He will do all the things he said just now.

So this is serious. This is scary.

Only I'm not scared.

Not at all.

Because this is better than I thought. This is a million fucking times better than I ever, *ever* thought.

Like him, I don't want it to end either. I don't want it to be just once.

I never wanted that.

Yes, I wanted him to give me my first kiss and then have things go where they may. But in my heart of hearts, I knew that once wouldn't be enough. I knew that his kisses would be addicting. His kisses would be hooking and I knew that I would want them and him over and over and over. And I wanted it so much that I was willing to compromise and have it only once if that's what *he* wanted.

But turns out, he doesn't.

He wants what *I* want.

And now it's even more imperative that it happen over and over and over.

Because I need to fix it.

I need to fix this pain. That I caused.

I need to fix his misery, cure the torture that I put him through due to my reckless, desperate actions.

It's my duty. It's *my* job.

To soothe my guardian.

So I bring both my hands down from his hair where I've messed up his curly strands, and cradle his jaw. Looking into his tortured, anguished, molten eyes, I whisper, "I was talking about you."

Breathing heavily, he frowns. "What?"

"Back in your office," I explain, reaching up and kissing the bump on his nose, shocking him a little. "When I came in to ask if I could go to the bar with my friends. And I said that I knew how it felt."

He finally understands, his frown clearing and his body going tight as if preparing for an impending blow, an impending knife to his gut, and God, my heart hurts so badly. My heart twists and turns, thinking about all the times I did put a knife in his gut, all the times I did deal him blows and bruises.

I press my mouth to his and kiss him lightly as I hold onto his tight body and keep whispering, "I said that I knew the pain, the longing of wanting to get close to someone when that someone doesn't let you. When I said that, I was talking about you, Alaric. I was talking about how I've wanted to get close to you these past days and you wouldn't let me. You'd keep saying no."

I go to his shoulders and rub the tight globes. I rub my thighs over his rigid sides, his spine, trying to ease him as I keep whispering in a soft, soft voice because I think he needs that. After all the rough and sharp emotions.

"And if you died, with your every no, then I died a little too. I died every time you said no because I thought that I'd never get to touch you. I'd never get to be close to you. I missed you so much, Alaric, this past week. I missed you so much that it was slowly killing me. It was killing me that you'd gone back to the beginning. When we were enemies and you wouldn't even look at me. You wouldn't even acknowledge my presence as you walked by. It was killing me that it was so easy for you to do that. So it was you, you see. Not him. I don't even think about him, Alaric.

"And you told me a secret, right? So here's mine: the moment you chose to kiss me, I came alive. The moment you put your mouth on me and filled me with your air and taste and gave me my first kiss, I fucking came alive, Alaric. You brought me back to the land of the living. And I don't wanna die again. I don't wanna do what we did last week, not talking to each other, not looking at each other like we would do in the beginning. I don't wanna come to you when I have school troubles or something only my guardian can handle. I wanna come to you because I can't stay away. Because when we're not close, everything hurts. Please, Alaric. Don't make me go back. Keep me here, with you. I'll be your Poe. I'll be your cute little whore. I'll be anything and everything you want me to be. I don't want new lipstick or a new dress. New nail polish or a tiara. All I want is you. Please."

I wasn't sure how he'd take my words.

I knew I had to say them. I knew I had to tell him everything that's inside of me, but I didn't know how he'd react. If my confession, my pleas would send him off the deep end. If they'd make him angry or push him away or send him running.

But I'm glad, *so fucking glad* and ecstatic, that they do the opposite.

They do what I hoped that they would.

No, he doesn't relax or lose the tightness in his frame or the sharpness in his jaw. But I know — I can feel — that his frustration leaches out. His self-recrimination, his hatred for himself, his helplessness at the situation that made him bargain with me in the first place goes away.

In its place, there's a new emotion.

A new tightness. A different kind of sharpness.

In its place, there's determination.

And destiny.

Yeah, that's what I see on his beautiful, stone-carved face. In his pretty eyes.

I see destiny. I see the stars aligning. I see planets revolving.

And this destiny isn't made of butterflies or little fluttery things. This destiny is made of fire. It's made of thunder and rain and landslides and stampedes.

This destiny is made of him and me.

I guess that's what I felt four years ago, when he appeared before me, up on the roof. And since I was so young, so angry, so immature, I chose to fight it.

Not anymore though.

I want it now.

I want my destiny.

"It wasn't easy," he rasps, his cheekbones flushed, his body heated.

"What?"

"To go back to the time when we hardly looked at each other."

"God, Alaric, please."

"You want me?"

"Yes."

My whispered *yes* makes the fire in him surge anew.

And this one's so hot and flaming that it makes him sweat and shake.

It makes *me* sweat and shake.

It makes me delirious and through that fog I hear him growl, "Well then, your wish is my command."

Chapter Twenty-Nine

His growled words hit my belly and his mouth hits my lips.

And I'm in heaven.

I'm floating above the bed. I'm flying high as I hold on to him. As I kiss him back.

As I pull him close even though there's no more closeness to be had. Even though I'm as entwined with him as I can be. My heels are digging into the backs of his thighs and my fingers are twined in his hair. His chest is pressing into my swollen tits and his pelvis is digging into mine.

I still try to climb him

And when I can't, I moan.

I whine into his mouth.

I ask him to fix it with these little horny noises I'm making.

And for a second I think he's listening, and he has all the plans of fixing this problem that I have. Because he tightens his fists in my hair, presses his body harder over mine.

But then he breaks all my happy and relieved thoughts when he breaks our kiss.

When he lets me breathe the air that doesn't come from him.

I'm about to complain that he should come back, that this is absolutely not what I wanted.

But then I'm appeased when his mouth hits my neck and sucks and kisses my fragile skin there, but only for a second. After that, he moves lower. His mouth leaves a trail of wet, hungry kisses on my chest. But since I'm not wearing a low-cut dress — because of him —

there isn't a lot of skin exposed. Which means there isn't a lot of area to be covered.

Which causes my dissatisfaction to grow.

So I fist his hair and whine, "Alaric."

By this point he's at my ribs, his open mouth is breathing on my stupid modest dress and since it's not happening on my bare skin, it's starting to piss me off a little.

So I roll and undulate under him, calling out again. "Alaric, come back."

But he has a mind and an intention of his own because instead of listening to me, he's moving down and down, his mouth now on my belly button, through the dress though.

God, I hate my dress.

I *hate* that he made me wear it.

"Alaric, please. You're supposed to make it —"

My words come to a screeching halt when I feel something. A smack. On my thigh. On my *naked* thigh.

Which jerks my eyes open — I can't believe I had them closed until now even through my complaints and irritations — and I look down, and what I see makes me clench my thighs closed.

Only I can't.

Because he's between them.

His big, impossibly broad shoulders are between my naked, pale thighs. That look and feel even more naked and even more pale because his bronzed hands are on them. His bronzed fingers are splayed wide and gripping my flesh so tightly, so possessively and authoritatively.

Although as hot and sexy and pussy-clenching and nipple-beading as that vision is, somehow the vision of his ring-sporting pinkie on my flesh, so close to the juncture between my thighs, is even more all that.

And then there's the dress I've been hating on.

It's all hiked up. All the way up to my lower belly. Meaning my panties, purple and lacy, are showing and I realize why he smacked me.

Why he shut me up without words.

Because he's looking at my panties.

He's looking directly at them.

No, he's *staring*.

He's unabashedly, without an inch of shame or reservation, staring at my panties and he didn't want to be disturbed.

But more than that I realize — now that he told me his secret — that maybe he's wanted to do this for a long time now. Maybe he's wanted to stare at me without an inch of shame or reservation for a long time now.

So I let him look.

And I know he's staring at the wet spot. He *has* to be staring at the wet spot. Because I'm pretty sure with how wet I am and how my pussy keeps clenching and spasming and pushing my juices out, my wetness has to be taking center stage down there. It has to be super obvious and glaring.

"Alaric," I whisper, my fingers clutching the sheet now that he's all the way down there, out of reach.

Still staring at my panties as if in a trance, he rasps, "I wondered about them."

"What?"

"Your panties." Finally he looks up, his eyes eaten up by lust. "The ones you were wearing that day. When you planted the camera in my office." His fingers tighten up on my thighs. "I wondered how wet they were. I wondered if you'd let me stuff them in your mouth."

I jerk at his words. "I would have."

His fingers tighten again. "Yeah?"

"Yes. Even though I planted that camera, I never wanted anyone to find out. I never wanted anyone to blame you."

A puff of air escapes him. "Blame me for doing things to you behind closed doors?"

I jerk again. "Yes."

Another puff of breath as he rasps, "Well they would've, yeah. But not for the reasons you think. Not because when they heard you moan and scream – and they would've because I still think you'd purr like a wildcat if I played with your kitty – they would've thought that Principal Marshall's got a student hiding in his office. Not because they would've thought maybe he's hiding a teacher in there. Or even a girlfriend. They would've blamed me but for other reasons."

"What other reasons?"

His chest pushes sharply on the bed. "Because when they put their ears to the door and *really* heard your moans and *really* heard your screams and needy little whines, they would've thought that it was someone else."

"Who?"

"A high-priced hooker."

I twist my hips again, almost shredding the sheets with my fist, whimpering, "Alaric —"

"They'd think that instead of working, instead of doing his job, the respectable Principal Marshall got so desperate, so hard up for a fuck that he called for a hooker. Because the only reason a girl makes noises like that, the only reason she moans like that, like she's dying and losing all sense, is when she's getting paid to and her john is banging her pussy doggy style, doesn't she?"

"But that's not—"

"Not true though, yeah."

"No, it's not."

"I know," he agrees. "I know it's not true, Poe. But they haven't met you yet, have they? They don't know that there's a girl, a cute little whore, a pretty doe-eyed diva, who moans for Principal Marshall like that."

"I do, I do." My thighs clench again. "Please, Alaric."

"And that Principal Marshall keeps her panties in his desk drawer. Because I would've kept them, you know." I jerk again, my heels digging and slipping on the bed. "I would've kept them so I could lock my door and take a whiff of them every chance I got."

I'm about to call out his name again.

But then he actually goes ahead and does it. He actually goes ahead and takes a whiff of my panties and then I can't. I can't form words. All I can do is twist and squirm under his grip and moan again.

Because he doesn't stop there.

He noses my panty-covered pussy and keeps taking drags of it, of my scent, as if he's an animal. A beast. A predator, and his next words prove it. "Although I have to say that as much as I would've liked those panties, Poe, and as many times as I would've smelled them while jacking off while my assistant told everyone who called that Principal Marshall was busy, I still wouldn't be satisfied." Another sniff. "I would've felt duped. Because I wouldn't have gotten the good stuff." Yet another sniff, this one followed by a growl as if he's really unhappy and dissatisfied with my imaginary panties. "The fresh stuff, see. The fresh, ripe scent of a snatch that I'm getting right now. That I'm fucking inhaling and snorting like coke. The scent of cherries."

At this, he licks it.

He licks the center of my pussy through my panties and I moan so loud that I'm afraid the ceiling will fall down.

That I'll wake up the whole household.

But I don't think he's worried about that. I don't think he cares because his growl is louder. And shakier.

It shakes his whole body, my taste, and in turn, the whole bed I think.

Me as well.

"Yeah, I would've been fucking disappointed, Poe," he says, looking up, his eyes belligerent, his jaw clenched.

Chest heaving, breaths scattering, I somehow manage to whisper, "I'll give it to you. I'll give you whatever you want."

I'm not even sure how or what I'm saying. All I know is that I'll give him anything and everything he wants.

"Yeah?"

"Yes."

"Every day?"

"Every day."

That makes him happy. That makes him breathe easier. "Good. Every day at lunch then. We have a standing appointment, yeah? I want you to come into my office, Poe, and hike up your school skirt. I want you to sit at my desk, with your thighs spread open so I can sniff your cunt and get my hit. So I can eat it too, your snatch. I need my lunch, Poe."

I'm shaking now. I'm trembling and I just want him to end this torture.

I just want him to take me.

I just want him to give it to me.

"I will," I tell him, my voice thready and barely there. "I'll do everything you want. Just please… Alaric, I want…"

"I know what you want, Poe," he says, his eyes glinting. "And I'll give it to you. But I'm going to prepare you first."

"P-prepare?"

"Yeah." He nods. "Because I'm your guardian, aren't I?"

"Yes."

"I'm the one who protects you."

"You do."

His hands on my thighs flex and tighten. His chest expands

under his shirt as well, before he rasps, "So I'm protecting you. Because you're going to need all the protection for what you want from me and what I can't fucking wait to give you."

With those confusing and slightly threatening words, his hands move away from my thighs and go to my panties. His fingers hook on the band and snatch them down my hips and legs before I can even comprehend his intentions.

Just as I notice him throw those panties over his shoulder, I feel it.

I feel the first lick.

It's hot and wet, wetter than even my pussy, and I whimper.

I twist when the first lick becomes the second and the third before he's sucking on my flesh. And then I'm shuddering under his ministrations as I try to keep my eyes open. As I try to watch his dark, curly head moving, going up and down and back and forth. As I watch his hands that are back on my thighs, keeping them spread and open.

Then I watch them move and slide and hook under my thighs so he can lift them up and put them over his impossibly broad shoulders.

At which point, I have to close my eyes and hold on.

I have to clutch the sheets and dig my heels in his back.

Because A: that just changed the whole angle and now I'm somehow feeling his tongue in my belly. And B: because he kisses like he eats pussy. Or maybe vice versa.

Maybe he eats pussy like he kisses, I don't know.

I'm very scattered. I'm very delirious and foggy and fucking restless.

Because he's eating me out.

He's sucking on my outer lips, vacuuming them in, lapping up the center of my pussy. When he's done with that, when he's satisfied, he goes inside. He thrusts his tongue inside and I dig my heels the hardest that I've ever done. Because I feel this pressure, see. This stretch of my hole, so that I can't help it.

And I guess I hurt him because he grunts.

And then he slurps.

And I lose my mind again except to say to myself that I was right: he does kiss like he eats pussy.

And the moment I think that, I come.

The dam breaks inside of me and I throw my head back,

moaning and whimpering, my body leaving the bed too. Or almost, because he puts his hand on my stomach to keep me in place so he can slurp down all my juices like he said he would. Like he said he'd prefer to do over lunch.

I'm not sure when I come back down to earth and into myself. But the next thing I know is that my pussy is still spasming and my heart is still thundering but Alaric is making his way up. And on his way up, he pulls and tugs on things as if he's impatient. As if he doesn't like how covered up I am.

He pulls my dress at my ribs.

He tugs at the bodice, the neckline, popping my breast out before going for a long suck of my nipple that threatens to send me into another orgasm. He finishes that by taking a bite out of my tit before moving onto my shoulders and my neck, pulling and pushing the straps of my dress.

Before coming full circle and putting his mouth on me, kissing the fuck out of me.

Making me taste my own juices and God, I love it.

I love my own cum. I think I taste amazing. I taste fabulous.

I've tasted my juices before but I never thought I tasted so good and so I can't take all the credit. I think I taste this fabulous because he's feeding it to me. Because his taste is mixed in with mine.

And this is getting me so hot that I go back to winding my limbs around him and humping his stomach. I go back to being all needy and demanding even though I just came.

But like before, Alaric has a mind of his own.

Because he breaks the kiss.

Only this time he doesn't go down, he goes up.

He pushes himself up on his arms and lifts himself up and off my body. Before getting completely off the bed and coming to his feet. I'd be asking him all sorts of questions right now but I'm super mesmerized by his athletic prowess. I'm super mesmerized by the way his body is so large and yet so graceful.

So powerful. So masculine.

Not to mention, I'm mesmerized by the fact that he's staring at me again.

In that erotic, hot way of his.

And again, I let him.

I even go so far as to come up on my elbows so he has a better look.

It doesn't matter that my dress is all rumpled and stretched. That my one breast is out, my nipple pink and throbbing from his mouth. It doesn't matter that my thighs are wide open and my pussy must be pink and glistening, again from his mouth.

And then as he's running his chocolate chip eyes all over me, his own jaw glistening with my juices, he goes for his shirt.

In front of my eyes, he unbuttons the top few buttons, making my heart stutter, before tugging at it and trying to snag it off his body. But I stop him.

"No, wait," I say, my lips dry at the peek of his bronzed skin.

He glances at me then, a frown between his brows.

I come up to my knees, just as I am, all disheveled and exposed, and continue, "All the way."

"What?"

Licking my lips, I look into his eyes. "Do it all the way. Undo all the buttons. I wanna see."

"You want to see."

I nod. "Yeah. And slowly."

"Slowly."

A small smile appears on my lips as I nod. "Like a striptease."

I'm not sure why I'm asking him to do this. It's only going to delay everything, the main thing, the most important thing that I want. But I have this urge. This naughty, diva urge.

To see him do this.

To slowly reveal the thing I've been dying to see.

As if it were a gift. A special gift for me.

And it is a gift, isn't it?

His body. The one he's built so patiently and with all his hard work over the years.

So yeah, I want him to open his shirt slowly.

He watches me for a second, his eyes glittering, his chest heaving up and down, his fingers paused while fisted in his dark gray shirt.

But then, he asks, his voice low, "Is that your final wish?"

My eyes go wide. My thighs clench.

At the fact that his words are so reminiscent of my own from the day in his office: *Is that your final decision?*

At the fact that he didn't say no: *I hate saying no to you.*

My eyes circled wide in wonder, I nod again. "It is."

His jaw goes tight for a second before he rumbles, "Well then, your wish is my command."

With those very erotic words, he begins.

His fingers move and go to the rest of the buttons and my eyes follow everything. My eyes take in everything. The deft masculine way he's unbuttoning his shirt. How those pesky little buttons don't stand a chance against his large strong fingers. How even his nails are masculine, square and blunt, and how that silver ring just makes everything so much hotter and sexier.

And then, God *then,* he pulls at the shirt fronts.

Not slowly and gently like I asked him to, like he's been treating his buttons, no.

He grabs them in an impatient, aggressive manner and tugs at them. He frees them from his dress pants and before I can even register that, his shirt is coming off completely.

His shirt *has* come off completely.

And holy God.

Holy fucking God.

He's. . . He's magnificent.

He's breathtaking. He's breath-scrambling and breath-scattering and breath-stuttering. And all the million other things that won't let me breathe. That won't even let me think or form words.

Because all I can do is feel.

And stare.

At the expanse of his spectacular body. His bronzed and muscled body.

At the perfectly round globes of his shoulders like small planets. Those broad tight arches of his pecs like the armor of a gladiator.

And then comes his torso.

It's broad and thick and ridged in a way that makes you think of buildings and pillars and tensile strength and I don't even know what tensile strength means exactly. But I know he has it.

I know that.

I also know that he has a six pack.

Holy God, yes.

There's a ridged ladder in his stomach and the rungs are so defined that I know my small fingers can grab one if they want. My small fingers can hold on to one if they want.

And I do want.

I do so, do so, want.

Not because he's a work of art or a beautiful piece of architecture. But because he's him.

Because he's built this body, cultivated it over the years. He's sculpted this with his own hands, his own hard work.

Because my Alaric wasn't always like this.

He built his body to be a symbol of strength. To be a symbol of what he wanted and needed when he was growing up.

And so I go to him.

I walk on my knees to go up to him and touch him.

But as soon as I do, my head is pulled back and he's leaning over me, his jaw clenched and his eyes shooting fire. "You done?"

His voice is a growl that vibrates.

In fact, his entire body is vibrating. I didn't realize that.

In my starstruck state, I didn't realize how his chest is heaving and how his abdomen is hollowing out. The abdomen that I'm touching, and which is all fevered and heated and sweaty.

My fingers slip and caress those ridges. "You have a six pack."

"Eight."

My eyes have never been this wide. "Holy shit."

"You —"

"You're a god."

"Poe, I —"

"No, wait. I don't think you're a god. I think…" I frown. "I think you're beyond that. You're beyond godly. You're… otherworldly. You're a big, sexy alien. Wait, is that better or worse? Than being a hot god."

He growls, impatient.

"You're just so beautiful, Alaric. You're breathtaking. Do you think I could watch you do your punching thingy some time?"

His jaw ticks at my ramblings. His fingers in my hair flex.

Then, "You know that you've made this way worse on yourself, don't you?"

I clutch at his sides. "Worse how?"

He leans even further down. "Kneeling there, giving me those fuck-me eyes while you make me strip for you. You didn't think that would come without consequences, did you? You didn't *think* that twisting me around your tiny little finger and babbling and being all cute little Poe would come without my cock swelling to four times its size, did you?"

He called me cute again.

He thinks I'm cute.

But there's something more important than that right now.

"F-four times. Is that…"

I want to look down and see if that's possible. Does that even happen?

And oh my God, how amazing if it does.

But he bends even further, a drop of sweat from his forehead plopping onto mine. "No, it's not. Not without medical help. But I guess you're fucking magical and better than western medicine, aren't you? And that's bad for you, Poe. That's bad because my raging monster of a hard-on is going to introduce you to a world of hurt tonight and that's exactly what I didn't want to happen."

So that's what it was.

The words he said to me when he went down on me.

He was preparing me for his cock.

God.

He's amazing, isn't he?

My otherworldly, alien, godly guardian.

My heart swells in my chest and I press my thighs together as he continues, "And this isn't a modest dress." He tightens his fist in my hair while his other hand comes to grab my bare breast, all rudely and obscenely. "If I could get at your tit with one pull of this useless dress, any other asshole could have too."

"Alaric, please. Now."

His jaw clenches with emotion and he simply stares at me for a few moments.

Before he descends on me and claims my mouth in a kiss.

And it's a kiss that goes on when he grabs my dress and drags it up my body with hasty movements, only breaking for a microsecond when he has to get it up my arms. It's a kiss that goes on when he unbuttons his pants, breaking for another second to drag them completely off. It's a kiss that goes on when he lays me down on the bed and comes to settle his muscular and heated bulk between my thighs.

He breaks it again though, waking me up from the drowsy slumber he'd put me in.

But only because he has to go up and kneel between my thighs.

That's when I get a good look at his cock.

And he's right.

It is big and swollen. And thick and standing up, touching his belly button.

It's duskier and darker than his bronzed skin and if it was someone else, anyone else, I would be scared. I would be scared by the length. By the ruddy knobby head. By the fact that it keeps throbbing, leaking pre-cum.

But since it's him, it's my Alaric, I'm not scared.

I'm impatient.

I'm horny and squirming on the bed.

When I look at his face to tell him to hurry, I notice that he's watching me writhe shamelessly. He's watching me twist my hips and bounce my tits as I clutch my sheets and rub my heels up and down.

"I'm clean," he says, breaking into my lusty thoughts. "I haven't had sex in months. I got so caught up in finishing everything in Italy before coming back that I didn't..."

"Okay," I whisper, trusting and completely uncaring and only because yes, it's him.

He swallows. "And I've never, not ever, not used a condom before so I'm —"

"Hurry, Alaric."

A puff of breath escapes him. "This is important, Poe. This is about your safety. This —"

"I don't care," I tell him, jerking my hips shamelessly. "It's you. So please, hurry."

And thankfully he does.

Maybe because he could see it on my face, how impatient I am. Or maybe he lost the battle with himself.

I watch him as he retrieves a condom from his wallet, lying on the floor — something he probably got from his pants in all the undressing and kissing — before rolling it down his length and coming over me.

"You had a condom in your wallet?" I ask as he settles himself over me.

"Been carrying it this whole time," he rasps, adjusting me now, opening my thighs up, hiking them up around his naked hips so his pelvis locks with mine. "Didn't want to take any chances around you."

By the time his meaning slams into me, that he's been carrying around a condom in his wallet all this time because he's wanted me, because I've been torturing him, his mouth is back to kissing mine and I forget all about condoms and wallets and everything else but him.

But the searing heat of his dick on my stomach.

Which doesn't stay on my stomach for long though.

It moves.

It travels down and then I feel it in my pussy.

Right at my hole.

At my tight, virgin hole.

That a second later doesn't stay that way because he takes it from me. He rips my virginity from my body with a sharp, stabbing push.

And the pain is so fierce and hot and fiery that for a few seconds after that I see and feel things in flashes.

I feel him break the kiss and shush me, licking my cheeks where my tears are streaming down. I feel his fingers caressing my hair and pushing my thick bangs away from my sweaty forehead. I feel his stomach juddering and hollowing out over mine, his chest vibrating and scraping against my nipples.

But there are two things that I feel the most.

One, the throb of his cock inside of me, stretching me, making my channel pulse in the rhythm of it.

And the second, his voice.

The deep, hypnotic hum of it when I whisper, "It hurts."

He lifts his face up from my neck where he was licking and leaving little kisses on my skin. His jaw is clenched, his forehead sweaty and tight, such a contrast to his soft words. "I know, baby. But it'll pass, I promise."

My belly clenches. "You called me baby."

His eyes go liquid. "You like that?"

I clutch his biceps. "Yeah. And you think I'm cute."

He kisses my forehead. "Because you fucking are."

"Say it again."

"My cute little Poe."

"Again."

"My baby."

"Again."

He whispers it in my ear and it makes me smile. "Thank you."

He whispers it on my neck and it makes my pussy clench and

I want to thank him again but I'm too lost in the sensations of it. And when he whispers it over my collarbones and throat and chin and lips, I move.

Which makes him move.

And as soon as he does, the pain recedes.

Magically, the pain goes down to a level where I start to feel things. Incredible things. Things that I've been feeling all this time but were overshadowed by the pressure, the sheer stretch of my pussy with his cock.

And then he does it again. And again, his dick sliding in and out in small inches.

All the while looking into my eyes, reading them, studying them like his favorite book.

And God, he's a fast learner.

He's a super fucking fast learner because one second, I'm only starting to feel good, I'm only starting to enjoy his slow glides, and the next, I'm craving them. I'm craving his moves. I'm juicing up for his moves. I'm swelling up and ripening for his length to invade me over and over.

Then he hits a spot in my pussy, a spot I didn't even know existed until he brought it to life, that makes it impossible for me to stay quiet. That makes it impossible for me not to throw my head back, digging it into the pillow. Impossible not to push back.

And when I do, it's his turn to grunt.

It's his turn to bury his face in my neck and clutch my face like it's the most precious thing ever.

Which only makes me push back harder, and soon we establish a rhythm.

Soon, my nails are scratching his back because this rhythm that we have is driving me crazy. This rhythm that we have is making me go feral and I'm digging my heels into his thighs, feeling his bare and clenching muscles, the coarse hot and hairy skin. I'm lifting and arching my pelvis to take him in deeper. I'm sweating and burning and feeling something in my belly.

Something like a tight fist.

A fist I recognize but it has never been this tight. It has never been this overwhelming and scary.

Yeah, it's scary.

I've never felt like this before and so I hold him tighter. I wrap my arms around his neck and bury my face in his chest, hoping that he'll protect me, hoping that he'll keep me safe from whatever is happening inside my body.

And he does.

God, does he.

He hugs me back.

His giant guardian arms wrap themselves around my tiny body as he plasters us together, both our skins sweaty and sliding against each other. And just the fact that I'm all cocooned in the heat of his muscles and bones and him makes that fist unfurl.

That fist inside my belly opens up and expands and I swear I feel fireworks burst on my skin. I feel every inch of my body waking up and climaxing in a mad rush, my limbs jerking and my hips twisting under him.

But most of all, I feel it in my pussy.

I feel it spasming and clenching around his rod as I come and come and drench him.

Drench my own thighs and the sheets beneath us.

But it's okay.

Because I don't think he minds and I don't think I've ever been this relaxed.

This drowsy and this happy that I'm smiling as my eyelids flutter and my vision goes in and out.

And then I feel him move.

I feel him shift and slide and come off my body.

When I notice a blur of his bronzed, sweaty body kneeling between my open thighs, I force my eyes to remain open. I force myself to remain still as well because it's his turn now.

I can't be hungry or greedy, asking him to come back over me and fuck me again; the first fuck isn't even over yet.

But God, the things he's doing while kneeling on the bed are so fucking arousing.

The way he slides off the condom — I see the drops of blood on it, that gives me a second of pride that I bled for him, for my Alaric — and grips his trunk of flesh. The way he jerks it in tight and fast movements, throwing his head back, groaning. The way every single muscle on his body is standing up and standing taut as he pleasures himself.

Jesus.

Is that how he looks when he's making himself come?

All sweaty and big and flushed. All horny and dark.

When he brings his other hand and grips his balls and tugs at them, I moan.

I have to.

My pussy is juicing up again and I can't help but rock on the bed, and I think that's what does it for him.

My moans and my little jerks, because he snaps his head back and his pretty dark eyes clash with mine. And the first sight of me, laying there all open, brings about the first jerk in him.

The first spasm that I see on his body, on his chest and stomach, but I feel on my skin.

Because he comes.

And his cream lashes out and lands on my belly.

Then it lands on my heaving tits and my trembling chest and finally on my puffy and swollen pussy, and I don't waste any time. I don't waste a single second to dip my fingers in it and rub his cum all over my body. I don't waste a second to douse myself in his scent and to revel in it.

By the end of it, I smell like him and my Alaric is so spent that he almost drops down on the bed but his arm shoots out and he catches his fall, hovering and leaning over me, his other hand still wrapped around his cock, his chest heaving and his groans echoing around the room.

I bring him all the way down over me by reaching up and winding my arms around his neck. And then we're kissing and making out and eating at each other's lips.

In the kiss, I whisper, "Best first kiss ever."

And into the kiss, he chuckles.

Which becomes the sweet, deep sound of his laugh — the first I've heard from him — when I lick his lips.

So yeah, totally.

Best. First kiss. Ever.

Chapter Thirty

Sunlight floods every inch of the room and I blink my eyes open.

The first thing I realize is that I'm smiling. I'm feeling all lethargic and sleepy and a good kind of sore.

I hear a voice.

"Good morning." Which then adds, "Well, good afternoon. Since it's 12:15."

I snap my head in the direction of the voice and see a blurry silhouette of a woman.

It's Mo.

She's standing at the window, pulling the drapes open, and holy fuck.

Am I naked?

I went to sleep naked, didn't I?

Fuck.

I don't want Mo seeing me naked. That's the last thing I want.

My smile falls off and I scramble to pull my blanket up to hide from her. But then I realize that no, I'm not naked. I have my favorite pajamas on.

And guess what, they're not purple. They're pink with white lace.

The only reason this asinine thought comes into my head is because this fact had come as a surprise to the man who dug them out of my drawers himself. Not to mention he also put them on me, because I was so drowsy and lazy and boneless after everything that he'd done to me last night.

Including the bath that he'd drawn.

God, the bath.

I go to smile again — my heart is already smiling — at the thought but I shove those thoughts away and focus on the present because Mo's here.

I spring up in a sitting position, and look for my glasses. Which I find half a second later because they're on the nightstand. Again courtesy of him; he'd found them on the floor last night — I probably took them off in all my crying and sobbing — and brought them up to my nightstand so I could have them within easy reach.

Again a happy thought I try not to focus on as I say, "Mo. What are you… doing here?"

Now that I can see her properly, I notice that she's in my walk-in closet, busy picking up the piles of clothes that me and my friends had discarded on the floor before completely giving up. "Okay, this is a mess. I'm going to send someone up here to straighten it all out."

"You don't have to," I tell her. "I can do it myself."

She turns to me then, smiling. "Well, I don't want you to. Because I hear that someone had a great night."

I freeze for a second. Then, "Um, you *hear*?"

What did she hear?

Did she hear me… you know, moaning?

Last night I mean.

God, did she hear everything? But wait, is that a bad thing or a good thing?

Is she going to be upset that…

"Yup," she says, breaking into my frantic thoughts. "That's why I brought you meds."

I'm so confused right now. "Meds?"

She points with her chin. "Ibuprofen. On your nightstand."

I glance over and sure enough, there's a little pill and a glass of water.

"Mr. Marshall said that you might need it after the night you've had," she says, and I snap my eyes over to her, my heart pounding. "I guess he was worried about a headache or something after the night out with your friends. So I'd take that," she points to the medication, "and then I'll whip you up some breakfast. Or maybe brunch, since it *is* lunch time."

Night out with friends.

That got interrupted.

I did text them hours later when I was about to fall asleep just in case they were worried. I'd also like to point out that I did it using my old phone, the one with the tracker because after the whole nude photo debacle, Alaric gave it back to me. Well, his assistant informed me that my phone was back at the mansion. I think it was his way of telling me that my photos are safe and he would never ever do anything with them. I already knew that but still.

But that's not important right now. I have other important things to worry about.

"Where is he?"

She frowns. "Who?"

"Uh, Mr. —" Then I decide to just do it. "Alaric."

It comes as a slight surprise to her.

I've never called him by his name before. Not even the night she chose to divulge his story and share some of his secrets with me. Mo has, of course. But usually, she sticks to his last name, and maybe I should've too. Especially after what happened last night and how we became more.

Than what we are.

That what we're supposed to be in the world's eyes.

And that's the thing, isn't it?

That's why he kept his distance. That's why he kept pushing me away last week even though he's wanted me for a long time now. Because of what we are to each other, guardian and ward, principal and student.

None of those things are the things I care about.

I don't care what he's supposed to be to me or what's acceptable in the world's eyes.

The only thing I care about is that he's my soulmate.

But.

I don't know how Mo will react to this. Or the rest of the staff here at the mansion.

I mean, people at school would definitely lose their shit, for sure.

And as much as I don't care about what people think, I also don't want to create any problems for Alaric. I don't want people to point fingers at him or make him out to be the bad guy. Which I know could happen so easily in a situation like this. And I also know that he'd take the blame. Not only because of his epic moral compass and his strong sense of right and wrong, but also because he'd do anything to protect me.

That's why he left last night.

After the bath, I mean. After he put me in my pajamas, cuddled with me and put me to sleep. I felt him leaving. I wanted to stop him, call out to him, but I was too drowsy to do it. And now I'm glad I didn't.

Although I wish I had this sense now.

I wish I hadn't called him by his name and given even a hint that things have changed between us.

But it's out there now, and Mo is watching me with a look in her eyes that I don't get. "I was hoping to talk to you about that."

Fearfully, I swallow. "Uh, talk about what?"

She approaches the bed and takes a seat on the edge, her eyes pinned on me. "About how you're doing."

I duck my eyes and bring my knees up to my chest, wrapping my arms around them. "I'm doing fine."

She places her hand on my knees in a silent command to look up at her. "I know you decided to stay. Even when he was ready to let you go. It came as a surprise to me, to all of us actually. And I'd like to know why. Because I want to make sure that you're okay. That you're —"

I grab her hand. "I'm okay. I promise." She still looks skeptical. "I swear, Mo. I'm fine."

She frowns. "He didn't force you?"

My heart slams in my chest when she puts it like that.

Force.

"No, of course not," I say, squeezing her hand. "He'd never do that."

"He has in the past."

"I know, but he had reasons."

"They don't justify what he did."

I squeeze her hand harder. "I know that too. But you have to trust me when I say it was me. It was my choice." Then, with a trembling breath, I add, "I wanted to stay."

I wanted him to kiss me and fuck me and I never ever want

people to assume otherwise.

I never want Mo to assume otherwise.

Not Mo.

She loves him. She's his greatest ally. She's been with him since forever and I can't have what happened between us turn into something that Mo might blame him for.

"He's a good man, Mo," I say before she can say anything, my eyes staring into hers with all the seriousness and intensity. "He's so good. He's so… moral and strong and determined. I've never met a man like him. I've never met *anyone* like him. My mom… I know I don't talk about it but she…" I swallow. "I loved her, okay? I admired her. She was my whole world. To the point where I was blind to so many of her faults. I was blind to how cruel she was despite her being cruel with me. Despite her being so neglectful and… I thought all moms were supposed to be like that. At least, all Hollywood moms. But they're not. Moms aren't supposed to be like that. Moms aren't supposed to cut you down. They're not supposed to make you hide who you are. And I never realized that. Not until him. Not until he gave me the courage to be myself."

I squeeze her hand again. "He sees me, Mo. Somehow, someway, he sees me. And that's all I've ever wanted: to be seen. To be acknowledged. And he makes me feel safe. Until him I was never safe, and until him, I didn't *know* that I was never safe. I'm safe now. I know we've had our differences in the past, him and me, but they're over now. They're done. And so please, don't ever, *ever*, think that he'd do anything to harm me. And I promise that I'd never do anything to harm him."

With pounding heart, I wait for her reaction. I wait for her to say something.

Usually I can read Mo but right now, she's not giving me anything. She's only watching me with the same look, and I'm about to say something more, but then she smiles.

It's her usual Mo smile, happy and warm.

But there's something more there too that I've never seen before.

A certain kind of knowing.

As if she knows a secret now that I don't.

Which makes no sense to me but that's the only way I can describe it.

Then, she says, "He's good, huh."

Eyes wide, I nod. "He is."

Her smile gets bigger. "Well, okay. I just wanted to make sure that you were good too."

I breathe out a sigh of relief. "I'm good too. I promise." Then, "You love me, don't you?"

I don't know where that came from.

Or why it took me so long to realize that.

I mean, the signs have always been there, that Mo loves me. That she cares for me.

But I'm only realizing it now.

That this woman, who I met accidentally, is someone closer to me than my own mother was.

She looks at me like I'm an idiot. "Well, duh, kiddo."

So maybe I'm not as unloved as I thought.

Maybe there's someone who does love me in a motherly way that I always wanted.

And look, it's all intrinsically entwined with him. Every good thing in my life right now is entwined with him.

My guardian.

I chuckle. "I love you too."

She chuckles too. "Okay then. Meds first. Then go freshen up and come downstairs for breakfast." Then, getting up and bending down she kisses my forehead and whispers, "And he's in the gym."

Chapter Thirty-One

Oh, he's definitely in the gym.

Definitely.

And he's doing the thing that I've been wanting to watch him do for a while now.

Four years to be exact.

Yeah, I've been wanting to see him punch his heavy bag for four years now. Ever since I knew there was a gym at the mansion and I saw the heavy bag hanging from the ceiling.

I hated him then but I still wanted to see.

I still wanted to watch him go at it.

And as I stand here, my back pressed to the door and my thighs clenched, and watch him go at the heavy bag after four years, I realize that I could watch him for the next four.

I could watch that tight black t-shirt that's stuck to his body like a second skin, highlighting every crest and dip of his muscles, rippling with every jab he takes.

It actually glides, that t-shirt. And it's only because his muscles are sliding underneath.

His muscles are fluttering and twitching underneath.

Especially the muscles of his shoulders, rolling every time he rears his arms back, one after the other.

Also his pectorals and his obliques.

They move too. They judder and shake at every impact.

And then there are his upper back muscles. What are they called again? I don't know. All I know is that they span out and flutter like wings as he keeps hitting that leather bag, much like his shoulders.

Fun fact: he's got two dimples on his back.

Yeah.

I saw them myself last night when he was drawing me a bath.

I also counted his eight pack. Just sayin'.

Another fun fact: I loved that he drew a bath for me after we had sex.

And not only that, after putting me in the hot water, he got in himself. He sat propped up against the tub before he settled me between his spread legs, propping my back against him.

Turning around, my arm pressed to his hot chest, I asked him, "Alaric?"

He looked down, his face misty and beautiful, dotted with droplets of water, all softened and relaxed. "Poe."

"Why are we taking a bath?"

He studied my face, his arms resting on the rim of the tub. "Because you need it."

"How do you know I need a bath?"

"Because you're going to be sore pretty soon. And this should help loosen up your muscles."

My eyes went wide and his lips twitched. "Oh, right. You mean after our very first sex."

"Yes, Poe, after our very first sex."

"You're so intelligent, aren't you?" Then before he could say anything, I said all breathily, "Thank you."

His arms came around me, turning me back around and splashing water everywhere. "Now, I want you to relax and close your eyes, all right?"

He put his chin on my head and held me tight, rubbing my arms with his rough but cozy fingers, and so I forgot what I wanted to say anyway. Until I felt him. At the small of my back.

His dick.

Growing hard.

Opening my eyes, I whispered, "Alaric?"

His chest vibrated with a deep hum. "Poe."

"I feel it."

"Ignore it."

I squirmed, rubbing my back against it. "I can't. He's my friend."

"What?"

I turned around to look up at him again. "What, are you saying he's not my friend?" I frowned. "I hate to break it to you, Alaric, but your dick is my friend. He made me feel good. And people who make you feel good are your friends."

He shot me a look like I'd lost my mind. "Well, *the people* will be glad to hear that. Why don't you try to relax now?"

I frowned harder. "And you're my friend too, just so you know. I know you were dead against it, so."

"Jesus," he muttered, looking up.

I poked his chest. "You are."

Looking down, he agreed, "Fine, Poe. I'm your fucking friend. Now shut your mouth."

Again, he turned me back around and wrapped his arms tightly around me.

I frowned at the tiled wall. "Well, that was mean."

"Never said I wasn't."

"And just for that I'm going to buy us a matching pair of friendship bracelets — another thing you were dead against. And force you to wear one."

"Fine."

"All the time."

"Got it."

"It's going to be purple."

"Poe."

"Just sayin'."

His response was to growl.

But I kept going. "It's too big though."

He squeezed his arms around me again. "For the love of God, Poe."

"It's a baseball bat." Then, "No, wait. It's a snake. An anaconda."

Finally, he turned me toward him himself and growled again, his jaw hard, "What the fuck do you want?"

I cupped that harsh jaw as I whispered, "To take care of you."

It clenched, emotions flickering over his beautiful face. "It's supposed to be the other way around."

"You're hurting."

"No, I'm not."

"It's going to bruise tomorrow."

"No, it won't."

"But —"

"If you go about taking care of me every time my dick got hard around you, Poe, then you'd be spending your life flat on your back, your thighs spread and your cherry pie snatch open for me."

At this, my mouth went wide too, in addition to my eyes, as I breathed, "No way. Really?"

A puff of breath escaped him and he responded as if this was the most obvious thing in the world. "Yeah."

"I didn't… I didn't know."

Tightening his arms around my body, he continued, "So I want you to stop giving me fuck-me eyes and go to sleep."

I studied his face, rubbing my fingers on his cheek. "I'm sorry I tortured you. I'm sorry I was so stupid that I ran after him. I'm sorry I didn't know. I'm —"

He pressed his mouth over mine to get me to stop talking, before he growled, "Sleep. Now, baby."

So I shut up.

But not before I thanked him again.

Because he called me baby. Because he promised he would and he did.

And I still hear it, hours and hours later, standing here in the gym, watching him pound his heavy bag like it's destined for hell. A second later, he stops though, his chest heaving, his hands that are wrapped up in white tape splayed wide on the leather bag, and his face ducked.

I think it's time for me to make my presence known.

I haven't yet.

Because as soon as I entered, I found him at the bag and I froze.

But I don't have to. He lifts his eyes on his own, landing them directly on me.

And in them, I see every single thing that happened last night.

I see every single thing that he did and made me feel flashing like glorious diamonds and stars and my skin wakes up with goosebumps.

"Hi," I whisper breathily.

His response is to straighten up and begin to unravel the tape from around his hand.

"I was… I just came in and you were…"

"I know."

"Y-you knew I was standing here?"

"Yeah."

"Oh." I swallow under his heavy, intense, *possessive* gaze. "Did I, uh, interrupt you? I —"

He shakes his head slowly. "I finished about twenty minutes ago."

I lick my lips. "Oh. But then… you were still going."

Again, he chooses to respond with silence. With actions.

Now finished with his tapes, he lets them fall to the ground and begins walking toward me.

Prowling toward me.

His thighs bulging under his workout pants, his chest heaving under his sweaty t-shirt.

And every step that he takes toward me somehow echoes in my belly. It echoes in my chest and beats like a drum.

So loud and so vibrating that I press my back against the door.

When he reaches me, he places his hand on the door above my head and leans in. "Because I knew you wanted to watch."

It takes me a second or two to realize what he's saying.

What he's referring to.

Do you think I could watch your punching thingy?

Something I said to him last night before I got distracted with other things, and forgot about it. He didn't, however.

He remembered and he delivered.

Like so many other things. Small and big. Crazy and whimsical.

Just because I wanted them.

Just because he can't say no to me.

Breathless, I crane up my neck and whisper, "So that was for me."

"Yeah."

Clenching my thighs, I whisper again, "Thank you."

His eyes flash as he leans further down. "Are you going to thank me every time I do something for you?"

I nod. "Yes."

"Because you're such a good girl."

"No."

"And you have excellent manners."

"No." I swallow. "Because it's you. Because you're amazing and because no one has ever done things for me. Not like this."

He studies my features, my eyes and glasses, my bangs. "Well then, it's about time someone did, isn't it?"

"Pampering," I blurt out.

He frowns, bringing his eyes back to mine. "What?"

"It's called pampering," I tell him like he doesn't know, like it's a bad thing. "What you're doing."

"What am I doing?"

"Fulfilling my every wish." Then, on a whisper, "It's called pampering."

His lips twitch. "Is it?"

"Yes." I inch up my glasses. "It makes me feel special."

"Yeah?"

"And spoiled."

"And?"

"And happy."

"What else?"

My belly hollows out on a breath. "It makes me feel like I'm your baby."

He leans even further down. "Good. Because you are, aren't you?"

"I am." Then, with wide eyes, "Alaric?"

I think he knows what I want. I want him to touch me. I want him to kiss me and oh God, fuck me.

Let's please fuck again.

It's obvious, by the way his eyes flash and his nostrils flare, that he knows.

But he ignores me.

Tipping his jaw down, he asks, "That for me?"

I want to bring him back to the topic at hand but then I remember that I have something for him.

A piece of cherry pie.

I look down at the dish I'm holding. "Oh yes. Mo said you haven't eaten yet and like, you've been working all day and then you came here for a workout. So I got you this. Because it's your favorite and I thought it might entice you. But Alaric," I add, looking up and going serious, "I think we need to talk about it."

We so do.

I don't think I like how he works so much. How he neglects everything else in favor of it.

This is same as his anger issues, his punching thingy.

He isn't serious though, I don't think.

Because there's an amused glint in his eyes and his lips are still twitching.

But before I can take offense to that, he grabs the plate from me and sets it down on a bench type thingy right next to the door. "What are you doing? I —"

Then he comes for me.

Putting his hands on my waist, he picks me up and my breath whooshes out again, my legs leaving the ground in a split second and my thighs hooking around his waist. Settling my hands on his shoulders, I go again, "What are you doing?"

He begins to walk. "Carrying you."

I wind my limbs around him tighter and curl his sweat-dampened hair. "Where?"

Reaching an oversized leather armchair on the far side of this big, industrial space, he sits down and settles me in his lap. "To this chair."

My knees hit the leather and my ass squiggles on his hard thighs. "Why?"

His hands tighten around my waist to stop my movements. "So we can sit."

"But did you hear what I said? I think we should —"

"And talk."

That settles me down some and I give him a thankful smile. Which he responds to by glancing down at my lips and flexing his fingers on my waist as if he can't bear it, my smile.

In a good way I mean.

But getting serious, I slide back on his thighs and sit up straight, folding my hands on my lap and hoping to portray that I mean business. But just as I open my mouth to talk, he jerks me forward so all sense of business is gone and I go flush with his body, my hands coming to fist his t-shirt on his shoulders.

Frowning, I look up. "I was going to talk."

Frowning as well, he growls, "So talk." Then, "From here."

I want to keep frowning at him but I have to admit that was sweet.

In a very caveman-ish way.

Losing my frown and resting my chin on his chest, I say, "I don't like this."

"What?"

"*This*, Alaric. It's Saturday."

"So?"

"So it's the weekend. You're supposed to take some time off. You're supposed to unwind. Instead you were working all day and you didn't even eat."

He watches me for a beat or two. "I had work to do and I wasn't hungry."

I shoot up and away from him then. "Are you serious?"

This pisses him off; I can see that.

His features that were all relaxed tighten up and he clenches his jaw. "Poe, let it go."

Frowning, I tighten my fists on his shirt. "No, I won't let it go. I wanna talk about it. You didn't let me talk about your punching thingy back in your office that day either. You have issues, Alaric. You have anger issues. You have control issues. And I wanna talk about them. I wanna talk about how you're always working. You're always doing things, attending meetings and conferences and —"

"That's my fucking job."

"Yes, it is, but you don't need to run yourself ragged like this."

"I'm not running myself ragged."

"You are. You do so many things and —"

"Poe."

"No, Alaric. Some of these things you don't even like. Mo told me, okay? She said that you were missing lectures this summer at your college because you are handling things at St. Mary's. But you love teaching. And she told me that the only reason you're doing this is because this is something your father would have —"

"Mo doesn't know anything."

"But —"

"And how about you come to me next time. If you want to dig up information on what I like or don't like."

I watch him for a moment or two. Then, "Do you love teaching?"

"Yes."

"Do you love working on your papers and conferences?"

"Yes."

"And what about being the principal of a reform school. Do you like that too?"

His eyes narrow. "No."

"See?" I throw my hands up. "Then why do you do it?"

"Because it's a responsibility and I take my responsibilities seriously."

"But —"

"And fine. I'll eat that fucking piece of cherry pie," he snaps. "Is that enough for you or would you like me to go take a nap too?"

I narrow my eyes at him. "That was mean."

"Never said I wasn't."

I study his unrelenting features, all tight and sharp.

The stubborn jut of his chin, the frown between his brows, the irritation in his eyes. He's obviously not a fan of this topic. He's obviously not going to listen to me. So I really have no idea what I'm supposed to do. And I also don't know how I'm supposed to let it go either.

Especially after everything that I know, that Mo told me that night. About his work. About how he lives in the town where he was hated.

How am I supposed to make him understand that he doesn't need to live like this? That he doesn't need to do the things that he doesn't like out of obligation, out of an extreme sense of responsibility.

Or out of whatever screwed-up reason he's thought of in his head.

"This isn't fair, you know," I tell him, swallowing. "That you keep taking care of me and you won't let me do the same."

"I don't need you to take care of me."

He does.

He so does.

And I don't know how to convince him so maybe I won't. Maybe I'll just do it without telling him.

Maybe I'll just take care of him in whatever little ways I can. Pamper him and spoil him and make him feel special.

"Is that your final decision?"

His body shudders with a breath. "Yeah."

My heart twists but I nod. "Okay."

And maybe he can see that. The pain he's causing me by saying no, and maybe it causes him pain as well, like he told me, because he jerks me closer and covers my mouth with his. He kisses me as if to soothe the sting, and I kiss him back because I want to do the same.

And I know that I'll always, *always* want to do the same.

When he's made me completely breathless and languid against him, he breaks the kiss and whispers, "You okay?"

My fingers as always have found their way into his rich, dark hair, and curling the strands, I nod, knowing exactly what he's asking. "Yeah."

His are tangled up in my dress. "Any pain?"

I squirm in his lap as lust leaches back to the surface after it got forgotten in our heated discussion. "No. I took the pill."

"Good."

"Thank you for sending that up with Mo."

In response, his lips pull up on one side in a lopsided smile before he brings me in for another kiss, soft and wet.

When we come up for air, I whisper, "Do you think Mo would be upset?"

"About what?"

"About us."

He frowns. "It's none of her business."

I wrap my arms around his neck. "I won't tell her. I won't tell anyone."

He wraps his arms around my waist. "I don't want you to worry about it. You're safe."

"But they'll blame you, won't they? At school. If they found out." Then, before he can say anything, I continue, "I want you to know that I won't let this, whatever we have, ruin things for you. I know you came to St. Mary's to make changes and I won't let things between us deter you from the job."

Thick and heavy emotions rearrange his features as he says, "I told you, Poe. It's not something you need to worry about. All you need to worry about are your exams, your classes, your future, okay?"

"What's my future?"

It's a question I've asked him before.

A long, long time ago when we were enemies and I thought that he was the biggest threat to it.

Now I know that he's the biggest shield, the biggest armor

that's going to keep it safe. I know that if it came down to it, he might destroy himself in order to keep it safe.

To keep me safe.

My guardian.

Who remembers as well. This conversation from long ago. His eyes glint and shine with the memory as he rasps, "New York. Fashion school and everything you want it to be."

My heart squeezes in my chest. At his answer. At the freedom he's given me.

At the emotion in his voice.

That clearly shows that I'm his baby. He'll give me whatever I want.

And he's right.

I *am* his baby. I am his diva.

And it's my job to thank him. To soothe him, to take his pain away.

To reward him for all the hard work, for all his little gifts.

"How many times do you work out in a week?" I whisper.

If he thinks my change of subject is weird, he doesn't show it. "Every day."

My eyes go wide behind my glasses. "Every day?"

"Yeah."

"For how long?"

"A couple of hours."

My hand goes down to his where he's gripping my waist, and I bring one up to my lips. Kissing his knuckle, I go on, "And then you work in your office?"

He jerks at my kiss. "Yeah."

I kiss his second knuckle. "Are you working on a paper right now?"

His jaw clenches as I lick his third one. "I'm always working on a paper."

I lick the fourth one and his other hand that's still on my waist tightens to the point that I moan. I grind on his lap.

Plus the taste of his skin is so good, see.

It's all salty and musky from sweat and hot from all the pounding that his epic hands have doled out.

It makes me all heated and horny.

"What is it about?" I whisper, going for the tiny one on his thumb.

His eyes narrow as he watches me pamper his beautiful fingers. "Something about… uh, the Medici family."

Since I've run out of knuckles, I go for the silver ring on his pinkie and circle the black stone that sits in the center with my tongue. I'm not sure how it's possible but his ring tastes like his sweat as well. And God, I could lick it forever.

I could lick every drop of sweat on his body and drink it down.

"Who are they?" I whisper next.

"They backed," he swallows, watching my tongue, "the Renaissance movement."

I smile excitedly, wiggling on his lap. "Oh, right. You're the Renaissance man."

He tightens his grip on my waist even more, effectively stopping me from making any movements. "What?"

I rub his knuckles on my cheek, all rough and hot. "You know, because that's what you study. The Renaissance era."

With that, I go for the gold and suck on his thumb.

I circle my tongue on the tip before taking the whole digit in. And I swear to God, it's so tasty that I have to moan. I have to close my eyes and grind on his lap again. I have to suck on it harder because imagine if he tastes so good here, how epic is he going to taste down there.

How epic is his dick going to taste.

But all my hot fantasies come to a halt when he snatches his thumb away and leans over me, pressing his chest into mine. Gripping my face with both hands, he nails me with his intense eyes. "That's not what that means."

I grip his wrists. "The Renaissance man?"

"Yeah."

"So w-what does it mean?"

"Why don't you find a dictionary and look it up yourself, yeah?" he growls. "But for now let's focus on what the fuck do you think you're doing?"

I grind on his lap again, rubbing my nipples against his chest. "I was… I was sucking your thumb."

"Why?"

"Because I was, uh," I squirm some more and a muscle jumps on his cheek, "thinking about sucking something else."

"Like what?"

I look into his dark eyes as I whisper, "Your dick."

Lust spills in his gaze, on the crests of his cheekbones, making them go even darker. "And so that was a preview, sucking on my thumb?"

"Uh-huh."

"And all this because I'm writing a paper on the Medici family."

"Yes. As a reward."

"As a reward."

I dig my nails into his wrist as I say, "Yeah. For all your hard work. You won't let me take care of you, but let me reward you at least. Let me reward you for all the things you do."

I'm sitting on the edge of my seat now.

Waiting and waiting for him to answer.

Squirming and licking my lips.

And he's watching me do all of that with lust-edged features and a wildly breathing chest that scrapes against my nipples with his every agitated breath.

Then he rasps, "You want to reward me, baby?"

I jerk in his lap, loving his *baby* and knowing that I probably won't ever get used to it. "Yes."

His fingers flex on my face. "Fine. I'll let you reward me. But be careful, yeah?"

"Why?"

"You don't want to reward me too much or be too good because then before you know it," he brings his face even closer, "you'll find yourself kneeling under my desk, sucking me off every time I work on a paper."

I shudder at the image he creates in my head.

At this graphic, erotic vision of me kneeling at his feet, tucked away under that big wooden desk in his office, sucking his dick while he focuses on his Medici family and the Renaissance movement.

"Yeah, I see you understand what I mean, don't you?" he rumbles and I nod. "I see you understand what I'm talking about. And let me tell you this too," he adds, his nostrils flaring, "I work on a lot of papers, Poe. A lot. I also work on a lot of lecture plans and presentations and conferences, and grants. I'm even writing a book, you know that, don't you?"

"You t-told me," I whisper eagerly.

"Yeah. So then you should really take my advice and take all the care in the world because before you know it, I might push your mouth down on my dick every time I finish a chapter. I might hump your mouth like a fucking animal every time I get a bunch of money for my archeological dig. And we both know that it won't stop at your mouth, don't we?"

"No?"

"No, Poe," he says like it's the most obvious thing in the world. "Your mouth won't be enough for me." With his thumb, he traces the lines of my throat; he even glances down at it. "You're going to have to let me throat fuck you."

"Throat fuck."

His thumb digs on my pulse. "Yeah. You know what that is, baby?"

"No."

"Well, Poe," he says and licks his lips, still staring at my throat, pulling my neck back even, stretching it as if he wants to examine every inch of my pale skin and my fragile tendons, "it's when a desperate and horny man with a big dick — let's call him Alaric, okay? — slides that dick into the pink mouth of a doe-eyed diva or his baby — let's call her Poe. But just sliding that dick in Poe's mouth is not enough for Alaric. He's too horny, too fucking insane for Poe. Because her mouth is fire, yeah? Her tongue is fucking insane and it drives Alaric crazy. So then, he goes in further. He grabs the back of her head, fists her pretty midnight hair and shoves that dick down her sexy little throat." His fingers touch the center of it, my throat, as if to point it out. "See? Here. He shoves his dick right here, Poe, and then fucks her throat like he owns it. Like he'd die without it. Like he'd expire right that second if he didn't hump and ride Poe's throat until his balls are smacking her chin and she's moaning with every jab, her nose buried in his pelvis, gagging and salivating."

"Oh God, Alaric, do you… Will you…"

Finally, he looks up and whatever he sees on my face makes him breathe so long and loud that he bends me backward, that his chest pushes and pushes into mine, flattening my big tits. "Will I what?"

"Will he come in her throat?" I ask, all shameless and wanton. "Please, please, will he?"

He frowns. "Fuck no."

Well, that pisses me off.

That makes me scratch my nails on his wrist and frown because that was the whole point of it. "Why not? I did all the work. I want it."

His frown grows harder and his one hand travels down to my ass and smacks it, making me moan. "Don't be a cute fucking whore, Poe. This isn't about you."

"But I —"

"This is about Alaric, remember?" Another smack, and even though I want to narrow my eyes at him, I don't. "This is about rewarding him, not you. So even after all the sucking and fucking that might make Poe's throat all sore and achy — so much so that she might need a fucking ice pack and hot chamomile tea to soothe it — she can't be a diva, asking for things, making her own demands. She has to wait."

"Wait for what?"

"For Alaric to decide," he rasps, "if he wants to come on her big fucking tits," he follows that with a squeeze and a jiggle of my tit and he does it in such a rude, obscene way that I can't help but whimper lightly, "or on her sexy-as-fuck librarian glasses."

"Oh God, glasses," I immediately answer, forgetting that I should be quiet right now because it's about him. "Please come on my glasses. *Please*, Alaric."

He watches me for a few seconds, his pretty dark eyes lined with lust and amusement but I don't even care. I don't care that I'm being so shameless and horny. It's all his fault anyway. He shouldn't have said the things he said if he didn't want me this way.

If he didn't want my belly to hurt with arousal and if he didn't want my pussy to swell and juice up, making a mess of my panties and thighs and my common sense.

"You can't help it, can you?" He squeezes my ass and my throat simultaneously. "You can't help being a greedy little whore."

"No. Not when it comes to y-you."

He smirks. "Fine. I'll come on your glasses, Poe."

I smile, relieved. "Oh, thank you."

That smirk falls off his face and something intense takes its place. Something potent and possessive and primal. Something that clenches every part of my body and I think it does the same for him.

Because he comes for my mouth.

But then instead of the tongue-lashing and teeth-clattering kiss that I was expecting, he gives me one that's sweet and wet and soft. Which makes everything even more intense.

I think I spoke too soon though, because what makes it even harder to breathe as my chest is being crushed under this huge pressure isn't the look on his face or his sweet kiss, it's the fact that he reaches up and inches up my glasses with his index finger like I always do.

It's the fact that he does it so tenderly and gently after all the vivid and erotic and deliciously brutal things he's said that I can't help but feel a sting behind my eyes.

But I ignore it all.

I put a stop to it all.

I have a job to do here. I have a reward to give him.

Plus he was all hard and hurting yesterday in the bathtub and I need to give him relief.

So I scramble off his lap and come down on my knees.

He opens his thighs wide, making them sprawl so I can settle myself between them.

My hands grope his hard thighs, pull at his workout pants, tug at the waistband until I have them down to mid-thigh. Until I reveal his bulging thighs and that trunk of flesh between them.

All hard and big and ruddy.

Leaking pre-cum.

My pussy clenches and throbs, making me press my thighs as I remember the stretch, the pain, the sheer pleasure I'd felt last night when that dick was inside of me. I'm not going to lie, I hated that the first time his cock was inside of me, it was sheathed. It was covered up in latex rather than sliding inside me all bare, all skin to skin.

"I loved it when you came on my tummy last night," I whisper.

With his nostrils flaring with arousal and lust, he grunts, "I came on your tight little tummy last night because I wanted to mark you. I wanted to see you all hosed down and covered in my seed."

And in this moment, I swear to myself that one day I will take his seed in my pussy. I'll take it and keep it safe and warm in my core.

But for now I'm going to feel his hot skin on my tongue right this second.

Running my fingers in the dark, coarse hair of his thighs, I reach for it and as soon as I wrap my fingers around his rod, he flinches. His hips jump in the chair and his abdomen, partially revealed right now with his shirt pushed up slightly and his pants pulled down, tenses.

More so than it was before. When I'd only slid down his lap and taken my place at his feet.

I can see all his muscles bulging and standing up in stark relief, his fists vibrating on the armrests, and I know it's only going to get worse when I put him in my mouth. So with my free hand, I massage his thigh, going up to his ridged stomach before I bend down and take him in my mouth.

His first taste hits me like a freight train.

And it hits him as well because he grunts loudly and I see him throwing his head back against the backrest, his fists opening and gripping the armrest.

But honestly that's the last visual I get before I have to close my eyes because my own veins are throbbing with lust. My own body is pulsing with his taste, with his size. With his scent and heat.

All of which is overwhelming.

All of which makes me think how naive I've been in thinking that his taste and scent of leather and cigar is thickest at the base of his throat.

It's not.

It's the thickest here.

It's the kind of thickest that might turn me into a junkie.

Because I'm already laving his head like one. I'm already tonguing it, sipping it, slurping that slit on the top like an addict, like I'll never get to do this again. And when that's not enough, when even his pre-cum won't satisfy me, I go deeper. I take him in further and he was right.

My mouth does drive him crazy.

Because those hands of his, that were gripping the armrest, come down to my head when he hits the back of my mouth. They clutch my midnight hair as his hips lift up from the chair.

And for a novice like me, it's too much.

Or it would have been if along with being a novice, I wasn't also a whore.

His cute little whore.

And since I am, I love that he pushes his dick into my mouth. I love that his hips flex and his abdomen clenches and so I try to open my mouth even wider. I try to even open my throat if such a thing is possible and then, I do feel him inching down further. I do feel him filling a tiny space at the top of my throat before he retreats and gives me some of my control back.

Which I don't need really.

I don't need my control at all. So I try to give it back to him. I try to push my head down even more so he'll take over and keep me at his mercy, and he does.

He takes over the reins and fucks my mouth. He fucks a tiny portion of my throat, his hips moving up and down, his fingers clutching my hair and his grunts echoing around us.

Meanwhile, I keep laving the underside of his rod, keep laving the thick vein on his cock, the tasty dark skin, the ridges that I didn't know he had.

Stupid condom.

And now that I know, I can't help but moan. I can't help but clench and clench my thighs together, scratch my nails on his thighs, twist the base of his cock, hoping that he'll go in further, he'll make me take him in further.

Just when I think that he's going to do it though, he erupts in my mouth.

His body arches up and I feel the first lash of his cum on my tongue.

It tastes all salty and musky and like it did last night.

But I know that that's all I'm going to get. He's made a promise to me and like always, he'll deliver.

So he knocks my hands off so he can grip his dick and take it out of my mouth so his second lash lands on my glasses. Followed by the one that lands on my cheeks, my forehead. My chin and my throat.

With every lash that lands on my face, I moan and knead my tits.

I whimper and press my thighs together, smelling him, tasting him.

Feeling pampered by him.

Chapter Thirty-Two

In four short weeks, summer school is going to be over.

And I'm going to graduate.

Before, when I hated this place and craved my freedom like air, I'd been counting down the days until my graduation. I'd been dreaming about it, longing for it, pining for it.

But now there's no dreaming or longing or pining.

Instead there's a strange sadness and dread.

I can't quite figure out why though.

Because yes, I don't hate this place anymore but I'd still like to graduate and move on with my life.

Besides, things are great. They truly are.

For the first time ever, I'm so content and happy with my life.

Ever since I started to pay attention in classes and do my homework and stuff, my grades have been decent. Nothing crazy like Echo's or Callie's and Wyn's when they were here. But I manage to scrape a B or a B+. Which is more than I did before.

So I guess I'm ready for the future.

Which is more or less set; another good thing.

It includes a city college so I can earn enough credits and transfer to a fashion program. Hopefully somewhere in New York. My future also includes living in my big townhouse that's been empty for the last four years because it's super close to the college that I'm gonna go to. I will probably have a few people on my staff for cooking and cleaning and doing all the chores for me. Oh, and a team of lawyers to help with my trust fund and all the estate.

Because investments are important.

They are wise and they will keep my money safe so I can have a nice nest egg for the future that comes *after* my future.

My guardian is very clear about these things.

He's very sure and he's planned everything out. He's not going to leave any stone unturned until he's made sure that I'm safe and okay and provided for.

He takes his responsibilities very seriously, see.

He also takes pampering me very seriously; yet another good thing.

Spoiling me, granting me my every wish. Whether big or small.

Like binging on my favorite TV show, *Supernatural.*

"I think you'd really like it, Alaric," I tell him one day in his cottage at night, lying on his leather couch, my thighs stretched over the thick armrest, my legs swinging.

Sitting on the armchair adjacent to the couch, my sexy guardian is reading a book. His tie is gone, his top two buttons are undone and his dark curly hair is all mussed up. Courtesy of me, because when I'd arrived at his cottage about an hour ago, I jumped into his arms and kissed the fuck out of him, plowing my fingers in his hair.

My own hair's all tangled and mussed up too, and my mouth is all swollen and throbbing, courtesy of him kissing me back.

But back to the fact that he hasn't answered me or looked up from his book.

I'm not deterred though.

Swinging my legs, I keep going. "It has like, demons and angels and leviathans." No response. "It has purgatory. And heaven and hell, Alaric." He flips a page. "Okay, fine. Forget all that. It has the Winchester brothers. Dean and Sam. I bet you'd love Dean. He's like you. All responsible, big brother-y. Being all crazy about his family legacy and all that."

He scratches his stubbled jaw with his thumb and I just wanna eat him up.

Why is he so sexy?

Why isn't he listening to me?

Narrowing my eyes and still swinging my legs, I say, "Okay fine, here's why you should watch *Supernatural*, Alaric: it has Jeffrey

Dean Morgan. And as much as I like Sam and Dean and will pledge my allegiance to them, I will pledge my allegiance *harder* for Papa Winchester and his dimples."

Nothing.

But it's okay.

I have a plan.

"Because let me tell you, Alaric," I say, drumming my fingers on my stomach, "that his dimples make girls' panties wet. Yup. They made my panties wet one time. And I'm usually super immune to Hollywood charm and all that. I mean, I grew up with these guys. I know how un-charming they can be in real life. But not Jeffrey Dean Morgan. He was *so* charming and I swear, the moment he touched me and smiled, I was —"

My words come to a screeching halt along with my swinging legs because his fingers are wrapped around my ankle and his eyes are lifted and on me.

Smiling, I whisper, "Hi."

His eyes narrow. "He touched you."

My smile gets bigger. "I thought you weren't listening."

His fingers tense around my ankle. "It's called multitasking."

My smile turns into a grin. "You're the best multitasker I know."

"I was also taking notes."

"About what?"

"About how a man touched you."

"Only my hand." When his fingers tense even further, I explain, "He shook my hand, Alaric."

"And you needed a change of panties."

"Hey, I never said that." Then, "And it wasn't from his hand per se. It was his —"

"Dimples, yeah. I heard that."

I bite my lip and a muscle dances on his cheek. "I was kidding though, I swear."

"Kidding."

"Yeah." Then smiling tenderly at him and undulating on the couch, I whisper, "I'd never get wet for dimples."

"No?"

"No." I glance at his nose. "I'm partial to bumps on a nose and pinkie rings."

In response, his ring digs into my ankle and his eyes flash.

"I was only saying that so we can watch my show together." Then, "I missed you all day in school. And now that I'm here, you're reading your book instead of paying attention to me." I rub my thighs together when I see a crimson flush on his features. "Please, Alaric. Watch my show with me?"

It doesn't even have to be my show, to be honest.

I just want to feel close to him.

Then, like the guardian he is who loves to pamper me, he rasps, "Is that your final wish?"

Biting my lip, I nod. "Yes."

His chest pushes out on a sigh and he shuts his book. "Well then, your wish is my command."

With that, he gets up from his chair and comes to pick me up from the couch. He settles on it before settling me on his lap with my back to his massive chest and my thighs straddled and on either side of his. And then he spreads them, my thighs, by spreading his and before I can even comprehend as to what he's doing, he switches on the TV with one hand and with the other, he goes under my purple skirt and grabs my pussy.

My legs swing and my toes curl. "Alaric, what —"

In my ear, he growls, "If I'm going to watch a show about angels and demons and leviathans and a man whose dimples you've mentioned in the same sentence as your panties and fucked with my head, I'm going to do it with my fingers up your cherry cunt and your ass in my lap, okay, baby?"

I moan because *baby*.

"And then," he continues, his fingers going up and down the center of my pussy, "we'll see how wet your kitty gets when I'm petting her." At this, his thumb flicks my clit and I jump and moan again. "And how loud you purr and how hard you scratch me like the wildcat you are while you watch your favorite show." He kisses my cheek softly. "Knowing you, you'll be bringing down the ceiling while you make me bleed and drench my lap halfway through this episode."

He isn't wrong about that.

Fifteen minutes into the show, I'm moaning up a storm and dripping on him like a leaky faucet.

I'm also scratching his forearms like the wildcat I am.

And since then we've seen so many episodes of *Supernatural* with me sitting in his lap and his hand under my skirt and his fingers petting my pussy. Sometimes he pets my kitty with his dick too, and makes me keep my eyes on the TV and tell him about the plot.

But that's neither here nor there.

What's important is that he'll give me anything that I want. See? A good thing.

Including letting me smoke.

Okay, before I tell this very interesting tidbit, I have to say that I'm not at all interested in smoking. And he's not at all interested in letting me smoke either. So it's not a regular thing.

But one night after he fucks me and we're in the bath — he draws me a bath every time and then proceeds to soap me up and shampoo my hair, running his beautiful strong fingers through my strands and untangling them — he's smoking.

Which he does sometimes.

He smokes after sex and every time he does, I watch him.

So this night as well, with my head resting on his strong wet chest and my face turned upside down, I watch him grip the thick brown stick of his cigar with all his fingers, rather than pinching it between two. I watch him take a drag and lift his face before exhaling and sending a thick cloud of smoke up to the ceiling.

"Alaric?"

At my whisper, he lowers his face and looks at me with hooded, drowsy eyes and rumbles, "Poe."

"Can I smoke?"

He studies my blue eyes, my upturned face and kissing my forehead sweetly, he rasps, "Absolutely fucking not."

"Well, you're smoking."

"I know."

"Why is it that you get to smoke and I don't?"

"Let's see," he begins, a light frown appearing between his brows as he sets his cigar down on the ashtray by the side of the tub, "because you're a girl and I'm a boy. And boys can do whatever the fuck they want but girls can't."

I narrow my eyes at him. "You did not just say that."

"And you did not just ask me to hand over my cancer stick to you." I go to protest but he speaks. "So shut the fuck up, Poe."

I purse my lips and take my head off his chest and look forward, miffed. "That was mean."

"Never said I wasn't."

I think about it and then, "You could feed it to me, you know?"

I go back to looking up at him, upside down.

My words have caught his attention and he's staring at me with his hooded eyes again.

Encouraged, I go on, "Like that thing they do on TV. Fuck, what is it called? When a guy takes a drag and then exhales it into a girl's mouth." My eyes go wide at my own idea. "Oh, let's do that. Please. Please, Alaric. It's so hot. And sexy and amazing."

He keeps watching me for another few seconds.

"Please? Just once. I don't even care about smoking. I just wanna feel what you feel. I just wanna feel close to you."

It's true.

That's the only reason I want to do this.

That's the only reason I want to do all the things.

I try to move away from him and turn around so I can make my point better. But he wraps an arm around my waist and his other comes to grip my throat and stretch my neck up even more. So he can come down and kiss my lips from above.

When he breaks it, he goes for his cigar.

He takes a big drag, his sharp cheeks hollowing out before his lips open and he sends a cloud of smoke up. With bated breath and a thumping heart I wait for him to come to me. I wait for him to give me his gray cloud of smoke.

And he does.

He comes down and with his eyes on me, he pours the rest over my lips. He exhales and God, I wish, *I wish* that I could keep my eyes open and watch him give me the smoke in his lungs but I have to close them because it's too much.

It's too intense.

So all I can do is open my mouth and suck in what he gives me, and get all heated up.

My lips, my tongue. My chest and belly.

Even my pussy.

When he's done, I open my eyes, all drugged and high, and he rasps, "Shotgunning. It's called shotgunning."

I give him a drowsy smile. "Thank you."

He responds by flexing his fingers on my throat, tightening

them, and kissing me once again.

And then he proceeds to take me out of the tub, carry me in his arms out to the bedroom. He deposits me on the bed, all wet and dripping, and fucks me into oblivion.

So he gives me everything that I want.

He gives me more than what I want.

Because I'm his baby.

And *because* I'm his baby, I give him things too.

I pamper him back and I reward him.

For his hard work. For all the papers he writes and all the research he does. For completing the chapters of his book. For outlining his lesson plans. For working out every day of the week, for laboring over his body.

Not to mention, I reward him for all the things that he doesn't want to do but does because they are his responsibility. All the city council meetings, all the board meetings, all the principal-y things that he has to do.

And over the past couple of weeks, I've realized that there are two Alarics.

Alaric number one is the one who takes my rewards with all the gusto.

He's the one who draws baths for me, watches TV with me, pampers me and spoils me. He helps me with my assignments and tests, and when I get things right, he smiles and calls me baby. He also calls me baby when I don't get things right though. But it's more of an exasperated endearment because I'm not listening to him while he's explaining things to me.

He's the one who poses with me for our selfies. For the record, he completely hates it but when I get in the mood, I grab his phone, cuddle with him and just go for it. And since he likes to indulge me, he doesn't protest. But neither does he smile. He simply stares at the camera in all his grumpy glory but I love it.

He's also the one who I tell about my designs and sketches. All the fabrics and colors that I'm thinking. All the new stuff that I make on my new purple sewing machine.

Oh and he's the one I seduce while wearing only his tweed jacket.

Remember the jacket he gave me that one time at the bar, when I was all provocatively dressed for Jimmy, I still have it. Sometimes I sleep in it to feel close to him and sometimes I wear it – and only it – to crawl up to him when he's all focused in his work. I like to push his books and files aside so I can get up in his lap and open the buttons one by one.

I've tried to strip for him like he did for me that first night.

But by the third button, he gets so impatient that I never get a chance to. So all I can do is hold onto him as he goes for my tits. As he sucks and sucks on the nipples, drinking from them, making them all hurt-y and sore and swollen.

But then there's another Alaric.

Alaric 2.0.

He's moody. And grumpy and even more silent than the first Alaric.

I think this is the Alaric that Mo was talking about, the unhappy one.

The one who has so many responsibilities and an extreme sense of duty.

I've noticed a pattern where I know that he comes out when he has to go attend all the board meetings and sit on all these councils and fulfill his familial obligations. Not to mention, they're building another branch of St. Mary's somewhere on the West Coast now; I noticed the files on the coffee table and after a lot of poking and prodding, Alaric told me.

He also told me that he's taken over that project.

Which is of course typical of him.

Because it's his family's name and legacy, and I know very well how crazy he is about that.

On such days, when he has to chase after all these things, he hardly talks or smiles.

He's tighter and tenser.

He's even less approachable as he walks down the corridors and around campus.

On those days, I so wish that I could go to him during school. That I could smile at him or talk to him. I so wish that we didn't have all these restrictions and rules to follow.

Because we do, don't we?

Because when the world is watching we can't be together.

Which means every day during school we behave the exact same way as we have been ever since he got here and summer school started. We don't look at each other or talk to each other in the hallways or in the cafeteria. For all intents and purposes, I still hate my guardian turned principal and he's still that aloof authority figure that all the girls drool about.

And as hard as it is and as jealous as it makes me, I know it's important.

To keep our distance. To pretend that things haven't changed.

I promised him that day at the mansion that I wouldn't let anything happen to him and his job — even though I know he does it out of obligation — and I intend to keep it.

And he in turn intends to keep me and my future safe, so distance during the day it is.

Which means when the world is sleeping is the only time I get to be with him.

But there's a problem of course.

Because that involves sneaking in and out of my dorm room. Which would've been fine in the olden days. But now with the bed checks back, it has become slightly trickier. I have to time my comings and goings. Plus I have to put pillows under the blanket, make it look like I'm sleeping under there while I'm really not.

This pisses Alaric off.

He never liked me breaking the rules anyway, but now with the new policy in place, he hates it even more.

So much so that he wanted to abolish it initially.

But I stopped him.

Because that would've been me and *this* — whatever this thing is between us — interfering with his job. And I'm not going to let that happen. I'm not going to let him make decisions based on our relationship.

It has to come from him, from within him, not because he was forced to do so by me.

To compromise, he's asked me to carry my old phone with me so I can text him when I leave that I got back safely. Cell phones or any kind of personal technology isn't allowed at St. Mary's. So technically I'm breaking the rules and he's breaking them with me, and I'm not happy about this either. But this is better than him revoking a rule completely just for me so I obey him.

So every night when I sneak out to see him, I initially meet Alaric 2.0.

But then I kiss him at the door and soften him up to bring out the first Alaric.

My Alaric.

But some nights, it's not so easy. To bring back the first Alaric, I mean.

Some nights Alaric 2.0 takes over.

Which means that even my kisses are not enough.

Which means that on those nights, he only lets me take a few steps into the cottage before he shuts the door and shoves me against it, going for my clothes.

Not that I mind, you see.

I don't mind him tearing open the buttons of my blouse to get at my tits or shoving aside my panties to get at my pussy. I don't mind him lifting me up in his arms and barely having enough sense to put on a condom and shove his thick and long length inside of me, and fucking me till we both shatter around each other, no.

I don't mind all that.

In fact once we're done, I make him put me down so I can fall to my knees and slide that stupid condom off — I still hate it; I still hate how it keeps us apart — before taking his still hard, still frustrated length into my mouth and sucking him off, giving him another bout of relief, hoping against hope that this might make him feel better.

Because I know if I go to talk about it with him, he won't listen.

I know that.

So I take care of him in these silent and passionate ways.

And even though he comes down my throat only a few seconds later, as if he didn't blow in his condom, he still doesn't relax. He still doesn't go back to being happy Alaric.

I don't think even working out calms him down on those nights.

And he does a lot of that after putting me to sleep for a few hours, before the time comes for me to sneak back to my dorm.

I usually wake up and let him be while lying there in the bed, my chest tight, my eyes stinging with tears. I don't want him to feel like I'm intruding on his space, in his downtime. If pounding a heavy bag gets him out of these dark moods, then fine.

But it's so hard.

So hard to lie there and pretend I don't hear the jabs and the pained grunts. So hard not to go to him and ask him to stop. Ask him to talk to me. To listen.

Because this isn't right. This isn't the way to deal with things, to deal with all these demons inside of him.

This *isn't* the way.

And tonight, it's much harder than ever.

I'm not sure what happened but he's been tense all day; I saw him during school.

And when I got here, his mood hadn't improved. He was agitated and antsy while he kissed me and then fucked me on the couch. And no, he wasn't rough with me by any means but I could feel that something was eating at him.

It's still eating at him.

He's been at his heavy bag for almost an hour now.

He keeps beating at it and beating at it, and I know if he doesn't stop, he's going to break something. Either that heavy bag will fall out of the ceiling or crack in two, or his bones will tear apart.

When a particularly angry grunt followed by a pant sounds through the cottage, I get up.

I climb out of the bed at my own peril.

I know there's a chance that he might not respond well to me interrupting him.

But it's a risk I have to take for his own good.

Besides, all I want is for him to stop. That's it. I'm not going to have that discussion again with him, about his work and responsibilities. I know that's not going to go down well. Maybe I can visit Mo next weekend and talk to her about it, about maybe devising a plan or an intervention of some sort. But for now, all I want is for him to stop and come back to bed, and get some sleep maybe.

With that hope, I walk into the living room and find him going at his heavy bag.

A blurry silhouette because I don't have my glasses on.

I walk closer until he becomes clear.

At some point he's taken off his shirt and I can see the muscles of his body darkened and drenched with sweat. I see the slick skin of his back and his shoulders stretching and relaxing over his dense bones as he delivers jab after jab.

"Alaric," I call out to his back.

But I guess he can't hear me over his panting breaths and his grunts and the thwacks.

So I go closer and try again. "Alaric, stop."

I know this time he hears me — his back tenses slightly and his jabs lose their steady rhythm — but he ignores me and keeps going. I go around him and come to stand directly in his line of vision.

"Alaric, stop. Please."

This time my voice has no effect. His eyes are trained on the heavy bag and his fists are furiously at work.

I'm not even sure how he's able to keep going because now that I look at his face, I realize that it's dripping with sweat. Thick rivulets are raining down from his hair and getting into his eyes. They travel the sides of his face and flow down to his veined neck, and his mountain-like shoulders.

Every time he rams his taped fist into the bag, sweat flies around him, his chest heaving and his jaw clenching.

"Alaric, please," I say, my voice all grave and tense. "Stop." When he still doesn't, I take a step closer to him. "Please. You have to stop. Just please. You're going to hurt yourself."

Yet again, he ignores me and keeps going, and having no choice at all, I approach him.

And put a hand on his arm.

As soon as I do, he jerks to a stop, snapping his head to face me. "What the fuck are you doing?"

My fingers burn at the touch of his sweaty and heated skin but I keep my hand there. "I was just trying to —"

"Are you fucking insane?" he growls, snatching my hand off his arm, gripping it in his fingers.

"You weren't stopping. I didn't —"

"So you thought that touching a man who's fucking punching a heavy bag is a good idea."

"I knew I was safe. I was —"

His fingers tighten around my hand as he growls again, his chest heaving, "Oh yeah, you knew that, did you?"

I take a step toward him then. "Yes, I knew. I knew you were ignoring me and I just wanted to get your attention. I —"

"Attention," he cuts me off, his eyes flashing. "Right."

"I just —"

"Because that's what you want," he goes on, his thumb mashing my pulse. "That's what you fucking live for, isn't it?"

I swallow at his tight grip, a grip that's slowly inching from tight to painful. "Alaric, I —"

"That's what you always want, Poe." His jaw clenches. "Don't you? Attention."

I take another step toward him and press my other hand on his wildly breathing chest. "Please let me talk, okay? I was just trying to get you to stop. I was just…" I study his tight, angry features; sweat is still dripping down his face, his mouth parted to drag in breaths. "You were going at it for so long, Alaric. I thought you were gonna hurt yourself. So I just wanted you to stop and maybe give it a rest. Something is clearly bothering you but you can't take your frustrations out on it and —"

"Yeah, something's bothering me all right."

"Please just —"

Leaning in, he rasps, "Would you like to know what's bothering me, Poe?"

I've come to a point now where my breaths are matching his. It could be his proximity, the fact that he's all bare-chested and sweaty. Or the fact that he's still holding my wrist in a punishing grip and his eyes are all feral now.

All wild and out of control.

Which makes me realize that as many times as I've seen him all angry and upset and agitated, I've never seen him this far gone. I've never seen him this on edge.

But it's okay.

It's him.

No matter how angry he is or how upset, he would never hurt me. He'd hurt himself first.

So I nod. "Yes."

A shudder overcomes him for a second at my easy acquiescence and his grip loosens from my wrist, but then his features tighten again and so does his grip before he says, "Yeah? Well, what's bothering me, Poe, is the fact that I had a meeting today. Early morning. And for the first time ever, I was late to it." I open my mouth to say something but he keeps going. "Which is fine, really. First time for everything, right? Besides, it was about the new branch of St. Mary's and technically, I'm the boss right now so people can wait. But then I got later because I walked into the wrong room." He nods as if to emphasize and mock himself simultaneously. "My screwed-up brain mixed up the floor numbers and I walked into a different conference hall than I was supposed to."

"But it's f-fine. It happens."

"Yeah, you're right. It happens. Not to me, Dr. Alaric Rule Marshall, with two PhDs and a post-doctoral fellowship from an Ivy League school who's gotten countless grants and papers published, but it does happen to people. So yeah, let's say that it's fine. *Again.* But it just so happened that along with getting the wrong room, I also got the wrong file. And turns out that it wasn't only for the meeting but also for people over in California who needed it urgently. So now I have to go to California tomorrow because the deadline to submit those papers that *should've been* in that file is tomorrow."

My heart drops. "You're going to California?"

"Yeah." He bends further down. "But that's not the worst part, Poe."

"It isn't?" I ask in despair.

Because it sounds like it.

That he's going to California tomorrow.

Why didn't he tell me before? For how many days?

Because suddenly I can't imagine not seeing him even for a single day. I can't imagine not being able to talk to him and touch him and be with him like this.

But wait a second.

Just *wait.*

Isn't that what's coming? In the future I mean.

The future that's all good and set and something that he's planned for.

And he's planned for everything, hasn't he?

Every single detail about where I'll live and where I'll go to college and who'll cook for me and all the investments, but he's never said a word about us.

He's never said anything about this.

I'm about to ask him that, I'm about to ask him, *what about us, is that in my future, are you,* but he doesn't give me a chance. "The worst part is why, Poe."

"What?"

His eyes turn all dark and somehow accusatory as he looks down at me. "The worst part is why I was late and why I walked into the wrong room and sent the wrong file to California."

"W-why?"

He studies my face for a few seconds, his taped hand a hot band around my wrist before straightening up.

Before letting my wrist go.

But only for a few seconds.

To take the tape off his hands as if he's getting ready to do something drastic, something dangerous with his bare hands. But I don't have time to freak out about it because soon, his hands are bare and he bends down again but much further than before and instead of trapping my wrist in his hold, he traps my waist.

He wraps his arms around my waist and picks me up.

He throws me over his shoulder, my belly hitting his hard muscles with an oomph, and with his arm now slid down to my bare thighs, he begins striding down the hallway.

Chapter Thirty-Three

I'm not sure what's happening.

I'm not sure why's he acting this way.

But still I hold on to his hips and my breasts drag against his back with every hiccupping breath I take. "Alaric, what are you d-doing? Where are we…"

Before I even finish my question, I get the answer to it.

We arrive in the bedroom and he throws me down on the bed. I go bouncing, my hands coming to grip the rumpled white sheets, my heels digging into the mattress to gain balance.

I don't even get a chance to catch my breath after this sudden turn of events when Alaric bends down again and grips my ankles. Before I know it, he yanks them forward to bring me closer, and then I'm propped on my elbows, looking into the darkest — and God, prettiest still — eyes ever.

"Because of you."

I don't have to ask him what he means by his rasped words or what he's talking about.

He's responding to my question, why did he miss all those things.

"M-me," I whisper, my chest going up and down.

"Yeah." His arms are now on the bed on either side of my waist. "It's because all I can think about is you."

My heart thumps. "What?"

He licks his lips. "It's because all I can fucking focus on is you. All I can fucking pay attention to is you." His biceps vibrate with tension, his shoulders straining. "Attention, yeah? That's what you wanted, didn't you?"

I swallow. "Alaric, I… I'm…"

"You've got it," he rumbles, his eyes still accusatory. "You've got my attention. You've got every little inch of it. Every little drop of it. You're the first thing I think about when I wake up in the morning, Poe, and you're the last thing I think about when I go to sleep. You're the *only* thing I think about when I'm awake. When I'm working in my office. When I'm walking down the hallway. When I'm sitting in on meetings. When I'm fucking writing my paper. You. You're the only thought in my head."

I put a hand on his jaw then.

It pulses under my touch like my heart is pulsing as I confess, "Mine too. You're the only —"

"Because it wasn't enough for you, was it?" he cuts me off, ignoring my confession. "It wasn't enough for you that ever since I came back from Italy, I couldn't take my eyes off of you. I couldn't stop watching you. I couldn't stop watching you smile and laugh and strut around the school like some sort of teenage fucking siren. It wasn't enough for you that I fucking lost my head and kept you here. That I fucking trapped you for the second time, no. You had to go ahead and do this."

"Alaric —"

"You had to go ahead and fuck with my head *so much* that now I can't even do my job right."

"Alaric, I think —"

"So are you happy now, Poe? Are you fucking *happy* that you have all my attention now, all of it?"

This time I can't even get any words out because he comes for my body again.

He comes for my waist.

He grabs it again but this time to flip me around on the bed.

My knees hit the mattress in a mad stumble and my arms struggle to catch my fall.

Although I shouldn't have worried about that, about falling.

Because he catches me.

And pulls me upright, my spine hitting his shuddering chest and his palm spreading wide on my trembling belly, keeping me plastered to his big body.

Then in my ears, he rasps again, "Are you happy that you've got me wrapped around your little finger, Poe?"

I hold on to his hand on my belly, my own chest heaving. "Alaric, listen —"

My third attempt at talking, at telling him to calm down and listen to me for a second, fails as well because his other hand goes down my body, past my heaving chest and hollowing out stomach.

All the way down to that place between my thighs.

I'm only wearing one of his workout t-shirts and no panties — I love sleeping in his clothes; they're all cozy and comfy after the bath — so his fingers find my pussy easily.

It's still wet and dewy from my bath, all soft and tender.

And despite being all rough with me, his fingers are tender too.

His fingers are careful and I close my eyes, moaning and resting my head against his shoulders.

"Tell me, baby," he whispers, his fingers going up and down my slit, juicing it up, getting it all wet. "Does it make you happy that I'm at your mercy now?"

He hits my clit and I jerk, my one hand reaching up and going around his neck. "Yes."

"Yeah?"

"Uh-huh."

As much as I don't want to see him all twisted up like this, all agitated and antsy, and as much as I don't want to interfere with his job either, I can't deny that I do like it.

I do like that I'm the center of his attention.

That all his thoughts are of me.

I've always wanted that. Always.

I've always wanted to be the center of someone's attention. I've chased after it, done things for it.

So yeah, I'm happy.

And the thing is that I never knew how much I wanted that someone to be *him* until he just said it. Yes, he's shared his secret with me, that he's wanted me for months, and that was why he wouldn't let me graduate early.

But he never said this.

He never said that I've consumed every waking second of his life.

And so I never knew that his sole attention would bring me the greatest pleasure, the greatest joy, the greatest happiness.

I never knew that his attention is the only kind worth having.

And I can't help but preen under it.

I can't help but wonder if this means he'll be in my future too.

Because God, I want that.

I want him.

I can't help but arch my back and undulate against him, whispering, "I'm at your mercy too."

Because isn't that the truth also?

That just as I'm his every thought, he's mine too.

And not only since I found out about him from Mo but for years and years now.

Only in the beginning my thoughts of his were laced in hate. But now they're laced in…

"You're happy that I spoil you?" he whispers, banishing my thoughts, his nose running up and down the side of my face.

I twist my hips under the assault of his fingers. "God, yes."

He licks the shell of my ear, sucking the lobe in. "Yeah, I live to spoil you, don't I?"

"Yes."

"I fucking breathe to spoil you."

"I…"

"I fucking breathe to pamper my baby."

"Alaric."

He groans. "And I fucking *live* for the way you say my name."

"You do?"

He's started to move as well, making me feel his big dick at my back like he's making me take his thumb in my hole. Only the tip of it and never taking it past the edge. As if toying with me, as if tempting me with the whole candy but never letting me get in more than a suck.

"Yeah," he says, rocking against me, rubbing his cock against my ass. "It's like you know Alaric will take care of you."

"He will."

"You know he'll give you anything you want. He'll make it all better. He'll conquer the world for you, he'll bring down the stars. He'll fight wars for you and he'll keep you safe, won't he?"

"Yes. I know he will."

"And every time you say it like that, like Alaric is the answer to all your prayers, I get hard."

"You never… I didn't…"

"Every time you say my name, I want to stick my dick in one of your holes."

My head rolls back and forth on his shoulder. "Oh."

"And it's hard work, Poe. It's real fucking hard work deciding which hole."

"What does that…"

"Mean?" he completes.

"Yes."

"What it means, baby," he begins, as his hand down below that's still playing with my pussy goes even further down. It goes from my tight little hole to the crack of my ass and I freeze for a few seconds, my eyes wide and open, staring at the ceiling.

But *only* for a few seconds.

Because the moment he touches my other hole with his wet thumb, my eyes fall shut and I shudder like I've been electrocuted. I shudder like there's a grenade inside of me that has been unpinned and exploded.

"That you have three holes," he goes on, his thumb now circling my hole in the back. "And when you're breathless and all doe-eyed, calling out my name, thanking me for making you a fucking cup of chamomile tea like I've built you a castle and claimed you as my queen, I can't decide where to stick my big fucking dick and make you come like my cute little whore. I'm always so torn between your cherry pie mouth and your cherry pie snatch. But then I think about this" – at *this* he stops circling the rim of my hole and starts pushing, making me clench my belly, making me dig my nails into his skin – "I think about your tight little asshole and I think, no, this is what I want. I want her asshole. I want to force my way in and take that cherry too. I want to claim that hole as mine."

And he does.

Only with his thumb though.

Only the tip, and the pressure is so immense down there, the stretch is so epic that it can only be pleasurable.

It only serves to make me all horny and whore-y.

So much so that I press my ass against him, against his invading thumb.

"Ah, I see you like that," he rumbles, his words vibrating his chest and in turn vibrating and caressing my spine.

I swallow, tucking my face under his chin. "Yes."

He kisses my forehead all sweetly as his thumb gains another inch of entry, causing me to whimper. "Yeah, you do. Because you're my whore, aren't you?"

I jerk out a nod. "Y-yes."

"But I have to warn you, Poe. Despite how eager you are, how you're humping my thumb and how your cunt is dripping for it, it's still going to hurt. It's still going to hurt like a mother."

"It's okay," I whisper, rubbing my nose in his throat, feeling my juices running down my thighs. "Because it's you."

His chest shudders again, an angsty puff of breath escaping his mouth. "Yeah, it's me, isn't it? And it's the least you can do, Poe, after everything that you've done, don't you think? Don't you fucking think that the least you can do is let me fuck your cherry pie asshole after you've fucked with my brain? That the least you can do is let me ruin it, like you've ruined my fucking life. Wreck it like you've wrecked me, my discipline and my control and all my goddamn plans."

His voice is guttural and tortured and everything inside of me is aching for him.

Everything inside of me is stretched tight and taut and I open my eyes to look at him. To explain things. To tell him that this doesn't have to be such a bad thing. That he shouldn't sound so broken up about it.

That it's okay.

It's okay if he's consumed by me because I'm consumed by him as well.

I'm surrounded by him as well.

I'm overwhelmed and drowning and suffocating and dying for him.

And it's such a glorious feeling, this death.

It's a feeling that I've never felt before.

It's a feeling that's so hot and intense that it feels like fire. And future.

Our future.

It feels like…

My brain tries to reach for a word and I know I'm so close to it, so close to figuring that word out, but I get distracted when his thumb gains another inch of entry and my lower body twists and jerks.

And he whispers, his face dipped and his mouth open on the side of my neck, "It's the least you can fucking do, baby, when you've turned me into this. This desperate and hurting man who doesn't know up from down. Who doesn't know what's right and what's wrong and what he should and shouldn't do. This desperate and hurting man who wants to grant you your every wish, fulfill your every little whim. Who wants to fuck you in his bed and put you to sleep every night. Who wants to bathe you with his hands and clothe you in his t-shirts. A man who wants to kiss your feet and lick your body like he's your daddy."

I jerk so hard at this, so fucking hard that I think I come.

No, I *know* that I've come.

I've come from his thumb in my asshole and his filthy erotic words in my ear.

And I think he has too because he jerks as well. He twists and breathes like a hurtling train as well as he says in his roughest and most tortured voice ever, "I am that, aren't I? I'm that man for you. You've turned me into that man. You've made me into your daddy, Poe, with your cute smiles and loud laughs and your doe eyes."

Oh God. Oh God.

Oh my fucking God.

I can't. I can't. I can't deal with this.

I need him right now. I need him right fucking now.

Even though I've just come.

"Alaric, please. I need..." I whine and hiccup, my head rolling back and forth again.

"I know. And your wish is my command, isn't it?"

And those are the last words spoken between us.

Those are the last precious words that float and thicken around us, turning the air all lusty and drenched. All foggy and somehow ours. Safe and cozy.

As he first kisses my mouth, eats at it like it belongs to him.

Before pushing me down on the bed, forcing me to stay on all fours as he goes down on his knees and kisses my pussy from behind. And as always, he kisses like he eats pussy or he eats pussy like he kisses, and with his mouth on my core, I come again, jerking and twisting.

But this is only the beginning, isn't it?

We have a long way to go.

In my drugged and high state, I notice him move around. I feel him lowering his pants and slipping the condom on. I want to tell him that he shouldn't. I want to feel his bare skin inside my body. I want to feel every ridge and that thick vein of his dick but I don't have the energy.

And then it doesn't matter because he's sliding inside of me.

He's pushing into my dripping pussy and starting to fuck me.

And it's so good, it's so wonderful that it feels like heaven.

His thick cock inside of me, his hips smacking into my ass, his hairy thighs rubbing against mine and his big hands on my waist.

Yeah, heaven.

And then he bends down, his sweaty and massive chest covering my back and those big hands of his moving away from my hips to grab hold of my jiggling tits.

I watch his dusky hands kneading my milky flesh.

I watch how even though my tits are big and plump, he can still cover them all with his hands.

Because he's so big and strong, you see.

He's my daddy.

He's my safety blanket and I'm his baby.

That's when I come for the second time, with those filthy, erotic words.

And then he's pushing me down on the bed, laying me on my stomach. Before jerking my ass up and adjusting it at an angle for his entry again.

So he can hump my ass like that.

With me lying flat on my stomach, and him kneeling over me like a bronzed god.

Him going deep and deep and deeper, as if all the way into my belly, as he watches his dick go in and out of my hole.

At some point, I drool, my head turned and watching him, his big thighs digging into the mattress on either side of me, looking so magnificent.

At some point, I also come again. I have lost count of what number orgasm this is though.

But I know that we're still not done.

I know all of this was in preparation for the big show, the main show.

For my ass.

I know he was preparing me by first eating me out and then fucking me into oblivion so it doesn't hurt as much.

Don't I know him so well?

For all his tortured thoughts and angsty and agitated emotions, he'll never hurt me.

And so I find myself rearranged once again.

He turns me onto my back and my eyes clash with his for the first time since he began saying all the things in my ears. Since he began toying with my pussy and fucking me.

And I know.

I know the word that I was searching for before he distracted me with his filthy words.

The word that felt so entwined with the future.

Our future.

It slams into my chest and throbs inside my body as I look at him.

He's kneeling between my thighs, all naked and flushed and beautiful, his cock still hard and jutting out and bare — I guess he took the condom off at some point — because I know he hasn't come yet; he was waiting for the main show.

His main meal, my ass.

He parts my thighs and pushes them up to my chest. My arms reach out on my own to hold my limbs and make it easier for him to take what he wants. To make it easier for him to focus on other things.

Things like pushing his dick into my asshole.

Pushing it past the initial resistance.

And then pushing it and pushing it some more until he's seated all the way.

And yes, there's pain and pressure and all those things but I don't care about that. I only care about paying the price of doing all the bad things to him by giving up my last hole.

But what he doesn't know is that I'm also giving him my heart.

What he doesn't know as he fucks my ass, all gently and patiently but steadily, is that I'm also giving him my love.

Love.

That's the word I was searching for.

Because that's what I've been feeling all this time.

And it's throbbing and throbbing inside of me as he fucks me with his eyes closed and his head thrown back as if he can't bear to look at me, and I watch him with my eyes all open as if I can't look away.

What he doesn't know is that when he's done, his cum filling my ass and my pussy dripping with yet another orgasm, this one the most violent of all as it comes squirting out of me, and he leaves me in his bed without a second glance, I'm crying in the sheets.

I'm crying and sobbing, thinking about the future that suddenly seems so bleak and so alone.

Chapter Thirty-Four

I love him.

I'm in love with him.

With Alaric.

My devil guardian, my tyrant principal and the man I've hated since the moment I met him four years ago.

Although now that I think about it, maybe I never hated him.

Which is extremely weird to say.

Because my life for the past four years has revolved around the fact that I hated him. Everything that I've done, every plot, every plan, every thought that I've thought is because I hated him.

And that's the thing, isn't it?

The fact that he's the only thing I've thought about in the past four years.

What's more — this one's a shocker — is that even when I loved, I thought of him.

Even when I thought of Jimmy, I thought of Alaric.

The whole reason I felt a pull toward Jimmy and his smile was because *he* never smiled at me. The whole reason I felt the need to talk to Jimmy was because *he* never talked to me. The whole reason I felt that I needed Jimmy's love was because *he* hated me.

Him, him, and him.

It has all been about him.

Alaric Rule Marshall.

My soulmate.

So maybe what I felt for him back then was this intense, magnetic pull. This intense, magnetic and *strange* rearranging of my molecules. This strange realignment of my cells and my organs.

And maybe it hurt, that strange rearrangement and realignment.

And that's why I named it hate.

And *maybe* it happens to everyone around the world. To every girl who meets her soulmate in a man. Maybe it hurts and aches and burns and so she thinks that she hates him, that she wants him to go away, that she wants to run from him.

When in reality what she wants is to get closer.

To merge her heart with his, and to fuse her soul with his.

This also solves the mystery as to why I've been feeling so sad about summer school ending and me graduating.

So yeah, I love him and he left me.

Naked and crying in his bed last night.

And he never came back. I waited. I stayed in that cottage, in that bed, smelling of him and me and our lovemaking, but he never showed. And so I left. I had to. Because of all these limitations that the world has put on us. And texted him to say that I got back safely.

I waited for him at the school as well.

Waited for him to take that walk from his cottage to the school building in case he'd come back at some point at night. Or show up later in the day. Although I knew that he was leaving for California today, I never got a chance to ask him all the details as to when or for how many days. So I was hoping against hope that he might still show up.

I was hoping against hope that we might get to talk about it.

And other things.

God, so many other things.

But again, he never came.

And now I'm here.

At the mansion.

It's Friday and it was an impromptu trip to go see Mo. I haven't seen her since she came into my room after my first night with Alaric and asked me if I was okay. That was three weeks ago.

Even though I have all the privileges that I want now and can come and go easily over the weekends, I refrained from making any overnight trips back to the mansion in favor of spending time with

Alaric on campus, either in his cottage at night, or at the library where he sometimes works or in the cafeteria where he eats; at both those places, we don't talk to each other and sit at different tables but it's always good to know that he's around, that I can see him and watch him.

And secondly because I've been doing this thing at St. Mary's.

It's crazy and exciting and I never thought that I'd be the one handling it all.

Well, with the help of Echo and Jupiter, and also my other two friends, Callie and Wyn, who have graduated but were eager to help when I told them about it; we've been meeting every weekend off campus; the one thing I wanted to leave St. Mary's for.

We're throwing an end of summer school slash graduation party.

Yup. A party.

At St. Mary's.

Who would've thought?

It's not lavish or big by any means. We don't even have the time to put something like that together in such a short period of time, but it's going to be fun I think.

We're turning the cafeteria into a party hall. Callie is handling all the invitations; we're inviting the seniors who just graduated and who live close by and can attend, and since Callie knows everyone, she's the best person for the job. Wyn is obviously handling all the decoration stuff with her artsy streak. Echo is helping Wyn with all that since Echo can be pretty artsy too.

Oh, and I roped Salem in as well. She is going to be our music person because we all wanted that sexy, heartbreaking feel of the Ballad of the Bards, and who better to handle this than the lover of sad songs herself? She's arranging everything from California and coordinating with Jupiter and guess what, she's going to be here for it next week.

Yay.

Lastly, I'm handling the food and setting the menu. Which is obviously coming from Middlemarch, meaning Mo and the rest of the staff at the mansion. And of course all my friends' costumes.

So yeah, I've been busy with the very first party at St. Mary's.

Which came together and became possible because of him.

The new principal.

Who apparently can't refuse his baby.

One night, while showing him my designs in bed, I had a

whim. A fantastical thought about making these dresses for all my friends. By then, I'd already told him all about Callie and Wyn and Salem, and also Echo and Jupiter. I'd already told him how even though I'd hated living here, these girls made my life so amazing and happy. And the only reason I did that was because I know that he still has guilt for sending me here. Even though he did it to protect me at the time.

So there I was, talking about it and telling him how amazing they would look in these dresses, and wondering where we'd even wear these lavish things, and he said, "Here."

"What?"

Bare-chested and propped up on the pillows, he looked up from my notebook and said, "Do it here. At St. Mary's. Like a get-together or something."

"Like a party?"

"Yeah. Whatever." He shrugged as if he hadn't just blown my mind. "You can have your friends here. Just tell me what you'll need for it and for these." He tipped his chin at the designs. "And I'll have them delivered."

I looked at him for a few seconds.

Okay, fine. It was *more than* a few seconds.

I mean, it had to be.

The man had just dropped a bomb on me and it was wonderful and otherworldly and oh my God. And so I just launched myself at him. I threw myself at him and hugged him so tight that I think I almost killed him. Or so I thought until he hugged me back at my whispered thank you, and then I showered his face with all the kisses and all the *thank you*s I had in me.

Which I guess made him hard and so he picked me up and dropped me down on his dick.

So it's not really a mystery that I love him, is it?

No one, and I really mean *no one,* has taken care of me like he does. No one has seen me and believed in me like he does. No one and *absolutely no one* makes me feel happy and safe and warm like he does.

The only mystery is that it took me so long, so fucking long, to realize it.

And now he's gone and I don't know when he'll be back.

Neither do I know if I'll get the future that I want. If he'll give it to me like all the other things that he's given me.

I don't know if he'll give me himself.

So I'm keeping myself busy.

I'm keeping myself *furiously* busy.

As soon as I arrived, I asked Mo to teach me how to make a cherry pie. If she thought it was weird or why or what it meant, she didn't let it show. So I spent hours learning how to make his favorite dessert.

So far I've made four practice cherry pies — all of them sucked but I'm not going to give up; I'm thinking of spending all day tomorrow making and remaking until I get it right — *and* finished sewing two dresses, one pink and one yellow. These turned out okay. I won't call them perfect but I did what I set out to do.

And it's only midnight.

I'm pacing the room like a maniac, trying to think of what to do next, my fingers aching and bruised, my heart aching and bruised as well.

When the door bursts open and the man my heart, *my entire body*, is aching for is here.

And it looks like he's in pain as well.

All disheveled and ruined with his hair rumpled and sticking up in places, a thick forest of stubble on his jaw and a heavy frown. He stands at the threshold, both his palms splayed wide on the door as if he burst it open with all the force inside his body, his tie swinging.

"Alaric," I breathe out, my heart soaring in my chest.

"I couldn't find you."

His voice, so raspy and thick and syrupy, hits me across the room, across the feet and feet of hardwood floor and a massive king-sized bed, all the way to where I'm standing by the far wall.

And I press a hand on my belly that's fluttering and tensing. "What?"

"I looked everywhere."

I don't understand. Why did he have to look everywhere? I was here.

"B-but I was here," I repeat my thoughts out loud.

His nostrils flare. "This isn't your room."

My eyes widen and my fingers press harder on my belly when I realize what he's saying.

Oh yeah. Of course.

I got so busy with all the things, all my revelations, that I forgot where I was.

"Is it?" he prods when all I do is stare at him in dumb silence.

"No."

He steps in then. "Whose room is it?"

"Yours."

"Mine."

My body trembles when he says that. All shivery and hot.

And then he closes the door behind him and I'm dripping with sweat.

He begins to walk toward me, prowl really, and I'm dripping with all these emotions and feelings, with love.

He goes for his tie, loosening it from around his neck and I whisper, "What are you doing?"

I know I should've spoken louder; his room is extremely big, much bigger than my room at the mansion. It's quite possibly the size of his cottage living room and dining room *and* kitchen combined.

But I know he hears me.

I know that.

Even though he's chosen to remain silent.

Even though after discarding his tie, he's now going for his shirt. He's now unbuttoning it, his fingers deft and sure, his eyes still on me.

Clutching the t-shirt that I'm wearing — his — I ask, "What are you doing, Alaric? How did you know where I was?"

"Mo."

I watch his fingers work quickly and he's only made it halfway to me. "I-I thought you went to California." I look up at his face, all sharp and beautiful, and so brimming with intensity and ferocity that it's going to bring me to my knees in a second. "I thought you had an important meeting there. If you're missing it because you're here right now then it's not my fault. You can't be mad at me and leave me like you did last night."

Now that he's done unbuttoning his shirt, he slides it out of his dark gray dress pants and, rolling his shoulders, he discards it on the floor. I don't know where it lands, the shirt, because I can't take my eyes off him.

I can never take my eyes off him when he reveals his body.

His massive gladiator chest, his ladder-like torso.

When he comes to a halt in front of me, I crane my neck, my

hands all clenched in my t-shirt and my toes all curled. "You didn't even say goodbye, Alaric."

No, he didn't.

He just left.

And now that he's here, I'm realizing that I'm mad at him.

I've been so busy with all the revelations and worries and anxieties and the sheer ache that he was gone that I forgot that I was upset too. I was, am, angry.

His face is dipped as he stares down at me. "The meeting's over for tonight."

"What does… Does that mean it's not over for good? Like you have to —"

"Go back tomorrow, yeah."

"So then what are you —"

"I forgot to run you a bath yesterday."

I draw back. "What?"

"When I left," he goes on. "I didn't get a chance to run you a bath."

"But that…" I frown up at him. "Is that why you came back? To run me a bath."

"I took your ass last night and it hurt. But I wasn't there to make it better."

"That's insane. That's —"

He picks me up then like he did last night, when he carried me from his living room over to his bedroom. But tonight, he does it gently. He does it carefully and tenderly as he wraps his fingers around my waist and drapes me over his shoulders.

I watch his back, all astonished and speechless.

At the craziness of this.

At the sheer madness that he'd fly back from California for the night just to run me a bath. Because he took my ass last night.

"It didn't even hurt that much," I tell him.

He carries me over to his en suite, and when we reach his claw-foot bathtub that I've only ever seen during my sneaking in and out, he puts me down and replies, "I'm going to run you a bath regardless. And then I will."

My fingers dig into his smooth dense biceps. "You will what?"

"Say goodbye."

My body goes numb at his words.

My body loses all function.

I stand there like a statue, like an inanimate doll, as I watch him turn the tap on. As I watch him go over to the closet under the sink and take out all the bottles and things that he knows I like.

Cherry blossom bath salts and bombs.

Even though it's not the fruit cherry, he still bought it for me. Because it's something I said to him in passing when we were taking one of our baths. "I wonder if they have like cherry pie bath salts or oils or something. Wouldn't that be cool?"

At the time, he was lying behind me, his eyes closed and his head resting on the rim of the tub. His only response was a non-committal grunt so I didn't think he'd paid attention. But the next night, there they were, tiny pink bottles of cherry blossom bath salts and bombs and oils.

"Well, this is the closest they had to the cherry pie that you asked for," he said when I asked him what they were doing there.

But the thing is that I never asked him.

I only expressed this crazy desire and he fulfilled it just because it came out of my mouth. And he has them here as well, even though we've never taken a bath in his room at the mansion and we never made any plans to do so.

But knowing him, I know he was preparing for any eventuality.

Because that's what he does.

He gives me whatever I want. He protects me. He pampers me and spoils me and grants me my every wish.

And as I stand here, watching him draw me the bath that he didn't last night because he left and for which he came back, I decide that I don't want to be mad at him. I don't want to waste my time being angry or fighting over stupid things.

As I watch him discard his pants, I decide I want to be his baby.

I want him to give me whatever I want.

And what I want is this one wish that I have.

One little wish.

When he comes to me and takes my glasses off, followed by my t-shirt before sliding my panties down, I decide that I want him to give me himself. I want him to give me his love. And when he puts me in the steamy, cherry blossom-smelling bath and takes his place at my back, I decide that I want him to take me as well.

I want him to take my love.

Because I love him.

I love this man.

And I want to love him and kiss him and touch him and pamper him and fucking take care of him for the rest of my life.

Is that too much to ask, that he let me do all of that?

That he stays in my future.

And not say goodbye.

Because that's what this is, isn't it? This is goodbye.

This bath is our last bath together.

And for what? Because his *one* meeting got screwed up yesterday? Because he went to the wrong room *once*. And that he sent the wrong file because he was thinking about me and his precious fucking school that — for the record, he doesn't even like — was put in jeopardy for like one fucking day.

That's bullshit.

That's so fucked up.

Fuck the school.

Fuck his responsibilities. Fuck his family legacy and his stupid stubborn sense of responsibility.

Fuck that he doesn't want to talk about it or listen to me or to anyone.

He's mine and I'm his and he'll stay here no matter what.

I'll *keep* him here.

My body that had gone numb jolts awake then.

My heart starts racing. My soul starts throbbing.

And I turn around in the hot scented water to face him. To look at his face that hasn't lost even a drop of its intensity.

His features are just as sharp and just as taut as they were when he'd burst that door open. If anything, they've gone sharper and tighter. If anything, his chest has started to shudder and his mouth has parted now that he realizes I'm not numb or sleepwalking anymore.

And his tension only grows when I press my fingers on his chest and whisper, "Alaric."

As if he realizes what's coming, what I'm going to ask him, his arms around me tense. They go rock solid.

I don't let it deter me though.

I want what I want and what I want is him.

So I forge ahead, "Alaric, I don't want to say —"

Before I can say *goodbye*, his mouth is on mine. His mouth is covering mine. His mouth is kissing and touching and licking and biting mine.

And I know.

I know he's shutting me up. I know he doesn't want me to say it.

Because if I say it then he'll have to give it to me.

If I say my wish, he'll have to grant it.

And this may be the one thing that he can't. One thing he doesn't have it in him to give so he won't even let me wish this wish. He won't even let me dream this dream.

So he's kissing me like his life depends on it. Like he's thirsty and I'm the last drop of water.

And I'm kissing him back because I'm thirsty too and he in fact *is* the last drop of water for me, isn't he?

He's the last drop of happiness and warmth and safety.

The very last drop.

And that's why I turn around or maybe he turns me around, the water splashing everywhere, so my trembling chest can crash against his shuddering one. So my arms are wound around the back of his neck and his are wrapped around my waist.

And then I start moving and rocking against him, or again maybe he does that, maybe he moves me against his pelvis. Against those ridged, hard muscles before sliding me down a little.

So my bare and soft pussy is aligned with his bare and hard dick, and then I'm moving and rocking my hips to rub my core over his length. To hump and grind and to go up and down, to chase that lusty pleasure that he always gives me.

And that pleasure is so easy to come by. Even now.

Even when my heart is breaking in my chest, my pussy is juicing up for him.

My belly is getting heavier and my nipples are swollen and sensitive.

My moans aren't that far behind either.

And neither are his growls and grunts.

Even though we're in the water that clings to every part of our bodies, I can still tell when his cock leaks pre-cum and when that thick and musky juice rubs over the center of my pussy. I can even smell it from here. His arousal and my lust.

I can smell us over the sweet cherry blossoms.

And we smell good.

We smell so good and he humps me so well against his dick that I come. I shatter around him, jerking and twisting in his lap and moaning and whimpering in his mouth.

The mouth that he's yet to break away from mine.

He kisses me all through my orgasm and he keeps kissing me as I go limp and lazy around him. Then, in a serious and sheer display of strength, he comes to his feet in the water, with me stuck to his chest and his lips. I hear water splashing and splattering all over the floor as he gets out of the tub and then he's walking back into the bedroom.

He's laying me down on his bed while he simultaneously lies down on me.

And because I've had so much practice over the past couple of weeks, I open myself up for him easily. My wet and dripping thighs spread and my rounded hips arch up so he can slide inside of me without a thought or hesitation or delay.

Without breaking this never-ending kiss.

In the back of my mind I'm thinking — crazily and irrationally — that if I keep kissing him and kissing him, he might never leave. And we might live like this forever, inside this kiss, inside each other's mouths.

But of course, he's not as romantic as I am.

He's not as crazy as I am.

Because he does break the kiss.

He comes up for air and I'm annoyed.

I wanna go back to suffocating each other with our cherry blossom kisses.

I blink up at him, at the magnificent splendor that he is as he comes up to his knees between my open legs, his muscles dripping with water and his cock jutting out. I see him twist and reach for his nightstand but before he can even open the drawer, I say, "No."

He turns back to me, his eyes intense, and I continue, "No condom." His jaw clenches at my protest but before he can say anything, I shut him up like he did back in the bathtub. "I want to feel you. Every part of you," *at least once before we say goodbye*, "and that's my final wish."

He watches me all still and frozen for a few seconds, his slick dark hair dripping water, his eyes intense.

And I stare back at him with all my defiance.

All the recklessness and poor judgement.

I'm his diva in this moment. His spoiled baby who doesn't think of the consequences of her actions.

And in the back of my mind, where I'm more mature and I have more sense, I know this is wrong. I know this is risky. But I don't care. If this is the last time that we'll ever be together this way — because he's a stubborn ass — then he has to give me this.

If he won't give me what I truly want then he has to give me this last rebellion.

And a moment later, he makes up his mind to do just that.

Instead of punishing me for this rebellion, my guardian decides to indulge me for the very last time.

His forehead now clear of the frown he had, and his jaw now relaxed, he comes over me then, like a dark but cozy cloud of rain. My thighs wrap around him again, my feet slipping and splashing the water on the small of his back.

With his eyes staring into mine, he adjusts his cock at my entrance.

I feel the head of it right there, right at the edge.

Braced on his elbows, he brings his hands up to join with mine on either side of my head.

I feel our fingers locking together, holding onto each other.

And then with one single smooth push of his hips, he's in.

He's inside of me and then I just feel.

Everything.

Every ridge of his bare cock. That vein that I love so much, all swollen and throbbing. That smooth and velvety skin sliding into my channel.

And it's so amazing, it feels so good that my eyes flutter closed.

My back arches.

And I moan, my fingers tightening against his.

This is heaven, his bare dick inside of me. It has to be.

This is death, so peaceful and resting. This is love, so hot and burning.

And I'm not exaggerating.

I'm so not exaggerating.

In fact, I might be understating the gloriousness of it, the sheer marvel of his thick cock pumping into me raw and unprotected because his moans are far louder, far more pained and erotic. His thrusts and pushes are far more potent and jerking. So much so that I feel my entire body shuddering. I feel my tits jiggling and my belly trembling with his pumps.

I feel my entire world shaking as he pounds my pussy.

As he commands, "Eyes."

At which point, they snap open.

And then I'm looking into his chocolate chip eyes. I'm staring into them as he fucks me for the last time.

As he moves and slides over me, our limbs slippery and sweaty and misty.

As he kills me.

I guess it's true what they say, that your life flashes in front of your eyes when you die. It's flashing right before my eyes. Starting from the moment I heard his name in my study, Alaric Rule Marshall, to the moment I talked to him for the first time, up on the roof of this very mansion. The moment he became my devil guardian because I decided I hated him.

Who three years later became my tyrant principal and my hate for him increased.

Then I see the moment all of that changed and he simply became my guardian.

He simply became the man who protects me and guards me and spoils me.

Who is now the man I love.

And as I see all of those things, those pivotal moments in time, I scratch my nails on his fingers like the troublemaking wildcat he calls me. I grind my hips against his like his cute little whore and I whine and moan like a diva, urging him to go faster. Urging him to bring me to completion.

And because I am all of those things to him, he does.

He grinds back, speeding up his thrusts, the water on his dense muscles evaporating and turning into sweat. The chocolate chips in his eyes melting and burning.

Something happens then.

Something shifts inside of me that not only makes me come, clenching and jerking on his cock, but also renders me temporarily insane. It renders me temporarily thoughtless and so fantastically reckless that I know I'm going to remember this moment for the rest of my life.

The moment when I died.

Of love. Of heartbreak. Of misery.

The moment I crossed my ankles at the small of his back and raised my hips, clinging onto him. The moment I decided to tighten, tighten, tighten my hold on his magnificent body as he pounded, pounded, pounded my pussy.

The moment he went over the edge and I locked him in my hold so he couldn't get out.

And he knew.

God, did he know.

And it's happening right now.

My body is all tightly wrapped around him, trapping him against me, trapping his dick inside of me and his eyes flare for a second as he understands my meaning. As he understands that I want him to come inside of me.

I want him to blow inside my cunt when I'm all unprotected.

When my pussy is unguarded and bare and raw and fertile.

When I know this can lead to dangerous consequences. Life-changing and future-breaking consequences.

And that's exactly what I want.

That's exactly why I want him to give me his cum, his seed so my life changes. So my future breaks and molds and shifts to accommodate him in it.

So I can keep him in it.

So he stays and never says goodbye.

I mean, he trapped me twice, didn't he? Can't I trap him too?

Can't I steal his seed and hope and pray that it sticks to my womb so I can take what I want from him?

Besides, he understands what I'm doing. He knows my intentions. I can see it on his face.

I can see it in his dangerous eyes and his clenched jaw. I see it in his sharp features.

Features of a predator.

Of an animal.

Of a desperate man, being tempted and tempted to the brink of insanity. And I would've done it too. I would've pushed him if not for that despair in his eyes. If not for the despair in my heart too.

If not for this heavy regret that's threatening to overcome our last fuck.

This is our goodbye. I can't taint it. I can't ruin it.

So in the last second, I loosen my hold from around him and he pulls out.

He manages to spill his cum on my belly.

And with every lash of it, tears drip from my eyes.

Chapter Thirty-Five

"I want you to go."

Those are the first words I've spoken since we finished saying goodbye to each other.

Since I tried to trap him inside of my body and inside of my life.

Before deciding to let him go.

Since that time, I've managed to put my discarded shirt back on. He's managed to don his discarded shirt as well. Although he hasn't buttoned it, nor has he buttoned the pants that he also pulled on.

Since that time, I've taken my place on the bed, pulled my knees up and wrapped my arms around them. While he's been pacing the length of the room, plowing his fingers through his hair, his features angry and distressed.

But at my words, he halts and turns to stare at me.

His eyes narrow. "What?"

I inch my glasses up and tuck my wet hair behind my ears. "I want you to go."

He stares at me for a few seconds before striding over to the foot of the bed. "Are you insane? Are you fucking insane, Poe?"

I know it's a rhetorical question. An angry question. But I still respond, "No."

He scoffs angrily. Harshly. "Do you realize what just happened? What —"

I dig my nails in my arms. "Nothing happened."

"Yeah?" he bites out. "Is that what you think?"

"You didn't come inside me."

He looks at me with such anger that I have to force myself not to shiver under his wrath. "No, I didn't."

I have to force myself to keep my tone even and calm. "So then as I said —"

"But I could have," he snaps then, cutting me off. "I fucking could have, Poe."

"I'm —"

"I could've come inside you and fucking got you pregnant," he says with clenched teeth, a vein beating on his temple. "I could've wrecked your future. I could've wrecked every single thing that I am trying to give you. Every single thing that you need to build a safe and secure life."

"But it was me. I was the one who —"

"Yeah, and that's the problem, isn't it? That I'm so blinded by you, I can't see straight. That I'm so wrapped around your finger, I don't know what's up and what's down. And I hate that." He plows his fingers through his hair again, tugging at them, pulling at them. "I fucking hate that, Poe. I fucking hate how you can mess with my control like this. How you can mess with my life, with my responsibilities, with what I believe is right and wrong. I fucking hate that."

I fucking hate you.

He might as well have said that.

And it makes me want to crumble. It makes me want to curl up in a ball.

But I can't blame him.

Because I hate myself too. For what I almost did.

For how desperate I became.

So yeah.

It's time for him to go and for me to let him.

"So that's why I want you to leave," I tell him. "You should go back to California."

His chest moves sharply under his unbuttoned shirt, his muscles flexing and bunching with the action. "Fuck California. We need to have a discussion about this. We need fucking boundaries. This can't happen, Poe. Not ever." He rakes his fingers through his hair again. "This was supposed to be fucking —"

"Goodbye, I know," I cut him off, finishing the sentence for him.

He winces at my correct guess. As if he thought I didn't know even when he made it quite clear.

He goes to say something but I don't give him a chance. "Do you know what unloved is?"

He's taken aback at my interruption, a thick frown emerging between his brows. "What?"

"It's, uh, someone who's not loved. I mean, it's self-explanatory, but still."

"Poe, what the —"

"I looked it up still. Since I got that other thing wrong, Renaissance man," I tell him, my eyes on his irritated and confused face. "I looked that up too. It's a man with many skills and talents. That's what Renaissance man means. And turns out, it still fits you. You are a man of many skills and talents, so. Anyway." I shake my head. "I'm rambling but," I look into his eyes, "I'm that. I'm unloved."

He freezes.

Irritation and impatience leaching off his features.

Maybe finally realizing that I'm not rambling for no reason. There is a reason for my rambles, and he is right.

There is.

I want to say this to him before he leaves for California tonight. I want him to carry this with him on the plane, and then into the meetings or whatever he still has left to do.

And hopefully he'll carry the things I'm going to say to him for the rest of his life too.

"I mean, it's not that hard to believe why," I continue. "Why I'd think that. You know all about my mom and how I grew up. You know that she was never very present or loving or kind or any of the things that a mother should be, I guess. In fact, she hated me. You know, because she got pregnant with me so young and how she got burdened with a kid when she was a kid herself. It ruined her relationship with her parents. It initially ruined her dreams of being this great superstar. She wanted to be a movie star, did I tell you that? But being a single mother and a struggling actress is hard. So when she landed a TV role, she took it. She was very unhappy about it in the beginning because it wasn't the big screen, but yeah. So you know all that. You know all about me being unloved. So that's not the point."

I pause here and take a deep breath.

I study his blank but tight features, his inscrutable but pretty eyes as he watches me. As he stands there so handsome and so strong in his unbuttoned dark shirt and dark pants.

"The point is, Alaric," I say to the man I love, "is that you are too."

His muscles flex.

As if I've dealt him a blow.

And maybe I have.

I'm sorry about that; I promise him silently that I'm going to make it better. I'm going to soothe the wound I'm causing right now.

"You never talk about your childhood. You never talk about how it was for you growing up in this mansion. I'm sure this place is full of memories for you. All kinds of memories. Good and bad, sad and joyful, right?" I swallow, hugging my knees tightly. "Although I suspect, from what Mo has told me, that the bad outweighs the good, and the sad outweighs the joy. You didn't have a good life here, Alaric. You didn't have a happy childhood. You didn't have good parents, a good father. You didn't have anyone to love you. Instead what you had was hate and loneliness and darkness and despair. And I understand it, I think.

"Not completely, you see. I can never understand *completely*. No one can. That's the thing about trauma. No one really gets what you went through, what you felt in that very moment. They can relate, sure, and make their own conclusions about it, but no one really knows what you experience in that particular moment. So I want you to know that I'm not trying to belittle it or to say that, *oh yeah, I know how you feel*. That's not my goal here. My goal here is to tell you that you're unloved and I know something about being unloved."

Licking my lips, I take a deep breath again.

Only because I don't think he's breathing. I haven't seen his chest move in the past however many minutes since I began.

So I breathe for him too.

"I know that it makes you do things. It makes you crave things. It made *me* crave love. It made *me* crave attention. It made me so desperate, Alaric, that I chased after love with a single-minded focus. I chased after love like my life depended on it. Like if I didn't have it, I'd die. That's why I hid myself, my talent, my passion from my mother. That's why I did all those stupid things to get her attention that only managed to push her away more. That's why I ran after Jimmy, and ignored all the red flags. Ignored the very fact that I didn't even love him."

I detect a movement then.

A slight rising of his chest, and something loosens inside of me.

To see that he's here, he's breathing, he's *listening*.

"Yeah, I know, right? It's a shocker." I give out a scoffing chuckle. "I chased after that guy for three years. I lied for him. I hid things for him. I broke all the rules for him and I was going to do some really horrible things for him. And turns out, I never even loved him. I guess I was so obsessed with the idea of being loved that I didn't care about anything else. I didn't care if I loved him or not, or if he was the guy for me or not, I just wanted to chase after him and be loved. But again, that's not the point. What I did and how it affected me. The point is, Alaric, that being unloved changed you as well.

"It made you do things too. It made you angry. It made you bitter. It gave you this extreme sense of responsibility, this extreme obsession with your duty, with family legacy. This need to always be working and working and never stopping. Not even for a single second, not even to breathe or to think about if this is really what you want, if this is really what you should be doing. If this is something that makes you happy. You came back to the town that almost killed you. You do the things you don't like. It's like you're punishing yourself for something, you know. You're torturing yourself for something. And I wish, *I really wish*, that you'd tell me. You'd tell me what you're punishing yourself for, Alaric, so I can tell you that you don't have to. You don't have to punish yourself anymore. You don't have to torture yourself. Whatever it is, just let it go. Just let it… free. But you won't tell me and I'm not going to force you to reveal your secrets. I will, however, reveal one of mine."

That's when I unwrap my arms from around myself and get up on my knees. That's when I climb off the bed and approach him. I stand before him, my toes almost touching his, looking up at him with all the love in my eyes.

And I think he gets it.

He gets without me having to say that I love him.

And he pales.

He blanches.

His muscles flex and shift before going solid.

But instead of backing away, I close the distance to the point where our toes go from almost touching to definitely touching. Where I crane my neck up and cradle his jaw as I whisper, "I want you to know that you're not unloved, Alaric. First, Mo loves you. Mo has always loved you even if you don't want to see it. But more than that there's someone else who loves you as well. And that's me. I love you."

I didn't think it was possible but he pales some more.

He even goes blue. As if all the blood and all the air is rushing out of his body.

As if I'm killing him.

God, I hope not.

I hope with this, he can find some peace.

He can one day see that he doesn't have to live like this. He doesn't have to live in the past.

I press my fingers on his bristled jaw and whisper, "I'm in love with you and I understand that you might not believe me. Because for as long as you've known me, the better part of our acquaintance, I was running after this loser guy that you already knew was a loser but I refused to see it. And I hate that. I hate I wasted so much time over someone who didn't even matter. I hate that I realized too late that the only thing that has mattered to me in the past four years is you. Whether in hate or in love, you're the only thing, the only man, I've thought about. You do something to me. Here." I put my other hand to the left side of my chest. "You affect my heart. You mess with my heartbeats. You make it race. Even when I hated you, or thought I hated you, you made it fly, and now that you make me feel good, my heart hasn't come down to the ground. It's hanging from the ceiling. It's hanging from the sky. It's up there, on the roof where we spoke for the first time. It lives there now. Because you make me feel safe and cherished and protected, Alaric. You make me feel seen and worthy. You make me believe that I can do things. That I can finish summer school, go to a fashion school, dress people for a living. You make me feel like I can be anything I want, I can do anything I want.

"And it was you who taught me not to run after things, not to be desperate enough to chase after things and people. So what I did today, I'm sorry for that. I let you down. I let myself down. What I did back there was wrong. I almost turned something pure, something so fragile and soft and sweet like my love for you, into something dirty. And I'm not an expert in love — God, I'm not — but I do think that love shouldn't be selfish. I do think that love shouldn't be destruction but the building of things. Love shouldn't be toxic but life-giving. And love definitely isn't what I almost did for Jimmy with the whole camera thing, it's what I want to do for you. And what I want to do is to give you this secret, okay? I want you to put it in your pocket and tuck it in your heart. This secret that there's someone out there who loves you. That there's a girl out there, in this world, who's in love with you, Alaric. And she pines for you and longs for you and dreams about you. She thinks that you're the most beautiful man that she's ever seen. The most intelligent and complex and infuriating and endearing man. She loves your leather-bound books and your tweed jackets and your silver ring. She loves that you're a history nerd and that you basically know everything there is to know in this world. She loves that you make the best chamomile tea and that you draw the best baths ever. She loves that you pamper her and spoil her and treat her like your baby. Like your queen. And she wishes that she could do the same for you and treat you like the precious man you are. Like her king. So I want you to stop, okay? Whatever it is that you're chasing after. I want you to take a breath and see yourself. Because you're loved. You're so loved, Alaric. By that girl."

With that, I go up on my tiptoes and press a soft kiss on his stunned and parted lips.

Our last one.

It's a tragedy, a catastrophe, a fucking blasphemy of apocalyptic proportions that our last kiss is such a short affair, when I waited for our first one for years.

And when our first one lasted for three weeks.

For the duration of this fever-like relationship.

It's a tragedy that I was so stupid for so long that I didn't realize.

I didn't realize that the man who's standing in front of me still as a statue, as a rock, so beautiful and strong and yet so fragile in a lot of ways, watching me as if I've destroyed his world, is the man I love.

But most of all, I didn't realize that the day I finally understand it will also be our last.

Chapter Thirty-Six

The Renaissance Man

"Are you leaving again?"

At Mo's voice, I look up from my desk, where I'm collecting all the documents and files I'm going to need for the upcoming meetings in California.

"Yeah, my flight isn't until later in the day but I'm hoping to catch something on standby," I say distractedly, not willing to lose my focus and mess up the files again.

Once was enough.

Once was all I could handle.

I can't afford to make any mistakes. Not on this project. Something so close and important to my family.

That's why I've decided to stay in California for a few more days to get everything settled and neatly wrapped up.

"But you just came back. I thought —"

I throw her a sharp glance, still busy collecting all the papers. "Yes. But now I'm going back."

Mo looks at me steadily. "So why did you come back?"

My body going alert, I glance down at the file that I've been flicking through. "Because I needed to do something here. Now if you —"

"What did you need to do?"

"It's none of your business."

"Must be very important if you flew all the way back for it. I mean, it's a six-hour flight and —"

I snap the file shut and look up again. "What the fuck do you want?"

She doesn't flinch at my tone as she says, "I want you to tell me why you came back."

Leaning, I put both my palms on the desk, fingers splayed wide, as I reply slowly, "It's none. Of your fucking. Business."

"For her." She nods, again without flinching or hesitating. "You came back for her."

I freeze at her words.

No, that's not true.

I don't freeze. I combust.

I erupt into flames.

Fire licks at my skin and rushes through my veins.

I love you…

Damn it.

Fuck. *Fucking* fuck.

I had just shoved her voice out of my head. I'd just gotten enough control to get back to my work.

And it fucking took me *two* hours. It fucking took me more than two hours.

To get my head, my body that wouldn't stop shaking, under control. To get my thoughts under control. To get this urge to go back up to her room — which she went to after dropping the love bomb on me — and demand that she take it back.

Demand that she explain herself.

What the fucking — what the *fucking fuck* — was she thinking?

First, she's too young to know what love is. Second, she loves me.

Me?

And yes, I came back for her, all right?

I did.

I came back so I could say goodbye.

So I could end this, whatever it is that we've got going on. Whatever it is that's messing with my head.

It's too hectic of a time in my life to be indulging in something like this.

This is exactly what they've all been waiting for, haven't they, ever since I came back and took this job. The board members.

This is exactly what they wanted, for me to fuck up. For me to make one mistake, however small, so they could all be proven right.

And on top of all that, it's plain wrong.

This thing between us.

She's my ward, my student. And it's fucking wrong how I have her sneak out of her dorm every night. Especially after that fucking bed check rule that I didn't even want to implement but did because I felt like I needed to hold onto my control. I needed to hold onto my responsibilities. So I let her take risks for me, break rules for me when I've punished her for doing the same for that fuckface that she doesn't even love. That's the only good news in this clusterfuck of a situation.

And then there's the way I pounce on her. How I devour her, eat her up without stopping. Without ever getting satisfied.

I knew this was a bad idea since the beginning.

But I got too weak — something I promised myself I never would be. And then I got so out of control — another thing I promised I wouldn't ever be — that I screwed up something so important.

So yeah, I came back to wake us up from this crazy dream and say goodbye.

"If you know," I manage to say after a few beats, "then why are you asking?"

She sighs, still watching me. "I guess that's my bad. I probably should've started by saying that I know."

"You know what?"

"About you two."

My fingers flex on the desk. They jerk.

Even though there's no accusation in her tone, which surprises me. It's very matter of fact.

"It's plain to see," she continues.

Well, that's fucking great, isn't it?

She knows.

She knows why I came here and what I've been doing to her all this time.

For the record I want to say that tonight, it was supposed to be just a goodbye.

No baths, no kisses, definitely no risky, unprotected fucks.

My brain fucking shuts down at the thought. My brain can't even comprehend the level of fucked-upness *that* was.

I knew what she was doing. I knew it.

And still for a second, for a microsecond, I wanted to come inside her. I wanted to give her my seed, breed her, trap her here. With me, under me. So she never ever leaves.

Jesus Christ.

I can't even think about it right now.

Not when I've got so much work to do.

Not when Mo is still standing here, watching me as if she wants me to say something. As if she wants me to confess all my crimes.

"I want you to know I struggled with this," Mo says when I hold my silence. "With things between you two. Not only because of your relationship to each other and the age difference but also because of how you were with her. In the beginning. But then I saw you. I saw that you'd changed these past couple of weeks. Every time you'd call, your voice would be so… different. So light. You'd laugh more. You'd chuckle and be more playful. And it's something I've always wanted for you. To be happy."

At this, I hear her voice.

Mo loves you…

It's not something that I've ever thought about. Or rather it's not something that I've dared to think about but maybe…

"And then every time Poe called," she continues, breaking my thoughts thankfully; I don't have time to think about love right now. "From her school. She'd sound so carefree and so happy, you know? It's something I've always wanted for her as well. And she wouldn't stop talking about you. How good you are. How you make her feel. How she's always sketching these days, making dresses, organizing her party at school. Yeah, it's plain to see. That she loves you."

At this, my fingers clench and I crumple the papers I was reading. "She doesn't know what love is."

A glint of satisfaction shines in her eyes. "So she told you."

I refuse to dignify that with a response.

But she isn't deterred, of course. "Good for her. I'm proud of her."

"Are you out of your fucking mind?" I snap at her. "She's my ward."

"I know. I told you I struggled with this. But she's eighteen now." She shrugs. "Old enough to make her own decisions."

"Doesn't fucking matter. She's still my ward and I'm still responsible for her."

"I know people would see it that way. It's not an ideal situation."

"No, it's not." I crumple the paper even more. "And I'm her fucking principal."

"But that's only for another week. Besides, this was a temporary job."

"It doesn't matter. It's still my job."

"You don't even like it."

I straighten up then, my hands fisted at my sides. "Are you done?"

"No." She shakes her head. "Because I'd like to know if you do too. Do you love her?"

I'm clenching my hands so tightly that my knuckles are cracking, throbbing. "Get out."

"Do you?"

"Get the fuck out, Mo."

She studies me for a few moments, her eyes scrutinizing and clear. Making me feel uncomfortable. As if I'm being analyzed. And I'm about to snap at her again when she speaks. "Because he does."

What the fuck?

Who?

"If you're talking about Jimmy, I swear to God, Mo, this will be his last day on Earth."

A small smile flickers on her lips before it vanishes and she shakes her head. "Not him, no. The old Alaric."

"What?"

"I might lose my job for this," she says, completely unbothered. "But I've decided it's worth it. Besides, I'm ready to retire. My knees are not what they used to be. So I'm going to say this."

"Say what?"

"I know you don't like to talk about him, the old Alaric," she says. "You probably don't even like to think about him either. I mean, look at you now. You don't even resemble him. And I know you think he was weak and a coward and —"

"He *was* weak and a coward," I snap out.

I can't believe we're talking about this.

I can't fucking believe that on top of everything else, now we have to talk about old fucking Alaric.

How did we even get to this?

"He was a kid," she says.

"Yes, whom other kids picked on. Whom his own father picked on."

More than picked on.

I don't remember the first time my father hit me, but I can't remember a time when he didn't.

When he didn't look at me with disgust. Anger. Hatred.

I remember how I used to hide under my bed when I knew he was home. How I used to run away from home and sleep in the woods when I knew he was in one of his moods. Which meant he'd find any excuse to hit me.

Not that he needed any.

The mere sight of me would set him off.

His wife's killer.

And it didn't help that I was so small, so sickly.

If I was stronger, bigger, healthier, my father would probably have been able to stomach my presence. But not only did I kill my mother, I was also such an anomaly in the Marshall family.

So yeah, that kid was weak.

That kid was a target who later got exactly what he deserved.

A beating within an inch of his life for being so fucking stupid.

"And that's their fault. Not yours," Mo says, breaking into my thoughts. "For picking on you."

"If I wasn't so tiny and weak begin with, they wouldn't have."

And she loves me. *Me.*

What a fucking joke.

The night when she fought with me on the roof, she was fourteen. She stood there, taking on the wrath of the sky and the man she thought was the devil.

And what was I doing when I was fourteen?

I was still keeping my head down while walking through the school corridors. I was still hiding in the library until dinnertime when I knew my father would be home. Kids were pushing me into lockers and I wouldn't make a peep because I knew giving them a reaction would only make things worse.

There's no way that she could love someone like me.

Someone as polar opposite of her as possible.

Someone so unworthy of her.

"I wish you saw it differently," Mo whispers, as if reading them, my thoughts.

And even though I know that she didn't, my reply still pertains to it. It still pertains to being unworthy of her. "Well, I don't."

"I wish you wouldn't hate him either."

"Mo," I warn.

"Or punish him for things that weren't his fault and —"

"Jesus Christ," I snap out, my fingers raking through my hair, pulling at it in clumps. "I'm not…" I sigh sharply. "So what if I am? What if I am punishing him, that boy? It wouldn't be anything less than he deserved. He killed his mother. Do you understand what that means?" I thump a fist on my chest. "I killed my mother. And then I had the audacity to be born half dead. I had the audacity to be born an anomaly. Do you understand how helpless it feels when your own body betrays you? When your body is so weak that you spend the better part of your childhood stuck to a hospital bed? When your own father doesn't visit you. So yes, maybe I'm punishing him, the old fucking Alaric. Maybe I'm fucking torturing that little boy for being born the way I was. But so what? So *the fuck* what? And can we please stop talking about me in third person?"

She has tears in her eyes now but her voice is as calm as ever. "Yeah, you're right. We shouldn't talk about old Alaric as if he were a different person. He is you. He is inside of you. Even though you have buried him under layers and layers of resentment. But as much as you hate him, as much as your father or this town picked on him or hated him, there's one person who loves him. One person strong and brave enough to love that sweet innocent little boy, and that's my Poe. That's my brave and courageous Poe who's up there right now, shut up in her room, probably crying over you. And I wish you could see what she sees."

With that, she leaves.

Finally.

But any control or focus that I'd gathered in the past couple of hours is gone now. And my head is full of her voice.

Her face. Her smiles and her laughs.

My head is full of her *I love you.*

And I wonder how easily that love might turn into disgust if she ever knew who she loves.

If she ever knew she loves a man like me.

Chapter Thirty-Seven

"You need to do it."

That's Wyn.

She has a pink strapless gown on with a lacy corset style top that accentuates her big breasts and her tiny waist. I also made satin gloves for her and I've left her hair all loose and curly, and paired her dress with Gucci sandals.

My girl looks like a Cinderella and so I named her dress The Dreamy Cinderella because Wyn is super artistic and dreamy.

Oh, and she's dressed up because today's the party.

St. Mary's very first graduation party, that we've all been working toward for the past few weeks.

Which also means that I graduated.

Well, I don't have my grades yet but I'm pretty sure I did.

And summer school is over.

All my girls are gathered here in my dorm room and I'm taking turns getting them ready, doing their makeup and hair, helping them with their dresses.

So basically I'm in my element and I'm loving it.

Which means I don't want to talk about what Wyn is talking about.

It's only going to make me sad, and I can't be sad because I have so much stuff to do.

"I don't need to do anything," I tell Wyn, who's looking at me with concern, as I finish up Callie's French twist.

Callie's wearing a light green ballerina-inspired gown — because she's a ballerina — with a sleeveless bust and a layered and puffy skirt. Her sleeves are embedded with shiny, emerald rhinestones that I found online and ordered specifically for her dress. I'm calling it The Fairy. Because her husband, Reed, calls her a fairy. And her sandals are from Prada.

Callie turns toward me. "She's right. You have to."

"No."

I point my finger at Salem who dutifully and very sweetly comes over and sits on the chair that Callie has just vacated in front of the mirror so I can do her hair. Just for that, I give her a hug from behind and she chuckles, hugging me back.

Although to be honest, I haven't stopped hugging her. Or any of us really, for that matter.

We're seeing Salem for the first time after school ended and she went away to California to be with Arrow, so we're all a little emotional. She arrived this afternoon and she's staying with Callie and Reed at their place in Wuthering Garden.

Anyway, back to her hair.

She's got big dark curls so there isn't a lot that I can do with it but I can make it all shiny and bouncy. I gather all the sprays and things and get to work, and while I'm elbow deep in her gorgeous hair, she says, "They're all right, you know. You need to do it. You need to give it to him. You made it for him."

It's a good thing I'm busy focusing on something else right now or I would have a hell of a time stopping my tears.

Like I had back when I told them.

That I loved him.

They were all understandably confused.

Even though they knew that I didn't hate my guardian anymore, they didn't think that I'd fall in love with him.

But they were supportive like they always have been.

Like they're being now.

Although Wyn did give me the side-eye. "I mean I called it. Accidentally but I did."

She did, yes.

Back at the Ballad of the Bards when she mistakenly thought I was talking about *him* when I was talking about Jimmy.

I chuckled. "You totally did, my hopeless dreamer."

Anyway I don't blame them for bringing him up. I blame

myself here, for being so emotional.

And I understand the wound is new. I do. I mean, it's only been a week ever since things ended but I really need to get a handle on things. I really need to get it together.

Am I going to cry every time someone alludes to him?

He's my guardian; of course people are going to allude to him for the rest of my life.

Clearing my throat and keeping my eyes on her hair, I reply to Salem, "I can always mail it to the mansion from New York. It's not a big deal."

"It was a big deal when I made one for Reed," Callie says, and despite myself I look up and find her watching me in the mirror.

"Made what for Reed?"

She's now sitting on my bed right next to Wyn. "The sweater."

Wyn turns to her. "Oh right. The white one. With a mustang on it."

"Yup." Callie nods. "It was a super big deal. I stayed up night after night to have it ready for him in time. Before his big game."

I stayed night after night as well.

But that doesn't mean I can just give it to him. He might pass out from my gift.

I still haven't forgotten how he looked when I told him I loved him, all betrayed and destroyed.

Like instead of love, I'd meant hate.

"And remember how he had it in his possession for like two whole years while you guys weren't together," says Salem in a dreamy voice, pressing a hand to her chest.

"I know." Callie blushes. "And I was so convinced that he'd thrown it away."

Wyn bumps her shoulder. "Reed can't throw away anything that belongs to his Fae."

"Right, like my brother can throw anything away that belongs to you," Callie retorts. "His truck still has that pink glitter paint."

And it's Wyn's turn to blush. "Shut up."

"I so wanna see that graffiti," Salem says. "I wish you'd taken a picture of it."

"No need to take a picture," Wyn replies, still blushing. "It was me. It was my face."

Callie laughs. "I so wish you'd taken Con's photo though. I

would've loved to see his face in that moment."

Yeah, there was this one time when Wyn — all calm and quiet — got so angry at Conrad, her now boyfriend, for denying his feelings for her that she snuck out of St. Mary's and went all the way to his house in Bardstown only to draw graffiti on his truck. It was such a gutsy move. It was a Poe move and I loved that for her.

Soon after that, Conrad came around, so a total win-win situation.

Then Callie turns to Salem, who's also laughing. "And don't forget how Arrow carries around your letters."

The smile that covers Salem's face is one that can light up any room. "I know. Like random letters. I'll find one in his pocket while doing laundry and it makes me so happy. And then some nights he wakes me up to ask me about them. Like, what was he doing when I wrote that letter; what year was it. It's so sweet."

Before Salem and Arrow got together, Salem had been in love with him for eight long years. And during those eight years, she wrote him a letter almost every day. She never sent them, of course; Arrow was dating her older sister at the time. She put them in orange envelopes and kept them tucked away in a shoebox.

But when they got together, Salem confessed about the letters. And from the looks of it, Arrow has been completely fascinated by them.

I'm so happy for her.

I'm so happy for all my friends actually.

They'd all loved and pined for their guys for years before fate brought them together. And if they felt anything like what I've been feeling for the one week ever since I realized that I loved him, I can't even imagine how they all managed to survive.

But I have to say, as painful as every breath is right now, I'd still take it.

I'd still take every painful breath and every stinging tear in the world to realize sooner.

To realize way before I did that I loved him.

I'd take years of pining and longing and crying in my pillow at night to realize that he was my soulmate. That he's as unloved as me, so I could fill his life with all the love. So I could tell him every single day that he is loved. That he beats in my heart and flows in my veins. That he's the flutter in my belly and the shiver on my spine.

Yeah, I would have.

And maybe in all of this, that's my biggest regret.

Not realizing sooner.

Not having enough time to fill his life with all my love.

"Okay, all done," I say to Salem, smiling.

"Have you been listening to what we're saying?" she asks, looking at me in the mirror.

I put everything aside as I say, "Yes. But your situation is different."

"How?" Wyn asks.

"Um, because all your guys loved you. They cared about you."

"Yes, but we didn't know that," Wyn reminds me.

"In fact, I thought my guy broke my heart on purpose," Callie goes. "Well, he did do it on purpose. But not for the purpose that I was thinking."

"Exactly," Salem adds. "And my guy was engaged to my sister."

"And my guy," Wyn chimes in, "never wanted to do anything with me. I was his little sister's best friend, remember?"

I look at all three of them and their eager and kind faces. "You guys are amazing and I love you. And I'm so happy for you that your love stories worked out, but no. He is," I swallow, wiping my hands down the skirt of my own dress, "different. He is hard. And impenetrable. He has walls around him and they are there for his own protection, I know that. But I also know that I can't climb them. I can't poke holes in them. I can't take them apart. Not unless he allows it. Not unless he's willing to let me in. And he's not. I've tried. So all I can do is let him go."

I want that for him.

I want that for him so badly.

I want him to just let someone in. I want him to not be so closed off, so lonely, so aloof.

I want him to be happy.

To build a life in the present and not live in the past.

And yes, if I'm being completely honest and selfish, then I want him to build a life with me. I want him to let *me* in. I want him to let *me* make him happy.

But it's not in my control, is it?

And I'm not going to beg.

He wouldn't want me to and I wouldn't want to make his life

even more difficult.

So I'll keep my promise and my distance.

And mail out the thing I made for him, the tweed jacket, from New York. Or maybe simply leave it with Mo to give to him once I leave.

"My only regret is that I wish I'd realized this sooner," I continue, my throat clogged with emotions. "I wasted so much time hating him and cursing at him and running from him. I wish I hadn't done that. I wish I'd realized sooner that he's my soulmate and… I wish I had had more time with him."

At this, my tears start to fall and I hate that.

I hate that I'm being such a spoilsport. It's the very first party at St. Mary's. I should be the life of the party right now but here I am crying, surrounded by friends who all take turns hugging me and shushing me.

But also if I was going to lose it in front of anyone, my girls would've been my first choice.

Because we're not only best friends, we're sisters, see.

We're the St. Mary's rebels.

Our bond is the kind of bond that I know will last a lifetime. No matter where we are or where we go, we'll always be in each other's lives. We'll always stick by each other through thick and thin. We'll celebrate each other's victories and happiness and wipe each other's tears.

Somehow we all manage to get ourselves under control and then in a flurry of activity, I'm re-touching everyone's makeup, and just in time too because as soon as I'm done reapplying Callie's dark green lipstick, Echo and Jupiter appear at the door.

"Oh my God, you guys look so amazing," Jupiter exclaims, looking amazing herself by the way.

I'm so glad I picked yet another shade of red for her. It goes so well with her copper hair, making her look like a sultry queen. I've named it The Sultry Siren. And Echo looks like such a good girl in her silver bell-shaped dress that I've named The Dove. Because she told me that her favorite bird is the dove.

"Okay, but we're late. Let's go," Echo says, clapping her hands. "It's time. Everything's ready."

They've been gone to check up on things at the cafeteria while I got everyone else ready, and well, the time is here. "Okay, let's go."

Then, "Oh but wait, let me get my satchel first."

My satchel holds all the emergency stuff that we might need in case of an unforeseen disaster like a broken heel, so I'm carrying a couple of extra shoes, tons of bobby pins, and lipsticks and brushes and whatnot.

At the last minute, I also shove his gift in it, as if I'm really going to give it to him.

If I saw him.

A: I'm not. No matter how much I want to. And B: he's not even here.

He left for California last week and he hasn't been back yet. I have no idea when he's coming back. Although I do know that we have a meeting with the lawyers set up — Marty emailed me — sometime next week, so he should be back for that at least.

The plan is that I'll be packing up and leaving for the mansion in a couple of days, where I'll stay for a while until things are ready in New York and my classes start. I'm not going to lie, I'm excited about college. Something I never thought I would be. I'm excited to take the step that will get me closer to a fashion school so maybe I can realize the dreams I never knew I had.

All because of him.

The man I love.

And the man who won't let me in.

But I can't think about all of that right now. I need to stay in the present and make this night memorable with my friends.

When I'm ready, we all head out of my room and walk down the hallway that's been our home for the past three years. The concrete floors, the brick walls, the beige doors. Some girls are still in their mustard-colored uniforms as they are rushing to get ready for the party. Some are already dressed.

There's laughing and talking and all this bustling activity that I realize I'm going to miss.

As much as I hated this place and all the rules, this was home for so many years and I made some long-lasting friendships here that I know I will carry with me for the rest of my life.

So yeah, I guess I'll miss this place as well.

We push open the glass door to the outside and there they are.

All the guys.

Well, this is a party, right?

Of course there are guys.

Again, who would've thought that St. Mary's would have guys coming in and out? But since it's a party that's going to have music and dancing, it made sense to invite guys also. All these guys are plus ones. Meaning no unauthorized guys, of course, and all of them had to show ID and produce their invites at the gates; it's a reform school, hello? There are rules that need to be observed and followed.

While waiting for their dates to emerge from the dorms, some guys are looking around as if they've stepped into a different dimension — a dimension made of concrete and cinderblocks — while others don't even bat an eyelash because they are more familiar with this school.

Like Arrow and Reed and Conrad.

All wearing black suits and light shirts, they're standing in a group together, Reed being the tallest — half an inch taller than Conrad — as they wait for their girls to emerge. And I swear to God, as soon as they do, all their gazes somehow land on them with a laser focus. And then, as if in unison, all their eyes flare for a second at the vision that their girlfriends — in Reed's case his wife — present.

Which makes me so happy.

Without a word to each other, they disperse and scatter, and walk over to their girls almost in a trance.

I notice that Arrow has a bouquet in his hand — of gardenias — that I'm assuming he's brought for Salem. But I think at the sight of her in a yellow/orange sunburst of a gown — named The Sweetheart because Salem is so sweet and that's Arrow's endearment for her — he's forgotten.

Because he simply stands there, looking down at her with parted lips.

"You're…" He swallows, his Adam's apple bobbing.

"Today *I'm* like the sun, huh," she says, smiling up at him. "Instead of you."

Salem calls Arrow her sun and it totally makes sense if you look at his sun-struck hair and his golden skin.

"No," he whispers, his eyes still looking hypnotized. "Not just today. You're always the sun. My sun."

Salem blushes and says, pointing to the flowers, "Are they for me?"

Arrow wakes up and nods.

And then I let them be.

This is such a private moment and I don't want to intrude.

And there's no shortage of private moments around me. While Conrad is gazing down at Wyn, his fingers stroking her cheek, Reed is smirking down at Callie, bending down to place a soft kiss on her mouth. After which she goes on her tiptoes and wipes the lipstick off the side of his mouth.

It starts up an ache in my chest.

Not because I don't want what's best for my friends but because I can't help but feel lonely, and empty.

Without him.

I can't help but feel hollow.

I can't help but want him here. Even if not as my Alaric then as Principal Marshall.

I mean, he's the one who made everything possible. He was the one who okayed this whole party idea, and then got all the staff working and cooperating with us. He should be here.

Once all the guys are over their initial shock and all the greetings have been made, we all walk over to the school building together. But when the time comes to climb the stairs, I tell my friends to go ahead without me because I'm going to need a minute. They are all concerned, but I wave it off with a smile and promise them that I'll be right behind them.

When they're all gone, I take a deep breath.

I take several deep breaths.

I'm not sure why I'm hesitating in climbing those stairs and going inside the building, but I can't help but think that once I do, once I get in there, it's over.

The wait is over.

And all the hope of him coming tonight will die.

It's a silly thought but there you have it.

So mostly just to appease myself, I decide to turn around and look for him one last time before I go in.

And as soon as I do, all breath leaves my body in a rush.

Because there he is.

Standing only a few feet away, in a brown tweed jacket and a black tie.

My Alaric.

He is here.

He came.

And Jesus Christ, he looks like… a god.

So handsome with such beautiful and sharp features. So powerful with impossibly broad shoulders and a muscular body, and so like the man I love.

"Hi," I whisper.

I don't think he heard me though.

Because he looks like he's in a trance.

He looks like he's hypnotized.

And by me no less.

My dress.

His chocolate chip eyes take me in slowly and methodically, from top to bottom, from side to side, from every angle. Then, "You look…"

I can't help but blush at his rough voice.

Rough and low and somehow reverent.

My own dress is purple and is a shimmery chiffon number with sequins studded all over the length. It's sleeveless with a high neck and a plunging back that's covered by my loose hair that I've done in tight curls. And I've got my suede heels on.

"You like it?"

He finally looks up, his eyes all molten and warm, shimmering as bright as my dress. Swallowing, he rasps, "I love it."

My blush intensifies. "Thank you."

Something flickers on his features at my *thank you*, something private and only meant for us to know. And instead of just my cheeks, my entire body blushes. I know I'm turning scarlet under my dress.

Under his intense gaze.

"What's it called?"

My heart thumps. "Well, I couldn't find a name for this. But since it's all shimmery and glamorous I thought The Purple Queen or something."

Because you treat me like a queen.

His eyes flash as if he heard it. "And what's that lipstick called?"

I touch it with my trembling fingers. "Uh, God of a Girl."

He takes a moment to respond. "You aren't the Purple Queen then."

"I'm not?"

He shakes his head slowly. "You're a goddess. A goddess in

purple."

A goddess in purple.

I like that. I love that.

I love him.

Why is he standing all the way over there? Why can't I get close to him?

Why won't he let me?

"You came," I say.

His trance breaks.

As if my words have woken him up, and I hate that.

"I… Yeah." He thrusts his hands down into his pockets. "I just got back from California."

"How was it? Did you get everything done?"

"Almost. Still working on it."

"You'll get it done though," I say, smiling and with all the confidence. "It's you. Of course you will."

He watches me for a few moments, my smile particularly. Followed by my eyes behind my glasses. Then, "I… have something for you."

"For me?"

He fishes something out of his pocket, a simple narrow case, and offers it to me. "A graduation present."

Despite the heavy melancholy, my heart leaps and floats in my chest as I take it. "A graduation present?"

He nods, rubbing the back of his neck. "Yeah, just a little something."

I watch him in astonishment for a few seconds before jumping to open the case. "It's a bracelet."

It's a twinkling row of diamonds seated on a blue velvet cushion.

I touch it with gentle fingers, my breath going haywire at the sweet, sweet gesture.

Looking up, I say, "I love it."

"Yeah?"

"Yes. It's perfect."

Like you.

His eyes flash again as if he heard this too. Followed by a hard clench of his jaw. Then, "It's just to say that I'm proud of you. I'm proud of everything you've done and all the things that you'll do. Because you'll do great things, Poe. In your future."

My future.

The period of time in my life that won't include him.

But I've decided over the last week that I'm still going to love him. I'm still going to pine for him and long for him. I'm still going to let my love for him grow and prosper and take root and blossom.

Because I don't want him to live in a world where he's not loved.

I'll love him so he knows that he's loved.

So maybe one day he'll see that he doesn't have to live his life this way, alone and unhappy.

And that's why I decide to give him his gift.

My friends were right.

It is a big deal. I made it for him and it shows that I love him. Which means he should have it.

"I have something for you too," I say, looking down and opening my satchel. I bring out the big white box. "It's just something I made for you."

When I look up, I find him staring at the box in a strange way.

In a helpless way even.

In a way that he doesn't know what to do with it.

There's a thick line bisecting his brows and his mouth is slightly parted.

He watches it and watches it like he's expecting the box to do something. Either explode or burst into flames.

"Alaric?"

That jerks him awake again and he snaps his eyes up. "I… No one's ever…"

I'm glad he takes it off my hands then, the box I mean.

Because my arm has started to tremble at his words.

At the meaning behind them.

That no one has given him a gift before this, before me.

That the man I love has never received a gift from anyone. No one has ever shown him this tiny bit of kindness that we show not only to good friends but to distant acquaintances. To strangers even. To new neighbors. To new classmates.

I'm not sure how I manage to contain myself, contain all these angry and miserable emotions, and say, "Well, it's about time someone did, isn't it?"

His gaze turns even more penetrating, even more compelling.

And I know I won't be able to contain it all and so, in my most cheerful voice, I continue, "Although I don't want you to get too excited. It's a little unconventional. It's a tweed jacket in your favorite color, brown, but —"

"Brown is not my favorite color."

That gives me pause. "It's not?"

"No."

"But then why do you wear it all the time?"

He looks down at his brown jacket. "I… I don't know. It's just…" He shrugs. "Serious."

"Serious?"

"Yeah. Intimidating."

"Is that why you also wear tweed jackets?"

"Yeah." Then, "That and a poor sense of fashion."

"Your sense of fashion is amazing," I defend him. "Because tweed jackets suit you. And let me tell you, that's what they're wearing in Milan."

"In Milan."

"Yes. All the time."

I'm not sure if they are.

But if they aren't, then they're all fools.

Everyone should wear tweed jackets. All the time.

His eyes glint. "I'll take your word for it. Since you're the fashion expert between the two of us."

"I am and you should." I nod regally and with all the poise. Then, "So what's your favorite color then?

A light frown appears between his brows again as if he's thinking about it. "I don't know."

"You don't know?"

He shakes his head. "I mean, I'm sure I had one at one point but I don't… remember."

And the meaning of *that* hits me so hard that I don't know how I breathe from one second to the next.

He doesn't remember his favorite color.

He doesn't remember the things that he liked at one point.

How is that possible? How is that even *allowed*?

No one should be allowed to forget their favorite color. No one should be allowed to forget the things that give them pleasure.

That bring them happiness and joy and a smile to their face.

No one. And least of all him.

The man I'm in love with.

The man who has protected me like no one ever has. The man who sees me and inspires me. The man with so much talent and dedication and hard work.

The man who's as lonely as me.

God, I don't know what to do.

I don't know how to fix this for him. I don't even think he'd let me.

But I wish he would.

I wish…

"Well, the jacket is brown but it has a subtle wine-colored pattern," I say, because again I have to say something, do something, or I'd just break down right here and now. "You could see if you liked that. If not, then you could always pick another one. A new one. There's this particular shade of pink that I like, that I also made into a dress. Maybe when you come inside and see all these colors, you can —"

"I'm not coming inside."

"What?"

"I just came here to give you the gift."

"You didn't come for the party?"

"I have a meeting right now and —"

"Oh," I say, my voice high, my head nodding rapidly. "Okay. Okay. Yeah, that's fine. You'll see pictures."

A stark look of regret washes over his face and he takes a step toward me. "Poe, I'm —"

I step back though. "No, it's okay. It really is."

He watches my retreat and his jaw clenches.

I don't have the energy to figure out what this means though. So I say, "Thanks for the gift. It's really beautiful."

I take another step back.

And he watches that too.

Then I say, even though I don't want to, even though it kills me to say it, "Goodbye, Alaric."

And with that, I turn around and make the climb.

Because it's over.

Already.

It has been over for quite some time now and there's no use

clinging to a little bit of hope.

Hope is cruel. Hope kills.

It's not the heartbreak that kills you, it's the hope that your heart will one day stop hurting.

It won't.

So I might as well get used to it now. Because I still stand by it.

I still stand by my decision to love him no matter what.

I hated him or thought I did for so many years, it's only fair that I love him for the rest of eternity to make up for that.

So I climb the steps and I go inside the school and I walk and walk and walk down the hallway, bypassing all the students to get to the cafeteria. But when I get to the threshold, something stops me from going inside.

Some force has its fingers wrapped around my ankle and I can't go forward. And I spin around, satchel and all, running back the way I came.

Running back to him.

I know, I know I said that I won't run after him. I said that I won't beg him or chase after him or make him take me back. But I can't keep that promise. I can't.

It's too cruel.

Crueler than hope.

He has to take me back.

He has to let me in. He has to.

I can't live without him. I won't.

I need to love him. I need to make him happy.

I need to pamper him and spoil him and give him all the gifts so he never says that no one has ever given him a gift. I need to make new memories with him, happy memories, so he never forgets the things that give him pleasure.

I burst out the door, rush down the steps and start to run toward the gate.

But I'm only able to make it halfway through when a figure steps in front of me. "Poe."

At first, I don't recognize him. Even though I know that voice.

I know that voice very well.

And I think it's because my mind is elsewhere. My mind is on the man I love.

But then I get it.

I know who it is.

It's the boy I thought I loved. He stands in front of me all run down and agitated, his eyes shifty.

"Jimmy?"

And as he steps toward me, I have this feeling in my chest.

A bad feeling.

A very, very bad feeling.

Chapter Thirty-Eight

The Renaissance Man

I never said thank you.

For the gift.

It didn't even occur to me until I got inside my car and started driving.

You say thank you, I realized then, when someone gives you a gift.

When someone gives you something so perfect that you think it can only be a dream.

A dream that you never had.

Because you don't know what dreams are. Or maybe you did. Once upon a time. But now you've forgotten.

I have forgotten.

Like I've forgotten my favorite color.

But this could be it.

The wine-colored pattern in the brown tweed jacket she made for me.

For *me*.

She made it for me and I never said thank you. I never said that it's beautiful. That it's gorgeous. It's perfect and that I love it.

Like I love…

"Mr. Marshall?"

"Alaric."

"What?" I jerk awake at my name being called, looking up

from the gift that she made for me.

It's on the table right in front of me and I've been staring at the white box for a long time now, I realize.

I also realize that I've carried it from the car. I've brought it into the meeting, into the conference room, because I didn't want to be apart from it. I didn't want to leave it in the car like an afterthought.

Like it didn't mean anything.

Like it isn't something special. Something precious.

But I see my mistake.

Because now the whole room is staring at it, at the box.

And I hate that.

I fucking hate that something she made for me is being stared at by this bunch of snotty assholes.

"Care to share with us?" one of the assholes, Robert Bailey, says.

Of course it's him.

I stiffen in my chair. "Share what?"

"What's in the box," he explains, his eyebrows raised. "Although I hope whatever it is doesn't come jumping out and make a mess."

Chuckles go all around.

Usually, I'm ready with a comeback. I'm ready to put this asshole in his place.

But today anger gets the better of me and I snap, "Eyes off."

He draws back in his chair. "Excuse me?"

I put a protective hand on the box. "Look the fuck away from my box."

I realize how childish it sounds.

How immature.

But I can't help it. It's *my* box.

It's my gift.

It's mine.

"Are you…" He looks around him at the others as if for support. "Is this a joke?"

The others are equally stunned. They don't know what to make of it, of me. Cynthia looks horrified. She's been looking that way ever since I put her in her place when she came to visit me at school. And Poe almost pounced on her.

My pocket-sized dragon.

But anyway, I don't care. That they all look horrified.

"No," I say.

His eyebrows draw together as he sits up straighter. "I'm not sure what's gotten into you, but I want you to know that I don't appreciate your tone."

"Yeah?" I narrow my eyes. "I don't give a fuck."

Anger is palpable on his face. "If I were you, I would."

"And why is that?"

"Because I'm very close to bringing the motion to table to dismiss you from the board. And after your last screw-up, guess what the results will be?"

There's a look of triumph on his face.

A look of satisfaction.

Like he's been plotting this for a long time.

And maybe he has been.

He certainly wasn't happy about my slip-up with the file. He was even less happy about the fact that I'm allowing a party to happen at St. Mary's.

Besides, he's never liked me.

Even though I've done everything that I can to prove him wrong. I've done everything that I can to prove all these people wrong. This whole town wrong. My father wrong.

And the truth is…

The truth is that I hate them. I hate this town. I hate these people. I hate St. fucking Mary's and all its bullshit rules.

I hate my father.

I do.

I fucking do.

And Jesus fucking Christ, it feels amazing. It feels like a weight has been lifted from my shoulders. All this anger, all this hatred that has been weighing me down for years, is lifted at this thought.

It feels freeing.

To acknowledge that to myself.

That I hate them all.

That I don't care. If they fire me from the board.

What's more? I don't care what they think about me.

I don't care if they think I'm weak and pathetic and unfit.

I don't fucking care.

The only thing I care about, the only person that I care about, is miles away, at a reform school, at a party.

That she has put together with all her hard work and joy and enthusiasm.

That she wanted me to attend and I refused.

Because I wanted to be here.

At this bullshit meeting with these bullshit people.

"You know what," I say to him, to all these people, "you don't have to. Because I quit."

Murmurs and gasps erupt across the room as I come to my feet.

As I pick up my box and tuck it under my protective arm.

But just as I step away from the chair, Robert Bailey bursts out, "Have you lost your mind? We need to discuss —"

"I don't fucking care." Then, looking at the room at large I say, "I should've done this years ago. I should've quit. Actually, I never should've come back to this hellhole of a town, but I did. And that's on me. But still I'd like to say, fuck you all."

With that, I turn around and stride out of the room.

Because I'm going back.

I'm going to her.

And I'm going to say thank you for the gift.

And then I'm going to say that I need her help picking out my favorite color.

And then, *then*, I'm going to say everything that she wants me to. All the things that she wants to know about me, about my past. All the shameful and ugly and cowardly truths. All the things that might disgust her, that might make her take away her love.

Because she loves me, doesn't she?

She said so.

And maybe she *will* take her love away after she knows all about me.

But it's okay.

Because I'll still tell her.

I'll lay myself bare for her.

It's only fair, you see.

Because she isn't unloved either.

My Poe is not unloved.

She can never be.

Because I love her too.

And I'm in such a hurry to go to her that it takes me a few seconds to realize that my phone is ringing. I fish it out of my pocket with irritation, ready to snap at whoever it is that's bothering me right now but their voice, their heavy pants stop me.

"Mr. Marshall?" the voice says.

I stand by my car, my hand halted in the act of opening the door. "Who is it?"

And with the following words, my world fucking falls apart:

"If you want to see Poe Blyton again, you'll do exactly as I say."

Chapter Thirty-Nine

I've been kidnapped.

Kidnapped.

I mean *what*?

How did that happen?

How did I get *kidnapped* from my school in broad daylight? By none other than my almost ex-boyfriend, Jimothy Wilson, who himself had confessed to me about his kidnapping plot.

Oh right, because I'm an idiot.

I'm a fucking idiot who believed Jimmy's lies.

When Jimmy appeared before me from out of nowhere back at the school, he told me that Big Jack would target Alaric if I didn't come with him. That Big Jack wanted the money and he was going to do everything possible to get it, including hurting Alaric. So if I wanted Alaric to stay unharmed, I needed to participate in the stupid kidnapping plot.

So I did.

I went with him.

Because the alternative was unthinkable.

The alternative was death.

Of me.

Of my heart. My soul.

The alternative was something happening to the man I love and God, no.

No, *absolutely not*.

I couldn't let that happen.

Only I should have known.

There is no Big Jack. As in Big Jack has no plans of attacking Alaric. It was one of Jimmy's lies. If Big Jack is going to attack anyone, it's going to be Jimmy, as Jimmy said when he brought me to this place. This dingy motel with gray walls and gray drapes on the border of Middlemarch and St. Mary's.

"I only said that so you'd go with me," Jimmy said while tying my hands to the plastic chair. "Look, I didn't wanna do this, okay? I didn't fucking wanna do this. But you forced my hand." I flinched when he tightened the knot around my wrists. "And now look where you are." He came to stand before me, his eyes red-rimmed and his nose sniffling. "Now, as long as you sit here and cooperate, everything is gonna be fine. I'm gonna call your fucking guardian and demand the money, and when he gives it to me, I'll let you go. And pay Big Jack off so he'll get off my fucking back."

I glared up at him, my wrists and my shoulders aching from all his stupid tying. "If you do something to him, Jimmy. If you fucking lay a finger on my Alaric, I swear to God, I will end you. I will fucking —"

He gritted his teeth. "Shut the fuck up, Poe, okay? Don't try to scare me right now. You can't do anything anyway."

I struggled against the bonds. "Oh, you think I'm not gonna get out of here? You think I'm gonna stay tied up forever? Because if you think that then you're dumber than I thought. I'm gonna get out, Jimmy, and I'm gonna find you and I'm gonna fucking strangle you to death, you understand? You stay away from my Alaric. You stay —"

He slapped me then.

Fucking asshole.

"This is your fault!" he screamed, sniffling some more. "If you'd just done what I'd told you to, none of this would've happened. So if something happens to your precious fucking Alaric, it's gonna be your fault." Then, "Now, sit tight. I'm gonna go make the call and get something to eat. I'm fucking starving."

I will say though that he wasn't wrong.

About the fact that this was my fault.

It *is* my fault.

That I'm sitting here, tied to a chair, in a strange motel room, waiting for my kidnapper to get back.

Not only that, if my kidnapper has already made the call, then right this second the man I'm in love with must be worried.

He must be worried *sick*.

And God, he has a meeting.

He has a very important meeting, but of course if he knows that I'm in danger, he won't be able to focus. He won't be able to give all of his attention to it and I know, I just *know*, that he'll beat himself up for it.

He'll be tense and frustrated and basically turn into Alaric 2.0.

And he doesn't need that, okay?

He does not need to be even more frustrated and angry than he already is. Definitely not because of me. Definitely not when I'm not there to calm him down, to take the edge off. Not that I'm always successful, but still.

God.

I need a plan. I need a fucking plan right now but my mind is too muddled to think of anything. Plus these ties are tight. They are super fucking tight and I've tried everything that I can for the past two hours — yes, Jimmy's been gone for *two hours;* I'm hoping he's passed out somewhere and never made that call — to loosen the bonds.

Just when I think to give it another try, the door bursts open.

And there he is.

All red-eyed and sniffling and shifty.

But triumphant.

Which causes my heart to sink.

He closes the door behind him with an unhinged and drugged grin. "Done. It's done, Poe. He's gonna give me the money. In about," he frowns, "two hours. He's gonna make the drop where I told him to and Big Jack will finally be off my back."

My chest tightens and heaves. "You called him?"

"Yup." He walks further into the room. "Twice."

"What?"

He shrugs. "The first call was just to scare him. You know, get him all upset and angry. The guy fucking punched me, Poe. He deserved a little bit of a scare."

Oh God, Alaric.

I swallow. "And the second call?"

He nods, putting his hands on his hips. "An hour later. Yeah, the second call was important. To tell him where to make the drop and not to call the police and all that crap. We had a long chat the second time around. I told him that I liked you. I did, Poe. I fucking liked you. I wasn't lying about wanting to try. Did I also want your money? Of course I did. But does that mean that I didn't like you or that I didn't wanna have a relationship with you? No. Why can't I have both? Why can't I have you and your money, Poe? Why is that —"

His words get cut off — brutally — when the door bursts open again and I freeze.

I stop breathing, stop thinking, stop feeling the pain in my wrists and my shoulders.

Because he's here.

The man I've been so worried about, who Jimmy tried to scare over the phone.

He stands at the threshold, wearing his tweed jacket and his dark tie, and such an angry expression on his beautiful face that I know Jimmy's in trouble.

I know that.

But I don't want him to be.

I don't want Jimmy to be in trouble, not because I have any soft spot for him but because I don't want my Alaric, the love of my life, to waste even a single second on him.

I don't want my Alaric to waste even a second thinking that he needs to exact revenge on Jimmy on my behalf or something similar because I know how he is, how angry he gets, how protective he is.

And it's as if Alaric knows.

He knows what I'm thinking, sitting here, watching him with wide eyes, because he swivels his gaze over to me.

His familiar chocolate chip eyes — right now hardened and even darker — find me and an emotion passes over him.

Over his entire body.

Causing him to shift on his feet and shudder.

Causing him to move.

And stride over to me.

I think it was relief. A big, gigantic wave of relief.

Because I'm feeling it too. As I watch him come closer.

In my peripheral vision, I notice that he's not alone. He might have burst the door open but there are other people here. Other people with guns and blue uniforms and loud voices and thumping footsteps.

But I'm not worried about them.

I don't care who they are, because the man I'm in love with has finally made it to me and he's kneeling down on the floor, his eyes wide and frantic, his jaw clenched. And then he touches me.

He puts his hand — and God it's shaking — on my cheek and I can finally breathe.

I can finally string some words together. "What… How…"

He presses his fingers on my face and asks in a voice as shaky as his fingers, "You okay?"

I nod. "Yeah. Yeah, I am."

It doesn't look like he believes me though; his eyes don't lose the franticness and his jaw is as hard as ever. "I'm going to get you out of here, okay? I'm going to…"

He trails off as if he can't speak anymore.

As if it's too much, and my heart twists so viciously in my chest that I have to gasp lightly. I have to whisper, "God, I'm so sorry. I'm so sorry, Alaric. Please don't —"

He stops my words, swallows them down with his mouth.

And Jesus Christ, I swear it feels like a balm. His plush mouth, his hard kiss — something that I thought I'd never get to feel again — is like an elixir. An aphrodisiac. My medication that I need to soothe all my aches and hurts.

When he breaks the kiss, I open my mouth to say something but can't.

Because those people that I've been ignoring until then push themselves into this little world that Alaric and I have created. And then there's no time or opportunity to disappear into that world again.

There's a whirlwind of activity after that.

From untying my hands to taking my statements as to what happened and how Jimmy got me to go with him; apparently these guys are cops. They also arrest Jimmy. Someone comes in to check my body for bruises even though I told them all that I was fine. They still insist on cleaning up my little wounds and the chafing around my wrists. Then they insist that I come down to the station right away, but before I can protest, Alaric does it for me. He tells them that I'm tired and that I need my rest and so *we* — he and I — will come down tomorrow but not today.

Because even though we haven't been able to disappear into our own little world like before, my guardian has still been by my side all throughout the questioning, the tending of wounds.

In fact from what I've gathered so far, I'm saved because of him too.

It was the tracker on my phone.

The one my guardian had put there years ago, and since he insisted that I carry my phone with me now, I'd had it in my satchel. So after that first phone call, Alaric had the presence of mind to check my location and call the cops.

So this is how they got Jimmy.

Such a simple solution.

Which makes me think what the fuck was I thinking? How the fuck did I think that I was in love with a guy who'd do something like this and not even well? I mean, his whole grand kidnapping plot came crashing down in a couple of hours. Yes, they were terrifying couple of hours of my life but still.

I'm so stupid or was. And God, it will never cease to amaze me how much.

But anyway, since Alaric couldn't have stood by while they came to get me, he insisted on coming with them to the motel. It wasn't an easy feat; again, that's what I've been able to gather. But I guess he was persistent and very angry. So in the end, they let Alaric come with them. Although they're sort of upset with him for barging into the room before them.

Oh well.

I don't care.

I'm glad he's here.

I'm glad he insisted on coming — even though I'm dying to make him feel better about his missed meeting — because I don't think I would've been able to get through it all without him being by my side.

After the cops and all the formalities come all the people who care about me.

And there are a lot of them.

Something I never had before. Not until I came to this strange town and met these strange people who have now become my family.

There's Mo. And there are my friends, Callie and Wyn and Salem; even Echo and Jupiter, who I only met a few weeks ago.

When I didn't arrive at the party like I'd told them I would, they all got worried, and so they contacted Alaric about it; I guess they got his personal cell number through Janet. By then Alaric had already gotten the phone call from Jimmy. So they all left the party — I'm sad about that — and drove over to the mansion to wait for me.

Not to mention, by then, Mo knew about it as well. Because Alaric called her after calling the cops.

So by the time I get done with the cops, they're all waiting for me at the mansion.

And before I know it, they're all hugging me and crying with me and laughing with me and there's so much loud chatter and exclamations and celebrations and anger at Jimmy that I almost lose track of him.

Almost.

But not quite.

Because as I said, he's there.

On the sidelines, with all the other guys, watching over me, guarding me, making me feel all safe and warm and cozy.

"He's watching you, you know," Callie whispers in my ear as we sit on the couch in the living room.

I swallow. "I know."

"I think he's got it bad for you," she says.

My heart jumps. "I ruined his meeting."

She smiles. "I don't think he cares about his meeting."

"I'm just —"

She stops me by giving me a tight hug and a sweet kiss on my cheek. "Just have a little faith, okay?"

A little faith. A little hope.

I don't know if I have that. I don't know if I even want that, see.

Because before Jimmy ruined everything, I was ready to run after Alaric. I was ready to beg him and plead with him to take me back. To let me love him. Even though his work, his responsibilities, are still going to be his priority.

And I still stand by it.

Because I can't not love him. I can't not be with him. I can't *not* try to make him happy and ease his frustrations.

He needs me, okay?

He needs to be loved. After everything that he's gone through, that's the least my Alaric deserves. And it's okay if he can't love me back. I have other people who love me, as evidenced by their presence here, so I'm going to be okay.

Which means that I've decided that I'm going to make my

case.

I've thought about it through all the whirlwind of things, and my plan is to plead with him. To make my case somehow and convince him that having me in his life is a good idea.

I just hope Jimmy and his stupid kidnapping plot haven't ruined everything.

So yeah, I'm determined.

Only I didn't know how exhausted I was, because after everything winds down and my girls and their guys go back home, I can barely keep my eyes open. I can barely even sit, I think.

And the last thing I remember before sleep takes over is my world tilting slightly and a pair of strong arms balancing me.

Oh, and a thick smell of leather and cigar smoke.

Chapter Forty

"Alaric!"

I spring up on the bed, my heart racing, my throat aching with all the emotions.

It's dark and scary but immediately, I'm enveloped in heat.

I'm enveloped by the strong pair of arms that I know — I remember — brought me up to my room. They smell of leather and cigar smoke, and they make me feel safe.

So safe and guarded that all these rioting emotions in me calm down.

All this churning stops and I wind my arms around his neck, clenching my eyes shut in relief. In gratitude, in an immense wave of love.

He's here.

He's got me.

And God, I love him so much.

I love him like I've never ever loved anyone before. Like I will never ever love anyone after.

Meanwhile, he's doing the same thing, I think.

He's holding on to me in relief. I can feel it radiating out of him in waves too. I can feel it in the big movements of his chest, in the tightness of his grip around me. In the way he brings me up on his lap and rocks me gently.

He's relieved that he was here to calm me down after my nightmare; I can tell.

He's relieved that I'm in his arms now.

"Hey," he whispers, turning on the lamp on my nightstand. "It's okay. You're okay. You're safe."

I rub my nose in the hollow of his throat. "I-I had the same nightmare. I couldn't… couldn't find you. I…"

He rubs his jaw in my hair, tightening his hold around me. "Shh, it's okay. It's okay, baby. I'm here, okay? I'm here. I'm never going anywhere."

I clutch his shirt then. At his *never*.

It sounded like a promise and never is a long time.

Never is forever.

God, please, please let it be forever. Please let me be here forever.

And then I can't stop myself. I have to tell him. I have to beg him.

"I'm sorry," I blurt out, looking up. "I'm so sorry, Alaric. I'm —"

He glances down at me, his eyes appearing so dark and liquid. "Poe, no. You don't have to apologize. You don't —"

I grab the collar of his shirt. "No, I do have to. I have to. Because you missed it. You missed your meeting, didn't you? And I —"

Something harsh goes through his features, his momentary relief evaporating.

Something really painful I think, because he winces and steals my words.

He flinches and grabs my face like I'm grabbing his collar, urgently, frantically, as he whispers harshly, "Fuck the meeting, okay? Fucking fuck it. I don't —"

I stop him again though.

It's like we have so many emotions inside of us that we can't contain them and so we're speaking over each other.

We're pulling and tugging on things, his collar, my jaw, and devouring each other's sentences.

"No, but you do care," I tell him, squeezing my thighs around his hips. "You do care, Alaric. And it's my fault. It's —"

"It's not your fault," he growls, his fingers digging into my jaw. "It's not your fucking fault, Poe."

"But Jimmy —"

"Fuck Jimmy, all right?" he says with clenched teeth. "Fuck him and fuck the meeting and fuck every *fucking* thing right now."

Then, swallowing thickly, "Do you have any idea what those couple of hours did to me? What that phone call did to me. I've been scared a lot in my pathetic life, Poe. A lot, and I'm not proud of it. But I've never been scared like that. I've never ever been terrified the way I was when I found out what he did. To you. When I kept thinking and thinking and *imagining* you in danger. Imagining you holed up somewhere, tied to a chair. He told me that. He..." He has to breathe and take a pause here and I squeeze my limbs around him; I bury my fingers in his hair. "He told me and I wanted to reach through the phone and fucking snap his neck. I wanted to hear the crunch of his bones breaking. I wanted to *see* the life going out of his eyes. But I couldn't. You realize what I'm saying to you, Poe? I *couldn't.* I couldn't touch him. I couldn't put my hands on him for touching you. For hurting you. I couldn't —"

I stop him again but this time I do it with my lips.

Like he did back at the motel.

I press a kiss on his mouth and he latches on.

He latches onto my mouth as if he needs it to breathe. As if he needs my lips to feel okay.

And of course I give them to him.

I kiss him until his breath goes back to being slow again. His chest goes back to moving up and down in a gentle rhythm rather than wildly, frantically.

And when he's lulled into relief, I break the kiss and whisper, "I'm okay. Look? I'm here. With you. And not once when I was with him, in that motel room, did I think that anything was gonna happen to me." His jaw clenches and I cradle it in my palms. "Because I knew you wouldn't let it. I knew you'd be worried and you'd turn the world upside down looking for me. I knew that, Alaric. You're my guardian. You're the man who protects me and keeps me safe. Of course I knew."

I did.

I wasn't worried about myself. I was worried about him.

About *him* being worried and tortured.

About being torn between saving me and doing his duty.

"And look, you did. You did save me. You tracked my location. You called the cops. You led them to me. You saved me, okay? You did." I sigh, studying his features. "But I know you. I know what you must've felt. When you got that call. You take your responsibilities so seriously and I know, I just *know*, Alaric, okay? That you must've just run out of there, out of your meeting and —"

"I quit."

"What?"

He takes a few moments before he answers. And in those few moments, he makes a few adjustments.

First, he pulls and hikes my thighs around his hips in a way that the space between them is now all pressed up against his abs. Before he goes for my spine, bowing it in a way that our chests press and breathe together.

As if he's aligning everything.

As if he wants us to be in sync.

Our breaths. Our bodies. Our hearts.

Like stars and planets up in the sky.

And then he comes for my face.

Which he cradles like my bones are made of fine china and I'm a fragile, silky creature that he's holding in his arms.

Then, swallowing again, he whispers, "I quit the board. I quit…"

My heart is pounding, racing as I ask, "Quit what?"

"Everything."

"Why?"

"I didn't want to do this tonight. I… You need your rest, but… When I got the call, I was about to drive back to you. I was about to drive back to St. Mary's. I wanted…"

He keeps trailing off as if he's running out of words. But I don't think that's it.

I think it's the opposite of that.

I think he has so many words to say that he doesn't know which ones to say first.

So I help him. I grab the thread he left trailing and prod, "You wanted what?"

His eyes flash and his jaw goes tight for a second. Then, "To say thank you."

"What?"

Another wave of emotion goes through him and we're so close and we're so perfectly aligned — courtesy of him — that I swear I feel his heart skip a beat.

Then, with his thumb making circles of my cheeks, he rasps, "I realized that I never said thank you. For the gift. For the jacket that you'd made for me. I never said…" He swallows. "But not only for the jacket. For other things too. For things that you do for me. For things that you do despite all the things that *I* can't do for you. All the things that I haven't been able to. And we both know that there are many things that I haven't been able to do. We both know that.

"We both know that I haven't been able to give myself to you the way you give yourself to me. I haven't been able to talk, to tell, to say, to bare myself like you do. For me. And that's because I… I don't know how, you see. I don't… I never learned and… But the thing is, Poe, *the thing is* that if I'd do it, if I'd learn it for anyone in this world it would be for you. But before I do that, before I tell you those things, all the things that I haven't been able to say, I have to tell you everything else. I have to tell you the truth. The truth about me. About the kind of man I am. The kind of man I… was."

My heart is twisting and twisting in my chest and I shake my head. "Alaric, you don't —"

But he doesn't listen.

He speaks over me.

And he speaks in a thready whisper, a whisper that chokes me with pain.

"In life, I've always struggled," he begins. "I've always struggled with… *everything*. First when I was born, I struggled to breathe. My lungs were weak. I struggled to eat. I struggled to regulate my body temperature. To grow. To gain weight. To be healthy. I struggled with that. When I somehow survived that, those early months of my life, I struggled to fit in. I struggled to… connect with people. To make friends. To be a part of something. To belong somewhere. At school, in classes, in study groups. But mostly at home.

"Yeah, I struggled a lot at home. I struggled with feeling safe. I struggled with feeling warm, with feeling… loved. And that's because I wasn't. I wasn't loved. I never was. And I deserved it, you understand? I *deserved* not being loved for killing my mother. I killed my mother. I was responsible for her death. I was *responsible* for all the blood that she'd lost. During my birth. How she looked like death before death came for her. My father used to tell me that. That she looked like death before death actually came for her. And I did that. *Me*. So yeah, I deserved his hatred. But that's not all. That wasn't my only crime, killing my mother. On top of that, being a murderer, I was so different. I was so… strange to him. So weak and sickly and pale. Like I was death itself. Again, something my father would tell me, that I was death. That I was born to kill. To kill my mother. To kill any hopes my father had for his legacy. And so I always thought that that was my due, you realize. That struggling, being hated, being hit and punched by the man who brought me into this world was my due.

"And when something is your due, you take it, don't you? You take it standing up. You take it with all the courage and bravery and dignity you can muster. I didn't, though. I couldn't. Because I was so afraid. I was always so *afraid* of my father. So I ran from him. I hid. I ducked for cover. I cowered. I crouched. I crawled. Every time my father came home, I'd hide under the bed. I'd hide in the closet. I'd hide up on the roof, in the woods. I'd hide. I'd just… *hide*, trying to disappear. And God, I hated that. I hated that so much. I hated myself for being so pathetic, so weak, so small. I wanted to be strong, you know. I wanted to be someone who could take it. Who could take all the beatings, all the curses, all the abuse and still stand strong. I wanted…" He chuckles harshly. "To be someone else. Someone different than who I was. So later, *years* later, when they came for me, my classmates, and beat me and broke me, I thought that was my chance. To die."

"What?"

"To kill myself," he says, his eyes far away now. "I wanted to die, you understand? I wanted them to kill me. I wanted them to fucking end my pathetic life. And when they didn't, when they couldn't do the job right and all I got at the end of it was a month-long hospital stay, I was so angry. At them. At myself. At everything. So much so that years later I punished you for it. I punished you for the things that others did to me but not well. Not in a way that got the job done. That gave me what I wanted: death.

"But anyway, I thought if they couldn't do it, then I would. I would kill myself. I would fucking die in this hospital bed myself. And be reborn. As someone else. Someone stronger. Someone people would be afraid of. Someone people respected and looked up to. Someone with no weakness, no softness. Someone who never lost. A Marshall. A true Marshall.

"So I did everything that I could after that. To kill myself. To kill old Alaric, the pathetic weakling. To forget that he ever existed. I got two PhDs, countless awards and grants and papers. I built my body. I sculpted it, honed it, made myself bigger and stronger. I came back to this town. The town that old Alaric hated. I sat on the same boards as my father, ran the same meetings, worked with the same people. Because these were the people, these were the things that old Alaric hated, you see. He liked books. He liked history. He liked being shut up in his own world but I forced him out. I *forced* him to become someone else. To become like my father. To value things that my father valued. Power, prestige, legacy. And I guess I did become like him. I became exactly like him because like *him*, I punished that boy. The boy that I was."

Finally, he focuses on me, his fingers flexing on my face. "You were right. When you said that I was punishing myself. I was. I have been. For being who I was. For being weak. For being a coward. For killing my mother. For being *born*. I have been punishing myself for all of these crimes. For all of these sins. And I want you to know that, Poe. I want you to know why. I want you to know who I was before I became this. Before you met me. Before you…"

His fingers flex on my face again, his gaze growing penetrating. "Before I tell you all the other things, I want you to know who you gave that gift to. The one that you'd made. Because it was your heart, wasn't it? It was your precious fucking heart. Your purple, polka dot heart that you put in my hands and I… I didn't even have the decency to say thank you. I want you to know who you gave your heart to. I want you to know that I'm not… like you. God, you're so brave, you know that? Do you have any idea how brave you are? How much of a fighter you are? You fight, Poe. You push back. You're courageous. You have a fire in you. No, actually that's not true. You *are* fire. You're a flame. A blue blazing flame. You're the hottest part of fire, Poe. And I'm not… I don't deserve —"

Finally I've had enough.

I've had enough of his words.

And I've had it to a degree that I put all my body into it. Into him. Into pushing him back.

Into overpowering him like I did that night.

The night I found out about his life.

About his story.

The night I realized that he was my soulmate.

So now he's down on the bed, flat on his back, and I'm over him. My thighs are straddling his slim hips as I sit on his eight-pack torso. As I lean over him, my hands fisted in his collar, my eyes glaring at him.

But maybe he doesn't get it.

He doesn't get how much danger he is in right now because he's not glaring back. He's not even breathing hard like I am. His features aren't tight like mine must be and his body is all relaxed under me.

And that makes me all the more angry.

The fact that he's simply lying there, gazing up at me with molten eyes while still cradling my face.

It makes me clench my teeth and twist my fingers in his collar as I say, or growl really, "Are you done?" I don't give him a chance to answer as I plow ahead. "You need to be done, do you understand? You need to be done talking right now. Because I don't wanna hear it. I don't wanna hear a single word against my Alaric. Against that little boy. I don't want to hear you say that he was a coward or that he was weak or that he deserved everything that he got. He did not. He absolutely did *not* deserve a single thing. Not a single punch, a single curse, a single abuse done to him by others. By you. He was a boy, okay? A little, innocent boy. And he did what he could to survive. He did what he could to *live*. Do you understand? And I want you to hear something else too.

"He's not dead. You tried to kill him, right? You tried to forget him, but he survived. He is inside of you. And I know that because he's the one who protects me. He's the one who pampers me. Who spoils me. He's the one who can't say no to me. He's the one who gives me my every wish, no matter how silly or how whimsical. He draws baths for me. He looks at my designs like they're the most precious things in the world. He's the one who watches my shows with me, who laughs with me, who teases me, who makes me feel like I'm his queen. Because I *am* his queen. I'm his baby, and if you say anything against him, Alaric, I'm not going to like it. I'm not going to take it, okay? So you have to stop. Just *stop*. Because you're wrong. You're so *so* wrong, God. He *is* a fighter. Don't you see that? He did fight back. He did survive. He survived everything. Every cruelty, every blow, every unfairness, all the hatred. He *survived* all that. And thank God for that. Thank fucking God because if he hadn't, then you wouldn't be here. You wouldn't be here, Alaric, and I… I don't…"

A sob escapes me then.

Which I'm not happy about.

I'm not happy about it at all. That I'm crying when I should be firm with him. When I should make him understand that he can't hate who he was, who he used to be. He can't hate that little boy, because that boy needs all the love in the world. That boy needs all the care, all the attention.

That boy is *him*.

That boy is my Alaric, the man I'm in love with, and God, please, I can't stand it if he hates him.

But I can't say all these things to him now because I'm crying like a lunatic.

I'm sobbing and he has to shush me now. He has to hug me and hide my face in the hollow of his throat. He has to caress my back, kiss my forehead and tell me that it's going to be okay. That I shouldn't cry. That I *am* his baby and it kills him to see me cry.

"You can't…" I say into his throat. "I won't let you, okay? I won't…"

He shushes me again. "Stop crying, Poe. Please, baby. Just stop crying. I'll do anything, all right? I'll do whatever you want. Just stop crying."

I look up then, my chest heaving. "I'm putting my foot down."

He frowns. "What?"

"I'm putting my foot down, Alaric. I've had enough. I'm going to be with you," I tell him, going back to glaring at him. "You and me, we're together now. I'm taking you and you're taking me, do you understand? And I'm going to pamper you and spoil you and love you. I'm going to do everything that I can to make you happy and you don't have a choice. I'm not giving you a choice here. Because I don't care what you think. I don't care what people think. I don't care that you're my guardian or whatever. I don't even care if you don't love me, because I do. I love you enough for the both of us and —"

"I do."

"What?"

At my quiet question, he tenses up, finally losing his relaxed demeanor.

His body bunches under me, his fingers flex over my face and I see things moving on his features. I see rigid lines appearing and disappearing but I don't know why. And neither do I get the time to analyze them because just like that night, it's his turn to overpower me.

It's his turn to push off the bed, his abs flexing as he carries me with him.

Then in a flawless, breathtaking display of his strength, he twists his torso and changes our positions, putting me down on the bed. So now *I'm* lying under him, my hair scattered around me and my hands clutching his shoulders, and he's leaning over me, propped up on his elbows and his body settled between my spread thighs.

And God, for a second, both of us simply breathe.

Both of us simply absorb the other.

The feel of our skins, the heat of our bodies.

The fact that we're once again locked in a position so intimate, so familiar to us. So heavenly and wonderful.

But then I guess the respite is over. It's time to say things and I'm so scared.

I'm so fragile right now. So vulnerable. So open under him.

"The moment," he begins, his eyes staring into mine, "I said that I couldn't go to the party, the one that you'd so lovingly and carefully put together, it felt like someone had taken a knife to my chest. It felt like someone had stabbed me, my heart, because your pretty blue eyes had dimmed. I could see that. I could see what I was doing to you but I couldn't stop myself. And then I couldn't stop myself from walking away, but every step that I took to my car, Poe, it felt like I was walking on broken glass. And then every second I sat there, in that conference hall, staring at your gift, it felt like I was burning. Like someone had set fire to my body, to my soul. And then I thought about all the other meetings that I'd sit have to sit through, all the other projects I'd have to handle because that's what a Marshall does, and I realized that I'd been burning ever since you walked out of my bedroom that night, a week ago. I realized that I'd been walking on broken glass, bleeding from my chest for a week now. And I couldn't sit there anymore. Not because of the pain, this excruciating pain, that I was feeling, but because I knew that there was a girl out there who was feeling it too. It was in her eyes, see. Her pretty blue eyes.

"I knew that there was a girl out there who thinks about me. Who dreams about me. She pines for me and longs for me and she was brave enough to tell me. She was brave enough to say it because she didn't want me to be unloved anymore. She didn't want me to be alone. And so I wanted to go to her. I wanted to say thank you. And I wanted to tell her that she isn't unloved either. She can't be, see. Because there's someone, a man — a *deeply* flawed man — who thinks about her too. He thinks about her smile, her laugh. He thinks about her midnight hair and her milky skin. He thinks about her obsession with the color purple; her glow in the dark nail polish; her purple lipsticks with weird-ass names. He thinks about her suede skirts and her polka dot dresses. He thinks about how imaginative she is, how creative and unique. How she names everything around her, her dresses and her hats.

"And this man, Poe, he *longs* to cherish her. He longs to take care of her, to spoil her, to worship her, to protect her. He longs to draw her baths every night, buy her her favorite cherry blossom bath salts. He longs to buy her a new sewing machine, new dresses, new shoes. He longs to be the man she comes to when she needs something, when she needs *anything*. There's a man out there who breathes and lives for that girl. Who breathes and lives to burn in her fire. To burn for her, because of her and with her. And I'm that man, Poe. *Me.*"

I jerk under him.

My limbs spasm.

As if they have been electrocuted. As if someone — him — shot a dose of adrenaline right into my heart.

And I realize, lying under him in this moment, that this is what it feels like. To get a second life.

To come alive after being at death's door.

This is the second time, isn't it? When he's brought me back to the land of living.

The first time was when he'd kissed me after keeping me at arm's length for a week. And now he brought me back with his words. With his 'me.'

"You?"

He swirls his thumbs on my cheeks, his gaze flicking back and forth between my eyes as he nods slowly. "Yeah." Swallowing, he goes on, "I know I don't know a lot about love. In fact, I know nothing. *Less* than nothing. I've never had it in my life and maybe that's why it's been so hard for me to accept that I found it. That's why it's been so hard for me to stop. Just stop hating, stop punishing myself, stop being angry. But I want to. I want to stop. I want to *learn* to stop. For you."

"For me?"

"Yeah," he rasps. "Because this love that I feel for you, I don't want it to be tainted by hatred or anger. I don't want it to be tainted by my past. Because that's all I want to feel, this love. So I'm going to stop. So I can love you the way you deserve to be loved. Without boundaries, without limitations, without any hesitation. You deserve to be loved like no one has ever been loved before. Like you're the only girl in this world. The first girl, the last girl. You deserve to be loved like a queen, *my* queen. Because you're my queen, aren't you?"

I jerk out a nod and a tear falls down the side of my eye.

He wipes it with his thumb as he goes on, "You deserve to be loved like my baby and I will, Poe. I will love you like that. I will love you like a dream, like a wish, like magic. Because you're all of that. You're my dream, my wish, my little bit of magic. And so, Poe, you don't have to put your foot down. I'm already on my knees. I'm already at your feet. I'm already here. Right here. I'll always be here, Poe. Always. And I know you might not believe me because I know I've fucked up. I acted like an asshole. I didn't come to you sooner. I let you think that I didn't love you. That you were alone in this. But you're not and I'm going to do better, Poe. I'm going to *be* better. For you. I promise. I'll show you. You'll see. I'll —"

I stop him then.

I lift my face up and put my mouth on him.

Because he's an idiot.

He's a clueless idiot.

Maybe that's why I love him so much. Because he's so clueless.

About how precious he is. How adorable and frustrating. How lovable and mine.

God, he's mine.

He wants to be mine. He wants to love me.

He *does* love me.

And so I kiss him harder. I pull and tug his collar, his hair, digging my heels into his thighs.

But like the idiot he is, he breaks the kiss, his chest breathing wildly, and pants into my mouth, "You hear what I said? I'm going to prove it to you —"

My chest is heaving too as I cut him off. "You don't need to prove anything."

His eyes go grave. "But Poe, I hurt you, baby. I need to —"

"Yes, you did." I fist his hair. "You did, okay? When you came to say goodbye that night. I was so angry at you. And then again, you said no to the party and walked away. You broke my heart then. But don't you see? You always make it better. Sometimes you're late. But that's okay. Because I was late too."

"What?"

I nod. "I was late too, Alaric. In realizing that I loved you. That I'd always loved you. I wasted so much time chasing the wrong guy and tormenting the one who's actually my soulmate."

"Soulmate."

At this, I cup his cheeks as well. I cradle his face like he's cradling mine. Like he's the most precious thing in the world.

And he is, isn't he?

For me.

And I'm the most precious thing in the world for him.

"You are," I whisper. "You're my soulmate, Alaric. Your soul matches mine. Your heart matches mine. Your *story* matches mine. We were both unloved, see. We were both alone."

He holds his silence for a couple of seconds, his eyes roving over my features, before he whispers, "Not anymore though."

"Not anymore."

"Because you love me."

"I love you," I say, still miffed. "And you love me."

With solemn eyes, he says, "I love you."

"So see? All better now."

"Yeah?"

"Yes." I press my fingers on the crests of his cheekbones. "So are you going to kiss me now?"

His lips stretch up on one side. "Yeah."

"Good. Because I think we've wasted so much time, Alaric," I tell him, still a little pissed. "We've wasted all this time fighting with each other and not understanding our feelings and then denying our feelings. And you're not gonna believe this but all of my friends, all of them, have been in love with their guys for like, years. *Years*, Alaric. And here I am —"

"Poe?"

"What?"

He smiles, a brilliant and bright smile, as he whispers, "I love you."

Oh God.

My heart is going to give out, I swear. He's so gorgeous. He's so beautiful and he loves me.

And he's smiling.

Forgetting my tirade, I bite my lip and whisper back, "I love you too."

His smile turns tender. "But now I want you to shut the fuck up."

I gasp but before I can retort, he gives it to me.

The thing I've been asking for but like an idiot, wasn't letting him give it to me.

A kiss.

Which I then sigh into. Which I then smile into as well.

Because I'm glad that the idiot that I'm in love with had enough presence of mind to put me in my place.

To love me.

And God, nothing could be sweeter. Nothing could be better than being loved.

By him.

By the man I love.

My guardian. My soulmate.

My Alaric.

Epilogue

"Okay, just give me one hint," I say.

"There's no hint to give," Jupiter replies.

"Come on," I plead.

"I swear."

"Seriously?"

"Seriously."

I narrow my eyes. "So are you saying that what happened was normal? You always do that?"

She widens hers. "Yes. Sometimes I do get overly enthusiastic when I meet people. It's no big deal."

"No big deal."

"Yes." She nods. "So are you gonna let this go now?"

Why don't I believe her?

Why do I think there's more?

There has to be.

I mean, the way she hugged Callie at the Ballad of the Bards the first time they met, and then again, when she got super excited about shaking Conrad's hand at The Horny Bard. That's no simple excitement. There's something there. Something Jupiter won't tell me. And I've asked her so many times now.

I sigh. "Fine. I'm gonna let this go."

She visibly relaxes. "Okay. Thanks."

And I would have, I swear.

She is clearly uncomfortable about it. She doesn't want me to pry and I respect that. I totally do.

But then she had to go and stare.

At one of the Thornes.

Shepard Thorne, to be specific.

Who is standing *all* the way over by the ice cream truck, while we're all the way over here, at the fortune teller's booth.

Oh, we're at this amazing carnival and by we I mean, me, Jupiter, Echo, Callie, Wyn and Salem. Plus all their guys and the Thorne brothers. The carnival was Salem's suggestion. And while thinking up ideas about one last thing to do before we all went our separate ways to college and whatnot, this seemed like a fun activity for the group.

And it has been.

We have had such a great time all day. Fun rides, fun food, so many laughs with my girls. Although there was this one little hiccup. We specifically came today to see this motorcycle stunt show — the very reason why Salem suggested to go here — but it turns out it was canceled.

Which is a shame because it was going to be amazing.

Like, really *amazing*.

I saw pictures of it online and oh my God, the guy could make the bike fly across spaces. I mean, *wow.*

His name is Zachariah Prince, and as breathtaking as his stunts are, the guy himself is pretty breathtaking too. He is hot, I'm not going to lie. With black hair and black eyes, he looks like a dark prince of some sort. Which actually is his stage name.

Oh, and the most amazing part: Salem knows him. Or rather she knows this guy's wife, Cleopatra Paige.

I saw her pictures too, and I think I may have a little girl crush on her and her fashion sense.

The girl has the most amazing blue hair — she is crazy about the color blue like I'm crazy about purple; her Insta is full of blue — and she rocks some serious biker boots. Not to mention I love her t-shirt, which I've come to find out she wears for all Zach's shows. It's a simple white t-shirt with 'Dark Prince's Cinderella' written across the bust.

I love it.

I absolutely love her show of support and loyalty toward her husband.

Anyway, prior to the show, Cleo was the one who told Salem

about this amazing fortune teller's booth run by a girl called Dove. So all my girls decided to stop by while all the guys decided to stay far away from it and stand huddled in a group six booths over.

Which is where Jupiter is looking.

And even though all the guys are standing in a group like I said, I still know that she's staring at Shepard. Because she's done that all day long. She's followed him with her eyes all throughout the carnival and the guy has zero clue.

Mostly because he's either busy shooting the shit with the guys — mostly Arrow, Salem's pro-soccer player boyfriend; apparently they played each other a few months back because Shepard is a soccer player too and have struck up a kind of friendship; also Reed because like Reed, Shepard is into cars — or playing on his phone.

And I think I know why he's playing on his phone.

So with my heart squeezing for my friend, I pull her away from the group and whisper, "You know he has a girlfriend, right?"

Jupiter is slightly surprised by both me pulling her and by my words. "What, who?"

I give her a look. "Jupiter."

She seems to be thinking about things before she sighs and says, "I know."

I tip my chin in his direction; he's playing on the phone right now. "I think he's texting her. Right now."

Her lips purse. "You don't know that."

"Are you serious? The guy's been stuck to his phone all day." I lean down and whisper super seriously, "He is texting a girl, Jupiter. And since he's got a girlfriend, I'm guessing it's her."

As much as I hate it for my friend, I'm fairly confident he's texting his girlfriend. Her name is Isadora and from what Callie has told me, he's crazy about her. Oh and she's also told me that there's some tension between him and Stellan – Shepard and Stellan are identical twins – regarding this whole Isadora thing. She has no idea why or what the hell is going on between her two brothers but she's sensed some conflict.

But anyway that's not important right now.

I'm more worried about my friend here.

Again, Jupiter seems to be thinking about things. Then, "Okay, so fine. He's texting his girlfriend. So?"

"So." I shake my head. "What are you doing staring at him?

This has heartbreak written all over it."

Finally my words get through to her and her shoulders sag. "I know. I already know. For more reasons than one."

I look at her speculatively. "You know you can talk to me, right? You can tell me all the reasons."

She gives me a small, sad smile. "I know. But some things are just better left unsaid."

Oh, Jupiter.

I wonder what it is. I wonder how I can help her.

Because I do want to help her. I want to help all my friends. I want them all to be happy.

As happy as I am right now.

And for the most part, they are.

Like, Callie just got the news from Dove that she might be getting some good news soon. Like the baby variety. Which completely stunned her. "But I already have a baby. I mean, that's crazy."

At which point, Salem pointed out, "But if you really think about it, look who you're married to. It's Reed. It's your gorgeous villain. Of course there's gonna be a lot of babies in your future."

And so we all stared at Reed for a while.

Who has Halo strapped to his chest and he's been carrying that little girl around all day without letting Callie take her even once, getting the brunt of it so she could enjoy herself with her friends. And God, he does look sexy with his one hand splayed on Halo's back while he plays with her fists almost absentmindedly as he talks and laughs with the guys.

So yeah, definitely babies.

And then, Salem and Wyn both got the news that there may be some serious commitment in their future. For Salem, it might come naturally and easily. Hello? Arrow is totally crazy about her. I bet he'll ask her to marry him the first chance that he gets.

But for Wyn, there might be some struggle.

So it was my turn to point out, "Well, we all know how Conrad is. He's super rigid about things. So you're gonna have to do some convincing."

Callie sympathized. "I know my brother. He's going to be all, oh my God, you're so young and whatnot. Just don't give up."

Wyn, like the calm and determined person that she is, smiled. "Oh, I'm never giving up." Then, looking at him from across the space where he was chatting with the guys, she adds, "Your brother is worth the fight."

So see?

Everyone is happy.

Well, mostly.

Because the moment Jupiter and I rejoin the group — all the girls are huddled around Dove's table and Echo is getting her future read — I hear Dove say, "Well, I think there's some confusion in your life."

I see Echo's shoulders stiffen. It's a slight movement but we all catch it. "Uh, what kind of confusion?"

Dove shrugs. "I don't know. Something. Like you're torn between two things." Then, "Are you?"

Her shoulders stiffen even more and she pushes her honey blonde hair behind her ears. "I don't think so?"

"Are you asking me or telling me?"

"Telling you."

Dove studies her for a few seconds. "Okay then. But if you were, confused I mean, I'd tell you to just go with your heart."

"Yeah, my heart is stupid, so."

Dove smiles then, sitting back in her chair. "It is, isn't it? But I'd tell you what I told Cleo long back. That hearts are stupid, yes. You never know where their loyalties lie. They have their own kings and queens."

Zach and Cleo have an amazing love story and Salem told us all about it. In fact, Dove here was the one who made Cleo realize that she was in love with Zach.

"And trust me," Dove continues. "It wasn't a happy realization for her. But I told her, as I tell everyone, that it's okay. You just roll with it."

"No, it wasn't," Callie adds, who stands propped against a table next to Dove and Echo. "A happy realization for me either, I mean. That I loved Reed."

Then Salem goes, patting Echo's shoulder, "I realized that I loved Arrow when I was ten. And I don't think that was a happy realization either. I mean, he was in love with my sister."

Standing beside Salem, Wyn shakes her head. "I don't think it's ever a happy realization when you finally find out that you're in love with a guy who wants nothing to do with you."

"Or with love," I chime in, leaning down to hug Echo. "That there are more important things in his life. Than you." I straighten up. "But sometimes you can be pleasantly surprised."

I can't contain my grin then.

And neither can my friends.

Callie raises her eyebrows. "Like our Poe here."

Wyn comes to squeeze my shoulder then. "Because she recently found out that the man she's in love with loves her back."

Salem shakes her head, chuckling. "Oh, he doesn't just love her back. He practically worships her."

"Oh my God, yes," Jupiter agrees. "Poe is basically his little queen."

"No wait, Cinderella," Callie goes then. "Because Cinderella is the one with the shoe, right? Where the prince goes down on one knee to put a shoe on her foot. To see if it fits."

"Uh-huh." Wyn smiles. "And he totally did that. In front of everyone. And Poe here blushed like crazy. Which is so rare."

"Yeah, Poe never blushes," Echo points out.

"Shut up, okay? All of you," I say, narrowing my eyes. "I did not blush."

I so did.

I had to.

It happened when we arrived at the carnival this morning. I climbed out of the car and my heel got stuck in something, making me stumble. And the first thing out of my mouth was his name.

"Alaric?"

But I don't think I even needed to say it. I don't think I even needed to call out to him because he was there at my side, in a flash, before I even finished calling out for him.

And then frowning, he came down on his knee and wrapped his large comforting fingers around my ankle, straightening my heel and fixing my buckle.

Looking up, he asked, "Okay, baby?"

I nodded, grabbing onto his shoulder. "Thank you."

That was when I blushed.

Because his jaw had clenched and his eyes had flashed.

And I know he was thinking about all the other times and all the other things that I say thank you for.

So yeah, I blushed.

Because he made me. Because he did go down on one knee for me.

Because I love him to pieces and I love being his baby.

Anyway, with Echo's reading done we all head back to the guys.

Honestly, I think the guys are all relieved as well.

Especially Reed, Conrad and Arrow.

Because their eyes swivel over to us and I distinctly see them breathing out and shifting on their feet as if relieved.

But that's all I catch because then my attention is stolen by this one man who breathes out the longest and shifts on his feet more restlessly than the others. As if he's been waiting for us — *me* — to get back more eagerly than the others. As if his eyes were waiting and just waiting to catch a sight of me and shine.

I wouldn't blame him if he was.

Because I was the same way.

I've been dying to get back to him ever since we separated. Dying to get back to touching him, smelling him, holding his hand, rubbing my nose into his shirt sleeves, kissing his biceps.

From what I gather about myself, I'm a super touchy-feely girlfriend who needs her boyfriend around her all the time. And from what I'm gathering about him, he's the same way as well.

So when I reach him, I go all the way.

As in I don't stop until the toes of our shoes are knocking together and my hands are on his ridged abs and I'm giving him my weight.

He's doesn't stop either. Not until he's gripping my waist, taking more of my weight, and leaning down, making my spine arch.

So we are all aligned in the way stars and planets are.

Because we're soulmates, see.

I'm about to say something when a strong gust of wind zooms in and threatens to take my hat away. But he saves it at the last minute. He puts his big guardian hand on top of it and keeps it glued to my head. Reaching up myself, I put my hand over his and when he's satisfied that my hat is going to be okay, only then does he go back to my waist.

But before I can thank him, his fingers on my waist tighten and he speaks with a frown. "What the fuck took you so long?"

Yeah, he missed me.

With my hair flying around my face, I breathe out, "Sorry. But I'm here now."

"Good."

"Thanks for saving my hat."

His chocolate chip eyes flash at my breathy words. "Are you going to thank me every time I do something for you?"

Still clutching my hat, I bite my lip at his repeated words from long ago. "It's my favorite hat."

He glances at my mouth for a second before he says, "I know. Lady Gaga Over Purple."

I smile. "You remember?"

"That you have strange names for all your clothes and accessories, yeah."

I frown. "Hey, you love that."

His lips pull up on one side. "I do." Then, "So what's the name of this one?"

I know what he's asking and licking my lipstick covered lips, I whisper, "Cute Corruption."

"I'm guessing there's a reason why you're wearing it."

"There is."

"Yeah? What is it?"

"Well first, because I'm cute."

"Is that so?" he murmurs, inching up my glasses with his index finger.

Something I'm finding out that he loves to do. And something I love to have him to do as well.

"Yes." I nod primly. "My boyfriend tells me all the time."

In the beginning, he had some trouble with the terminology. As in, me calling him my boyfriend.

He said that it made him sound like a teenager.

But I told him to suck it up. Because he is my boyfriend and I am his girlfriend.

Have been for two weeks now.

And it's been the best two weeks of my life.

Ever since he told me that he loved me, I've been living in a dream.

I told him that night that we'd wasted so much time being away from each other, fighting our feelings and whatnot. When we could've been together. When we could've made new memories to replace his old ones. Something I'm very determined to do.

So now he makes sure that we spend as much time together as possible. Sort of like a catch up.

And I love it.

I love waking up with him at the mansion and spending the day with him. I love exploring the woods and the grounds. He takes me out on dates and shopping sprees. We go for long drives, long walks. We go to the movies because he told me one time that he'd only been to the movies on a handful of occasions and oh my God, I had to rectify that.

Not to mention I love staying home with him. Especially when he's in his study, working, and I'm sewing my dresses or sketching them. And now that he's quit the school board and all the other responsibilities that he never liked but fulfilled nonetheless, he only works on things that he loves — his papers and grants and his book. And so I get to see him all relaxed and fun all the time.

I mean, yes there are times when he gets agitated and angsty. Especially when a few days ago he showed me all his hiding places around the mansion and the woods. I could tell he was embarrassed by that. He was angry at himself, and even though I wanted to break down and cry and sob for all the cruelties he had to go through, I pulled myself back. I got a handle on my emotions and told him that he had nothing to be ashamed of.

That I was proud of him.

For surviving. For protecting himself.

Besides it was the fault of his abusers, his father, this town. Not his.

I know it was hard for him to believe me, but we'll get there.

We'll get to the day when he believes me wholeheartedly. Until then I'll keep reminding him.

He hums. "Well, he sounds like a smart guy."

"He totally is."

"Tell me the second reason."

Oh, right.

Why I wore this particular lipstick?

"The second reason is that I'm out to corrupt you." Then, grinning and pointing to my lips, "Get it? Cute Corruption."

His lips twitch. "Corrupt me."

"Yup. I mean, look at you." I widen my eyes. "You're hanging out at a carnival. Who would've thought?"

He squints his eyes as if in thought. "True. This is wilder than the movie theatre."

Which he looked so uncomfortable in. And then he frowned through the entire plot of the superhero movie we were watching.

Well, until I leaned over and kissed him.

Then his focus shifted and he seemed happy.

"I agree. And," I tell him excitedly, "you tried my cotton candy."

"I did."

"Did you like it?"

"Absolutely fucking not."

I swat his chest and he chuckles.

God, I love to hear him chuckle.

It makes him look younger and more boyish somehow, his lips smiling, his chocolate chip eyes amused.

"Plus you're relaxing," I say.

"Oh, is that what this is called?"

"On a Saturday."

"It is Saturday, yes."

"And you don't have your tweed jacket on," I add, toying with the silver chain of his locket.

Oh, did I mention that I gave him a locket?

It's to replace the ring on his pinkie.

Because that ring was a symbol of all the things that he never wanted to do, what his father wanted him to be, and so when he quit all his responsibilities, he also gave that ring up. And since I promised to myself that I'd make new memories with him, I got him this tiny locket on a silver chain that he now wears around his neck all the time.

"Only because my girlfriend threatened to throw them all away if I put one on."

I totally did.

He was actually going to wear a tweed jacket to a carnival. I let him have his way at the movies but not here. Not today.

This is supposed to be fun and he doesn't need to look all principal-y or professor-y.

So he's only wearing a dark gray shirt and his dress pants.

And I have to say he is the most handsome guy here.

With his scruffy jaw and his fluttering curly hair, he's like my personal eye candy.

I raise my eyebrows and bat my eyelashes. "And you agreed because you love your girlfriend so much?"

"I mean, my first thought was my tweed jackets but okay."

I narrow my eyes. "You're mean."

He chuckles again. "Never said I wasn't."

I melt at that deep sound and shake my head. "I'm being serious, okay? Did you have a good time or not?"

At this, he brings me even closer, both his arms tightening around my waist as he bends further down. "I did."

"Really?"

"Yeah."

"Do you like my friends?"

"I do." Then, "Conrad's nice."

I grin. "Yeah? You liked hanging out with him?"

I had a feeling that he might.

Callie's oldest brother, Wyn's boyfriend, is close to Alaric's age. Plus from what I know about him, he's very big brother-y and responsible and family's super important to him. And while Alaric's family was shit, he still has a very strong sense of morality and responsibility. So I thought they might hit it off.

And it makes me want to squeeze him in happiness that they did.

That feeling only grows when right in front of my eyes, my man's majestic cheekbones flush and he nods. "We're hanging out again. Next week."

Oh my God.

I'm going to tear up, I swear.

I'm so happy. My Alaric is going to hang out with someone.

He doesn't have friends, see.

He's always been alone. He's always struggled.

And I don't want him to.

Not anymore.

I want him to feel like he belongs, because he does.

He belongs with me.

And not only that, I want him to find friends. To have fun. To go out. To be happy.

To *see* that people will accept him for who he is and not who he always thought he should be.

Plus he never got to do these things before, back when he was a kid. And this makes me so emotional, that he's finding it in Conrad and hopefully the other guys.

"So what are you gonna do?" I ask, smiling.

"Play soccer."

My mouth falls open. "You know how to play soccer?"

His eyes look amused. "Yeah."

I swat his chest again. "Shut up."

"I played some in college."

"Holy shit." I grab his shirt. "You got at least seventeen times hotter just now."

"Yeah?"

"Is there anything that you can't do? Like, anything at all?"

He shakes his head slowly, his eyes still teasing. "Not much, no."

I sigh. "You're seriously the Renaissance man, aren't you?"

The man who can do all the things.

The man who is not only a scholar, a fighter, now a soccer player, but also someone who has the power to make me do things. Who has the power to jack up my heartbeats. To make me feel all fluttery and breathless and safe and heated and cozy and protected.

My Alaric is the most powerful man in the world.

"Well, at least you're using it correctly this time," he murmurs.

I give him a dreamy smile. "I'm so happy, I'm not even gonna take offense at that." He chuckles again. "But do you realize something?"

"What?"

"Conrad and Wyn are gonna be in New York too." I hop up and down. "You can play all the soccer that you want with him over there."

Because that's where we're going. Along with Wyn, who's going to start art school in the city, and Conrad, who's going to be the coach for the New York soccer team.

Now that summer school is over and I'm a high school graduate — yay! — I'm moving to New York to start community college. And he's going with me. Mostly because he doesn't want me to go alone, but also because I don't want him to live here. In this town. In the same mansion that contains so many bad memories for him.

So we're starting fresh.

Which means he's also quitting his job at Middlemarch College so he can get something in New York. And while he's already got offers lined up — everyone wants to snap up Professor Marshall — he's not in a hurry to accept any of them. He wants to work on his book for a few months before committing to a college.

Plus he wants me to travel with him.

That's another one of the things that I found out about him.

Alaric loves to travel. He traveled a lot when he was in his graduate program, mostly on grants to all these historical sites, and so he wants to share that with me. And of course, I'm all in.

Actually I can't wait.

Living with Alaric — not in my old town house though; Alaric hated that idea and found a place for the both of us which I don't mind at all — traveling with him, studying fashion at some point in the future, learning all the new and old things about him.

Nothing could be better.

Plus all the things that I was worried about turned out to be okay.

Like people at school finding out about our relationship. Not that it matters much now, because not only have I graduated but also Alaric isn't the principal anymore. But still I worried, when he came to pick me up from the dorms on moving out day, that people might raise their eyebrows and blame him. Well, they did raise their eyebrows but mostly it was because I was in love with the man that I'd hated for years and years and very vocally.

And secondly, the fact that Mo wholeheartedly approves of our relationship.

She's so happy for us and has mentioned many times that she loves to see Alaric and me smiling and being happy together.

Although she did have the talk with me about the birds and the bees and all that. I think she frowns upon the fact that Alaric and I not only share a roof over our head but also a bed. Alaric thinks it's none of her business, but I did try to put her at ease. I mean, she's the only mom figure in my life and I can't have her worry over me like this.

So all in all, I'm the happiest I've ever been.

"We're gonna have so much fun in New York," I continue.

He brings his hand up to cradle my cheek. "Is that what the fortune teller told you?"

"I didn't have my future read."

"Why not?"

"Because I know my future."

His thumb skims the bottom of my lip. "Yeah? What is it?"

I go up on my tiptoes. "You."

"Me."

"Yeah." I nod. "And I know that as long as I have you, I don't need anything else."

He presses the pad of his thumb on my lips, parting them slightly. "Fuck yeah, you don't. Because I'll give you everything."

My heart skips a beat. "Why?"

"Because you're my baby."

"And your little queen."

"And my little queen."

God, I love him so much.

So so much.

"You're my king too, you know?"

"Yeah?"

"And so I'll always thank you for everything you do for me."

I stare into his eyes.

He stares back.

I bite my lip.

He clenches his jaw at the action.

"Alaric?"

"Poe."

"I love you."

"I love you too, baby."

And then he bends down to kiss me. And I finally let go of my hat and kiss him back.

I feel the hat fly away in the wind and he breaks the kiss for a second to maybe go back after it. But I fist his hair and bring him back.

Fuck the hat.

Fuck everything.

I wanna kiss my soulmate.

And I want my soulmate to kiss me back.

But a few seconds later, I break it myself and whisper, "So speaking of corruption, what would you think about having sex with no condoms?"

He stiffens. "What?"

"You know," I begin hesitantly. "I never liked condoms and I was just thinking that one time that we did it — although it was a bad move — felt so good. And so amazing and —"

"No."

"But Alaric —"

"No."

"I'll go on the pill," I say with wide eyes.

That seems to piss him off even more. "Fuck no."

"Why not?"

His nostrils flare. "Because I don't want a fucking pill to protect you."

"What? That doesn't —"

He crushes me to his body then as he growls, "When it's *my* job."

Oh God.

He did it again, didn't he?

He can't stop doing it.

He can't stop being adorable. It will only make it harder for him to put me off my mission: have unprotected sex with the man who wants to protect me from everything.

I fist his hair. "Why are you so awesome? You make it so hard to stay mad at you and —"

"Poe?"

"What?"

His chocolate chip eyes flash. "Shut the fuck up."

And then he covers my mouth with his, swallowing not only my lips but my gasp as well.

It's okay though.

Because as I said, it's so hard to stay mad at him.

So I'll let him kiss me and I'll kiss him back.

But we're coming back to this conversation.

In the future.

Which is bright and full of laughter and smiles. It's full of leather-bound books, colorful dresses, cherry pies – I finally nailed it – and exotic places. And I don't need a fortune teller to tell me that.

Because it's him and me.

Alaric and Poe.

Alaric

There's a girl who loves me. Who lives and breathes for me.

She tells me that I'm a fighter. A survivor.

That I have the same fire in me that she does.

And maybe I do.

I'm learning, see. I'm learning who I am. I'm learning who I want to be.

I'm *learning.*

For her.

For that girl.

Because I love her too. Because I live and breathe for her too.

Because she's the beat of my heart and the air in my lungs.

My wildcat, my troublemaker.

My siren and my doe-eyed diva.

My Poe.

THE END

(For Alaric and Poe)

Echo

When: A few weeks ago; First sighting of Reign Davidson
Where: The Horny Bard

Everything is going well.

Actually, everything is going better than well.

Everything is going great.

Unexpectedly great.

I mean, when I came here tonight – to The Horny Bard – all I wanted to do was to catch a glimpse of him, look at him from afar.

And I'm doing that.

After two long years.

Ever since he broke up with me and walked out of my life.

But.

But *he's* looking at me too. He's noticing me too.

And in the same way he used to back when we were together.

With adoration and want.

And oh my God, oh my *God*, I'm going to freak out.

With happiness I mean.

With giddiness. With love.

My ex-boyfriend, who I never ever thought would look

at me the same way, is looking at me.

He's staring at me and he's staring at my wonderful dress like he can't look away.

And that's why I had to hide here, in the bathroom, away from him and everyone else out there. Lest I do something crazy like grin like a lunatic and hop up and down in my spot with the kind of joy I can't contain.

Standing at the sink, I stare at my reflection in the mirror.

"Lucas is looking at you," I tell myself with wide eyes and flushed cheeks. "Maybe he misses you. Maybe he has missed you like you missed him and maybe…"

Okay, no.

I'm not going there.

I'm not going to jump and leap and weave dreams of a reunion, standing at a bathroom sink, just because Lucas looked at me a few times over the last hour.

Instead I'm going to stick to the plan.

Or rather the plan my friends, Poe specifically, came up with.

When I told her that my ex-boyfriend was going to be at The Horny Bard and that I wanted to see him, Poe went into her plotting mode. She planned and devised everything, starting from what dress I'd wear – a blue suede corset style number – and what my makeup would be – smoky and sultry – to how I'd act around him.

She said to be aloof and confident.

She said not to appear desperate or clingy or to throw looks at him. Let him come to you, she said, don't let it show how much you still love him.

And since I love him a lot still, I decided to follow her advice.

Which means I'm not going to jump the gun or break character.

So yeah, I needed this little bathroom break to rein my thoughts and my feelings in.

Exhaling and patting my hair and my flushed cheeks, I decide it's time to go back. I walk out of the bathroom and immediately come to a grinding halt.

Because there's a guy here.

He stands leaning on the opposite wall, his black stomping boot propped up on the bricks, his hands shoved down into his pockets and his eyes trained on the bathroom door.

Or rather, on me since I'm standing on the threshold now.

I know he's waiting for me.

Because that's what he does.

He waits for me.

In darkened corners, in lonely hallways, in empty rooms.

He waits and he pounces.

Although since this is a bar and it's a Saturday night, I can't call this hallway lonely. There are people coming and going. I even have to step aside to let some other girl into the bathroom.

So not lonely.

But still dangerous because I have a feeling that he doesn't care if there are witnesses present.

He will still pounce.

Damn it.

"Nice dress," he drawls, his eyes going up and down my body.

I fist my hands and press my body into the wall so as to stop the trembling that overcomes my body at his voice.

Low and deep.

Rough like sandpaper.

"What do you want?" I ask, trying to sound all confident and calm.

His eyes come back to my face. "It's pretty."

Of course he completely ignores my question.

Because again, that's what he does.

He ignores things and people and feelings and does what he wants to do.

"Pretty," I repeat.

"Yeah," he says, nodding his head slowly. "Blue suits you."

Okay, I don't have time for this.

Shaking my head, I ask again, "What do you want?"

Something dark flashes in his eyes and he cocks his head to the side. "I want you to say thank you."

"What?"

"It was a compliment."

"Yeah, right," I scoff.

He frowns slightly. "What, you don't think so?"

"No."

"And why's that?"

"Because it's you."

"And?"

"And you never give anyone compliments."

His lips twitch as if on the verge of a smile. Which can't be true.

If anything, they're going to be on the verge of a smirk.

Because this guy hardly ever smiles.

He smirks though.

All arrogantly and condescendingly.

Because he thinks he's better than everyone.

"I'm pretty sure I do," he replies.

"Well okay, so let me rephrase," I say, raising my eyebrows. "You never give compliments to me."

And there it is: his smirk.

All dark and in its glory.

"Ah," he drawls again. "I hear hurt feelings."

"There are no –"

"Well, allow me to rectify that."

"You don't –"

Again, he speaks over me. "You look pretty in blue," a pause, "Echo."

I clench my teeth. At the way he says my name.

Like he owns it.

Like my name belongs to him. Like he's going to keep it and say it whenever and however he wants.

God, I hate him.

He runs his eyes up and down my body again as he murmurs, "Very pretty."

Steeling my spine, I go, "What do you want, Reign? Why are you here?"

Now it's his turn to clench his teeth, his jaw. Narrow his eyes slightly, even.

As if me calling his name causes the same effect in him.

Which I know is ridiculous.

I don't say his name the way he does mine. I will never say his name like he does mine.

I don't even like his name, and if I had my way, I'd never say it.

I'd never even look at him.

At his dark hair and bronzed skin.

But he recovers quickly and his features – which have always been so sharp and defined, so masculine – go all relaxed and nonchalant.

"To say hi." I open my mouth to say something but he goes on, "I mean, how long has it been, huh? Since we saw each other."

"Two years," I say. Then, "Not long enough though."

He chuckles. "And you were sitting out there, surrounded by all your friends. We didn't get a chance to talk, let alone catch up."

I *was* sitting out there, surrounded by my friends like he said. And it was on purpose.

To protect me from this guy.

I came to the bar with all my friends from St. Mary's and their boyfriends. Again, this was Poe's idea. I needed all the moral support, hence the girls. And we needed entry into this bar, hence their boyfriends who know people here. But when we realized that the guys from our group know the guys from *his* group, my friends decided to literally surround me and barricade me against him.

Which means that I never should've left that cozy little nook.

Stupid Echo.

"If I wanted to talk to you, I would have," I tell him.

"Now that wasn't very nice, was it?" he says, shaking his head slightly. "I give you a compliment and you break my heart."

"You don't have a heart."

"Yeah?"

"Yes. You're heartless."

Oh God, he is.

He has been ever since I've known him.

Which is practically all my life.

At my words, he takes one hand out of his pocket and puts it on his chest. On the left side of it. He splays his fingers wide and with sparkling eyes, he says, "Well, whatever it is, it's racing right now."

I swallow at his gesture.

I don't know why.

It makes my throat go dry. His large, dusky hand on his sculpted chest.

"I hope it's racing fast enough for a heart attack," I retort.

He chuckles again. "I wouldn't rule it out, no. Especially since I'm seeing you after so long."

"Are you –"

"Because I wasn't lying, Echo. You are pretty." Then, in a grave voice, the kind I've never really heard from him before, he says, "You are fucking breathtaking."

Before I can respond to that, he steals all my words by pouncing.

By getting closer to me.

In a flash, no less.

One second, he was standing at the opposite wall and the next, he's standing right in front of me with hardly any gap between our bodies.

I straighten up, my eyes going wide. "Get away from me."

Putting a hand on the wall, above my head, he dips his scruffy jaw and rasps, "I see why he loved you."

I stiffen. "Don't talk about him."

His eyes swipe across my features. "Why he went for you."

"Reign –"

"But I hope this dress was a gift."

I'm thrown by the abrupt change of subject. "What?"

"It's for him, isn't it?"

"No," I lie.

"Because you came here for him."

"I came here with my friends, okay?"

"I'd believe you, you know." His lips pull up once again and of course, in a smirk, as he continues, "If you didn't reek of a little thing called desperation."

I flinch. "Get away from me right now."

"And that's why I hope it was a gift. Because I'd hate to see you waste money that you don't have. For something you'll never get."

Of course, he'd say that.

I knew he'd find a way to taunt me about my lack of money, or rather my family's lack of money. Mostly because he loves doing that. To remind me how poor I am.

I'm pretty sure if I stand here long enough, he'll also remind me how my father works for his father and how rich he is.

Asshole.

But still I can't help asking, "And what is that?"

He leans down then. "Him."

My nails are drawing blood on my skin. "Get away from me. I'm not going to ask you again."

"I mean, don't get me wrong," he keeps going, his eyes swirling over my face, his voice all rough and low. "It was pretty fun to watch you out there. Pretending to be all aloof and unaffected, pretending that you don't care, that you don't notice. When we both know that you do. You did."

"He was noticing me too, you know," I tell him.

Even though it's completely ill-advised.

Completely thoughtless and reckless.

To say that Lucas is still interested in me.

"Well," he says. "You can't blame him, can you? You look pretty as fuck."

"You know what, I –"

He shrugs. "But I don't think he's going for desperation these days." I flinch again and he goes on, "So really, I'm saving you all the trouble here. I'm saving you from getting your heart broken again."

Yeah, right.

He's saving me.

Him.

The guy responsible for breaking my heart the first time.

The guy responsible for breaking up me and Lucas.

"Why do you hate me?"

I can't believe I asked that. But the question is out there now.

And I need an answer.

It has always been this way, see.

He's hated me since the first time he saw me, and he hates me still.

Only I don't know the reason.

I don't know what I could've possibly done to him to make him hate me to a degree where he took the love of my life away.

Darkness flickers through his features, making them taut for a second or two before he replies, "Take my advice, return the dress and forget about him."

"You can't tell me what to do."

His eyes sweep over my features again.

As if for the last time.

And then he steps back. Shoving his hands down into his pockets again, he says, "It was nice seeing you again, Echo. I hope we don't have to do it again." Then, "And it's been two years, two months and twelve days."

With that, he leaves.

And I stand there. All trembling and heated and sick.

With hate.

Because that's what he does.

Reign Davidson, my childhood nemesis, my ex-boyfriend's best friend, the guy responsible for breaking us up, makes me sick with hate.

He makes me sick with loathing.

He makes me want to get back together with my ex just so I can win against him.

And you know what, I will.

I will win against him.

If it's the last thing I do.

To be continued in…
The Hatesick Diaries
Coming November 15th 2022

Echo Adler hates Reign Davidson. He's the reason the love of her life left her all alone and brokenhearted two years ago.

So it should be easy to stay away.

It should be easy not to dream about his dark and mean eyes, or his cruel but sexy smirks. It should be easy not to think about the guy who ruined her happily ever after.

Only it's not.

Sometimes his intense stares make her heart race, and those smirks of his make her breathless.

But it needs to stop.

Because she has a mission: to get back together with her ex-boyfriend. And Echo will be damned if she keeps dreaming about Reign.

The guy who not only makes her sick with hate but who also happens to be her ex's best friend.

To be continued in The Hatesick Diaries

Coming November 14th, 2022

Bad Boys of Bardstown

St. Mary's Rebels Spinoff series
Coming soon!

You've met the good guy of Bardstown, Conrad Thorne. Now, it's time for the bad boys:

Ledger Thorne

Shepard Thorne

Stellan Thorne

Ark Reinhardt

Homer Davidson

Byron Bradshaw

And the girls who will reform them:

Tempest Jackson

Jupiter Jones

Isadora Holmes

Lively Newton

Maple Mayflower

Snow Jones

Add the series to your TBR

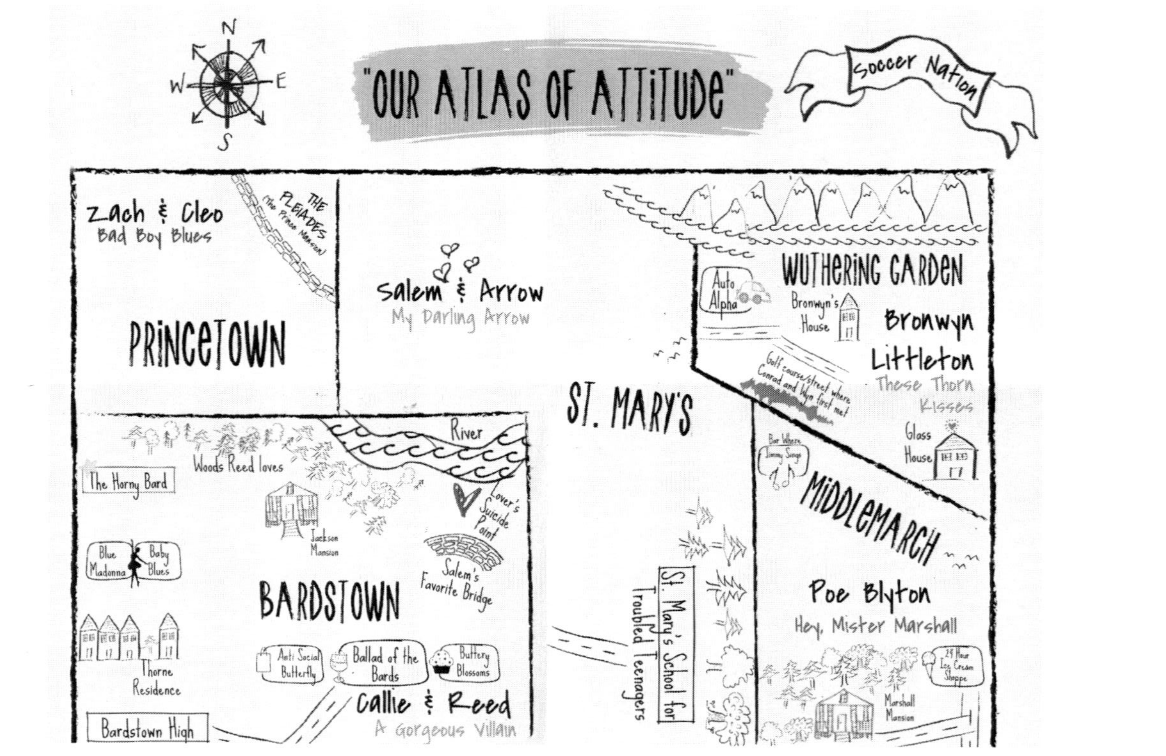
"OUR ATLAS OF ATTITUDE"
Soccer Nation
N
E
S
W
Zach & Cleo
Bad Boy Blues
THE PLEIADES
(The Prince Mansion)
PRINCETOWN
Salem & Arrow
My Darling Arrow
WUTHERING GARDEN
Auto Alpha
Bronwyn's House
Bronwyn Littleton
These Thorn Kisses
Golf course/street where Conrad and Wyn first met
Glass House
ST. MARY'S
Bar Where Jimmy Sings
MIDDLEMARCH
Poe Blyton
Hey, Mister Marshall
24 Hour Ice Cream Shoppe
Marshall Mansion
St. Mary's School for Troubled Teenagers
River
Woods Reed loves
The Horny Bard
Jackson Mansion
Lover's Suicide Point
Salem's Favorite Bridge
Blue Madonna
Baby Blues
BARDSTOWN
Thorne Residence
Anti Social Butterfly
Ballad of the Bards
Buttery Blossoms
Callie & Reed
A Gorgeous Villain
Bardstown High

Acknowledgements

Dani Sanchez of Wildfire Marketing Solutions, thank you for always having my back and for always giving me awesome advice.

Leanne Rabesa, my editor and fact checker, thank you for checking and rechecking my timelines. Also for constantly telling me that hair's singular. Sorry I always forget!

Olivia Kalb, for reading and re-reading my story and for giving me such great advice about how to make it stronger. My writing is better because of you.

Najla Qamber, my cover designer, thank you for not ditching me when I kept changing my vision of the cover on you. Thank you for putting those gorgeous lips on the cover. If anyone could do it and portray the sexiness and angst of the book, it was you.

Virginia Tesi Carey, my proofreader, thank you so much for being so flexible about dates and for reading this long, long, loooooong story.

Melissa Panio-Peterson, my fearless PA. What can I say about you that I haven't already said. You're a constant source of happiness and encouragement to me in this industry.

Ayesha & Katie, thank you both for being so supportive and for always having my back. I can't imagine doing this without you guys. You're always my first thought when I think of an idea or a scene. Your thoughts and enthusiasm keep me going.

ABOUT THE AUTHOR

Writer of bad romances. Aspiring Lana Del Rey of the Book World.

Saffron A. Kent is a USA Today Bestselling Author of Contemporary and New Adult romance.

She has an MFA in Creative Writing and she lives in New York City with her nerdy and supportive husband, along with a million and one books.

She also blogs. Her musings related to life, writing, books and everything in between can be found in her JOURNAL on her website (www.thesaffronkent.com)

www.thesaffronkent.com

Made in United States
North Haven, CT
05 July 2022